THE VANITY
ROOMS

THE VANITY ROOMS

PETER LUTHER

To Beci

First impression: 2013

© Peter Luther & Y Lolfa Cyf., 2013

Cover design: Y Lolfa

The publisher acknowledges the support of the Welsh Books Council

ISBN: 978 0 95601 256 2

Printed on acid-free and partly recycled paper
and published and bound in Wales by
Y Lolfa Cyf., Talybont, Ceredigion SY24 5HE
e-mail ylolfa@ylolfa.com
website www.ylolfa.com
tel 01970 832 304
fax 832 782

I

Gathering around the hut

DURING THE FURIOUS drive through the undernourished roads of Cardiff's docklands he wondered at the name the woman, after much persuasion, had finally volunteered.

Fabrienne!

She was working her old Fiesta with grinding shifts of the gearstick and whispered curses to the engine, having pointed out that French names were commonplace – Charlotte, Denise, Harriet... – but it was, he decided, the most improbable name for someone who looked like a Bollywood star from Butetown.

"Where are we going again?" he asked, one hand on his seat belt, the other wrapped around his mobile. This odd turn of events, where barely ten minutes ago she had been leading him around the show apartment of a city centre development, had already prompted half a dozen texts: several to drinking buddies to describe the "shockingly tasty Indian bird" who had spirited him away – one to his twelve-year-old daughter from his first marriage to describe the show apartment he'd just seen – "when I'm minted, going to buy you one of these sweetheart"; and one to his wife, soon to be his ex-wife – "Found a place to live. Satisfied?"

"To the Bay," Fabrienne replied cheerily with a slightly raucous Cardiff twang. "To show you something more within your price range."

He shifted uncomfortably, the suspension of the small bucket seat struggling under his weight.

"What's the rush?"

"Tight window: they said we'd only have an hour."

She bit her lip.

"Who's *they*?"

She gave her answer to the clutch.

Bemused, he mentally replayed his tour of the show apartment. She had been going through the motions as she mechanically sold the cosmopolitan cafes below, the city skyline ahead, her professional antennae having identified that he had neither the intention nor the means to purchase; that he had wandered in simply out of boredom.

Gripping his seat belt, he concentrated, searching for the moment that had changed the dynamic, which now had them racing down Bute Street.

It was a name...

Out of habit when in his thoughts, he visualised his mobile. He tapped out 'na' on the imaginary text keyboard, pulling it up as predictive 'name'.

Yes, it was something to do with *his name...*

His mind tapped 'kn'.

Knight.

During the tour he had been texting to arrange his Saturday date, occasionally muttering the sweet overtures produced by his thumb; he put his mobile away on hearing her sigh of exasperation.

"You're probably wondering why I'm not in work. My day job's only in the mornings." He threw her a speculative glance. "I'm an actor. Afternoons is when I do my auditions and stuff." He produced his actor's union card.

"Really?" she said, without looking at it.

"Yeah, I'm a writer too: I've written this docudrama for the BBC."

She didn't comment.

"The Beeb are all over me. Seriously. It's set in the French Revolution and I'm playing the lead role: guy called Chaumette; great role, a real butcher. Going to be on the telly at the end of the year." He paused, discouraged. "Anyway, my name's Kris Knight. So, you know, watch this space."

She blinked as he put his union card away. "Kris … *Knight*? With a 'k'?"

"Yup. Kris Knight, both with a 'k'."

He now gripped his seat, the Fiesta taking the Bute Street chicanes too tightly.

Yes, that was it. That was the moment…

Her eyes had been interrogating the beech laminate floor of the show apartment. "Do you want to buy one of these apartments?" she asked bluntly. "Yes or no?"

He opened his mouth in response.

"Good." She produced her car keys and, as an afterthought, a huge smile that was slightly out of sync with her eyes. "Let me show you something else."

And with that he had followed her quickly out as she walk-ran, her hand at the right side of her head to keep her long hair in place; down in the service lift, reading the workers' graffiti on the gaffer tape to negotiate the awkward silence, then into the gabled reception of the sales office where she fleetingly acknowledged a large bearded man in an overcoat sitting patiently near the water cooler. He was the only other person in the building, admitted through the intercom and camera during their viewing: a necessary security measure, she had explained, because she was the only member of staff on a Monday.

"I'm sorry, I have to lock up," she said to the overcoat. "If you don't mind waiting next door, I'll be back within the hour."

The overcoat nodded, getting up to follow them out. His right hand made a protective fist, as if he was squeezing something precious.

Fabrienne's hand tightened on the steering wheel. *Christ that was close,* she thought, inwardly shaking with a mix of shock and relief.

I almost missed him. After three months of waiting, oh God I almost missed him…

Her anxiety was causing her to speed and miss her gear changes.

"Almost there," she said sweetly, making a conscious effort to slow down as they turned into the Bay.

He was studying his mobile. "Selfish bitch," he muttered eventually, furiously texting back. "Sorry, it's the ex," he explained.

She nodded grimly. "Don't apologise, had a bad divorce myself."

He stretched his shoulders, only vaguely registering the response. "Her lawyer's got his greasy mitts on the house. *Our* house. That's why I'm looking for somewhere. Anyway, I was just telling her about the gaff you showed me…"

She reduced her speed to a crawl, deciding they had plenty of time. Her nerves steadying, she now reflected on the man who had turned her day on its head. He was in his early forties, overweight, his hair receding: very ordinary looking if it wasn't for a cherubic face with an engaging smile. In some ways he reminded her of a child, with his muttered texts to women, which were clearly for her benefit, and his boasts of screenplays. And if he was a child then that mobile was surely his teddy: it hadn't left his hand once.

This was the man *they* were interested in. The man who fulfilled the criteria of the Russian Trustee, Renka Tamirov, when she had deposited £10,000 in her account as advance payment for delivering him to the building.

He is wanting to be artist.

His name is chess piece.

The man had done a lot of talking and, from a well of tedium, she now tried to draw as much detail as possible. He was from Southend and had met his Welsh wife working abroad; they had returned to the city to live near her family. Things hadn't worked out, but he was still here because he had some business with BBC Wales…

"So the BBC have taken your play?" she inquired thoughtfully. "It's actually in production?"

"Yeah, absolutely." He put his mobile away. "Well, I've got a meeting next week, you know, just to dot the i's and cross the t's. But it's a done deal. I'm sure of it."

The small car park was near a dirt track of underdeveloped ground reserved for port storage and warehousing, which was the Cardiff Bay Barrage coastal path. In the January chill, with the engine turned off, the harbour front was silent save for the squawk of seagulls as they fought the cold for scraps. With her head slightly bowed she turned in her seat to look in every direction before unbuckling her seat belt. He looked round too, in confusion: the old Norwegian Church was behind them, the new Millennium Centre in the distance, but there was no one around.

"Are you expecting someone?" he asked.

With a quick shake of her head she got out of the car and

led him over a small pedestrian bridge, then shortly diverted from the path through some open fencing. She looked round impatiently as she waited for him to catch up, a hand partially covering her face: he was texting again. Shortly their feet found frozen grass and the view improved with the light shimmer of the sea.

She waited, knowing that she didn't need to say anything.

To the casual observer the building might simply have been a taller version of the decrepit warehouses and storage units, the martyred derelicts that lined the coastal path like crucifixions, but on closer inspection its appearance improved. The carefully worked stone was carved with elegant lines, though weathered beyond all remedy.

"Tall, isn't it?" she said. "I'm sure the views of the harbour are stunning."

He looked up. The arch windows began about twenty feet up, the smeared, opaque glass creating a grimy camouflage in this wasteland. He shivered in his North Face puffer jacket, not from the cold but from an extreme case of déjà vu. The building had the breath of ancient fatalism, the stone sighing with the disappointment of the world.

"I know," he heard her whisper. "It grows on you, doesn't it?"

He pulled himself away. "Look, Fabrienne, I'll be honest with you, I really don't think I can afford…"

"It was like built in the eighteenth century," she said quickly. "Probably looked really tidy in its day."

He hesitated and smiled in spite of himself, the 'like' and 'really tidy' all Butetown. "What, it's not a converted warehouse or something?"

"Oh no. People lived here. Wealthy people. Maybe even

famous people." She looked round nervously, anxious to go inside.

"In the eighteenth century? I doubt if this was prime real estate way back then: the only residents would have been prostitutes and muggers." He smirked as he checked his iPhone, a full three minutes having passed since he last examined it.

"I think they wanted privacy," she said, with an irritated flash at his mobile as she led him to the entrance. This was a wooden door that shared the greasy dirt camouflage of the windows, except for a small plaque that was gleaming and bore an inscription in a French script:

Gathering
The desire for inequality

"Gathering?" he asked.

"That's the name of the building ... and the charity."

"*Charity?*"

"Well they're not registered or anything, unless it's like under a different name, but they've got some kind of arts funding program. They're non-profit, anyway."

The door opened to the soft touch of her finger.

"It's left open?" he asked.

She shook her head. "They told me it would be open for an hour after you introduced yourself. That's why we had to rush." She grimaced at the inconsistencies in this explanation.

"*What?*"

"Look, they've got their own rules, okay?" she snapped, then produced another big smile in apology. "Come on, I'll show you around."

The door closed softly but quickly, squeezing tight behind them to create a vacuum seal. The darkness was sudden and absolute.

"It's okay," she whispered. "The lights will come on."

A recessed light in the ceiling glowed in the distance, then another, then another, sufficient to reveal a long, windowless foyer with a floor of bronzed marble, gleaming and immaculate. The walls and ceilings appeared to be decorated with a luxurious bronze paint traced with gold leaf. More lights appeared, each a little closer than the last at irregular intervals, so that their approach resembled the careful footsteps of a predator. As always when she entered this building, she was transfixed by their progress.

"Faaaaantastic," he muttered, thinking that only history could produce such a decadent waste of space. "Has it been restored?"

"I don't know. I suppose so. The door's hydraulic and the lights are on sensors." These were merely her assumptions; Renka had declined to comment on the mechanics of the building, other than to offer the throwaway comment, *It just works.*

The lights now picked up a line of elegant French chairs, neatly arranged and equally spaced along the left wall, casting tall and irregular shadows. An impulse that it would be impolite to do otherwise prompted him to count the chairs, the only feature in the bronze foyer. There were thirteen.

"There are thirteen residences in all," she said, as if the number had jumped from his head into hers. "Two or three on each floor. The building's even higher than it looks, I think."

"Listen, babes, I'm not going any further until you tell me what's going on. Is someone pulling my chain?" He considered her with suspicion. "Has my wife put you up to this?"

As the lights shone overhead her hand instinctively went to the right side of her face, partially concealed by a sweep of her lustrous black hair and carefully held in place with hairspray and clips. She decided to let the 'babes' go. "I work for the people who own this building," she explained. "Well, maybe they just manage it…"

"And tell me what this *Gathering* does again?" he asked, but in a reflective voice. He was sure that he had glimpsed the rough texture of scarring on her right cheek and ear when her hair had moved slightly with her touch; he now recalled that she had been holding that side of her head as they hurried out of the show apartment.

She seemed to find his change of tone significant, for she turned to present her left side to him. On this profile her hair was swept back to allow her cheekbones to celebrate the alluring smoke of her eyes.

"It sponsors struggling artists. Well, it like gives them free accommodation and support."

He smirked. "Well that's generous, but I never really thought of myself as an *artist* before."

His eyes darkened momentarily as a solid truth hardened in his subconscious.

Just want to be somebody… Show my bitch wife I'm someone to be respected… Show them all…

"You're a historian…" she suggested cautiously. "Or actor, writer. Whatever." Again she remembered herself and smiled, this time with encouragement.

He shrugged. "Just want to get on the telly, to tell you the truth. That's all I've *ever* wanted." He felt his mobile vibrate but he didn't answer, feeling it would be inappropriate. "So

13

why's it called Gathering?" he asked, having surprised himself at resisting the call of his iPhone.

"I think it's got something to do with *that*." She looked up at the ceiling to indicate an inscription in the same script as the door plaque, but this time proud and noisy, carved in letters large enough to be read twenty feet up:

It became customary to gather in front of the Huts or around a large tree: song and dance, true children of love and Leisure, became the amusement or rather occupation of idle men and women gathered together. Everyone began to look at everyone else and to wish to be looked at himself, and public esteem acquired a price.

"What's this?" he asked. They had to walk to read the inscription that ran in a line down the centre of the ceiling.

"It's Rousseau."

He had heard of Rousseau: a philosopher who influenced the French Revolution. He made to speak, then hesitated, realising this was pretty much the extent of his knowledge.

"Yeah, Rousseau, of course."

"Of course," she murmured dryly.

The one who sang or danced the best; the handsomest, the strongest, the most skilful, or the most eloquent came to be highly regarded, and this was the first step at once toward inequality and vice: from these preferences arose vanity and contempt on the one hand, shame and envy on the other.

He massaged his neck to hide his embarrassment, wondering if she was getting her revenge for those smirks over her accent. For someone who'd written a play about the last Dauphin his knowledge of Revolutionary France was thin on the ground. In fact, it was confined to an old book he had found in a junk shop.

"We can leave, if you want," she said.

"What?"

"Kris," she said, her first use of his Christian name summoning his full attention. "It's important that you know that. In fact, they told me to *say* that. You don't have to see the room. You can just go."

"What, after coming all this way? Don't you want to show me it?"

"I'm *instructed* to. That's not what I'm saying."

By the time they had reached the end of the foyer she had taken his silence for his answer. In a recessed shaft of the far wall was seated a black iron cage; it revealed itself as a lift as its front folded up on their approach.

"Don't tell me, sensors…" he said, as impressed as he had been with the ceiling lights. "Retro cage lift with a modern suspension. Outfuckingstanding!"

"Please Kris, don't swear," she whispered.

"Oh sorry, I didn't mean…"

She shook her head, her hand going instinctively to her hair. "No, I don't mind, honest. Just don't swear here, in the foyer. In the rooms upstairs, that's okay: they're *yours*." She meaningfully lowered her voice. "And you need to speak quietly."

He smiled with confusion.

"This is where they gathered," she explained, with a glance at the chairs. "It doesn't like… Look, just imagine you're in church or something."

They stepped into the lift and turned. There were no

controls inside the cage: no buttons, not even a lever. The foyer was returning to gloom, the animal on the ceiling retracing its steps.

"Which floor?" he asked.

She didn't answer, her eyes glazing over at the approach of the darkness. The dream always started here in this lift, the chairs blinking out one by one.

"Fabrienne...?"

"I have no idea," she replied, distracted.

They waited.

"Sorry, did you say –?"

"Kris, think of something."

"What?"

"Look, I know this sounds odd, but just concentrate. Try to find a connection with the building."

He looked from her to the foyer ceiling, mentally reciting the inscription until he gave a shudder of exhilaration. Three competing tugs of passion put hooks in his skin: they were attached to long threads of empathetic familiarity, cast by the building as a line fisherman finds his catch.

The first tug was his name.

Knight.

He felt the second tug: it was his eighteenth-century French play.

The Dauphin's escape from prison.

Yes, the building remembers that.

And the third tug, the strongest of all, actually painful in his imagination.

His ambition.

The need to be celebrated, just as the inscription said.

The lift door closed.

11

The Chess Room

Y ES, IT'S HIM.
    And no, we shouldn't follow. Fabrienne will see us: she has hunted eyes.

These were the answers to two questions the bearded man had asked his notebook, as he sat in the Starbucks next to the sales office. As always, the questions were posed in the front, the answers written in a rapid hand at the back. Occasionally he punctuated these answers with a smiley, which would always result in a curious but delighted raise of his eyebrows. The book was expensive, brushed suede with thick watermarked paper, and entitled *Gracie's Book (3)*, for it already had two predecessors hidden under the back seat of his Land Rover.

He closed the book and thoughtfully tapped its cover, then reached into a small buttoned pocket in his waistcoat to locate and discreetly nestle in his palm a small porcelain-like figurine of a teenage girl. She had tightly pinned red hair, her hands behind her back, one hand squeezing a finger of the other. Her expression could be described as one of bored curiosity.

"But how do we know it's him?" the man asked, his North Wales accent stretching the 'how' and applying a pause before 'it's him'. The Starbucks was all but empty but he spoke quietly, his voice deep and breathy. His huge hand closed around the figurine with the closing of his eyes, before he sighed and returned the girl to his waistcoat. The book was open at the back. He waited, his hand poised with his pencil. Shortly it went to the page.

His name is KNIGHT. Honeyman, the room showed me a chessboard. Remember?!

"So it did," he muttered thoughtfully, smiling at her use of his surname, his preferred appellation. "So it did…"

And don't forget that Chelsea London's occupancy of Gathering started with HER surname too. The building needs to find things it recognises.

He nodded as he wrote. Chelsea London was an international movie star and lived in rooms of the building once occupied by an author of romantic novels. That author's last novel had been entitled *The London Address*.

His eyebrows rose in amusement as he received a belated rebuke.

We've been through all this before!!

Replacing the notebook in his overcoat pocket, he sat back and observed the shopping precinct, content to await the return of the striking sales assistant, when he would adopt the guise of a prospective purchaser. Alternatively, he might take advantage of a business card which read 'theatrical agent' if it prompted her to reveal a snippet of information on the actor Kris Knight. Then with a grunt of dissatisfaction he thought better of it: he should come back at a later date, when he had had a better opportunity to monitor the man's progress.

He closed his eyes, deciding that was the better course, though he would doze for a while before he left. Gracie had identified the actor a week ago and insisted on a pursuit through pubs, cafés and stores, even camping out at his place of work, until the man had at last wandered into The Pavilion to make his connection with Gathering.

Yes, I'll come back another day. Now I can sleep a little...

He smiled contentedly, partly to block out that detested suspicion that his process with the notebook was a fantasy he had devised.

A fantasy where Gracie wasn't dead, and he wasn't a child murderer.

★

Kris counted three floors that dropped beneath the rising bars of the lift cage.

"We're here," Fabrienne said, as they came to a silent stop. The ascent had been quick and smooth but he felt a tremor of draining energy, as if the lift had pushed through something difficult.

He let out a short gasp of weary disorientation. "How many floors are there?"

Her journey in the lift was always to the top floor. "Six," she said immediately, the fleeting glimpses of walls, corridors and doors beyond the bars a revolving movie in her head. She was always accompanied in this lift, finding it curious that her host invariably seemed to find the smooth, seamless journey tiring.

Kris looked around. To his left was bare stone, the chaotic dimensions of the building having produced the jutting elbow of a wall of a room. The short corridor ahead ending in a teak door was lit, but the corridor to his right was in gloom. Its door, like some of the others he had spotted on his ascent, was boarded up.

"Are you sure the building's safe?" he murmured. The planks were irregularly cut and damp, brutally hammered in with long rusted nails bent into the wood.

"Not all the building's in use, that's all."

"It's listed?"

"I suppose." Again, she was merely guessing.

He turned a full circle, supposing that the cage lift was designed to open in three directions, depending on which corridor it was accessing. Like the folding of a metal accordion, its front now quietly opened. They stepped out into the lit corridor to find that the door at the end had a brass plaque, which as with the plaque on the entrance was shining as if it had just been polished:

La Pièce D'échecs

"The Chess Room," Fabrienne translated.

"You speak French," he muttered rhetorically, but thinking that he wouldn't have needed the translation: the name, which he now mouthed soundlessly – *La Pièce D'échecs* – was buried in his subconscious. He shrugged mentally, thinking that he probably knew more French than he realised.

She glanced back at the lift. "You don't have to go in, Kris," she reminded him quietly. "We can still go back."

The door had no handle or keyhole: it was opened with a wrought iron thumb latch. She again took his silence for agreement as she pushed it.

The cloud of dust belonged to a room locked up for centuries. The faint outline of the arch windows was traced by the sunlight captured in the glass.

Fabrienne seemed to share Kris's surprise at this unexpected barrage of haze and light, though the dust settled quickly, sucked into a draft in the corridor. Painted white walls emerged, a Rococo frivolity playfully concealed in the shell-shaped ceiling cornices and small discreet wall murals. The room was huge.

His jaw dropped. "There's no way I can possibly afford this..."

"I told you, it's free."

If the walls were restrained, the floor was as loud as a trumpet, laid with the bronzed marble of the foyer but etched with friezes. Some showed chess pieces; others games of chess, the participants hunched in concentration. He turned to Fabrienne, who had followed him in cautiously as if she feared she would trip a burglar alarm. "But the service charge? The council tax?"

"All free. Provided your references are accepted." Now inside and having carefully closed the door, she looked around in undisguised awe. "Wonderful, isn't it? The Trustees call this room the *salon*."

"Salon?"

"Like the building it means 'gathering': in this period, a literary or philosophical gathering under an impassioned host."

He stretched his shoulders in bemusement. Dramatic chaise longues in brown velvet and regency striped chairs in the centre of the salon were served by walnut coffee tables with delicately thin legs, and were all, she explained, restored original pieces. The framed oil paintings were originals too and she briefly closed her eyes to assemble the information she had memorised: Renka had fully briefed her on the description of the room while declining to actually show her the room. *Not appropriate without chess man*, had been the explanation.

"They're different artists, though painted at around the same time," she said. "Late 1780s, just before the Revolution. They're all of Paris."

The paintings didn't as much show the city, as its activities. There was the ascent of an air balloon, theatre productions, orchestras, garden readings, a chess tournament. They all had one common denominator: cheering crowds. The applause of wildly clapping hands echoed from the paint.

"Well, so long as there's room for my plasma," he remarked. "And my sofa. It's okay if I bring my gear up?"

She didn't know the answer to this question. "Provided nothing's moved," she suggested as a safe compromise.

Ornamental pieces were placed to strategic effect against the walls; as he walked the perimeter he was drawn to a wooden cabinet with gilt-bronze feet. The two front doors could be opened to display four drawers, each with an alpine relief: rocks and mountains, the snow applied in silver leaf. He tried one of the drawers, it was locked. "Japanese lacquer cabinet," he muttered. "Exported through the Dutch East India Company. Shows a relief of Mount Fiji."

"Really?" she asked with surprise.

He cleared his throat, having no idea where that information had come from. Concentrating, he realised that many things were more than just familiar: they were *known*. At the next wall ornament, a console with various objets d'art, he examined a porcelain inkstand with two celestial globes. The zodiac globe would contain ink, the constellation globe silver-gilt. Another object, something that appeared to be a gold enamelled shell, he recognised as a snuff box.

He stopped himself, forcing his mind to empty as he waited for logic to come to the rescue. He must have read about this room somewhere; it was probably famous. Perhaps he'd fallen half-asleep watching a history arts programme.

Alternatively, perhaps the information in his head was all nonsense and he was just on a high of creative adrenaline. Maybe someone had been smoking something in the lift. He returned the snuff box to the console, remembering the rush before the lift doors had closed, then the feeling of exhaustion during the ascent.

"Does the furniture belong to a heritage trust or something?"

"I don't know. Perhaps."

"So I suppose this charity is set up to look after all this furniture. Do they want me to be a caretaker or something…?"

"No, it's like I said: they help struggling artists. This is to be your home. Everything here is to be *used*."

He walked to the windows and marvelled briefly at the view: he could see Penarth Marina across the barrage, to the north the skyline of the city centre. The windows themselves were solid glass in fixed lead panes. He breathed the air and it was fresh; there must be an open window somewhere.

Stepping back, he realised that the glass was clear. The weatherworn smears he thought he saw from the ground must have been a trick of the light; either that or the outside was coated with something clever to maintain privacy.

"Through those doors is the bedroom and bathroom," she said, indicating doors at the far end on opposite walls. He turned expectantly. "You can't see them, Kris. Well you can, but only when they've given me the keys." She made eye contact. "So what do you want to do?"

He breathed out expressively. "What can I say? It's free and it's big and it's faaaaantastic, even if it does feel like a museum. Of course I'll take it." He decided to press his luck. "On one condition: that you show me how the kitchen works on our next visit? Supper maybe? I make a shockingly good Thai green curry."

She smiled politely.

"What do you think, babes?"

Her response was pre-empted by a memory, where she was back in her dream, bound and naked in the foyer, masked men and women sitting on the thirteen chairs chanting the Rousseau inscription. A knife was at her breast, tracing her heart. She would wake suddenly to the echo of screams...

"Sure, that would be nice," she said, not relishing the prospect of explaining to Renka that their target hadn't moved in because she wasn't prepared to accept a dinner invitation, or because he had called her 'babes'. "But they'll be checking your references first," she reminded him.

"No problem. D'you want some names?"

"Oh no, nothing like that." She paused, remembering another part of her instructions. "I don't know how long it will take, but it might be a while. Do you have somewhere to live in the meantime?"

He shrugged with embarrassment. "Staying in the YMCA, to tell you the truth."

From her purse she took a piece of paper with a handwritten telephone number and the name 'Mason'. "Ring this man. He's got a room available in Roath and he's cheap."

"I really don't think I can afford..."

"He's *very* cheap," she emphasised. "I think he's just

grateful for the company, to tell you the truth. There won't be any bonds or six-month tenancies or anything."

She waited for him to pocket the note before making her next statement.

"And there's something else you need to see before you make your decision."

Near the centre of the salon there was a narrow section of wall with a feature wallpaper of black flowers. It contained a discreet panel door.

"It's through here," she said, pushing the panel partially open to reveal a dark alcove. Squeezed in at the back was a contraption which appeared to be a partially closed cabinet, its open panel displaying antiquated gears and cogs. On top of the cabinet was a chess set.

"What is it?" he asked. "I can't really see…"

As the door was fully opened a powerful recessed light brought the alcove to life. A life-size figure sat behind the cabinet, its right hand resting on a cushion, the other holding a long smoking pipe.

"Fuck me," Kris groaned, catching his breath.

"I know," she whispered. She had jumped too, even though she had been told what to expect. The figure Renka had explained would be waiting in the alcove was perhaps made of china, its skin shining ebony, and was dressed in exotic robes and turban. The head was slightly bowed, the glass eyes levelled on the chessboard. "It's called the Turk," she explained. "It was the first automaton."

He frowned suspiciously. "Automaton…?" he murmured. "You mean it's a robot or something?"

"It's from the eighteenth century and very famous. Invented by a man called Kempelen."

"What does it do?"

"It plays chess, Kris. The Turk would use its free arm, the one on the cushion, to move the pieces. It hardly ever lost, and it played in all the best courts of Europe. It's said it even played with Napoleon, though Napoleon tried to cheat."

Kris looked at the Turk, then at Fabrienne, then back at the Turk. "What?!" he said incredulously.

"There was a man inside the cabinet," she said dryly. "Obviously. See the different panels? He'd move around in the cabinet when each panel was opened to make it appear there was nothing inside but levers, which dropped into place when the seat was moved. Those cogs and gears are fake and just fold away. It's a magic illusion."

He nodded with thoughtful appreciation. "But how did the guy inside play?"

"The chess pieces are magnetised: each has a string underneath the board to show its position on the grid. The chess master had a metal pointer that would move the Turk's arm."

Kris gave a groan of appreciation as he imagined the crouched chess player concealed in the darkness, unable to sneeze, trying to understand the dynamics of the chess game from pieces of string. "The poor sod must have been brilliant."

"But never seen," she agreed. "Rempelen got all the glory."

"Right, very much *behind* the camera. And you say Napoleon played on this thing?"

She shook her head. "No, *that* Turk was destroyed in a fire. This is another machine. A prototype, I think." Her voice lowered. "Not many people know about it."

He looked at her pointedly. "So where'd this come from?"

"Gathering believes it was Rempelen's first machine, that it was stolen and found its way here. The design of the chess set dates to the early part of his career."

She inwardly breathed her relief. Renka's explanation of the contraption had been very precise; the instructions, with her now for over three months, could finally leave her head.

"It doesn't bother you?" she asked.

"Why should it bother me?"

"It has to stay here, Kris. Everything has to stay. You'll have to live with this thing."

"It's locked away, isn't it? If I manage to nick a bird one night I'll make sure she doesn't wander in here by mistake when she makes my morning tea." He chuckled. "Or maybe I will, if she's a hummer and I want her to make a swift exit." He leaned into the alcove to examine the chess set, reluctant to step inside but close enough, with a stretch, to reach the chessboard. The white pieces facing him were eighteenth-century Europeans, the black pieces presenting their backs, some turbaned Eastern exotics.

An ivory Dieppe chess set, he thought, carved in the day when the French colonial wars against the Moors made such racist representations fashionable.

He straightened up, his heart pounding, perplexed at this strange new library of knowledge. Taking a deep breath he noticed something on the nearest edge of the board.

"The mobile is yours," she said, referring to the object he had spotted.

"Mine?"

"The charity will ring you, on that, when they've checked your references." She waited. Renka had been very clear that she wasn't to hand him the mobile, that she wasn't even to touch it.

"There's really no need," he said, reaching inside his jacket for his iPhone.

"No!" she said firmly. "They'll ring you on that: *only* on that."

He threw her a curious look, then shrugged and took a long step into the alcove. Snatching up the mobile, he quickly stepped out.

"Just keep it safe and they'll call when they're ready," she said, having noticed his aversion to the alcove. She empathised: this was a dark place in the salon, cold with anger and regret.

"Sure," he replied nonchalantly, weighing the mobile in his hand. It was heavy and seemed to be made of ivory, the slightly discoloured white bone giving it a bizarrely old appearance. It was also minimalist: just a numbered keypad and a display. "Are you sure the charity just doesn't want me here as a caretaker? I mean, the stuff in this place all feels very familiar."

"Does it?" she asked cautiously, having difficulty reconciling his knowledge of the Japanese cabinet with her initial assessment of him.

"Oh I don't know," he said, wary at venturing further into this territory. The detail and history of all the salon's furnishings had slotted neatly into his mind, as if his computer brain was downloading data. He even knew their date of construction: not just the year, but the month, the tools used... If he concentrated, really concentrated, perhaps he would even see the faces of the artisans...

He returned to the mobile, deciding that it was just another bad case of déjà vu brought on by the dust and mothballs. "Does this thing even work?" he asked.

In answer, the display illuminated to show a white Dieppe knight on the chessboard: a bewigged troubadour astride the upper torso of a horse. The display briefly changed to a traditional schematic of a chess game ready to start. A white knight faded out then reappeared in its move.

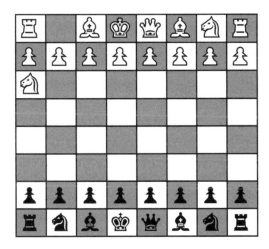

He blinked with shock. "Nice app," he muttered as the display faded then went dead.

"What did it do?"

He didn't answer immediately. "It showed a knight. It moved."

"A knight? And it moved? Then it could have been made for you."

He nodded slowly, buying time as he struggled to regain his composure. He had felt a rush of adrenalin as the knight moved; it was a strange type of high, a charged cocktail of ambition and creativity. In that moment he felt he could conquer the world.

"Our hour's up," she said gently, seeing his dazed expression, with a touch of his elbow leading him to door. As she closed the salon door behind them he caught a glimpse of a full-length mirror opposite the wallpaper feature. It was plain and innocuous, a wooden frame without even a bevel in the glass – the reason, no doubt, he had missed it.

Going down in the lift, the sense of weariness returned, that feeling of pushing through invisible barriers. In his imagination he turned and rotated his memory image of the mirror, acquired through only that one fleeting glimpse, but unlike the rest of the furniture in the salon it was inscrutable, refusing to reveal its secrets.

An alien, setting up residence in the strangely familiar room.

III

The Game of the Little Prince

K RIS'S MOBILES WERE both laid out neatly on his desk as he typed. From under his headphones he gave them the occasional protective glance, as a parent might check on sleeping children.

Neither mobile was working.

Infuriatingly, when he had taken his iPhone to the Apple store it had started up as the smug, acne-ridden teenager tested it, with dozens of messages noisily announcing their arrival. When he got home it promptly went off again and he spent the evening with the charger and the manual until he resorted to walking to a payphone to ring his daughter Lucy. It was 10p.m. and she was asleep, her stepfather angrily putting the phone down, though Kris was reassured just to get through. Walking home, he mentally composed on predictive text the message he would send her when he was connected again. His hand ached to feel the promise of his mobile's vibration.

The following afternoon he had returned to the Apple store; the iPhone again obligingly sprang into life, this time with a pornographic film being moaned out at high volume. The assistant looked with astonishment at the display, then with equal astonishment at his Gathering mobile brought out along with it. Kris snatched both back and hurried out, the porn stars grunting from inside his pocket.

The iPhone shortly shut down again but the experience

made him reluctant to return to the store. That evening, as he sat on his bed and considered his iPhone like some dead pet, he supposed the Gathering mobile had done something to damage it: perhaps its frequency messed with other networks. He would just have to live with it until the charity rang; in the meantime, recalling the astonished look of the kid in the store, it would probably be safer if he kept their mobile secret. After all, it was unusual and looked expensive: maybe someone would steal it.

Now in work, still waiting for his call, he turned from his computer screen to consider his ill-fated iPhone. The sense of isolation of that first week had been unbearable, his withdrawal pangs tapping out message after imaginary message, yet now in his second week he didn't feel so bad about his inability to call and text. In fact, he was starting to realise, he didn't feel so bad at all, a subliminal message telling him that there was nothing that might arrive on his iPhone that could possibly interest him.

He shook his head to banish this ludicrous notion. Lucy rang him twice a week: nothing was more important than that.

With lightning speed he tapped his mouse, switching out of his screenplay and reopening the minutes he should have been typing. Someone had stopped outside, perhaps to study the noticeboard; he decided with irritated resignation to turn the transcription machine back on.

He waited for the sound of footsteps, eyeing the minutes with hatred. It was one of those curious quirks of fate that at 42 years of age he had ended up here, as a part-time typist. His passport still stated 'actor' – a standing tribute to an undergraduate course entitled 'Acting and Stage Combat' from the University of Essex – but his thirties had been mainly spent in the Canaries selling timeshare, a quick stopgap to clear his debts turning into a career while he collected rejection letters for his film screenplays with himself as the lead. He had returned from Gran Canaria with just three things: a suntan, a young wife and a typing skill acquired as a result of a year's enforced placement in the resort's contract department. His wife Trish wanted to live near her parents and their savings went into a new build semi-detached.

He had quickly lost the suntan; within a year, he had lost the wife. Trish insisted he had changed, that she was sick of him being so restless, so dissatisfied with his life. Maybe it wasn't his fault; perhaps the British climate was to blame.

Yeah, that or the six-foot-four bodybuilder you...

He froze, muttering the fractious but secretive curse of the unrepentant sinner as he heard two voices in the corridor, one belonging to his young, officious supervisor. He reluctantly returned his headphones to his ears and his foot to the pedal, his whole body groaning with tedium as he was returned to the scheduling meeting. He sighed as he listened, then typed. An executive was lamenting the lack of public awareness of radio's quality programming: superbly acted plays, incisive documentaries, the most frank and penetrating interviews...

Kris slowly shook his head to the tap of his fingers, thinking that the executive was completely missing the point about television: its unique ability to create community through the most banal and vulgar spectacle. With television the mob was back in the Roman arena: the thumb that once slit the throats of gladiators now pressed the phone, gifting careers to aspiring singers or ejecting some disliked contestant.

Out of the corner of his eye he saw the loose hanging suit of his supervisor pass his open door. He removed his headphones; it was 11 o'clock, which today meant a strategy meeting when all the suits would be squeezed into room 3A for about twenty minutes.

Out of habit now rather than expectation, he used this window of opportunity to check the Gathering mobile to see if there was any indication that he might have missed a call or received a message. He didn't really know what he was looking for; the keypad had turned out to be a facade, just numbers carved in the ivory. The thing had no power source, no battery case and not a single button; if it didn't feel so heavy he would have been sure it was something out of a Christmas cracker.

He sighed and sat back. He could always pop into The Pavilion sales office, but he didn't want to seem like a stalker. He had returned to the sales office later that first day to thank Fabrienne for the accommodation tip – a dirt cheap room in a house in Roath with a geek landlord – but the brief conversation was conducted solely through the intercom. He had then bumped into her quite by chance on the weekend, when he was out in the Bay with his date at The Comedy Club, a particularly uninspired choice of venue given that he was feeling distinctly out of sorts because of the loss of his iPhone. His date, an ebullient divorcee wearing too much black make-up around her eyes and determined not to talk about her kids or that *bastard* she had married, had started the evening enthusiastically enough, but by the time they had eaten she had contracted his sour humour.

The evening got worse when they hit The Comedy Club, in spite of how eagerly he had been looking forward to it. It was a private function with a select audience, booked only by calling in several favours through his actors' guild in the hope of making some media connections. Indeed, before the first act came on there was a small commotion as the presence of a celebrity, Cardiff Bay's own Chelsea London, was announced. He became animated on seeing the actress, a black woman in late middle age sitting alone at a booth. She had no drink; she was watching the stage with her arms crossed, her long, elegant face a mask of mild derision.

Without explaining his actions to his date, he got up with the intention of approaching her. He had his sales patter ready: he would rave about one of her more obscure television parts to demonstrate that he was a true fan, hopefully to secure an address where he could send her his screenplay.

He didn't make it very far, instead catching the eye of an astonished Fabrienne returning from the cloakroom. In the sales office she had worn a shapeless blue and yellow sales uniform and minimal make-up; this evening she was in slinky black number with heels and looked fantastic.

"Hey, small world," he said, his stomach fluttering.

She opened her mouth to speak, then shook her head instead.

"Is everything okay?" he asked. "I haven't heard anything yet. From the charity, I mean."

"Kris, I really can't talk. Not now." In spite of the fact that this was effectively a private party, she looked distinctively uncomfortable at being out in public, casting furtive glances to the corners of the club.

"Look, I appreciate this is your own time, but I just wanted to say…"

"No, no, it's not that. I mean I really can't speak. I really *can't*. I'm with someone."

He shrugged, hiding his disappointment. "Sure, so am I," he countered, though reluctant to identify the lucky woman. "I was just going over to say hello to our local celebrity over there."

She glanced at the booth, then looked back to Kris, pulling in his full attention with her eyes. She waited a few moments, then whispered, "Got to go!" and rushed back to the cloakroom, her hand to her head.

He watched her hurry out of sight, struggling to process what had just happened, then looked at the booth, to see it was empty. He turned back to his date. She was gone as well.

It had been a strange evening, leaving him on his return home with an unfulfilled longing that went beyond loneliness. His reflection in the mirror of his wardrobe door returned the burning desire to be someone else.

Someone with their own booth. Someone who beautiful women didn't run away from...

At his computer he glanced at the clock to banish the memory of his downcast reflection, thinking that everyone had the odd bad Saturday night. In the time remaining to him he returned to his screenplay *The Game of the Little Prince*. He hadn't been lying to Fabrienne, he did have an appointment lined up with a television executive this Friday, but the executive, Lisa Buoys, had an office on the third floor and had agreed to give him a fifteen-minute slot just in order to stop his constant haranguing of her PA. The suggestion he had given to Fabrienne that the play was a done deal was a complete lie. In fact, he wasn't even sure if Buoys had read it.

Submitted with his treatment to Buoys was an article from *The New York Times* dated 15 January 1922, headed 'Unsolved Mystery of The French Revolution'. This was a critique of a then-topical novel by one Georges Lenotre, which explored the mystery of the fate of the Dauphin, Louis-Charles. The article unreservedly supported Lenotre's view that the

Dauphin had escaped from his captivity at the hands of the Revolutionary Commune.

Lenotre's analysis of this old and long-debated mystery was compelling. The agreed facts were that after Louis XVI was executed in January 1793 the Commune, in fear of foreign powers recognising the Dauphin as king, separated him from the rest of his family, to include his sister Marie Therese, who would miraculously survive the Revolution and keep an account of these days. Traditional wisdom had it that the Dauphin, or Little Capet as he was called by the Revolutionaries who preferred to use his ancestral name, was under the custody of the leader of the Commune, Anaxagoras Chaumette: a man so fiercely atheistic he had changed his first name to banish the biblical 'Pierre Gaspard'. Chaumette used his creature Antoine Simon, a cobbler, to teach the young innocent uncouth habits and lurid songs, but this was just the beginning of his degradation. In January 1794 Simon left the prison and Little Capet was now treated appallingly, bricked up in solitary confinement. When the Commune fell six months later, the heads of Chaumette and Simon falling with it, the prince was released from his cell though still kept away from his family and servants. His changed, withdrawn demeanour – no longer the precocious child reciting Tacitus – was thought to be the psychological result of his confinement. He died of tuberculosis a year later.

That was the official line, but on reading Lenotre's book it was extraordinary that anyone could have been sold this pup: with Chaumette's connivance Simon had clearly taken the Dauphin with him when he left the prison in January 1794.

Kris reviewed his two-page treatment, the synopsis that would hopefully have persuaded Buoys to read his hour-long dramatisation where he took the part of Chaumette, with

Rhys Ifans being at the top of his wishlist for the cobbler Simon. His finger ran down the bullet points that referenced the key inconsistencies Lenotre had identified, which he needed to be fully familiar with in case she interrogated him.

He closed the document, taking a breath of wishful expectation, then as an afterthought googled 'Gathering'. Once more, and in spite of numerous variations, he wasn't able to find a single reference to a charity that helped struggling actors. In fact he was starting to suspect this was some sort of elaborate hoax: perhaps Trish had friends who had engineered it.

He took a moment to seriously consider this proposition. No, that was ridiculous. The building was real; perhaps Gathering just didn't care for his references, whatever they might be.

His eyes did a double-take. One last search, googled as 'Gathering Rousseau', had at last produced a link. The link for some reason took him to a website entitled Message Gong, where the home page was blank aside from the website's name in French script. Numerous link tabs merely gave the same message in large letters: 'Awaiting'.

He again typed 'Gathering Rousseau', then nodded as he found no link. The Message Gong thing was just a misdirection error.

He logged off and with another glance at the clock, which told him the meeting in 3A would be coming to an end, reluctantly switched the window to his minutes. He considered his two useless mobiles, as dead as the Dauphin and his double, then put on his headphones and returned to the meeting. The executive was rambling on about scheduling and he went into autopilot as he tapped away.

Shortly he frowned. A faint but discordant crash had

interrupted the executive. Two bells followed, the second very shrill. He waited for someone in the meeting to say something, to comment on what was presumably an alarm, but the meeting went on as if nothing had happened.

He replayed the tape, to hear the dialogue without the interruption. He waited, listening to the voices, until another sound, this time a deep, shivering gong, gatecrashed the meeting.

With a gasp of comprehension he quickly pulled off his headphones. Gathering's mobile was ringing.

I V

Message gong

I T WAS THREE fierce chimes. He heard its second repeat. The first was a bass note, a low and resonant gong. Then a chime, its sustain dull and flat as if the bell was heavy with rust. Then, a shrill high note, sharp and off-key, ruining any sense of harmonic expectation.

But this wasn't the alarming development. The mobile's three-note clarion, repeated insistently after a pause of a few seconds, was so *loud*: the small device seemed incapable of generating such power.

"Kris, what the *hell*...?"

It was his ferret-faced supervisor, Dylan Hughes, standing in the doorway with a hand at his ear. The noise had interrupted the planning session. Kris snatched the Gathering mobile into his lap, just as it was re-arming its brass throat. It vibrated momentarily in his palm, then went silent.

"What *is* that?" Dylan asked in a thick West Wales accent.

Kris presented his palms. "Sorry mate, it's my mobile. I must have got it connected up to my computer speakers by mistake."

"No mobiles in office time," Dylan barked back, with a suspicious glance over the desk to see what he had snatched. Kris quickly stuffed the mobile into his roomy puffer jacket hung over his chair. "I won't tolerate this sort of behaviour, Kris," the 'tolerate' finding physical expression in an extended bony index finger. "And I'm not your *mate,* Kris. We're on first name terms here, but don't abuse it. Clear?"

Kris mentally counted to three as he regarded the pock-marked young man in his baggy suit, which he wore oversized to disguise a skeletal frame. "Right. Sorry, Dylan."

The ritual of chastisement seemed to satisfy his supervisor, though he left with a puzzled expression as the explanation of the computer speakers was digested. Kris took a relieved breath, sneaking a look at the mobile display as he pulled it gingerly halfway out of his pocket. The screen was illuminated and read:

Message for you

The text faded and a chess piece appeared. It was an ebony head and shoulders caricature of a negro; it had a saturnine face with white lips and eyes that glowered hideously.

"Black pawn?" he muttered, recalling the Turk's chess set, the Europeans against the Moors.

As before, the schematic chessboard briefly presented itself to show an enemy pawn moving forward two spaces, although this time he experienced no shock or disorientation.

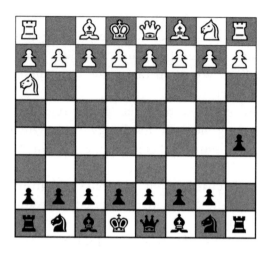

The chess piece returned to the display and now flashed expectantly. His thumb tentatively touched the screen and the image was collected up in a box and pulled into a far corner. A message appeared:

Address book created

He pressed the text and was taken to a page that was blank save for one name:

Lisa Buoys

He raised his eyebrows with anticipation, wondering if Buoys' PA was sending him an agenda or something for their meeting. Then he frowned: next to the name was an icon, the image of the Moor pawn. If this was an address book, it was as if the executive was actually represented by this chess piece. He pressed her name and a new page appeared, headed:

Details for Lisa Buoys

It read, simply:

Ugly lesbian bitch

★

"I have absolutely no idea who sent it," Fabrienne assured Kris once again, as they looked at each other through the glass cased model of The Pavilion development in the sales office. He had insisted that this conversation be face to face, refusing to explain the reason for his visit over the intercom. Once in, the Gathering mobile let him down, stubbornly refusing to switch on to display the message. "It must have been a crank call," she suggested, reluctantly prepared to accept his story. "Perhaps someone hacked into the network."

He made an effort to calm down, conscious that the 'ugly lesbian bitch' message had unsettled him. "It wouldn't be so bad if this thing actually worked; if I could make a call or something. It's just my luck that my iPhone's gone down at the same time. I feel lost."

"That may not be a coincidence," she conceded. "Gathering's network is very strong: other networks don't get through in close vicinity."

"Hey, that's no good, I can't –"

She wasn't in the mood for games. "Well give it back then."

He paused, then shrugged, pretending a casual examination of The Pavilion model to see if he could identify the show apartment he had seen. He shook his head with distaste; they all looked the same, unlike his glorious, unique salon.

Yes, it is a salon…

My *salon*…

He picked up the ivory mobile, which she hadn't touched or barely acknowledged, even though he had at first placed it inconsiderately in the centre of her papers. "Anyway, I haven't heard from your people," he complained, "and if this thing isn't working how are they going to get in touch?"

"It'll work, Kris. They'll be in touch."

"You seem pretty confident."

Walking around the glass case towards her she automatically put a hand to her right hairline as she turned to face him. "Do you think they'd have gone to all this trouble otherwise? Do you know how much they paid…?" She looked away.

He was making a concerted effort to ignore the sweep of her hair over her right ear: there was so much hairspray keeping it in place it looked like cardboard. "So is this some kind of test? Have I got to do something to satisfy them before I can move in?" He stretched his shoulders. "Do they want to make sure I'm an *artist*, or whatever you call it? I've got an acting class this Saturday, if that helps."

"I'm sure it will," she replied, but with little enthusiasm.

"D'you wanna come? It's in Chapter Arts Centre: we can have lunch afterwards."

She smiled, the blink of her eyes answering in the negative.

"Maybe some other time then," he muttered. "Perhaps when I've moved in, and you're not conflicted with any professional entanglement." He nodded to himself, considering this to be a perfectly valid reason for the rejection. And, now he thought of it, for last Saturday night. "Is that why you couldn't speak to me in The Comedy Club?" he probed. When she didn't answer he smiled with satisfaction, choosing to believe his propaganda. "I *will* move in, you know."

"You will," she agreed. "You'll castle."

He did a double-take. "Did you say *castle*?"

She returned to her desk and sorted through her brochures. "It's like ... just an expression," she said to her papers. "One we use in the trade," she added. "You know – when a king moves into his castle."

"Right," he said, unconvinced.

"Anyway, Kris, I'm sure they'll be in touch, and when they do I'll be delighted to show you the rest of the rooms." She searched for an appropriate way of ending the meeting. "And best of luck with your acting class."

As he pocketed the mobile he registered that the sales office was empty once again. "Are you actually open, Fabrienne? You seem very quiet for a sales office in the centre of town."

She stiffened. "It's mainly appointment-only on Mondays, though if someone buzzes and I'm satisfied they're not troublemakers I'll let them in." She hesitated. "I ... I only work here on Mondays. Other staff are here the rest of the week."

His eyes narrowed with a moment of insight. "Only *you* use that intercom, don't you? The rest of the week the doors are open."

"It's health and safety, because I'm here alone."

He felt both satisfied and confused as he returned to the busy shopping centre of The Hayes. He paused to take out his dead iPhone: if it wasn't going to work there was hardly any point in having it, he decided, for he had no intention of giving up Gathering's mobile and the chance of the call confirming his tenancy. He turned the iPhone round in his hand, considering how uninteresting, how vulgar the plastic contraption was.

He dropped it into a waste bin.

★

As Honeyman strolled past the sales office, with just a glance to check that the saleswoman had returned to her desk, a moving shadow through the opaque glass, he wondered whether she would remember him. He had been an overlooked potential viewer when she had hurried out of the building with Kris Knight and was gone by the time she returned.

Should he play the same role, or slip into some other guise? He had planned on paying her his visit much later, when he knew more about Kris Knight, but Gracie's figurine, warm and contented in his hand, was demanding this meeting immediately. She had predicted that the woman's phone would ring on the hour, that he needed to be talking to her at exactly that time.

There were several seconds of silence after he buzzed the intercom; he imagined his face being studied through the camera before the door clicked open. Fabrienne smiled in greeting as he stepped in, standing to the side to keep herself out of view of the street. Her eyes creased slightly as a bulb of uncertainty glowed dimly in her memory.

"I'm sorry, have you been in before?" she asked.

He smiled through the undergrowth of his beard. "I was here for a viewing last week," he answered, having realised there was a way he could refer to his previous visit while still creating his subterfuge. Within the pocket of his overcoat a business card he had selected found its way between his fingers, as he relaxed his grip on Gracie's figurine.

Fabrienne blinked, trying to remember: shortly her mouth opened in both surprise and embarrassment. "Oh yes, you were the gentleman who was waiting that time I had to rush out. I'm so, *so* sorry about that." She quickly cleared away the papers to indicate he had her complete and undivided attention. "You must believe me when I say that I really did have to leave…"

"Oh I understand completely."

Again her eyes creased.

"Honeyman," he said, offering a hand in greeting.

"Fabrienne," she replied cautiously.

"That's a charming name. Unusual, but charming."

She hesitated, accustomed to defending her name like a lioness defends her cubs. "Well, perhaps I can give you that tour of the show apartment now?"

He checked his watch: it was one minute to the hour. "I confess I'm a little pressed for time today," he said slowly. "Perhaps I could make an appointment?" As he made full eye contact, her hand went to her right hairline, just a flicker of his eyes in the wrong place enough to trigger a defence mechanism that the years had made as responsive as a web. Perhaps he should just admit Gracie had told him all about her: that her real name was Vaishali and that she worked for Gathering.

He decided against it, instead checking his watch once more with a shameful sense of cruelty. Two seconds to the hour…

"Oh!"

Her eyes widened in alarm, her hand going to the inside of her jacket. She had recognised the unusual throb, the quick double pulse like a heartbeat, that warned of a call from one particular person.

"Or perhaps I could take some literature?" Honeyman asked suddenly, throwing her off balance. She opened her mouth to answer, then stepped back, but as she again reached into her jacket she knew it was too late. The mobile was about to ring.

"Please take your call," he said. "I can wait."

She frantically shook her head. "Shut up! No, I mean I'm sorry…" The moment was all confusion: she had never received a call from *her* when someone was present. Renka had explained that would never happen.

Her Blackberry was in her hand. It vibrated with a passion, making the veins in her hand go iridescent blue, as the ringtone, the voice of a black woman in late middle age, shrieked out.

"ANSWER ME BITCH!"

Honeyman turned away in pretended embarrassment as Fabrienne muttered to the mobile.

"Can't speak … no, can't speak … someone's here… someone's here someone's *here!* I know … I know!"

"I'm sorry, is this a bad time?" he asked gently, as she returned her mobile to her jacket and her mortified expression found a half-smile.

"That was my crazy niece. She likes to send me silly texts. I'm so sorry."

He nodded. "In fact it is I who should apologise. I'm here under somewhat false pretences." He handed her his business card, which she took with a look of shocked exhaustion.

Tristyn Honeyman
Theatrical Agent

"I'm not really here to see one of your apartments," he confessed. "Which I'm sure are lovely, by the way. I'm interested in the actor who was visiting you just now."

She thought about this. "So last time you were here, you were waiting for *him* ... not for me?"

"Yes indeed."

"I don't understand."

"I've heard interesting reports about him, you see," he said, always attempting to keep as closely to the truth as possible when he was in one of his necessary deceptions. "But before introducing myself I'd prefer to see him in action. Did he give you any indication of when his next performance might be?"

She was still in a state of shock. Her caller had been furious, saying she'd take the matter up ... take the whole matter *up!* ... with Renka Tamarov. "I didn't think he has much going on like," she muttered, her accent finding a comfortable fit within her bewilderment. "Without wishing to say anything that might damage his chances," she added quickly.

"No indeed," he said reassuringly.

"Eh ... if it helps, he said he had an acting class on Saturday."

"Ah, perfect. Where is that?"

"Chapter Arts Centre."

They shook hands. As she buzzed him out she apologised again for her niece.

"She sounds ... needy," he remarked, with a squeeze of an eye in farewell.

In the surveillance camera she watched him go.

"More needy than you could possibly know..." she muttered as she returned to her desk.

V

Address book

"**Y**OUR PHONE'S TURNED off!" Trish snapped. "You avoiding me?"

She punctuated the question with three finger jabs to Kris's shoulder. He had only discovered she was a poker *after* they had married.

"Changed my mobile," he said defensively. They were in the car park of the Chapter Arts Centre and he was looking suitably embarrassed as the students from his workshop wandered past. "How did you find me here?"

"Spoke to your agent." She smiled pointedly as she took her mobile out of her bag: his agency was a company that traded above a chip shop in Grangetown and which accepted every type of theatrical *artiste* on payment of a monthly fee. "Okay, give me your new number." When he didn't answer she stuffed it back into her bag. "Playing games are we?"

"Trish, what do you want?"

"The papers are waiting to be signed. Did you get a solicitor, like I told you?"

He shrugged.

"I'm having the house, Kris. My solicitor tells me I'm entitled to it."

"Can't your personal trainer boyfriend put a roof over your head? We both slogged our guts out for the deposit on that place." He smiled ironically. "That was a good year, Trish. Remember the 'grub for a grand'?"

Her eyes softened momentarily at the memory of their first year of marriage, when they had eaten out in a fancy restaurant each time they saved £1,000 towards a house deposit. She had worked in the sales office on salary, but Kris, energised and on commission, had hunted unsuspecting holidaymakers with a carnivorous ferocity.

"Leave Stuart out of this," she said.

"Really? I thought he was the *reason* for all this?"

She looked at him aghast.

"Anyway, can't he put something into the pot?" he pressed, "I'm not making money anymore, Trish. Got a part-time typing job, which just about covers my payments for Lucy. I came back for *that*."

Came back for *you*, he thought.

"You can't be that hard-up. You drove here."

"Caught the bus, Trish. The only thing you left me was the sofa and the stereo. Remember?"

Trish considered him with suspicion. "I'm sure I saw your car..." When she noted his exasperated expression she said, "Anyway, you can always return to timeshare."

"You know I can't, Trish." He had left on bad terms with the management, breaking a notice period because Trish had insisted she'd found their house. The timeshare industry was as gossip-hungry as a sewing circle and as unforgiving as the Mafia.

"Anyway, Stuart hasn't got any money," she muttered to her fingernails.

No, no money, he thought ruefully: *just muscles.*

Stuart was some five years her junior and the biggest numbskull he'd ever seen; or rather glimpsed, as they came out of his favourite Thai restaurant, tipsy and loved-up. Trish, her face too horse-like to be considered conventionally pretty, still had the sexiest smile and those fantastic legs; she was wearing that short denim skirt that got him so...

"Get a solicitor, Kris. I mean it."

He winced as the 'mean' landed with a finger to his shoulder, then nodded in reluctant assent. "Got to go," he said, seeing that only the two of them were left in the car park.

She glanced mischievously at the Chapter door. "Can I watch?" she asked.

"Watch?"

"The acting class. Your agent told me it was an acting class."

Kris mentally cursed High Hopes, thinking he wouldn't bother reporting in with his schedule in future. They didn't care anyway; he only did it because it made him feel like he was doing something proactive. "Just brushing up," he muttered.

She was smirking. "Kris, you can't act. What are you thinking?"

"Watch this space. I've got my screenplay into the Beeb."

"So you're a writer too?"

"Best way to get a role."

"Oh please!"

"Anyway, it's a workshop. No spectators."

He was wrong, as the tutor, a young man called Carl with a ready smile and hyperactive hands explained when she inquired. It was important for budding actors to get used to an audience, the reason why the workshop was held in the largest theatre, the actors taking the front seats. Kris was the last in: when prompted to introduce himself, he rose to tell the class about his screenplay; when Carl expressed interest he explained it was about the escape of the last Dauphin, based on the theories of Georges Lenotre.

"And what made Monsieur Lenotre so sure he escaped?" Carl asked.

Kris happily took up the challenge, addressing the group to test the information crammed in his head. "The Dauphin's sister, Marie Therese, kept a lifetime diary. She was convinced to her dying day that her brother had escaped."

"That could have been the wishful thinking of a sister who didn't want to believe her brother dead," Carl suggested.

Kris nodded. "Okay, but it's difficult to explain why after the Commune fell the Dauphin shouldn't be reunited with his family, or at least have some contact. Think about it. It was clearly in the interests of the Revolutionaries for people to believe the Dauphin was safely imprisoned, rather than wandering around Europe seeking support from foreign power. Yeah? Revolutionary France was at war: the last thing it wanted was Royalist pretenders springing up everywhere." He presented his palms. "All this separation achieved was speculation. The prince was just as safe locked away with his sister, wasn't he?"

The class reflected on this with a group murmur.

Kris was animated, delighted at having this opportunity of a dry run before his meeting with Buoys. "Now this is incontrovertible fact. When the Dauphin died – that's to say when the boy in the *prison* died – the jailers let his body be identified by a few guards. These guards had only glimpsed him from a distance, walking in the gardens a few years before. This was in spite of the fact that on the upper floor of the prison they've got his sister and three longstanding servants ready to identify him."

"So?" the tutor asked.

"Don't you see? All this did was fuel the rumours, when the Revolutionaries could have scotched them then and there. Why ask virtual strangers to identify him?" He turned appreciatively to greet another group murmur, this time locking on to Trish at the back, who was yawning with boredom. "Oh yeah, and the doctor that had been called to examine the sick Dauphin died in mysterious circumstances the following day. Is it a coincidence that he was the royal family's family doctor?"

"He saw the boy was a double and refused to play ball?" a student suggested.

Kris nodded. "Got it in one. So when the Dauphin dies a few days later they got another doctor in. The one who removed his heart and kept it in his surgery."

"Removed his heart?" Carl asked with mock astonishment.

"Yeah, that was a tradition for French monarchs. By the way, when the grave of the eleven-year-old Dauphin was later excavated they discovered the bones of a rickety sixteen-year-old."

"That's unconfirmed," came a voice from the back. "There's dispute over the location and the source of that information."

Kris turned to the well-informed man in the overcoat at the back of the hall. He recognised the mass of hair and beard from somewhere.

"So what do *you* think happened?" Carl prompted.

Kris returned to the group, momentarily thrown off course by the interruption. "That's what my play is about. The Commune leader Chaumette, with the help of his right-hand-man Simon, smuggled the kid out of the prison in January 1794. This was purely for political advantage:

Chaumette believed that when the Revolution had run its course there'd be a call for the return of the monarchy. Anyone who had access to that monarch would be the power behind the throne: I know this might seem odd with two hundred years of hindsight, but back then no one believed they were creating a republic that would run and run.

"But things didn't go according to plan. Chaumette and Simon were guillotined and so the location of the kid was lost. When Chaumette's successors visited the prison to find the Dauphin missing, they had no choice but to put up a cover story, this solitary confinement bullshit, to explain away the period when no one, not even the Commune guards, had seen him. Then they substituted him. The last thing they wanted were rumours that the Dauphin was free." He paused for breath. "Anyway, no one knows what happened then, but in *my* story Simon's wife – she was childless and loved the kid – rescued the Dauphin from wherever her husband left him."

He smiled to say he was finished; from his screenplay he heard his final voiceover, as a boat headed for the New World.

Carl checked his papers. "And in this drama you're playing…?"

"Chaumette. I'm hoping Rhys Ifans is going to play the cobbler."

There were appreciative whistles.

"He hasn't confirmed yet," Kris conceded, sneaking a glance at Trish, her face all derision.

The man in the overcoat spoke again, gently but loud enough to be heard.

"But do you think Monsieur Lenotre and the reporter of

The New York Times would have been so confident if they had been writing in the year 2000?"

The North Wales accent placed heavy emphasis on the words 'two thousand'. The group turned towards the voice.

"Two centuries of speculation, rumour and theory..." the overcoat continued, "...come to an end with abrupt certainty."

This time the emphasis was on 'abrupt', the word causing Kris to wince. "Yeah, the gentleman at the back's referring to the DNA testing, when the heart of the kid who died in the prison was tested against the DNA of Marie Antoinette." He paused. "That threw me for a while, I won't deny it, but then I realised what must have happened. That's why my screenplay's so exciting, because everyone thinks the case is closed."

"I'm sure it will be wonderful," Carl declared, moving from his perched position at the end of his desk to a chair, where he quickly sifted through his notes. "Now, Kris, you're playing the part of Chaumette, and I see you describe him as 'a radical who hated all notions of rank and organised religion'. So, in getting inside this man's skin, this man as leader of the Commune would have been a street politician, so he would have been an orator. We can also assume that he was cunning, domineering..."

"And French," Kris added, lapping up a laugh.

Carl smiled. "So you want to play him with a French accent?" he inquired patiently.

"Absofuckinlutely."

More laughs, this time dampened by a strained look from Carl. Kris stretched his shoulders, having always loved playing the class clown. He turned to look at the overcoat again, but he was gone. Sitting near his place was Chelsea London: his inclination to gawp was curtailed by the fact that she was staring right back at him with a deadpan expression.

"Ladies and gentlemen," Carl announced, "I've a lovely surprise for you. Miss Chelsea London, Cardiff's own Hollywood star, has offered to drop by to watch the workshop. Big round of applause for Miss London." The group complied enthusiastically. "Please, everyone, face front. Miss London's only here to observe. Now, Kris, why don't we read your extract?"

Kris walked up on stage to more applause, the group lubricated with goodwill; he took his place at the end of the desk, leaning on it with one hand.

Carl was holding his extract. "Okay, I'm playing the crude cobbler, Simon, you're playing Chaumette. You're discussing how you're going to deal with the Dauphin. Now if you don't mind I'll deliver your lead line with an English accent."

"No problem. Not all of us can do accents." Kris winked at a pretty young girl in the front row, who accepted the flirtation good-naturedly. Out of the corner of his eye he collected another very different look of derision from his wife.

Carl took a breath; his words emerged as a sort of coarse Cockney, though sufficiently subtle to bring an admiring murmur from the group. "Let me take him under my wing, Patron. I'll teach him all my words and songs."

"Hey that's pretty good," Kris declared. "Maybe I better call off Rhys Ifans."

Some laughter and scattered applause.

"Okay, okay, settle down," Carl said to the group. "Kris, this time in character." He reset. "Let me take him under my wing, Patron. I'll teach him all my words and songs."

Kris took his hand from the table, raising it to his shoulder like a Roman consul. "Yeez, make Leeetle Capet looze his idea of rank. Better he be a cobbler than a poet."

This time the laughter was delirious. The only people not laughing were the tutor, who was maintaining a professional composure, and Chelsea London, whose deadpan expression remained in place, though she took this opportunity of getting up and leaving.

"I think you might need to work on that accent," Carl suggested at length. "And perhaps your delivery…"

Kris didn't reply, his cheeks flushing red.

"But that's why you're here, okay?" Carl added diplomatically, with reproving glances to the group. "Shall we try it again?"

Kris's eyes came to rest on Trish; she was physically shaking, her hand over her mouth.

Bitch…

"Kris?" Carl pressed.

"Look, it's been a while since I acted. And as you say, brushing up is why I'm here.'

"Oh, absolutely."

Guilty murmurs of encouragement.

"And perhaps I *should* lose the accent," he conceded.

Carl nodded. "Speak it in French with subtitles if you're using an accent. Otherwise there's a danger of it sounding like Monty Python."

Kris took it in good humour as the tutor now received the laugh, but he was anxious to get off the stage without losing face. With an uncomfortable flash of insight he had seen the clumsy dialogue of his screenplay, how badly written it was: he was faced with an honest realisation of his talent.

I can't write. I can't act.

"So are you ready, Kris?"

"Okay."

He hesitated as a pinprick of foreboding told him to look at his puffer jacket, folded on his chair in the second row.

"Kris?"

The three discordant chimes of the message gong brought the auditorium to silence. The repeat brought half of it to its feet.

He had a three-second window of opportunity before the gong sounded again. He managed to collect his jacket, just a touch of his pocket enough to disable the mobile, while privately vowing never to let it go off in public again.

A bus was mercifully pulling in across the road as he hurried out of Chapter, the jacket under his arm. By the time Trish came out to the car park he was safely on the back seat of the bus, checking his message.

It was another chess piece: a white infantryman with wig and shouldered musket.

White pawn, he thought. A chess move was displayed on the schematic, the king's pawn moving one space.

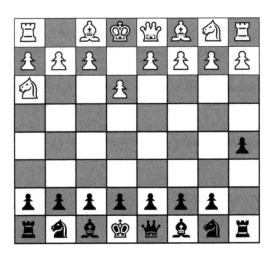

The pawn was bundled up with the message 'sent to address book'. The display now became a faint chessboard, a background of squares in marble off-white and taupe. Two icons appeared, in the top left and top right hand corners. In the top left was a bright red cartoon heart, which he supposed was the battery monitor, in the top right a miniature painting of a leather-bound book. This revealed itself as an address book since touching it produced an ornate desk with quill, ink and a curling page of parchment, which then took him to his names.

The bus's engine stopped and he looked up. *This must be a timing zone for the route*, he thought, but decided that no one would see him up here.

He returned to the display.

Lisa Man-suit
Mason Flower

Mason was his new landlord, a buck-toothed history lecturer – or perhaps he was just a researcher or something because he had a speech impediment – who he had secretly nicknamed 'the Goof'. His number was on his other mobile and he supposed Gathering had somehow transferred the details. This idea was dispelled when he touched Mason's name to reveal what appeared to be a detailed CV, though as he scrolled through the list of impressive academic qualifications, the information became wholly confidential in nature: extracts from tutors' reports and letters from literary agents.

Kris exhaled with appreciation. If half of the praise he was receiving on his academic papers was justified, his goofy landlord was clearly brilliant. The comments also appeared to be urging him, in vain, to get himself published on a commercial level: 'Mason's literary skills, combined with his passion for research, would make him a successful author in popular as well as academic circles. Sadly, his painful shyness, which appears to stem from a perceived failure of his social skills, is preventing him taking any professional step that might bring him even by accident into the public spotlight.'

Kris felt a tremor of unease: the Goof was probably the exact opposite of himself. Then his unease turned to embarrassment as the information became frank reports from the Goof's psychiatrist, analysing his problems with social interaction. Reference was made to his collapsing in a sobbing heap during counselling.

Kris looked up thoughtfully, wondering why he was being given this information, remembering that Fabrienne had passed him Mason Flower's details. Perhaps she had been prompted to do so by Gathering.

He returned to the mobile. Next to Mason's name was his chess icon, the white grenadier pawn, and Kris wondered if anything would happen if he accessed the icon. Touching the pawn revealed a message:

Go to the Mountain

His thumb thoughtfully massaged the off-white bone of the mobile, aware that 'The Mountain' was the term for the Jacobin majority who sat in the highest benches of the Revolutionary Assembly. Perhaps Gathering was telling him he should check some points of historical research on his screenplay with Mason. Perhaps that was why they had pointed him in his direction.

A touch returned him to the address book. He had noticed it immediately but he now gave some thought as to why

'Lisa Buoys' had been replaced by what was presumably a nickname, 'Lisa Man-suit'. He wondered if it was a glitch as he accessed her details; unlike Mason she had no information, just the original message:

Ugly lesbian bitch

The aggressive insults were bothering him: they didn't sit with his theory that this chess game was some sort of entrance exam Gathering had set. Gathering was a charity, after all; nice people who offered free accommodation to struggling artists.

He thought it through. Buoys' name had been accessed just after he went on the internet in the office: perhaps the chess game was hosted through an internet site and the black pieces were being downloaded by people visiting the site. Gathering only controlled the white pieces, which explained his receiving the Goof's helpful background information; with the white pieces he got help with his screenplay, with the black pieces he just got something stupid, nasty and ultimately irrelevant.

He nodded, thinking that this was possible. He wondered if Buoys' Moor pawn icon had a message too. His thumb gave him the answer.

Make the bitch cream in her man-suit
Show her the proving documents

He huffed with irritation, this vulgar nonsense both confirming and disproving his theory, having no idea what 'the proving documents' might be. With another touch of the display he was returned to the screen with the marble chessboard, which he now assumed was the menu screen. It produced a third icon in the centre of the display. Perhaps this home screen showed the systems that were being downloaded and would allow him to access the mobile; with a measure of excitement he supposed it might work like a normal phone in a few days' time.

The third icon was the painted miniature of a thumb latch, similar to the iron latch on the door of the salon. He pressed it, but while the paint faded slightly, nothing happened. He pressed it again and the display went off, and no amount of prodding could bring it back. He put the mobile away with a sense of resignation, and with his mind no longer distracted, he ruminated on his humiliating episode in the workshop.

This unwelcome interruption to his composure coincided with the bus's engine starting up, though his discomfort didn't last long. There was a switch in his mind that protected his self-image, which had taken him safely through life. On a general level it had always allowed him to believe that he was handsome, charming and talented; specifically, it told him that Fabrienne had declined the night out because she was professionally conflicted; it now translated the workshop episode into a bunch of unfriendly students who didn't appreciate a virtuoso performance.

Anyway, sod acting lessons, he thought. Far more important was moving in to his new apartment: if Gathering only sponsored artists, then moving in would prove he *was* an artist...

As he travelled past Chapter he nodded at his inverted logic. He glanced down as he passed to see a red Fiesta parked on the road, then turned around in his seat to look properly. He was right: it was Fabrienne's car. She was in the driver seat, he recognised her blue and yellow sales uniform. He couldn't be sure from his angle at the window, but she seemed to have her head bowed submissively, someone in the back seat haranguing her with expressive fingers.

As the bus turned the corner he stretched to his side for one last look. He reacted, sure that whoever was in the back had just landed a blow across her mouth. Maybe he should get out at the next stop.

He thought better of it, remembering that Fabrienne had mentioned something about a bad divorce when they first met: maybe that was her ex-husband in the back of the car. If she was trying to escape from one of those arranged marriages there might be a lot of angry relatives in the mix; better to stay well clear until he was fully aware of the position.

He smiled. Perhaps the ex was jealous because she'd furtively made her way down to Chapter in the hope of seeing him. He stretched his shoulders reflectively, prepared to believe it was a logical fit.

With this nutritious parcel of information safely stored away, nourishing his self-image, he settled back in his seat. His thoughts returning to his mobile.

Mason, his white pawn, had just moved. That meant that black would move next.

V I

The castle on the mountain

T HE MOBILE DIDN'T ring for the rest of the day. The display was dead the next day too and Kris spent most of his Sunday in an internet cafe. Still nothing came up: he even went through numerous variations of 'message gong', wondering now if that had been the activation trigger for his first message, some kind of app that was downloaded directly from the internet to his mobile. He was unable to find the website.

Two miserable days in work followed, the mobile refusing to ring. When Tuesday eventually took him to bed, he wondered if it wasn't enough just to wait or surf the internet, as he had done to access Lisa Buoys. Perhaps he had to physically do something to access the next chess move.

He fell asleep and dreamed of a fortress filled with enemies, on the crest of a high mountain.

"I shouldn't be watching this. I suppose I should be swatting up for my production meeting." Kris's eyes switched quickly to Mason to test his reaction.

The bay of the terrace house looked out at a chip shop which blew its smell of cod and vinegar into the room. They were each seated in tired chairs with different faded chintz facing a portable television: Kris had got to the room first but had taken the chair with the loose spring, leaving the better chair enticingly for Mason.

"Right, right…"

Kris considered his landlord and housemate without looking at him, pretending to be absorbed in the episode of Casualty. He was an odd looking chap, barely five foot and, although only in his late twenties, already completely bald. He had the ginger wisp of a beard and moustache, which he had clearly taken great effort to grow and which he constantly needed to wipe because of a dribble he couldn't seem to control. Kris thought this might be something to do with his very prominent buck teeth: it was a struggle not to call him 'Goof' by accident.

His most prominent handicap, however, no doubt setting the seal on a lifetime of social complexes, was a speech impediment made hilarious by a high squeak of a voice. Maybe it was his teeth, but he couldn't say words beginning with a 'sh'. This was particularly unfortunate given that his pet subject was the Carolingian king Charlemagne. Kris had had some fun in his first evenings here quizzing him on the relative virtues of 'Tharlemagne'. The answers had been squeaked out deliriously with the Goof's belief that he had found a kindred spirit.

Kris had gained the impression that the Goof enjoyed company. His decision to call for lodgers was curious given that he had a good university job, but as Fabrienne had indicated perhaps he just enjoyed the hospitality of a shared house. The gadgets, magazines and items of clothing left scattered around the house, together with a cluttered kitchen that was never clean, attested to the existence of the university students who also lived here.

Kris shifted as the spring poked against the cloth. Crammed

into his bedroom upstairs, making for a very small walkway, was his prized soft leather sofa, the only piece of furniture he had salvaged from his marriage and only then because it was black and Trish thought it looked like 'bachelor death'. He wouldn't bring it into the front room in case one of those scutty students used it.

"When's your meeting then?" Mason asked.

"Eh, this Friday. Afternoon." He had waited in this damned chair for an hour in the hope Mason would emerge from his bedroom for a bit of communal time and he now sighed inwardly with relief, the man having at last taken the bait and asked a question. "I hope my historical research stands up," he added casually. "You've read some of my screenplay, haven't you?"

Mason had readily offered to look at his screenplay when they found some common ground with their interest in history. "What about your new place?" he said in his high voice. "Heard anything yet?"

Kris cursed silently as the subject was changed.

"Not yet."

"You will tell me when you're thure you're moving out?"

"Of course," Kris said, forcefully suppressing a smirk at the Goof's 'sure'. This evening there would be no piss-taking, even if the Goof wasn't aware of it.

They watched the television for a few minutes. "You agree with my theory then?" Kris asked at length. "About the Dauphin, I mean?"

Mason's eyes wandered slightly from the television. "Are you thure you've got round the DNA problem?" he asked uncomfortably.

The DNA test in 2000 had revealed that the heart of the

boy who died in captivity *was* related to Marie Antoinette. All the conspiracy theories over the prince's substitution had vanished in a puff of anti-climax.

"That wasn't the Dauphin's heart they tested," Kris replied. "That's the whole twist on my story: it was the heart of his brother, Louis-Joseph."

"Louis-Joseph," Mason murmured in sceptical agreement.

Kris returned to the television, annoyed at this challenge to his peace of mind; he simply wanted to find out what Mason had to say about The Mountain. "Louis-Joseph," he confirmed. The Dauphin's older brother had died, age seven, of tuberculosis in 1789, and as with all French princes, his heart had been removed.

"And you say that *his* heart was swapped with the heart of the commoner posing as the Dauphin?"

"Correct."

It was historical fact that the surgeon, Pelletan, who had removed the heart from the boy who died in prison, had kept it – but years later it was stolen by one of his students. This student confessed to the theft on his death bed and the heart was returned. Kris's screenplay had the theft being engineered by a Royalist society, infuriated that the heart of a commoner should be mistaken for a royal artefact. Later, they came into the possession of Louis-Joseph's heart, which had been lost after the Basilica of St Denis had been sacked during the Revolution. At this point they had the idea of returning Louis-Joseph's heart to a suitably regal resting place, under the cover story of a repentant thief.

Mason appeared troubled by this elaborate theory. "Louis-Joseph's heart was embalmed. The heart kept by Pelletan was pickled in alcohol."

"So?"

Mason had been wondering how to break this news to his housemate. He took a steadying breath in an attempt to stop his voice going off at a high octave. "This isn't my period, but I do know that Louis-Joseph's heart was mummified. The mitochrondial test wasn't carried out on a mummified heart."

"Mito*what*?," Kris muttered, then began to picture Lisa Buoys' abrupt dismissal of his screenplay on the ground of scientific impossibility. He went cold: his chat with Mason was merely meant to build on his research, not destroy the whole premise of his work.

A few minutes of television passed.

"Just because the DNA showed the heart was related to Marie Antoinette doesn't mean it was her son," Kris said eventually. "She had a big family. Perhaps it was some Austrian backdoor squib or something…"

"But why would the jailers go out of their way to substitute the Dauphin with a relative?" He paused. "And there's something else that just doesn't fit with this old escape theory. Something which *never* fitted, even before the DNA testing."

"Which is?"

"Well the myth of the free Dauphin is like sightings of Elvis. Wouldn't he have been seen by someone who recognised him, if he was alive?"

"Not if he escaped to the New World."

Mason's face crinkled. "Perhaps Huckleberry Finn met him. Who did the pretender tell Huck he was? The *Dolphin* of France?"

"Okay, cute."

Mason, deflated, decided to tread more carefully.

"Seriously, he would have turned up somewhere. And why go to the New World? Why not visit his sister after everything settled down and she became a ruler in Austria?"

The colour had drained from Kris's face. Mason offered him a sad smile in consolation. "You might be right about the Dauphin being moved from the prison at some point. All the evidence points to it. But if so, I think he was brought back. The boy who died of tuberculosis in the prison, who had his heart removed, *was* the Dauphin."

"So why didn't they get his sister to identify the body? Scotch all the bloody rumours about him being free?"

Mason returned to the television. "Sometimes people are just stupid."

"That's not very satisfactory, Mason."

"The truth rarely is."

Kris considered the ceiling, the image of the wigged grenadier flashing in his mind. "You know, we should work together," he said at length, finding the idea appealing. He had no inclination for research: for every minute spent reading Lenotre's book – the extent of his research apart from watching a YouTube clip on the DNA testing – he had spent an hour pacing the bedroom trying to get into the skin of the cold, magisterial Chaumette. And perhaps Mason could even give the dialogue some electricity: after all, the tutors had raved about his literary as well as his academic skills. "Perhaps we could rewrite the screenplay together? Maybe think of a different ending?"

Mason seemed to find the notion amusing as he got up with his empty coffee cup. He motioned with it to Kris, who shook his head.

"Not really interested in going on television or anything," Mason admitted.

Kris threw him a furtive glance. "You wouldn't have to do any publicity or anything. You wouldn't even have to be credited if you didn't want. You'd be my silent partner."

"Partner?"

"Yeah, like Elton John and Bernie Taupin. You'd write it, I'd present it. I'd do all the talking at interviews, and all that stuff. You'd be credited and paid of course, but you'd be in the background." He cleared his throat. "Mason, does *The Mountain* have any relevance to the Dauphin story?"

"The *Montagne*? The third estate in the National Assembly?"

"Right. The ones who sat in the high gallery."

"I suppose," Mason said as he left the room. "Thaumette came from The Mountain, if that's what you mean. Robespierre too," he called from the kitchen.

Kris tutted, dissatisfied with the answer, his irritation translating at annoyance that Chaumette received the same lisp treatment as Charlemagne. He sat back with a scowl, wondering if he should rephrase his question, then jumped out of his seat and dashed upstairs.

He had heard the message gong.

He was on his black leather sofa, curled up for the lack of legroom. He activated the message

*BBC Llandaff accessed through your research
It is greedy and full of secrets*

then the chess piece. It was a sort of dark pagoda, a tiered tower with eaves. Suspiciously alien; the warning seemed to suit it.

Enemy castle…
The schematic moved a black castle two squares forward.

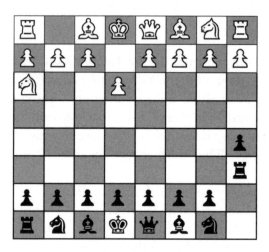

He wondered who in the BBC the castle was meant to signify: if Buoys was the black pawn, perhaps it was her boss. He accessed the icon for his leather address book but nothing had been added; the list remained just 'Lisa Man-suit' and 'Mason Flower'.

"A castle has no face," he whispered to himself.

It's the BBC itself. In this game a castle is either a place or an institution.

Returning to the chessboard menu he noted a new address book in the bottom left corner, this one with 'Chapter Emile' engraved in the leather. He nodded thoughtfully, progress clearly having been made as a result of his tackling Mason, the research the message referred to, though the 'Mountain' reference remained a mystery.

He wondered how Gathering was even aware he had followed its advice and talked to Mason. His eyes narrowed.

Perhaps Mason was in on it, had texted them from the kitchen while pretending to make his coffee. He nodded once more, this time with suspicion. When the time was right he would tackle the Goof on his relationship with Fabrienne, in the meantime would keep a watchful eye. He pressed the thumb latch icon but it refused to respond, the paint just fading with his touch; he huffed, thinking that whatever the app was it couldn't have downloaded properly. He pressed Chapter Emile.

The list that rolled out after the quill and parchment seemed never ending. He scrolled through over a hundred names

Emmanuel Joseph Sieyès (astronomer)
Jean-Sylvain Bailly (philosopher)
Louis-Pierre Deseine (sculptor)
Mlle Raucourt (actress)
Napoleon Bonaparte (army colonel)
Nicolas-Edme Rétif (novelist)
Jean-François Marmontel (historian)
Saint-Just (idealist)

and at 'Saint-Just (idealist)' he stopped, losing interest. He returned to the chessboard, then paused and pushed the Chapter Emile icon again. He'd heard of Saint-Just: Robespierre's young, handsome right hand man in the Terror. And as his memory reviewed his weary trek down the list, he was sure that he'd seen the name Bonaparte as well.

He cursed, the leather fading slightly but the address book refusing to open. Then the mobile went dead, the opportunity lost as punishment for his laziness.

That night he dreamt of Fabrienne.

She rode him under the sheets, one hand to her hair which was wet with perspiration, her brown skin glowing with exertion. Time passed gently before she rolled off, her head tucked contentedly into his chest. She wouldn't let him stroke her hair, so he caressed her shoulder; she had long bones and her skin smelt of almonds.

"Answer me," she whispered sweetly.

"Yeah I love you, babes," he said. It was his stock answer in such situations, but he meant it. He had never been with a woman so beautiful.

She seemed to briefly consider the response. "Answer me," she repeated, in a louder voice.

His eyes remained closed.

"No, I mean it, babes. Honest I do."

The duvet formed a mould around their damp bodies. It seemed to increase in weight, as if it was slowly setting into rock.

"Answer me!"

He sat bolt upright and snatched the mobile from his bedside table. It was vibrating with a passion.

It's ringing! he thought. *This isn't a message – that's the gong and bells. Someone is actually calling me!*

The display showed a white chess piece: a serene woman, her hair an outlandishly huge creation of jewels and finery. He stared at the display, mesmerised by the beautiful chess piece that reminded him of Marie Antoinette.

So Fabrienne's my white queen…

He was certain it was Fabrienne calling: the ringtone was her actual voice.

"ANSWER ME!!"

Now it was a high-pitched screech. He pressed the display,

aware that he could hear movement from Mason's room. He raced to the door and opened it.

"Sorry, TV on too loud!" he called, closing the door and moving to his sofa, his eyes on the display. The white queen moved four squares into the game.

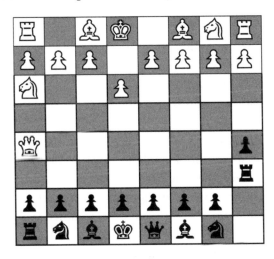

"Hello, Kris?" Fabrienne said quietly.

"Hey, Fabrienne. This is a nice surprise." The speakers on the phone were superb and he was able to watch the display, which still showed the white queen, as they talked. He imagined the piece almost talking to him.

"I am so, *so* sorry for ringing you this late. I really am."

He reached for his watch and squinted. It was 3a.m.

"But one of the Trustees just called me," she continued. "There's an opening for you to view the salon again, but it has to be first thing tomorrow morning. That's why I thought it best to ring you straightaway."

He put his watch aside, not caring about the time or

why the Trustee couldn't give him more notice. "No problem, honest. Shall I meet you outside Gathering?"

"Fine. 9a.m?"

"Right." He'd have to be late for work and take his lumps from Dylan Hughes, but it would be worth it. He considered the mobile with a mischievous air. "So, have I *castled*, to use your phrase?"

She laughed uncomfortably. "Not quite, Kris. They're still checking your references, but they have given me permission to show you more of the rooms."

"So we're making progress. I must be doing something right?"

She laughed again, unsure what to say.

He wondered if he should tell her that someone had sampled her voice for the ringtone. He decided against it, electing instead to give her a demonstration tomorrow by asking her to ring him. "Okay, see you tomorrow. And thanks."

As he was returned to the menu, after another useless rub of the thumb latch, he accessed his own address book. He smiled, seeing that Fabrienne had been added with the white queen icon.

Lisa Man-suit
The Goof
Fabrienne Iqbal

Then he frowned, seeing that Mason's name had been replaced with the Goof. It had been Mason Flower when he last looked and he recalled Lisa Buoys mutating to Lisa Man-suit when his landlord had been added: logic told him that the last name turned into a nickname when a *new* name was added. He supposed that made sense; the mystery was how Gathering knew his secret nickname for his landlord. He shrugged, supposing it was an obvious nickname for a man with buck teeth and no social skills. Maybe someone in his university had already come up with it.

Reassured by this analysis, he accessed the Goof's details to see if anything new had been released with the change of name. He guessed correctly: the CV was gone, replaced with just a note:

Confidentiality agreement!

Filing the note for future reflection he returned to the address book, far more interested in 'Fabrienne Iqbal'.

Her details were sparse in comparison to those originally offered for Mason. Pressing her name revealed that she was thirty-two, just over his initial estimate, and her real name was *Vaishali* Iqbal. Nodding as his theory of a name change was confirmed, he scrolled down. She had a first class degree in classics and a master's degree in French literature, which impressed and intimidated him in equal measure; she must have been inwardly laughing when he attempted to bluff an understanding of Rousseau in the foyer.

He returned to the address book and pressed the white queen icon. He shivered, imagining that the display momentarily went so cold it seared his skin.

No message this time: the link was to a photograph. It showed a younger Fabrienne in her graduation cap and gown and its caption read: 'When she was Vaishali'. The cap was carefully positioned over the right side of her face. He pressed the display and another photograph appeared, this time more natural and more recent: she seemed to be speaking normally, unaware her photograph was being taken. It was entitled: 'At her writing class.'

He lay back and curled up, loving the soft hide of his sofa. Perhaps these photographs were part of her CV, stored on the Gathering network along with all other employees.

The next photograph dispelled that idea. It showed her in what appeared to be in the middle of an argument, her face contorted with fear: 'Vaishali planning her escape from her husband.'

"Bloody hell, how did this get on?" he muttered, noting that the image was slightly blurred, taken in the heat of the moment. He hesitated, and looked closer. Her hair was everywhere and he saw the scarring over her right ear and cheek. He counted six small blister clusters, four on the skin around the ear and two on the ear itself. They looked like burns.

Poor kid, he thought, but finding the discovery somewhat endearing as he thought of the lengths she went to hide this part of her face, just as she tried to hide her real name. Maybe she had become estranged from her family and was trying to build a new life, something really difficult for a woman from her culture. Anyway, the scars weren't nearly as bad as she probably believed, but someone had illegally downloaded this photograph and she needed to be told.

The fourth and last photograph dispelled that idea also. The caption read: 'Vaishali giving head.'

Her eyes were squeezed tight and she didn't seem to be enjoying it, her hair pulled tightly up and held off camera, probably by the man. He wasn't sure how long he looked at the photograph before the mobile returned him to Fabrienne's CV.

Maybe she's a porn star or something. He shook his head;

it just didn't fit. Someone was spying on her, had a secret camera somewhere. Perhaps it was an obscene practical joke by her ex-husband.

His stomach was twitching at this discovery. At the bottom of Fabrienne's CV details, he noticed something new: an envelope with a wax seal. He touched the envelope and a piece of blank parchment unrolled.

"What…?"

The word 'What' appeared on the parchment as he said it, written in an elegant handwritten script.

"Remove?" he said, and the word disappeared. He raised his eyebrows, realising the text messaging was voice activated.

With the third and fourth photographs still stamped on his eyes, he said in a shaking voice: "Hello Fabrienne, Kris here. Just want to thank you again. Look forward to seeing you at 9a.m. tomorrow." He watched the words roll across the parchment, hearing the scratch of a feather nib; it wasn't the most exciting of messages but at least it might start a line of communication. He waited, unsure what to do next, then said, tentatively, "Send?" The software understood his inflection and the parchment rolled up. The display faded to the distant sound of hooves.

As he sank into bed he tried to shut out the photographic images, feeling ashamed at his intrusion into her life. The reaction was more extreme than it should have been; he was actually shaking with self-disgust, yet feeling more aroused than he could remember. He reset his thoughts. While he couldn't shake Fabrienne from his mind, he could think of something more innocent … something … anything… Yes, Fabrienne's phrase: *castling*.

She had been lying to him in the sales office. Castling wasn't a sales term at all, it was a chess move: the king switching with a castle.

He closed his eyes contentedly. Perhaps the white castle would represent his new apartment; perhaps he wasn't just a knight in this chess game, but the king too. After all, wouldn't he be the most important piece in his own game?

"And a king must have his castle," he murmured dreamily. He tried to recall the chess schematic, to remember where the pieces had moved. He mentally moved his knight, his pawn, and his queen. A white bishop stood between the king and his castle; the bishop could move out through the space created by the pawn.

"White bishop has to move," he thought as he drifted into sleep.

His forehead creased as he wondered who the white bishop might be.

VII

Audience

THE RUSSIAN, RENKA Tamarov, sat in an apathetic hunch, one shoulder lower than the other, her gaze aimed just above his head. "Ten minutes," she announced, showing the wrist which held her watch.

She was a tall, sinewy young woman with cropped black hair and strong features; she had a certain rough glamour, Tom thought, though she had applied not an inch of make-up to her pale skin. In her designer combat fatigues, with her stern demeanour, she reminded him of a sexed-up terrorist.

Far less interesting was her client, the famous Chelsea London.

The interviewer from *Review* magazine was carrying a professional half-smile as the actress talked in a monotone. He had discovered that she was quite intensely boring without her scripts: lately, a superbly crafted and critically acclaimed American police drama where she was playing the role of a drug corner boy's failing mother.

Skin cream and photographs…

He wondered how he would be able to sneak these more interesting observations into the article. Throughout the interview she had been rubbing a cream with an aroma of burnt almonds into her hands and bare arms, her ebony skin glistening with gratitude. Occasionally she would dab a spot or two under her eyes, or drag a fingertip down her cheek, the result briefly animating her expression.

As with her agent, she was also looking beyond him as she talked, pausing only when she noticed he had stopped scribbling, then waiting until he resumed. Her agent had refused to let him tape the interview.

"Would you like me to discuss some of my older projects?" she asked flatly, having finished her monologue on the police drama and turning to adjust one of the vases of flowers at her dress mirror, one of many bouquets wishing her luck. She was rehearsing for a play in Cardiff's New Theatre, where she now had this dressing room, in order to fill the three-month wait before her US drama proceeded to its next season. She was a renowned workaholic.

"Certainly," he sighed, with a weary turn of his notebook which rested on the laptop case on his knees.

"You not use stock material?" Renka suggested from her corner, eyeing the laptop suspiciously. She considered his business card once more. "Mr Tom Singer," she read, "perhaps we send you quotes, which you write as interview. Miss London tired now."

"Fine," he said, feigning disappointment but relieved at not having to sit through a regurgitation of London's back catalogue. The sixties star, a contemporary of the Shrimp and Twiggy, who had changed her name from Betty to Chelsea in tribute to both her surname and the swinging city, was famous as much for her work as for having had the most fortunate of careers, when weighed against what many regarded as her somewhat doubtful talent. Her luck began with the moment she was picked out as the unlikely central role of an edgy film about teenage drug abuse, one which perfectly suited her then vulnerable and alienated persona – she came from an abused childhood and had been sleeping rough since her early teens – and which brought her acclaim, though everyone assumed she would be a one-trick pony. But her luck continued with a succession of minor roles in dramas which were all outstanding works, very often the signature projects of up-and-coming writers and directors.

The respect for her as an actress had almost grown by default, her reputation protected by the successful productions with which she was associated. In fact, a number of hopeful biographers over the years had instead sought out her agent, the star-maker with an unerring eye for quality scripts, only to find a dead end. London seemed to have no permanent agent, rotating them frequently.

Tom's attention returned to the actress, who now, and with obvious effort, managed a reluctant eye contact in anticipation of the audience coming to an end. Several people had drifted in and out of the dressing room during their meeting, some to bring refreshments, others to bring messages and flowers, yet he had gained the distinct impression that she barely noticed any of them.

This was not just some diva-like aloofness, he had started to realise. It was as if she was actually unaware of them, her body language not even registering their presence as they milled around like so many phantoms. Her eyes simply wandered from the door, where she found her words, as she applied more of her skin cream: stuff which she should probably market because she didn't look a day over fifty. When her concentration faltered, her eyes drifted to the two photographs on her dressing mirror held in position under a string of lights. There were no people or pets in these photographs; they seemed to show sections of a room, ornately furnished with antiques.

He thoughtfully rubbed his designer stubble. "Are those photographs of your home?"

"They are private," Renka muttered. "Different question please."

Tom nodded compliantly, shifting his position and that of his laptop. "Okay. Now you're famous for spending most of your time in Cardiff, even though you were born in the East End. Your Hollywood friends say they never see you socially; that you always fly back, even if it's for the weekend."

Not that you have any friends, he thought. His inquiries, built upon a body of research, had confirmed that Ms London barely had a single acquaintance outside her career. No friends, no family, no significant other, not even a dog…

"This is my home," she answered simply. She had turned to face the dressing mirror on the pretence of collecting up her belongings but her eyes were switching between the photographs and her reflection.

He considered her awhile, imagining that she spent a lot of her waking moments in front of mirrors. "Is fame important to you, Miss London?"

She secured the lid on her skin cream and returned it to her handbag. "I don't know what fame is, anymore," she said to her reflection.

"You don't know what it *is*?"

She shook her head. "I *am* fame. There is no desire or hunger in me anymore; no wish or need. It is *me*."

He cleared his throat, his own question having been a southpaw but completely thrown by the answer. He noticed a brief smile of satisfaction from the agent. "Eh … can I quote you on that?" he asked, checking his notes to ensure he had accurately recorded the strange response.

"No you may not," Renka said. "As in contract terms, we require advance proof of interview. And we supply photographs." She stood up, losing her hunch; her back was straight, her long chin jutted towards him.

"Oh, right," he said, collecting his laptop and standing up also. He and his publication had been required to sign a lengthy confidentiality agreement with strict requirements on protocol to get this rare interview.

"You are aware that only *we* supply photographs?" the Russian repeated. Her finger tapped her cheek, expectantly.

"Absolutely. The contract was very clear."

"You read contract? You understood it?"

"Absolutely," he repeated defensively, tucking his laptop under his left arm. He was about to offer his right hand to one of the women when he was diverted by a loud and muffled ring; it was like the excited shake of a handbell.

TA-DING!

"Is that a fire alarm?" he gasped.

"Not fire. Don't worry," the Russian said.

Chelsea had reached into her handbag and collected her mobile. At least this is what he had assumed she had done, for she went behind a dressing blind, holding her mobile to her chest. The ring was louder and an odour invaded the room, yet behind the curtain she seemed reluctant to answer; instead, her shadow through the white linen showed her moving stiffly like some oriental shadow puppet.

TA-*DING!*

In fact, she was savouring the perfume, the same almond cologne of her hand cream, though now so intense it seemed powered by flames. Her face dropped as the reek of something sour and rancid broke through, prompting her to quickly answer the alert. The sound and the smell vanished, and shortly she appeared from behind the linen curtain and addressed Renka, who had made no attempt to interfere. "Someone's here. Downstairs."

Tom looked from agent to actress, then back to agent, in confusion. "Stay here," Renka said, the command directed to Chelsea, for she had opened the dressing room door and was efficiently marching the interviewer out. He managed a satisfied glance at the dressing mirror as he left.

The crisis over, Chelsea took her mobile back out of her bag and held it lovingly in both hands. She returned to her seat where her vacant gaze again found the mirror. With the assistance of her photographs she imagined herself at home, in her salon, where nothing could intrude on the reflections of herself.

A long time passed before she blinked and took up her mobile. She regarded the cartoon heart monitor for a while, transparent save for a diminishing line of red at its bottom, then accessed her address book. She adeptly scrolled down a long list of names until she found what she was looking for.

Her eyes returned to the mirror as she waited for her call to be answered.

"Food," she muttered immediately as the call connected.

"Food, yes, of course…" came the nervous response. "What time?"

The face of her reflection changed to one of sly derision. "One hour. And you can read to me, bitch, from your *ghastly* novel."

The theatre was closed to all but a few ticket purchasers in the downstairs foyer and the cleaners who had left their mops and buckets on the red carpet of the first floor intermission bar. In one corner of this bar sat a casually dressed young woman, a baseball cap with a very long lip covering her eyes. To her left sat a stick-thin middle-aged woman in a Chanel suit; to her right a hulk of a man with heavy eyebrows and deep sallow eyes. He was wearing a suit and reading a paperback.

The New Theatre was more than a hundred years old: Sarah Bernhardt had once trod these boards. The young woman, who was a Hollywood actress, through some professional DNA felt an affinity with the building, imagining that she smelt the greasepaint and heard the five-minute calls. Indeed she found the fusty sense of familiarity faintly uncomfortable, stripping away as it did the security blanket of a devoted entourage and increasing her already stratospheric levels of stress.

Her American colleagues, her agent and bodyguard, were ambivalent, content to sit wherever their pay cheque sent them. Her agent, Erika, hadn't at first thought too much of the starlet's sudden desire to return to Wales: Josie was Welsh after all, though she hailed from near Chester and was estranged from her family. The substantial bribe they had forced on the usher to allow themselves to wait here, in the hope that the elusive Cardiffian Chelsea London would appear, was just the latest item in a list of the unexplained.

Erika finished her email, saving it for later transmission from her hotel, and with an inward sigh at this foolishness, started another draft, this time to her accountant with an update of her reclaimable expenses on this Welsh adventure. Perhaps Josie was organising a project with London, rather than just paying a touristy visit to the capital; if so, she would be sure to talk her out of it. Josie Hannah had more talent in her little finger than the tired, overrated B-star.

Erica gave a satisfied tap of her Mac Air. It had taken three years to move beyond the stereotype inevitably created by a young, stunning blonde: Josie's acting ability, now that she had found suitable roles, was starting to astound. A few more key roles and she would rule Hollywood.

Tom Singer of *Review* magazine agreed, catching Josie's eye as he trotted down the stairs, the actress looking up suddenly in expectation before realising her mistake and once more shading herself under her hat. He paused, even in the fleeting moment of opportunity recognising the improbably beautiful blonde who had prompted his male colleagues to rip down their pictures of Megan Fox and Jessica Alba.

"Josie Hannah?" he asked. He had a good five years' experience of interviewing celebrities but his heart was pounding.

The bodyguard was up instantly, the paperback on the floor. "Whoa there, buddy." A large hand projected in front of him.

Tom produced a laminated ID, while pulling tight his suede jacket. "Tom Singer, *Review*."

Erica looked up, closed her Mac and smiled. *Review* was the most widely distributed film publication in the UK.

"What brings you here, Miss Hannah?" Tom asked. "Not thinking of treading the boards just yet, surely?"

Agent and bodyguard turned to look at the baseball cap, which gave a quick tremor. "Mikey, please ask him to go away," Josie whispered to her bodyguard. "I'll gladly speak to him when I get back to LA."

"Sorry buddy," Mikey said good-naturedly, turning back round. "You heard the lady. Bit busy right now."

"We'll link up back home," Erika said, her teeth so large that her smile threatened to turn her bone face into a skull.

"Sure ... thanks..." Tom murmured.

"We'll even do that whacky *pint of milk* thing you do, okay cupcake? Oh, your British sense of humour..."

"Sure, okay…"

"He is leaving anyway," came a voice from the stairs. Renka walked down to the bar and Tom, acknowledging the statement, made his way down to the foyer. "Remember contract, Mr Singer," she called grimly. "Remember you have *read* it."

He paused on the steps, repositioned his laptop under his arm, and went to the exit.

Renka turned to Josie, now looking up. "I am ready for you," she said. "Follow me alone."

"Well excuse me, Miss Siberia," Erica said, her accent all lower east side New York. "We're here to see Chelsea London. Don't know who the hell *you* are, whether you're her D-girl, but my girl ain't going nowhere without us."

"Erica, shut up!" Josie hissed and Erica stepped back as if she had been slapped. It was the first time she had seen Josie lose her composure; she actually sounded frightened.

"She comes, and she comes alone," Renka confirmed. She thoughtfully considered the beautiful actress with a tap of her cheek. "Yes, you are picture. The Father was indeed victorious in you." Bodyguard and agent exchanged concerned glances. "What did they call you, in incubation? What name Dr Mays give you?"

"The first Trustee, an older man, named me," Josie answered in a weak, shaking voice.

"Yes, that's correct, you were first child. What name?"

"The Valkyrie," Josie confirmed, briefly closing her eyes.

"Then I call you that."

Erica stepped forward, putting a hand on Mikey's arm for support. "Now listen here, missy…"

She was silenced by a flash of Josie's terrified eyes. "Don't, Erica! I've come a long way to speak to this woman."

Erica raised a skeleton digit in protest. "But cupcake, you came to see Chelsea London."

"No, she come to see me," Renka agreed. Her eyes went to the ceiling. "I have commandeered box."

When the actress had left with the Trustee, heading for the highest box that overlooked the stage, agent and bodyguard returned with baffled resignation to their chairs and to their Mac and paperback. Tom, meanwhile, had walked a few hundred yards down the road to his hotel, The City Plaza, where he decided to have a drink before returning to his room to check his notes and begin his article. He was now planning on staying another night, just in case he got the chance to interview Josie Hannah.

He was sitting contentedly by a hearth fire in the lobby when he was joined by a man who introduced himself simply as Honeyman. The man asked him how his interview with Chelsea London had gone.

"You'll be able to read about it in next month's issue," Tom said suspiciously. "I'm sorry – who are you?"

"Honeyman," he repeated, with his free hand patting his waistcoat for a business card. His right hand was settled on his overcoat on the seat, and was a fist.

'No, who *are* you? Why are you interested in Chelsea London?"

"I'm just a fan, Mr Singer." The large moustache crooked into a smile. "And of your publication too. I'm a great film enthusiast, although I confess I believe the golden age has long passed."

"Really," Tom muttered. "Look, Mr Honeyman…"

"Just Honeyman."

"…right … now don't get offended, and I'm really flattered that you've obviously recognised my photo from the magazine, but I just don't talk to strangers. Just don't do it. Even if they are film fans. And I've got work to do."

Honeyman considered this with a nod and appreciative murmur. "Miss London wasn't what you were expecting, was she?" His fist tightened, keeping it under his overcoat so as not to alarm the young man.

Tom hesitated, rethinking what would have been an automatic, sarcastic response. His brain was yet to fully process London's strange monologue, her moisturiser and that mobile phone. And that po-faced Russian who sent erotic shivers down his spine. "What do you mean?"

"She's a different person when she performs, you see. When she is displayed." He grunted, philosophically. "There's nothing left for her now outside that, you see."

Tom shrugged. "Well, that's the price of fame, I suppose."

"No Mr Singer, it is the price exacted by Temple Thirteen Thirteen, which is called *Gathering*."

Tom nodded and swigged the rest of his lager. "Well, as I said, I've got work to do."

Honeyman leaned back, raising a submissive hand. "Thirty seconds, then I'll be gone." His words had no effect, Tom continuing to gather his things. "No doubt you were also surprised to see Josie Hannah."

Tom paused, then picked up his glass, inviting him to continue.

"Poor Josie is also connected with the coven, Mr Singer, though through a different temple, one called Precious Cargo." He breathed in hard through his nose, to help him fight back his tears. "She's terrified, you see. Precious Cargo has fallen. She was the oldest of six adults it produced, all very beautiful and very talented, and the other five are dead. Murdered."

Tom considered his empty glass. "What are you talking about? No one close to Josie Hannah has been killed. She's got paparazzi all over her: we'd have heard."

Honeyman grumbled in response. "The first death was in London. A promising writer called Carl Tyrone. The latest death was an engineer in New Zealand."

"Engineer? What's an engineer in New Zealand of all places got to do with Josie Hannah?"

Honeyman shook his head sadly. "Let me ask you a favour, Mr Singer. Please, please … don't look at the photographs you've taken."

Tom cleared his throat. "Photographs?"

Honeyman's right hand squeezed tight. "The photographs you've taken with the micro camera hidden in the lining of your laptop case."

"How on earth…?" Tom stopped himself. This guy was probably working for London, was her head of security or something, playing some mind game by pretending to be mad. "I don't know what you're talking about, but I do know my rights. You need a search warrant if you want look at my case." He paused. "Anyway, why would I take photographs? That Russian woman has to approve the article before it's published. The contract's very clear…"

"Clear indeed," Honeyman agreed. "The coven sets great store by its contracts, for they are ordered with rules and believe themselves to be holy; they have forsworn violence unless their temples are trespassed upon."

"What on earth…?"

"And you need to be aware that you would be trespassing, Mr Singer. The contract you read and signed has put you on notice."

Tom considered Honeyman carefully, now more interested in his delivery and demeanour than in his words. He had a churchman's gentle conviction. "You *don't* work for her, do you?" When Honeyman shook his head, Tom got up. "I'm not sure where you got your information," he said with a trace of admiration, "or perhaps you're just guessing, but I'm going now. It's been nice meeting you."

Honeyman remained in his seat and ordered tea, his mind turning. Eventually Gracie's book was taken from his pocket and, with a furtive glance around the hotel lobby, he discreetly placed his Gracie figurine on the glass table. He wrote:

You shouldn't have spoken to him, Honeyman.

"I had to try," he sighed.

You should have just stolen his case. You can't talk about the temples to bystanders – they won't believe you. You KNOW that.

Honeyman closed his eyes in acknowledgement of this fact, feeling helpless. There was a long wait, then he wrote:

Do you think that Franklyn is killing them?

He was aware that she was referring to the Precious Cargo children. "I'm sorry, Gracie. I know how this upsets you, but it seems likely, doesn't it? On the command of Dr Mays, no doubt," he added, as a sop to the memory of the young man she loved so unconditionally. He waited, but no more words came to the notebook; fully aware of his ward's dejection he returned it to his jacket. In the presence of the building that was called Gathering she had been able to uncover the most useful information, most recently the covert intentions of this film journalist, but when it came to Franklyn Tyde, her love and her nemesis, there was no help.

He considered the figurine on the table with a mix of fascination and sorrow, snatching it up as the waiter appeared with his tea.

★

Renka was balanced on her midriff on the wall of the theatre box; lifting her legs and stretching her arms, she was arcing from side to side, simulating her flight over the theatre. Her expression remained impassive, only the light of her eyes attesting to the sensation. "Do you ever try this, Valkyrie?" she asked. "It is liberating."

"I don't like heights," Josie said uncomfortably, seated at the other end of the box. "And don't call me that."

With a spring, Renka found her feet as a frail old man entered the box, making no eye contact with either woman. Renka helped him to sit down by steadying his chair and taking his walking stick, then stood behind him like a guard, her arms folded.

Josie's breath left her chest.

"You remember me, my winged Valkyrie?" he said in a thin, breathy whisper. His face was a nest of wrinkles in yellow skin and he sported a wig of thick red hair, greased with a side parting combed carefully across his forehead.

"Yes, I remember you."

"I named you, did I not?"

Josie nodded.

"And you are as beautiful as I would have expected," he

declared. "And as talented, no doubt. I haven't seen your films," he admitted, "but I am sure it is so."

"I thought you were retired," Josie remarked. His name was Mr Ovenstone and her prevailing memory was how terrified her parents were of him.

He pulled on the joint of an index finger, until it clicked. "I am a Proctor, Valkyrie; I never retire." He weakly held up his hand and Renka took it and squeezed it erotically. "And there are always consolations in hard work. In our society, rank has its privileges."

He retrieved his hand and Renka folded her arms once more with a satisfied smile. Josie shuddered as she considered the chemistry between them: though she had been very young she vaguely remembered a similar relationship with a beautiful woman called Dr Lauren Mays, his then junior Trustee. He had looked decrepit even then.

"Why do you bring her to me, my dear?" he asked, his eyes indicating that the question was intended for the Russian.

"She come of own accord," Renka answered.

"Ah." Mr Ovenstone considered Josie with bemusement. "And what could you possibly want from us?"

"You know what I want!" Josie blurted, losing her composure. "The others are dead. Dead! Murdered! I want your protection!"

"Protection?" he asked, feigning surprise. "But what about your guardian?"

"I don't have a guardian anymore. A fact you're fully aware of."

"Ah, this is true." He recalled the puppet theatre that was once the toy that protected and nurtured her, now useless pieces of wood. "Precious Cargo has turned to heresy. Its Trustee thinks the temple she served has produced something ... special. You need to understand that we take that most seriously. Recall, some renegade Jew had the same idea two thousand years ago and look at all the fuss *that* caused..."

"That's not my fault!" Josie protested, tears coming at last. "It was Franklyn Tyde, and the Trustee you're referring to was one of your own, Dr Lauren Mays..."

He was shaking slightly with mirth from his last remark. "Yes yes, but you are part of the temple nonetheless. You have taken its gifts; now you must pay its debts." As if he had just been suddenly possessed by a malevolent spirit, Mr Ovenstone's expression changed, his eyes widening with fury, his breath coming in short gasps.

Josie recoiled. "What can I do?" she whispered.

He considered her with vicious abandon, until at length his expression softened, returning to that of a benign old man. With a raise of his index finger he indicated that Renka should answer.

The Russian considered Josie's question carefully. "Perhaps use balcony," she suggested at length, leaning a little to take a peek at the seats below. "Maybe winged Valkyrie will fly."

"What...?" Josie gasped.

"Ah, what a sight that would be," Mr Ovenstone sighed. "Your decorative limbs, your beguiling face, all broken."

Josie brought a hand to her mouth. "Mikey," she muttered automatically, but knowing that against the Trustees her twenty-stone minder would be as helpless as the day he was born. Fear now turned into panic; she bolted out of her chair and ran out of the box.

Renka paid no heed to her departing footsteps, choosing instead to amuse Mr Ovenstone by positioning herself once more on the balcony edge, as if finding flight over the theatre.

VIII

Thumb latch

FABRIENNE OPENED THE front door of Gathering and stepped in, barely as Kris raised his hand in greeting. She walked briskly into the foyer, briefly disappearing into the darkness before the lights found her.

"Everything okay?" he asked breathlessly as he joined her in the lift. The cage closed and she looked up, without speaking, as they made their ascent. He groaned, again feeling the loss of energy during the journey, but wondering at her silence. "Babes, what's wrong?"

"I am *not* your *babes!*" she snapped. She closed her eyes as he made an expressive gesture of placation. "I've been told to show you the salon again," she said calmly. "That's what I'm doing."

"Fine, but tell me…"

She was out of the lift as soon as it opened. He darted ahead of her, pressing down on the iron thumb latch and swinging the salon door open.

"Right, that's it," he said. "Unless you tell me what's wrong, I'm not going in." He decided to roll the dice. "Go back to your employers and tell them they can move someone else in."

She considered him for a while, weighing her anger and her fear. Fear easily tipped the scales.

"Look, I'm sorry," she managed. "I'm tired, I didn't get

enough sleep." She closed her eyes once more and when she opened them she was smiling, thinly. "Honestly, I'm just tired."

"Okay," he said cautiously. He watched her walk towards the windows, to the door on the far right, then re-ordered his mood, wanting to enjoy this moment; a moment he had visualised since his first visit. He stepped in and his eyes went immediately to the wall mirror, the one part of the salon which held an inscrutable place in his memory.

His reflection was a stranger looking back at him.

No, not a stranger. He felt as if he was looking at Chaumette; or, to be precise, himself in role as the Commune leader.

He resisted the temptation to speak his lines from the workshop; with this man looking back at him he knew instinctively that the words would come out differently.

No doubt it was the surroundings that had put him into character, from the crease in the right eye to the arrogant tilt of the head, but the sensation was a snort of artistic cocaine. The image in the glass went out of focus as he turned to the sound of a door opening. He moved away, feeling it inappropriate to linger.

The bathroom had been opened with a key Fabrienne declined to hand over. She said that once opened, the door could never be locked. He shrugged, assuming it was a fire regulation.

He glanced at the double doors on the opposite wall.

"Those open into the bedroom," she explained. "I haven't been given the key for them yet."

"You haven't...?"

"This is the bathroom," she said abruptly. "Shall we go in?"

The polished stone bathroom was at least half the size of the huge salon and housed a bronze tub in its centre. At first sight the tub looked cold and uninviting, even morbid, but shortly he realised he could easily spend hours of reflection soaking away in that thing. It boasted five porcelain taps attached to copper pipes rising from the floor: four were shaped in what appeared to be scantily dressed harem women, each figure in different colour silk; the fifth, a fat-bellied man with crossed arms, was presumably their eunuch.

"No shower?" he asked.

"No shower," she confirmed.

He looked around, referencing the turn in the wall that identified the location of the Turk's alcove. "And where's the loo?"

She looked too and shortly they located a wooden commode in the corner. He put a hand to his forehead. "Fabrienne, are you honestly saying that no one's lived here since the eighteenth century? That I'm living in a bloody museum?"

"Do you want to go?"

"I didn't say that!" he growled, a splinter of irritation sharpening his tone. "Sorry," he said immediately, realising that he had expelled something cold that he had collected with his reflection a moment ago. "Maybe the bedroom has an en suite," he suggested placatingly.

She shrugged, her frostiness returning as she recovered from her surprise over his outburst.

He was desperately trying to rationalise what he was seeing, wishing to find no fault with his new home. "And I'm assuming the commode's all plumbed up, yeah? The design's just retro, like the lift?"

She raised her eyebrows, finding her chilled revenge. "I don't know. Maybe you should test it."

He shook his head. "I'm sure everything works just fine. After all, the apartment's warm and I haven't seen any radiators." He paused. "And you say you can't open the last door to let me see the bedroom and kitchen?"

"Not until Gathering's ready to let me move in."

He looked up at the ceiling. The murals were in the style of Botticelli but of a distinctly erotic character, *The Birth of Venus* having Venus surrounded by overly-excited satyrs. "So are you going to tell me what I've done to piss you off?"

"You *know* what you've done."

He gave a sigh of relief at having at last lanced the boil. "Honestly, I don't." He turned away with an appreciative tap of the onyx wash basin.

"Just leave it," she warned.

He raised his voice. "Fabrienne I want to know! I can't talk to you if you won't tell me what's wrong!"

Her accent was now pure Tiger Bay, raucous and pronounced, as something snapped. "Don't screw with me you English fuck, I'll…"

She jumped.

The sound, which was like a creaking pipe, had come from the salon. They both turned in confusion.

They started at the sound of another longer creak.

"It's coming from the alcove!" she cried. They raced into the salon, to the black wallpaper, and with a look dared the other to open the panel door. With the third creak they pressed the door together.

The sound was the Turk's arm moving. The automaton had already performed two moves, the first to collect the chess piece, the second to deposit it on its square; now its hand was returning to the rest cushion. Its glass eyes flickered up suspiciously at its opponent as it did so.

"Oh, of course," she whispered. "Renkelen deliberately made the machine noisy to give the chess master the opportunity to sneeze or whatever." She almost smiled with relief, before she remembered she was still angry.

"Right."

"Gathering must have installed a computer program: perhaps they present it at trade fairs or something."

"Right."

From a distance he considered the chessboard. The pieces were arranged exactly as the last schematic on his mobile, the last play being the white queen moving four spaces. He made out the Marie Antoinette piece; he had opened the door in time to see the Turk's hand moving away from it.

"It must take a while to catch up with the network," he muttered. "I had that move when we spoke on the phone last night." He blinked, a question occurring as he looked up at the Turk, something about the chessboard making a long observation of the pieces uncomfortable.

"What?" she said, seeing the question in his eyes.

"Who plays black?" he asked.

She looked sullenly at her feet. "The real Turk, the one destroyed in the fire, used to go second: it played black. The prototype must have been designed so that the automaton went first."

He shook his head. She had misunderstood the question.

"No, I mean *who's playing black?*"

Fabrienne had no more to say, other than that they had already outstayed their allotted time. He was too weary, too confused, to press her further; they left the building in silence.

The mobile's message gong activated as soon as Fabrienne had departed in the direction of her Fiesta, parked in the same space behind the Norwegian Church, with no offer of a ride. He decided to stay in the Bay and risk Dylan's displeasure at being irredeemably late, so he strolled down to the front and found an empty bench next to a large ornamental anchor.

The sea air was bracing and he armed himself with several lungs of it before he accessed his message. He had disabled the mobile before the gong sounded and the message was waiting for him on the display.

Snapping, scribbling suck up

He pressed the message and was given a black pawn, identical to Lisa Buoys' chess piece. The schematic moved the black king's pawn one space.

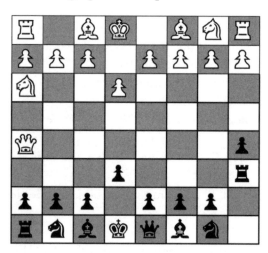

While the pawn was identical, through the schematic he registered it as a different piece. He wondered why the Turk hadn't let him see this new black move.

Who moves black? he wondered again in irritation.

As he accessed his address book it occurred to him that there would be a new entry. After all, this was another pawn but it wasn't *Lisa Buoys'* pawn. She was the black castle's pawn.

Yes, she stands in front of the castle…

Guarding the BBC…

He stretched his shoulders, wondering if that was significant. Going to the address book he found that his guess was correct: a new name had been added.

Lisa Man-suit

The Goof

Fabrienne

Tom Singer

Fabrienne Iqbal was now simply Fabrienne. So, queens mutated in a different way: no derisory nickname, rather a dropping of formality.

He dreamily considered this assessment a moment, finding it vaguely romantic and erotic, notwithstanding Fabrienne's incomprehensible behaviour. He considered the new entry: he had no idea who Tom Singer was, though he memorised the name, aware that when the next name was added it would probably change. Pressing the name, Tom Singer's details simply repeated the message: 'Snapping, scribbling suck up'. He pressed his black pawn icon to see if he could access something else. The text offered was:

Watch his eyes

He shrugged, positive that it was some rogue element on the internet hacking into Gathering's network. Returning to the chessboard menu, out of habit his thumb hovered over the thumb latch. A cold gust of salt air made him hesitate.

This is getting weird, he thought. *I'm winding myself up...*

He was thinking it was significant that he had a little while ago opened the salon door, that he had pressed its thumb latch. Fabrienne had opened the salon door on the first visit.

He took a deep breath through his nose, then pressed the latch.

This time it responded with a click.

The display was impervious to the glare of the early morning sun and, as Kris concentrated, the screen seemed to increase in size. It was disorientating. His logic told him that the screen remained some two inches square, but his understanding and interest seemed to engage it to create panel extensions that folded out in his imagination. He felt as if he was in a room where the solid walls were the screens of the mobile, his thumb on the display being his thumb on the latch of the room door. Yes, it was definitely a thumb latch: his thumbnail scratched its old, rusted surface.

He blinked and looked away, frightened by the wholly immersive experience. Squeezing his eyes, feeling a little dizzy and taking deep gulps of the smarting sea air, he supposed it must be some prototype magnifying effect, something that could be standard on all phones in a few years' time. The thumb latch meanwhile was merely his imagination cross-referencing the salon door.

With this readjustment made, he opened his eyes, now accepting the experience. He went into the Chapter Emile address book, determined this time not to leave prematurely.

The immersive experience told him he was sitting at a desk, flicking through letters, notes and calling cards, all handwritten with a quill. There were hundreds of papers on the desk.

In his mind he scrolled right to the end; he lost track of time but he guessed it took about fifteen minutes, such was the extensive list of contacts of the chapter. At the very end of the list, numbered and in a larger hand, were thirteen names, identified as being hosts of rooms.

He pushed away the papers on the desk and instead, with the push of a dummy ink pot, accessed a drawer in the desk. It slid out to reveal thirteen large calling cards, all engraved in glorious gold ink.

The cards replicated the address book. The host of the Magic Room ... the host of the Hydrogen Room ... the host of The Perfumery ... the host of The Chess Room...

He returned to the drawer, sorting through the cards. The host of The Chess Room ... that must be the member of the chapter who had occupied *his* room.

In his mind he found the list of computer names and pushed The host of The Chess Room.

He saw his hand taking this calling card out of the drawer and he was momentarily redirected to his mobile display with the message 'contacting the host'. Almost immediately he was told 'number unavailable'. He smiled a sigh of relief at what seemed to be a joke, then rang The host of The Magic Room for good measure, to receive the same message. He touched The host of The Perfumery. This time the dial tone didn't disconnect.

He was back in the room, which he now realised was in darkness; he had only been able to read the papers because he was holding a candle. He braced himself. The ringtone was unusual: an insistent handbell made with a quick shake of the wrist every few seconds.

No amount of concentration was able to break the illusion. His fear, combined with his fascination, made him as light as a feather; he was in flight, tossed on a rogue wind.

The ringtone was getting louder: two angry shakes of the wrist.

Ta-ding.

Ta-*ding*.

Someone was going to answer, his stomach told him.

Someone was *about* to answer.

He returned the calling card to the drawer and shut it, terminating the call. The candle blew out, telling him his time was up; he felt his hand rattle a door handle.

He was back on the harbour, underneath the anchor, taking deep gulps of air. Whether that app was a vision of the future or not, he would never access it again. The level of submersion made him suspect that there was some element of hypnosis involved; perhaps the app emitted a hypnotic pulse.

The mobile display was still lit but it was just a mobile again. Taking a few moments to readjust, he returned to the Chapter Emile address book. He smiled at the list of names, deciding this was just a joke app and he was taking it far too seriously. He scrolled up to where he had seen Napoleon, described as an army colonel. When he found it, with another smile he pressed the name and was immediately connected to what sounded like a battlefield. Once again he was surprised at the mobile's speakers as he put his hand over it in a vain attempt to muffle the noise. Fortunately there was no one around. Cannon fire, cheers and cries could be heard in the distance, shot spinning overheard, through what seemed to be some extraordinary wave sound technology.

No one came to the phone.

So old Boney isn't available to speak, he thought wryly, pressing the screen to remove the battle. He scrolled further up until he came to a name which made him pause:

Louis-Charles Capet (Dauphin)

He murmured with interest and pressed the name, connecting immediately as with Napoleon: apparently only members of the chapter were provided with a dial tone.

He waited, wondering where this app would take him.

The silence lasted a long time, until he realised it wasn't quite silence: frail breath could be heard, along with a water tap of condensation.

Then commotion, the mobile vibrating in his hand. The scurrying sound of rats, a loud creak, perhaps a heavy handle being turned. Something was pushed roughly along the floor.

The frightened voice of a child.

He was sobbing quietly.

The rats squealing excitedly.

"Sick joke," Kris muttered, as he touched the screen to return to the chessboard.

"Aidez-moi…" the boy wailed, as he departed.

★

Fabrienne was still struggling with her anger as she performed her bedtime ritual in her small bedsit opposite Canton police station, where she was linked to a permanent panic alarm. Her panic buttons were situated in the lounge, bedroom and bathroom, while her front door had a reinforced steel lock, which she always double-checked with two firm pulls before she turned off the lounge lights.

The ritual then took her to the photographs on her dressing table, where she would kiss the female members of her estranged family, to include her mother, several aunts and numerous cousins and nieces. There were no men in these photographs. Then from a locked drawer she would take her printed manuscript, the incomplete novel entitled *The London Address,* and sift randomly through the pages with their faint, elegant font, editorially checking paragraphs at random. Occasionally she would pause and smile, as a section drew her in and she read purely for pleasure. The book was her life; it was *her.*

Then she slipped into bed. At last she smiled, able to picture the next section of her novel which she would work on the following evening. She had five day jobs, one for each day of week, to allow her to build the necessary cash stockpile that would one day allow her to emigrate and live without fear. Of the day jobs only the Monday position in The Pavilion was in Cardiff, but they were all entirely flexible, allowing her to leave immediately if necessary; for she had a sixth job which was 24/7, the one which necessitated her living in Cardiff, notwithstanding its perils.

This job created the final part of the ritual, which was placing her Blackberry under her pillow in case it should ring. It wasn't unusual for her to receive a call in the middle of the night, demanding her immediate attendance, though more often than not her sleep would be uninterrupted, with nothing to prevent her dreaming of her ritual murder under the Rousseau inscription in Gathering's foyer.

I X

White bishop

K RIS IMMEDIATELY LOOKED for the suit: first he found the jacket, hanging on the back of the door that he was directed to close, then, turning, the pinstripe waistcoat tight around Lisa Buoys' plump torso. She hadn't risen from her desk, but he pictured her suit trousers ending in lace-up men's brogues.

Lisa Man-suit, he thought, deciding that the network clearly knew what she looked like.

"Kris. Do you consider yourself an historian or an actor?" she asked brusquely.

Disarmed, his presentation fell out of his head. He placed his hands on his knees as he sat down. "Eh, actor, mainly, Ms Buoys."

"Actor, mainly," she repeated, considering the screenplay in front of her. She turned the pages with an impassive expression, speed reading.

"I've got the treatment here," he suggested. "It gives a summary of the plot and an outline…"

"Don't patronise me, Kris. I know what a treatment is and I don't need a summary." Without looking up, her finger went questioningly to the paper. An eyebrow raised and she continued

Inwardly he cringed, embarrassed and uncomfortable. With her red cheeks and short permed hair his stomach told him she was the most repellant woman he had ever seen, while his logic told him that the network had orchestrated his view through the creation of a sexual stereotype.

Ugly lesbian bitch…

In his mind he shook his head in confusion: he regarded himself as liberal and open-minded, but her association with the chess piece, combined with the network's message, was making his skin crawl. Was the chess game warning him she was an enemy?

His mind wandered as he questioned what a black chess piece necessarily meant in this context. Perhaps the woman was just someone he had to overcome, just as the black BBC castle was something to be captured. He imagined a reassuring throb of his mobile as this thought distilled.

"Your dialogue is stilted," she remarked. "Your pacing is bad."

"It does need some polishing," he conceded.

With a huff that suggested this was a gross understatement, she continued and his eyes wandered helplessly around the office, his fingers touching the pocket of his jacket which held his mobile. He tried to concentrate.

"Wrong. Wrong. Wrong." She turned the page irritably. "Louis-Joseph's heart was *embalmed.*"

Perhaps it was the residue of the immersive experience with the thumb latch, but something took him out of his chair, away from this room.

"Nonsense!" she muttered.

He was looking at Buoys' pawn icon, his anger summoning understanding: *Show her the proving documents.*

She put aside the screenplay, then by way of final autopsy briefly examined the treatment before putting that aside also. "I agreed to see you as a favour to Dylan…" she began.

"It's okay, I know the script isn't right."

She looked at him imperiously, inviting him to explain why he had wasted her time.

"I've spoken to a history researcher, who explained my mistake with the DNA testing. With his help I'm going to rewrite the script."

She tutted. "It's not just…"

"He's going to help me rewrite *everything*," he clarified. "Help me with the style too. He's brilliant." His fingers again found his pocket. "Ms Buoys, I know you're just going through the motions…"

"I beg your pardon?"

"That you've seen me because I work here and because I've been pestering your PA. But I really think I'm on to something with the Dauphin mystery and I think it would make great TV. Go into any Waterstones and you'll see two types of books outselling the rest: history and mysteries. This has got both."

"This isn't a mystery, Kris! The DNA test cleared everything up!"

"The prince did escape, nevertheless." He smiled to defuse her outburst. "I've got a theory about how his heart came back to the doctor, Pelletan. I hope you'll just take a look at my new script."

"I'm not interested in theories," she said curtly. "*No one's* interested in theories…"

He nodded, getting up and putting his jacket on. He paused on an afterthought. "I take it you might be interested if I could offer you proof?"

The timeshare industry had made him adept at telling lies: his statement was delivered with earnest conviction. Her response was suitably hesitant.

"Proof?"

"Absolutely. My historian friend and I have uncovered some historical documents which completely overturn conventional thinking." He paused for breath, unsure where all this was coming from. "We're in the process of getting them authenticated before the reveal, but we've agreed that we want BBC Wales to have first refusal. I take it that's okay?"

She shrugged with an expression of bemused annoyance.

"That you'll take another look once the proving documents are available?"

She shrugged again. He offered his hand with a smile; she took it, though her face remained a mask of irritation.

After he closed the door behind him he brought his ear close to a door panel, his eyes squeezing in concentration. Shortly he raised a fist in triumph.

The woman had rung someone and was asking about latest research on the lost Dauphin.

He'd make the bitch cream in her man-suit.

For the next hour he was mercifully spared the ordeal of his headphones, having been tasked by Dylan with filing. He walked around his office in a flurry of inefficient activity, uselessly moving papers between cabinets and in-trays, attempting to work off his adrenalin.

He had at least obtained Buoys' attention, while wishing he could text her to thank her for seeing him. What was the use of having her in his address book if he couldn't contact her?

He gave a reflective sigh, thinking that finding the documents he had promised was more of an immediate concern. The Goof must know of something he could use:

even if the document was already in the public domain he could use it to bluff his way into another meeting on the third floor, this time with a better script. He sighed once more, finding the plan only half-satisfactory, though at least he was still in the running. He continued with his filing. Shortly he paused, making a quizzical face as he heard a woman whispering. He put his head round the door to look into the corridor to see who the voice belonged to.

There was no one there. He paused and listened. The voice was getting louder. It was definitely female and … *Russian.*

"I take your eyes."

Perhaps someone was on speakerphone, he thought, but there were no lights flashing on the intercom. He shrugged as he pulled open a cabinet drawer.

"I take your eyes!"

If the woman spoke any louder she'd have Dylan on her arse: this was about the time that he patrolled the corridor.

"I TAKE YOUR EYES!"

He froze, then his eyes widened as he dashed for his puffer jacket to disable the mobile.

"I TAKE –"

From the display he saw that it was a call announced by a new white chess piece: a bespectacled country parson with a wide brimmed hat and an open smile.

White bishop, he thought, his stomach fluttering. Just touching the mobile had disabled the ringtone, the anti-social alert that demanded attention, but the chess piece was throbbing to indicate the caller was waiting. His thumb pressed the display to connect the call; the schematic showed the white king's bishop move three squares.

"Hello?" he ventured.

"Mr Knight, this is Renka Tamirov. I am Trustee of Gathering."

"Oh, hello." He went to the door and gently closed it. If Dylan came in he'd say his mother had died or something. "Please, call me Kris."

The Russian ignored the invitation. "Do you like salon, Mr Knight?"

"Like it? I love it. I can't believe you're being so generous…" He hesitated. "Assuming, of course, you're happy with the checks you've made. Have I passed everything okay?"

"You are close."

He nodded, encouraged. With the bishop having been put into play he pictured the next available white move: castling, the king swapping with the castle, which Fabrienne had hinted meant 'moving in'. He considered running this theory past the Trustee, but decided against it; it would seem gauche to confront her with something that was obviously not meant to be discussed.

"You have an unusual ringtone," he said as a compromise to his curiosity.

"Yes? What is it?"

"Don't you know?" he chuckled.

"If I know, I don't ask."

He cleared his throat, deciding that the woman wasn't one for small talk. "Eh, it's your voice, and you say 'I take your eyes'." He waited for her to say something. "What does it mean?" he asked at length.

"The ringtone translates caller's thoughts and feelings."

He recalled Fabrienne's appeal for him to wake up. That was an amazing piece of software, though he doubted whether it would catch on: there would be too many people becoming enemies.

"My reference to eyes is, perhaps, telling of something important," she conceded. "It tells of need to keep our dealings secret."

"Confidential, sure," he agreed.

"Secret," she repeated.

"Secret, okay." He mulled over Fabrienne's reference to the prototype Turk being confidential: with such valuable artefacts being stored away, maybe the chess game was designed to test the level of his discretion. He was relieved that he hadn't mentioned the chess game a moment ago, which must have impressed her. As if in confirmation, she said:

"Meantime, why not stay few nights?"

"Faaaaantastic!"

She seemed unsure of what to make of this response. "Not moving in," she said at length. "Just suitcase. No *things*."

"No things," he agreed. A dreamy wandering around the salon imagined a wall plasma and some modern art, all the old paintings taken down and stored in the alcove with that chess machine. His leather sofa in the centre…

"I have instructed Fabrienne to meet you outside Gathering at seven this evening with key."

So she had taken his agreement as read. "I really can't tell you how grateful I am, Miss Tamarov. In fact, I really don't understand why you're being so…"

"Did not Fabrienne explain, Mr Knight?"

"Oh, absolutely, but all the same…"

She spoke rapidly. "We are charity. We help struggling artists. You are historian and we help. Is it understood?"

"I'm an actor, as well…" he suggested.

She didn't respond and he decided not to press his luck: if they wanted a historian, that's what they'd get. "Would you mind giving me some background to the building?" he asked. "Fabrienne said it was never a commercial unit and I see all the furniture's still there. Who used to live there?"

"We are happy to answer all your questions." There was a short silence which told him she wasn't happy about it at all. "The building was leased by a chapter of émigrés from Paris."

"Paris? And they came *here*?"

"They need complete anonymity."

"What, were they involved with the Terror or something?"

"They knew Saint-Just," she remarked, but he gained the impression that he was on the wrong track. He frowned, feeling he should attempt to justify their assessment of him as a historian.

"Saint-Just? He was Robespierre's right-hand man, wasn't he? Robespierre's top assassin?"

"More philosopher-politician."

"Same thing, back then," he countered defensively, wishing for all the world that he could call on that store of knowledge he seemed to possess with the antique furniture in the salon.

"Is there anything else, Mr Knight? I will give you all the time you need."

He considered the image of the bishop, the friendly country parson smiling up at him from the display. "No ... no, and I'm sorry for keeping you."

As she terminated the connection he immediately accessed the address book.

Lisa Man-suit
The Goof
Fabrienne
Little Tommy Snoop
Renka Tamarov

Renka's details were blank and pressing her white bishop icon delivered the message: 'no information available'. Bishops clearly kept things under their hats.

Tom Singer had mutated to Little Tommy Snoop, the reference to the snapping and snooping still under his details. He had written 'Tom Singer' on a post-it note and once again he wondered who he was. He also wondered if he could now send that message to Lisa Buoys. He accessed Lisa Man-suit to be given the envelope icon. Clenching a fist in triumph, his second of the day, he pressed it and spoke his message.

"Dear Ms Buoys. It was a pleasure to meet you. I promise you'll love my second script. Kris." He read the message, nodded, then said, "Send". The parchment rolled up with the clop of hooves as the mobile went dead.

Fifteen minutes into his filing he heard the desk tremor. He snatched it up to disable his mobile before he received the message gong. No chess schematic this time, just the black Moor pawn and a message:

J'attends avec l'intérêt!
Lisa

"I wait with interest," he said, surprising himself with his translation, then thinking that it was hardly a difficult one. All the same, he wondered why Buoys would choose to text back in French.

Perhaps she was already liking the idea of a French play and the fact that she had ended the message with 'Lisa' was encouraging. Maybe she wasn't quite the gorgon she had presented in the meeting.

"Lisa Man-suit," he chuckled as he returned to his filing, no longer feeling intimidated by the executive on the third floor.

Fabrienne had a studiously impassive expression as he approached with his suitcase. She didn't make eye contact.

"I'm here with your key," she said.

"Yeah, the Russian rang."

A shadow crossed his path. A large man took off his dark sunglasses with a friendly smile.

"Sorry buddy, can ya help us? We're a bit lost."

Kris acknowledged the American, cautious at being approached in this deserted location by a stranger, especially someone so imposing. He relaxed somewhat as he noticed the American's three friends standing some distance down the dirt path. One was a thin woman looking on intently, the other looked younger, though a baseball cap obscured her face. A trendily dressed young man with a stubble beard was staring at the building.

"What are you looking for?" Kris asked, gesturing to the harbour. "The Bay's that way: the Millennium Stadium and the Welsh Assembly." With no reaction from the American, just the smile remaining in place, he added, "Techniquest is just a bit of a walk along from there…"

"Right," the American answered, with a brief glance at his friends. "We're actually looking for something else; a bit off the normal tourist route."

"Mikey, what's happening?" the middle-aged woman called, to be silenced by the young woman placing a darting hand on her elbow. Kris's heart missed a beat as he saw her eyes. Was that Josie Hannah? The *film star* Josie Hannah…?

The group seemed to notice his moment of recognition and the young man who had been holding back quickly approached. The American accepted the passing of the relay batten with a finger salute to an eyebrow, returning his huge bulk to the women.

"We're looking for a sort of arts council place," the young man said. "We've heard there's a studio, or something, that helps young actors." He paused, deciding to be more direct. "It's called Gathering."

"This is Gathering," Kris replied, turning to Fabrienne for confirmation, but she was gone, having presumably walked around the side of the building.

The young man rubbed the stubble on his chin. "What … this?" he asked, looking up at the tall building but without any sense of surprise.

This is bullshit, Kris thought. The two women were

keeping their distance, had now turned to look nonchalantly out to sea.

The young man produced his ID and offered his hand with a broad smile. "Sorry, Tom Singer, *Review* magazine."

Kris hesitated, then looked at the ID. "Tom Singer," he muttered, cautiously taking his hand. "This is a private residence. It's not open to the public."

"Right," Tom murmured, his eyes straining to make out the windows towards the top of the building. The building couldn't even be seen with binoculars from a distance, the three of them having chartered a boat this morning to explore the coastline. It must be something to do with its positioning off the coastal path. He greedily breathed in the building's air. "Any chance we could have a quick look round, all the same?"

Kris glanced at the space previously occupied by Fabrienne. "I'm sorry, but I'm sure that's impossible."

"No problem." Tom smiled farewell and strolled back to his party. The two women were already walking away; shortly the bodyguard followed with a final finger salute to his eyebrow.

Kris waited for Fabrienne to emerge from behind the building. "I don't talk to strangers," she said immediately by way of explanation. He nodded thoughtfully as she opened the door, sure there was an ex-husband in the mix somewhere. As he followed her down the foyer he felt a warm sense of comfort and familiarity at the gradual appearance of the lights, no longer questioning the odd physics of the building.

"I'll leave you here," she said coldly, stopping two thirds of the way down. She handed him a key. "This is for the foyer door. You know the way."

He turned the small bronze key round in his hand. "Still not going to tell me what's upset you?"

She left him with a sarcastic smile and with a sigh of resignation he walked to the lift. He stopped to look up to the sound of levers. The lift was moving. It came to a halt, but didn't open.

"Hello?" he ventured.

"Who? Who?!" It was the tired voice of a woman in late middle age. He tried to make her out within the shadow of the cage; he smiled amiably, wanting to create a good first impression for his neighbours.

"My name's Kris Knight. I've just moved in."

There was no response.

"Are the lift doors jammed?" he asked. "Would you like some help?"

"I don't want anything … from *you*…" the woman hissed.

The cage opened and his jaw dropped as he was faced with Chelsea London wrapped inside an ermine coat. He stepped back; an overpowering perfume, a cloud of burnt almonds, had wafted out of the lift.

"Miss London, I had no idea you lived here. My name is…"

She barged past him with an expression of disbelief. The ceiling lights flicked off to follow her passage until she paused thoughtfully halfway down the foyer, where she hovered near one of the thirteen chairs. She reached into her bag for her mobile and she looked at it, expectantly.

He watched her from the lift, until it took him up.

★

The four tourists were sitting in a corner of the Millennium Centre cafe, Josie wearing oversized dark glasses, one hand on the peak of her baseball cap. Mikey sat next to her, leaning across the table, his bulk providing further protection from curious eyes.

"Honey, this is crazy," Erica said again. "If you could just tell me what we're trying to achieve."

"I told you," Josie whispered. "Chelsea London lives in that building."

"So?!"

Josie shook her head, not caring to elaborate.

"Honey, if meeting that has-been is so important to you then that's exactly what we're going to do." She stirred her cappuccino reflectively, her call to duty overcoming her reservations.

From under her cap Josie's eyes flickered to Tom sitting opposite, and he dutifully produced the colour copies of the photographs from London's dressing table mirror. He handed them over with a magnifying glass.

He tried to conceal his resentment at her constant requests to view the pictures, which he now regarded as his property. The revelations contained in the photographs had made him forget he was sharing time with a beautiful superstar. Josie Hannah was relevant to him only in that they shared a common purpose.

To see inside Chelsea London's home.

To see the wonders...

X

Black bishop

As Kris opened his eyes, he waited for the grumble in the small of his back. It didn't arrive, the stiff velvet chaise longue having been surprisingly comfortable, in fact he had fallen asleep as soon as his head touched the backrest. His eyes flickered to his chest, where he held his mobile. It seemed unaffected by his night's sleep, carrying no trace of his palms' perspiration.

He sat up to regard the double doors that led to the bedroom and wondered when he would get the key. He shook his head, thinking that the doors would just be unlocked and left open, as with the bathroom.

Keys seemed unnecessary inside the building. The lift took him to the correct floor and corridor, there was no danger of wandering into the wrong room by mistake. There must be hidden cameras, probably with a security guard watching from some control room somewhere, activating the lift and the lights as required.

He looked round uncomfortably, then decided they wouldn't go as far as putting surveillance in the rooms. The extreme security was required because of the historical artefacts being stored; not only the antiques but treasures like the prototype Turk. That idea of helping struggling artists was all bullshit: the charity was looking for a caretaker and the Russian Trustee was testing whether he could keep mum. He yawned, not really caring; he loved these rooms and he wasn't going to disappoint her.

He wandered happily to the windows and breathed in the view of the Bay. He knew he was high up but the world seemed surprisingly small: the people setting up stalls and putting out chairs to their franchise businesses looked like so many dots. Conversely, his long view across the Barrage to Penarth Marina seemed too close, the townhouses clearly in view; with a squint he imagined he could read the names on the yachts.

He stepped back. The glass in these windows must be concave or something, he reasoned, magnifying near or far depending on the angle; perhaps this was the fashion in the eighteenth century. The glass certainly looked old, the odd hairline scratch and air bubble suggesting the hand of a craftsman. Once more he searched for that open window to find where the fresh sea air was coming from, but all the glass was fused to lead panes. He supposed it was in the bedroom.

He checked his watch: he had overslept and only had an hour before his meeting with the Goof over in Penarth Marina, a good thirty minutes' stroll along the coastal path and across the Barrage. With no time for a bath he groaned as he remembered there wasn't a shower, so at the onyx vanity console he filled the ewer of rock crystal and gold for a strip wash. The water spurted out of the single tap and was exactly the right temperature. As he splashed and dabbed himself he realised the water was perfumed; shortly he felt as clean as if he had been blasted in a power shower. He didn't bother with deodorant, deciding he didn't need it; with that sweet-smelling freshness all over his body it would have been crass to spoil it with product.

Some clever soap dispenser was no doubt built into the console, he thought with a smile, The Chess Room continuing to surprise him. As he dressed from his open suitcase he pondered on his lunch meeting with Mason. Yesterday evening the mobile display had illuminated Mason's page, with a message waiting to be written. It snatched an idea that had been floating round in his head, that it would be a good idea to take the socially challenged academic for a fancy lunch to pitch his idea for the new screenplay. He had sent a text, 'Join me for a steak, Pier 64, 12 noon, my treat?' which had come back eventually with Mason's cautious agreement.

Having dressed, he picked up the mobile to put it in his jacket, pausing to consider its dead display. He had no means of accessing it; it was as if the mobile decided when it would be used. The wall mirror had the same aura of stubborn aloofness. He had fallen into the habit of studiously avoiding his reflection as he walked around the salon; he would look in the mirror when *it* was ready.

He made ready to leave. What was he hoping for from this meeting? What did 'Go to the Mountain' mean? He huffed, perplexed, deciding that he'd really quiz the Goof about the National Assembly over lunch as the price for the best steak in the city, but at the door he paused and frowned. He turned to consider the Japanese lacquer cabinet, specifically the locked drawer with the alpine relief of Mount Fiji.

He went to the cabinet and tugged on the drawer handle. He muttered a curse, it was still locked. He shook his head, then as an afterthought tried the bronze foyer key. It fitted.

"Go to the mountain," he murmured, pulling out the

drawer to find what appeared to be a handwritten letter, tied in a ribbon and secured with a wax seal. He picked it up carefully, the paper crisp with age. The seal was broken but he was reluctant to open the letter, the pages possibly bonded with time, though he whistled as he saw the date on the fold, which in faded ink was '13 Prairial'. Prairial was a month in the short-lived Revolutionary calendar.

A sudden misgiving had him glancing round guiltily as he made to put the letter in his jacket, then thought better of it and took a clear plastic bag from his suitcase, gently wrapping the letter up before pocketing it.

"It became customary to gather in front of the huts..." he muttered, unconsciously repeating the memorised ceiling quotation as he walked down the foyer. "Everyone began to look at everyone else and wish to be looked at himself..."

Kris felt the warning vibration message gong on the yacht basin, when he was a few minutes away from Pier 64. He disabled the message gong efficiently and, to avoid the joggers, ducked into a dry dock where he could read the message in privacy.

The display showed a black chess piece: a turbaned Moor with hoop ear rings. His hand was on his heart, his mephistophelian head tilted back with a dissembling smile.

"Bishop," he muttered. "Enemy bishop."

The piece reminded him of a snake charmer. He pressed the display and the chess schematic showed the black bishop move out from the ranks.

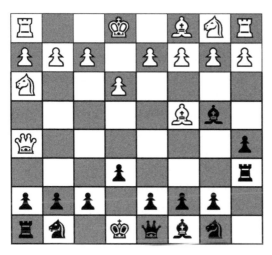

The display presented a message

The Baptist is here

before he was directed automatically to his address book.

Lisa Man-suit
The Goof
Fabrienne
Little Tommy Snoop
Second Trustee of Temple 1313
Tristyn Honeyman

He accessed 'Tristyn Honeyman', the fresh entry with a black bishop icon, but as with the Russian there were no details under either his name or chess icon. Perhaps in this chess game the bishops had a special role, or held a special significance.

He allowed this analysis to filter. Unlike the nicknames, insults and informal first names, Renka Tamarov had mutated into something which looked very official: 'Second Trustee of Temple 1313', whatever that might mean. Perhaps the reference to a temple meant that she belonged to some religious organisation, hence her being assigned as a bishop, although she seemed a most unlikely Bible-basher.

He put his mobile away and walked to the glass door of the steakhouse, locating Mason sitting on a high table near the bar, devouring chips in an animated fashion while speaking to a large bearded man seated opposite. The man was nodding occasionally, listening attentively but without speaking. He was glancing round regularly.

Kris remembered the man from the Chapter workshop: it was too much of a coincidence to assume he was anyone other than the Baptist.

"Black bishop. Enemy priest," he muttered silently, imagining that he felt the mobile throb in agreement.

The bearded man saw him as he entered the restaurant. The man hesitated, patted Mason's hand, then got up from the table. With his head down he left the restaurant via a different exit, moving swiftly notwithstanding a slight limp in his right leg.

"Who was that?" Kris asked Mason as he joined him at the table.

Mason's voice was an excited squeak. "History buff. He wanted to know all about my papers on Tharlemagne!"

This went over Kris's head in a puff of disinterest. "I see you've already ordered," he remarked with an air of exasperation, noting Mason's half-eaten sirloin and supposing he didn't realise it was polite to wait for your dinner guest. Mason was speaking a little too loudly and eating too quickly, his peppercorn sauce spraying from his teeth. He was usually perfectly calm; Kris wondered whether this was his way of coping in public.

"You okay?" Kris asked.

Mason nodded, deciding not to mention that he had paid the taxi driver to wait up the road. He wasn't sure why he was here, except that he felt a bond with his latest tenant that he rationalised as an interest in his screenplay, but it was something else, something inexplicable. He had the notion that he was looking for something important, something *new*, and only Kris Knight knew where it was to be found.

Sorry, Kris mouthed discreetly to a couple nearby who were looking over uncomfortably. Out of the corner of his eye he noticed Mason pile too many chips in his mouth and Kris tapped his forehead meaningfully without humour. The couple nodded with vague comprehension and looked away.

He turned back to Mason and leant forward. "Mason, just keep it down, okay?" he whispered. "This is a restaurant."

Mason paused, then nodded.

This guy isn't fit for the outside world, Kris realised, deciding he didn't want to eat after all; he'd let Mason finish his steak and then they'd get out. A waitress came over and he grimaced while touching his belly. "I'm just going to wait for my friend to finish, then we'll have the bill," he said pointedly, his eyes marking his intentions and inviting her not to question his decision. "I'll just have a glass of house red." The waitress hesitated, looked at Mason, then smiled and sidled away.

The waitress had good legs and Kris watched her go until his eyes were shovelled up by a tall, striking woman in army fatigues sitting outside on the deck terrace, notwithstanding that there was a cold drizzle. She gestured with her eyes to the waitress who dutifully stepped out to attend her. The waitress looked back at their table as the woman whispered something in her ear, then nodded mutely.

"I've already paid for my steak," Mason said as he pushed his plate away. "I didn't expect you to pay for me. Nice just to be asked."

Kris nodded. As with the tenants, he had suspected that money wasn't an issue with the Goof: he was simply pleased to have what he would regard as a cool, worldly-wise friend. He managed another glance outside at the woman in fatigues, but only briefly, as her expression made it clear she didn't welcome his observation. "How did you get speaking to that guy in the first place?" he asked.

Mason was surprised. "He was sitting at the bar and he came over: he said he knew *you*. Asked me about your pitch to the BBC. That's when we started talking about the Dauphin, which got us on to your Thaumette theory. He had firm views on that."

"Yeah?" Kris asked suspiciously. "What's that then?"

Mason smiled shyly at the pretty waitress returning with the wine, who studiously avoided his eyes. "Just the usual," he said. "The Dauphin died in prison; ineptitude and bureaucracy stopped the body being properly identified."

"Sorry, unconvincing."

"True, but then he said that the first thing you have to understand about the French Revolution is that nothing makes sense. A crazy time built on mistakes and accidents, which can't be logically analysed with hindsight."

Kris glanced back at the door, the image of the turbaned snake charmer causing him unease. "How did that guy say he knew me?" he asked casually.

"He said he met you at Chapter Arts Centre."

Kris sipped his wine, savouring it appreciatively. He had always liked wine but recently his appetite for it had increased, in fact to the exclusion of all other alcohol. "He just sort of heckled from the back, to tell you the truth, but that's how he knows about my script." He paused. "Did he say anything else?"

"Such as?"

"I don't know. Anything unusual?"

Mason shook his head, wiping his mouth with a serviette that was stained with sauce. "He just seemed interested in you. I assume he's involved with your production or something?"

Kris sat back, wondering whether he should share the chess game with Mason, but deciding that wouldn't be a good idea given the Russian's warning about keeping secrets. Maybe he was even being followed and that character, who the address book told him was called Tristyn Honeyman, was working for the Russian. Perhaps that's what a bishop signified: an employee of Gathering. "There *is* no production, Mason," he said at length. "At least, not yet."

"Your meeting didn't go well?"

Kris sighed. "It went a lot better than it should have. I got her interest at least; got a window for a further script." He stretched his shoulders. "That's really why I wanted to meet up. I want you to help me write it. We can be a production team: you as writer-researcher, me as the producer-presenter, like I mentioned the other day."

Mason answered immediately. "I am interested," he conceded, "but where have you got left to go with this Dauphin idea?"

Mason hadn't ordered a drink so Kris quickly collected

another glass of wine from the bar. Mason looked at it suspiciously.

"Look," Kris began, "you agreed that the circumstantial evidence is compelling. Chaumette and Simon smuggled the Dauphin out but then were bumped off. The Dauphin died in whatever place he was left."

Mason sniffed the wine. "That's feasible, but how...?"

"How do we get round the DNA testing?" Kris paused. "You're the history whizz kid. I was hoping you might have some ideas... Perhaps there's some old documents lying around...?" he added enticingly.

"Thanks for the compliment, but I can't conjure evidence. Kris, I really think you're going up a dead end with this. Why not choose a different subject?"

Kris shook his head. Gathering was clearly convinced that there was mileage in the Dauphin story, otherwise they wouldn't be sponsoring him. He ran his finger round the rim of his wine glass, realising that they hadn't actually said anything complimentary about his screenplay other than inferring he was a historian; what really gave him his solid floor of confidence was that memory of the first time in the lift, when the building itself reached out and found a hook with the Dauphin. "Look, if I draft some ideas will you at least have a look at it? Even if you don't want to be involved, tidy up the dialogue? Make it more natural; more authentic." He shrugged, a little unhappily. "Even if we haven't got a new slant, it's still a good mystery."

Mason looked unconvinced as he took a long draught of his wine, spilling it down his chin. Kris grabbed the glass off him, feeling the tremble of Mason's fingers in the glass, and pulling it towards him with another embarrassed apology to the couple on his left. The Goof was actually shaking with nerves, he realised; maybe he was on medication and something in the food or drink had upset him. He felt like a grossly negligent babysitter.

"How's your new place?" Mason squeaked, trying to compose himself.

"Good," Kris said at length, the affirming nod more for his own benefit then for Mason's. "Weird, but good."

"Weird?"

"Hmmm. Some curious shit's going down, which I'm still trying to figure out." He considered Mason for a few moments, then brought out his mobile and laid it on the table. "This thing, for example, is the craziest phone I've ever…"

Kris regretted his action immediately, snatching it up as he saw Mason reach for it. The mobile was vibrating with excitement as he closed both hands protectively around it and returned it to his jacket. "Sorry, I forgot, it's downloading some apps." This was the first time he had brought out his mobile with the intention of someone else looking at it, but the idea of another person touching it was… It was…

He shook his head, unable even to find the words. Although the mobile belonged only to him, existed only *for* him, instinctively he knew it could be touched by others, could be stolen or abused, that it needed to be guarded. A black space in his mind would throb with danger with the memory of that fleeting moment when the Goof almost took it: it would break his mind if he were to lose it.

Another shake of his head dispelled this curious fear, then he put it away completely. He was vaguely aware that his brain had developed a new muscle in the last few weeks, one that managed to either rationalise or ignore the inexplicable.

"New apartment is fantastic, to tell you the truth," he said with a grin. Out of the corner of his eye he noticed the fatigues woman retake her seat, having stood up at some point in the commotion of the last few seconds. "I'll show it to you sometime. Hey, and I found something in one of the drawers which you'll be interested in." He took out the letter wrapped in its clear plastic bag and handed it to Mason.

"What's this?"

"A letter, I think. It's in French, and it's old."

"What?"

"Could you check it out? It might belong to the original occupant of my rooms: a chap who liked his chess."

"What?" Mason repeated. His eyes widened as he silently mouthed the date on the fold of the letter: *13 Prairial.*

"Oh yeah, I forgot to mention, didn't I? My new gaff is a sort of eighteenth century museum. You'd love it. Found that thing locked away in a Japanese lacquer cabinet." He watched Mason turn it carefully around in his hands. "Well, aren't you going to open it?"

"Best I do it at home," Mason suggested, with a guilty glance at his wine. "Don't want us spilling anything." He carefully pocketed the letter in the rucksack he had brought. "Or perhaps in the university lab, in controlled conditions." He was shaking with excitement.

"Mason?"

"I'm going to go now."

"Go?"

"I want to look at this letter."

"Suit yourself. It's just a letter, probably nothing important. You don't mind if I stop here and order something?" he added, secretly relieved. He motioned to the waitress that he was ready to order after all; he felt like celebrating, even if he had to do it alone. Unaccountably, given the obstacles he faced, he was feeling exuberant. Somehow the salon had gifted him with a sense of destiny, a feeling that his success was guaranteed. That problems which a few weeks ago would have been insurmountable were now merely pot holes on the road.

Provided I accept their direction…

That reflection rang a memory bell as Mason rose from the table. "It's just on loan, mind," he murmured. "In fact, would you mind signing something for me?" He produced a detailed confidentiality agreement. "I got this printed off at the internet cafe. It's pretty standard."

He was lying: the confidentiality agreement was one of many that had been found in the Japanese cabinet this morning when he checked more of the drawers. This one had Mason's name on it.

"You can trust me," Mason said, sounding hurt.

"I know. I'm just following instructions."

"Instructions?"

"From the owners of the building: the Trustees, whatever. They said that anything I found in the apartment was mine but I'd need a confidentiality agreement if I showed anyone."

He offered a pen. Mason shrugged and took it. "Could you give me your number?" he asked as he handed back the signed agreement.

"You've got it. You texted back last night."

Mason shook his head. "Strangest thing. My mobile didn't recognise your number."

"It must have recognised something: you replied to my text."

The academic raised his hand in a shy farewell. "Your number's thowing on my mobile as one three one three. It's meaningless."

1313.

Thirteen thirteen…

The number rotated in Kris's imagination as he felt the excited throb of his jacket.

"Meaningless," he agreed, returning the farewell wave. He sighed, noticing that the fatigues woman had also got up to leave. Her food and drink had been left untouched.

X I

Writing bureau

"I DON'T BELIEVE he's going on the telly," the girl giggled to her friend, their arms enlocked as they walked the coastal path.

"Me neither, Trace," her friend replied, but soberly and without humour. "Let's go back and get a taxi."

"But we're almost there," Kris insisted, turning round and walking backwards to face them. "Just have a nightcap. Seriously, you'll love the place." His voice was slightly slurred from the wine he had drunk in Cardiff Bay, where he had found the two women merry from the vodka bottle concealed in their bag.

"Just a quick one then," Tracy confirmed.

Her friend huffed but complied, not fancying walking back by herself. As they came to a stop she looked up at the building in disgust. "It's an old warehouse. It's a fuckin' dump."

"Shut up Debs," Tracy said, but unable to resist another giggle. "Show some respect: it's the boy's home!"

Kris was taking it in good humour, making an effort to steady himself as he produced his bronze key from his trouser pocket. "Don't let appearances deceive you ladies," he declared. "I live in a palace."

"There you go, Debs: he lives in a palace." Both girls laughed.

He was surprised that the exterior of the building hadn't wowed them: perhaps they couldn't fully appreciate it in the dark, or maybe they just couldn't see beyond the weathered stone. He grinned as he turned the key, picturing their faces when they saw the bronze foyer.

The door didn't open.

"Come on Kris," Tracy said, "I'm freezing me tits off."

The key turned in the lock but the mechanism refused to engage, nothing catching on the key's teeth. Time passed as he persisted. He was sober now, the problem with the door like a bucket of cold water.

"I'm not liking this," Debbie muttered. "I'm cold and it feels like we're miles from nowhere. I want to go home."

Kris persevered with the lock; he was starting to mutter and curse.

"Yeah, me too," Tracy said, now with a cautious tone.

He wasn't sure how long he continued turning and pressing the key: the key that had worked easily when he came home from Pier 64 earlier that day. Eventually the door opened and he turned round with a groan of relief, but both girls were gone, already over the pedestrian bridge and heading for the taxi rank. He gave a couldn't-care-less wave and went inside. The door squeezed tight behind him and in the darkness he waited for the foyer's lights.

The lights didn't appear.

"Hello?" he said as quietly as he was able, but his words were a noise ball bouncing off the walls. He swallowed in the realisation he had no means of leaving the building: the front door had always opened on his approach and in the pitch darkness he stepped towards it, trying to trigger the mechanism. Nothing worked.

He took out his mobile and was relieved to see that the

display was shining, so brightly in fact that it was effectively a pocket torch. He made his way down the foyer, guided by the shapes of the thirteen chairs as a navigator charts a coastline, until he found himself at the lift. He heard the cage slide open; it closed as he stepped in, the lift taking him up.

The ascent seemed longer than normal, even more exhausting. When the cage opened he held up his mobile to shine into the corridor and he saw it wasn't his floor. The corridors ahead and to the right ended in boarded up doors. The cage had opened to his left, facing a teak door. Stepping out, his mobile illuminated the door's plaque:

La Parfumerie

"The Perfumery," he muttered, again unsure whether his translation was inspired or just a lucky guess, though he recalled the thirteen hosted rooms in the chapter on his address book, one of which was The Perfumery. He contemplated knocking, changed his mind and returned to the lift, huddling into a corner to wait for it to move. For the first time the building was making him afraid.

Time passed. "Hello?" he said eventually, wondering if this was Chelsea London's floor. He again contemplated knocking but it felt like an appalling intrusion; he shivered as he imagined his salon's outrage if a stranger were to knock on *his* door. Instead, he waited, until with a twist in his stomach he realised his mobile's display was fading. When it went out, the darkness would be complete.

"Don't go out, don't go out," he whispered to the mobile, and it burst back into light. Such was his relief, at first he didn't hear the handbell announcing a call. It started very quietly, becoming louder with every insistent ring.

Ta-ding.

Ta-*ding*.

It was the ringtone he had heard when he tried to call the host of The Perfumery. He checked his display: there was no chess piece, rather an antique apparatus which reminded him of an ornate bunsen burner, a candle under a gilded cup that might have adorned a lady's dressing table.

He swallowed. A woman who had lived in the eighteenth century was apparently calling him. A very loud ring prompted him to touch the display.

The handbell ended with an echoed clatter.

"Hello?" he whispered. He briefly heard breathing before the call terminated.

"What have you done?!" came a woman's voice from beyond the door. It was loud, almost hysterical.

"Is that you, Miss London?" he called, getting up. The display was still lit but the candle and cup artefact had vanished. "Why are the lights out?"

"The lights are out because of *you*, you ghastly little man!"

"Me? What have *I* done?"

London's voice had come down in pitch but was still shaking. "You've offended the building!"

"The building…?"

"Of course! Of course! Have you said something? Brought someone? Have you? Have you?"

He thought about Debs and Trace, probably now in their taxi, imagining how they would be reacting if they were here. "Yeah, sorry," he muttered. "Sorry," he repeated, in a louder voice. There was no response: the mobile faded, putting him in complete darkness, though he heard the cage close and felt the lift going down. With an ache of relief he realised he was back on his own floor. The cage opened and he felt his way down the corridor until he found the thumb latch. Inside, the salon was in gloom, the windows framing the night sky.

"Candles," he muttered. "Must be a candle here somewhere."

He remembered there was a candelabra on a plinth in the far corner of the bathroom. He stopped at the door, considering the copper tub with its harem taps. In the shade it looked very appealing indeed; a warm tingle went through his body as he imagined sitting in its steamy water.

The lights went on.

"You bring the darkness."

The display showed a black Moor pawn.

"You bring the darkness!"

He answered after the second ringtone, recognising the voice.

"This is Chelsea London," she announced as the call was answered. Her voice was chilled, but controlled.

The schematic showed a flashing black pawn in front of the king's castle, but it didn't move.

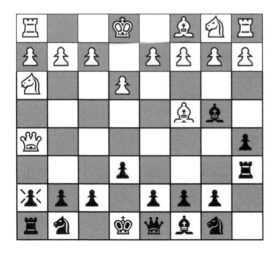

White moves next, he thought, noting the grounded pawn. The schematic was merely identifying her as a player in the game: a pawn guarding the enemy castle.

"Chelsea London of The Perfumery, in Gathering."

"Okay…" he agreed.

"I am, I suppose, your neighbour…"

"Look I'm really pleased to meet you…"

"… and you will *never* inconvenience me again."

He opened his mouth to speak but was lost for words. This woman was famous after all: it didn't seem right to argue with her.

"This building is to be treated with respect," she continued. "We are but its guests. Do you understand, Kris Knight?"

He wanted to ask her how she knew his surname - he didn't remember giving it when she was observing in Chapter; instead, he said, "Yeah, sorry."

The call ended, though the display remained lit. Without hesitation he went to the address book, taking care to avoid the thumb latch.

Lisa Man-suit
The Goof
Fabrienne
Little Tommy Snoop
Second Trustee of Temple 1313
The Baptist
Chelsea London

Noting, without surprise, that 'Tristyn Honeyman' had now mutated to 'The Baptist', he knew that this would probably be the only time he would see London's real name in his address book. He lingered awhile at Renka Tamarov's title, 'Second Trustee of Temple 1313', the number taking on a vague significance with the number on the Goof's mobile. Perhaps '1313' wasn't meaningless at all: it was a special number for this network. When he had the chance he'd ring it from a landline and see what happened. Perhaps he should google it too.

He returned to the chessboard menu and paced the room. He accessed Chapter Emile, scrolled down to the end of the list and tentatively pressed The host of The Perfumery.

This time the number didn't ring; he was directed to a page which had the antique that looked like a fancy bunsen burner.

"A perfume burner," he muttered, cross-referencing the artefact against her name now that he was at leisure to make the deduction. He touched the icon to see a brief entry:

Claudine de Tour du Pin
1754–1812
romantic novels

His thumb flitted over the name, prompting a distant but irritated *ta-ding*. He pulled his hand back and the text faded, to reveal a message.

Time to lock up

He frowned, picturing the boarded-up doors. The text faded once more, now to present a series of photographs. He flicked: they showed close-ups of a striking middle-aged woman with white powdered cheeks, wearing a feather hat with a half-veil. The veil covered the right side of her face.

He jumped as her eyes flickered.

"Bonsoir, Monsieur Knight," the woman said.

He touched the screen, realising that this last photograph was actually a film of whatever actress or model had stepped in to play Claudine. He was returned to her details. At the bottom of the screen was a message: 'access your bureau?' With a groan of delayed shock he pressed, to be taken to a page with a wax seal. A writing bureau had a space for text composition, while two partially open drawers were labelled 'received' and 'sent'.

In the sent drawer he glimpsed, in a flowing ink script, the opening of his text to Lisa Buoys. At least he assumed that was what it was: he recognised her first name.

So, this was where his texts were stored. He touched the drawer and it sprung out. Continuing to pace, his nose greedily inhaling the crisp, fresh air circulating the salon, he discovered his text read:

Salut Mme Buoys. C'était un plaisir de vous rencontrer. Je promets que vous aimerez mon deuxième script. Kris

He was nodding as he paced; he was pretty sure this was his exact message in French, which explained why Buoys had replied in French. The mobile must have an app, or possibly a bug, which automatically translated English to French.

He slumped onto the largest chaise longue which doubled as his bed and breathed a sigh of relief. At least Buoys didn't seem annoyed; in fact his French erudition had clearly impressed her.

Pondering on this, he wondered if this was why Fabrienne was angry with him. Receiving his e-mail in French might have made her think he was a snob or something, or that he was taking the rise out of her degree in French literature. He shrugged, thinking that in that case her reaction was extreme: after all he had merely thanked her for ringing and to confirm he'd meet her outside the building the following morning.

He touched the Buoys letter, moving it down and back into the drawer; then switched to his left to find his message to Fabrienne. His fingers tingled at the memory this simple message invoked – composed, as it had been, after he had seen her private photographs.

He accessed the letter to confirm it was also in French. His face dropped in horror. It read:

Fabrienne,
I put my tongue to your scars.
And I lick.

★

There was no view of Gathering from Honeyman's digs in Cardiff Bay, a studio apartment in a new development opposite the Millennium Centre. Even taking the let unfurnished had put a severe dent in his savings, but there wasn't anywhere else he could live where he could imagine a view of the eighteenth century building. It was in fact impossible to see it, tucked away from the coastal path between empty derelicts.

At least, that was how his logical mind rationalised why such a large building couldn't be seen from any distance. The building's camouflage had only become apparent when he realised he was continually walking past it, that he needed a mental effort to see it.

The building didn't care for being observed. It had been built, Gracie had told him, to hide thirteen people from the world and time had given it a flinty mindset of secrecy, guarding its anonymity with powerful methods of persuasion. To the majority of disinterested observers it would appear dirty and unimportant, dropping quickly out of memory. To the overly curious, a shock of revelation would achieve a similar memory loss, but with something sharp and painful. The building only revealed itself to those within the orbit of the temple.

He gloomily considered Gracie's figurine on his window sill as he reached into his holdall and pulled out his camera with its telescopic lens. She no longer had any of her old powers now that her temple Precious Cargo had fallen: her sole reason for continued existence was to be reunited with Franklyn Tyde, for whom the term 'soulmate' was a literal truth. But because she knew about Temple Thirteen Thirteen she had been able to lead him here: strands of knowledge ran through the DNA of all those connected with the coven.

Inspection of the building's exterior had told her that two rooms were awake. When he scribbled this in his notebook, asking her to clarify that statement, she explained that they were either occupied or ready to receive a guest. They were called The Perfumery and The Chess Room. There was a common link to both these rooms: someone who worked in The Pavilion sales office in the Hayes.

The link had turned out to be one Fabrienne Iqbal, a solitary woman who seemed to have no family or friends.

On his wall chart he had pinned a long range photograph of The Pavilion's sales office, its door open. This chart displayed his research, the work of eighteen months, and had thirteen names. They were all French émigrés and he had traced their names from one remarkable document in the council archives, a computer search of scanned archive documents finding them by cross-referencing the words 'thirteen', 'émigré' and 'Bute'.

When the 2nd Marquess of Bute had been developing Cardiff Docks in the early nineteenth century, Bute's engineers had investigated the isolated, uncatalogued building that they had come across almost by accident. Bute's lawyer recorded that it was held in trust for thirteen people and couldn't be purchased.

The lawyer had also provided their occupations. Ink squiggles and question marks were on the lawyer's letter at this point, to query why such information needed to be given, though clearly the lawyer had thought it necessary. The lawyer ended his letter with a blunt warning to his employer that he was to stay away. The warning probably resulted in the lawyer's retainer being terminated, if Bute's scratched exclamation marks were any indication.

The émigrés had different professions, but the common factor was a link to celebrity through the mediums of art, entertainment and discovery. There was an actor, a poet, a balloonist, a chemist, a theoretical mathematician, a philosopher, a satirist, a magician, a sculptor, a painter, a composer, but two names had been ringed with Honeyman's charcoal pencil: a romantic novelist and a chess master.

One was the obvious candidate for The Chess Room. The second had been found when he had ordered from a Paris bookstore a novelette by Claudine de Tour du Pin, contained within a 1930s volume reprint of many long-forgotten writers. It was a curio that had as its heart the theme of contemporary Parisian living in the late eighteenth century as seen by some of its (now forgotten) residents.

There was also a brief foreword on the authors and subscribers, which had enabled him to identify not only The Perfumery but Fabrienne Iqbal's position on this chart, which was directly underneath the French author. Claudine de Tour de Pin, it was said, was renowned in French society for her exotic perfumes which she imported from India through the patronage of several celebrated perfumers. Her novels, written under the pen name Madame Claudine, were mainly purchased by those who wished to be invited to her salon gatherings, which, it was said, were fronts for Romanesque orgies, before she retreated from society after a heated argument with her longstanding rakish paramour resulted in her disfigurement with acid.

A postscript completed Madame Claudine's epitaph. It was said that her final novel, which her publisher had no interest in after she abandoned society, was a true masterpiece. It was called *The London Address:* disfigurement and despair had sharpened her talent to an extraordinary extent, an official biographer had recorded, one of the few to have read the work.

Sadly, *The London Address* manuscript had never been found. It existed now only in the memory of the dead.

Honeyman distrusted computer storage and Madame Claudine's one surviving novella, an early two-dimensional romance, was printed out in the ring binder marked with her name, stacked next to the twelve other ring binders, some empty save for his own notes and questions, others thick with details he had uncovered through Paris archives. A balloonist who was disabled through a helium explosion, his inability to raise finance for a second project recorded by his creditors. Critics' reviews and notices of the various artists. A fairly thick dossier on a brilliant chess director, the records reasonably detailed because he had been connected to Kempelen, the celebrated inventor of the Turk.

All thirteen were compiled in his last largest file, a lever arch entitled Chapter Emile. Some of the documents in this file consisted of his own research on Rousseau, especially extracts from his work *Emile*, all prompted by the discovery that Claudine had belonged to a Revolutionary chapter of that name: Chapter Emile was more passionate than the Girondins, more radical than the Jacobins.

The chapter's history and constitution, and its violent destruction, were matters of public record; cross-referencing had revealed that membership of this chapter was another common feature of the thirteen émigrés.

That was his research, but for his inspiration he now relied on Gracie. He turned her figurine to face the wall chart and Fabrienne's photograph. He had no idea whether the figurine could see, or whether it was just a lodestone for Gracie's essence, but the action felt right. When he was dressing or sleeping he always turned the figurine away.

"Tell me about Fabrienne," he asked gently.

He patiently allowing the minutes to pass. Eventually he stiffened and collected his notebook. In the back of the book, Gracie's section, he wrote:

Her heart belongs to The Perfumery.

XII

Tom's eyes

"I KNOW WHY you're angry with me," Kris called to the intercom, "but I didn't send that text." He waited, there was no response. "Do you really think I'd be that stupid?" he pressed. "Fabrienne, you know I like you: do you really think I'm *that stupid?*"

He let the seconds pass, sure that he could hear her breathing.

"If it wasn't you, then who was it?" came the eventual response.

"Someone's hacking into the network: that was your own explanation, remember? Some rogue element on the internet."

She let out a long, confused sigh. "But how could you … how could they *know…?*"

She didn't wait for an answer, buzzing open the door. She was standing by the glass-cased model by the time he had collected himself and walked through.

"They must be close to home," he said. "Remember when I told you about that Lisa Man-suit message? Well that was a bullseye, because the woman *was* wearing a suit. Whoever's doing this knows who all the players are." He paused, seeing she was unconvinced. "And maybe you don't hide your thing as well as you think," he suggested gently, having thought of countless variations on the word 'scars' on the bus in and eventually deciding on 'thing'.

She put a protective hand to her hairline. "My husband threw hot water over me in the first year of our marriage, in case you're wondering. I was married young," she added gloomily.

He nodded cautiously, trapped in a furious internal debate as to whether to tell her there were pornographic pictures of her on the network. He had eventually decided against it, with a mental groan at yet another secret he was forced to keep: if she knew he had seen that last photograph their relationship would be over before it had started, no matter who was to blame. "Are you sure it's not your ex-husband hacking in?" he asked.

She shook her head decisively.

"Other members of your family?"

"I never see any of them," she muttered. "My ex-husband's in prison and I've got court injunctions against the rest." Her face registered her surprise at how much she was telling him: perhaps it was the fact that he shared a connection with Gathering, that he had seen the building; she had been thinking about the building a lot lately, more than she used to. That made him closer to her than anyone else in her life.

He concealed his satisfaction over the progress he was making. "Then maybe it's Gathering that's orchestrating all of this. It's their network, after all. Fabrienne, what's your relationship with these people? How did you get involved with them?"

She froze.

"Okay, so don't tell me," he groaned, raising his hands in placation.

"I *can't* tell you, Kris."

They both paused for mental breath. "Do you still want to move in?" she asked at length.

"What, castling?" he said slyly.

"Castling," she admitted. "I know about the chess game."

"Yeah, I guessed."

"And whose move is it now?"

"Mine. A black bishop moved last." He smirked. "Would it interest you to know that you're a queen ... *my* queen ... while my landlord's just a pawn?"

"Why do you think I'm a queen?"

He stretched his shoulders. "Maybe you're just important to me...?"

She looked down glumly, choosing to misinterpret the statement. "Feel rather useless, to tell you the truth. Don't think I've been any help at all." Her eyes darkened. "Who's the black bishop?"

He smiled, content to play out the fiction that he had been referring to her professional skills when he mentioned her importance. "Oh, him. Someone who's been stalking me. Doesn't seem to want to talk to me though; he ran off the last time I saw him. I'd think he was working for Gathering if wasn't for..."

"Wasn't for what?"

"Well, if it wasn't for the fact he's listed as an enemy. As a black piece, I mean."

She tapped the glass case, reluctant to make eye contact with Kris, her anger having turned to embarrassment. "He's a bishop. Maybe that's important. Is there anything – how can I put it? – anything *spiritual* about him?"

He shrugged. "Not that I'm aware of: he seems to know his history, but that's about it. Anyway, that Russian bird's a white bishop and she doesn't sound like a nun or anything."

Fabrienne nodded slowly but didn't comment.

"I still think the building's beautiful," he said, in case she thought he was having second thoughts.

"It is," she whispered.

"And you believe me about the text?"

"I believe you."

He readied himself. "Fabrienne, I know we started off on the wrong foot, that you think I'm some kind of wide boy. And I know you've got a degree in French literature..."

"How do you know I've got a degree in French literature?"

He hesitated. "You told me."

"No I didn't."

"Fabrienne, you must have." In his mind he cursed his stupidity. "Or maybe I just guessed because you knew all the translations in the building."

She reluctantly accepted the explanation. Renka had said that a reason she had been selected was because she was fluent in French. That was *one* of the reasons...

"I'm just trying to say that you've misjudged me," he said, eager to regain the initiative and reminding himself not to call her 'babes'. "There's more to me than you think."

Her eyes went to the ceiling in thoughtful acknowledgement.

"And pretty soon I'm going to be famous," he added, but regretting his desperate boast as soon as it left his mouth. She went to her desk, explaining that she had work to do; her resigned smile in farewell suggested that something had been reordered in her mind.

The crank of the Turk's arm greeted him in the corridor as the lift doors opened.

That's my move, he thought excitedly, notwithstanding the weariness of the journey. *I'm castling!*

As he made his way into the salon, heading for the black wallpaper, he felt the warning tremor of a message. He slowed to disable the gong, then glanced at the mobile display and frowned, losing his step. The bespectacled parson with the wide-brimmed hat was looking back at him.

Bishop?

The schematic showed the white bishop move to the square occupied by the Tom Singer pawn. The pawn blinked out and disappeared.

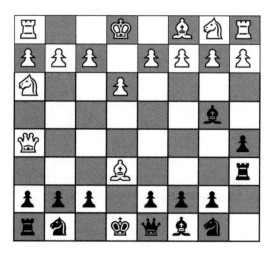

With the next loud creak he pushed open the alcove door to see the Turk's hand returning from the bishop to its cushion, the game configuration in line with the schematic. The Turk came to a stop, just a flash of white eyes having briefly checked his opponent's reaction to his move.

So he wasn't moving in yet after all. From the safe distance of the salon he briefly examined the dynamics of the game: it was a pretty poor move on the part of the white player; the bishop had taken a pawn but would certainly be taken in its turn by either of the two pawns or the castle.

He closed the alcove door. If it wasn't a move that he would have made, then perhaps he wasn't the white player after all. Rather, he was just a chess piece, one part of a game completely outside his control. He checked the message left by the moving white bishop, who he knew was Renka Tamirov. Indeed, even the message carried her broken English:

Look on floor

He did so. The black pawn that had been taken had rolled off the cabinet and onto the salon's etched marble floor. He picked it up and at the same time reopened the panel door to return the piece to the nearest edge of the board.

The Moor chess piece was heavier than it looked. Both its eyes had been bored out.

★

An extended stay in The City Plaza went far beyond Tom's expense account, but this was the closest hotel to The New Theatre, where there was always the chance of meeting Chelsea London. Josie Hannah had now taken the penthouse suite under a pseudonym for the same reason, though she was decidedly slumming it. He wished she was staying elsewhere, starting to tire of her attention.

The photographs were best viewed alone.

He had obtained enlarged prints of the photographs he had clandestinely taken during his interview with Chelsea London: the two photographs of her home, pinned under the string of lights on her dressing table mirror. He had two sets:

the polaroid-sized snaps he carried round with him and the two paper enlargements on his hotel wall, printed on the best quality paper he could find.

The enlargements occupied the place reserved for a desk console and television, now consigned to the bedroom, and he was studying them from the desk's hard-backed chair when the door was knocked. It would take a fourth knock before he finally opened the door: it was a strange feature of the photographs, the two rooms they pictured, that when you studied them the outside world seemed to fade. Well, perhaps not fade, just become less real. His eyes narrowed, his body rigid as he sat a few feet away from the wall, just far enough to take in the whole of the enlargements. No, even *real* wasn't the right word.

Less *relevant*...

Yes, less relevant. Anything that wasn't important to the rooms, to what they represented, was to be disregarded.

His mouth twitched as he vaguely became aware of the first knock on the door, three firm knuckle raps.

He had taken the photographs with a concealed camera during his interview with London. There was an urban myth in film journalistic circles that London became so homesick when she was working she carried photographs of her home: a number of interviewers had spotted these photographs, to be given a firm rebuff when they attempted a closer look. No one was even sure where she lived, her records containing no single address; all official documents were sent care of her agents, lawyers or accountants, and she had plenty of all three.

He had been sure that this was some elaborate hoax she had concocted to arouse media interest, fame hungry as she had always been. The interview contract predictably stipulated that no photographs could be taken: his snaps would be for his financial posterity when the actress died. No one could access her date of birth, but she was no spring chicken given that she had been doing the sixties circuit, posing with Minis in miniskirts. She looked in her early fifties at most, but during the interview her hands had provided a glimpse of her true age before they greedily sucked up the skin cream.

A second knock, this time with the flat of a hand. His mouth opened slightly in acknowledgement.

The rooms the photographs presented were beautiful. The first showed a long space with chaise longues and intricate furnishings, ending in a window of arched lead panes; the second, a bedroom with a magnificent oak four-poster bed framed with pink taffeta curtains.

Both rooms were sumptuously decorated with white and pink Rococo facades, spotless and free of clutter, but that wasn't what made them extraordinary; what had caused him to fall in love with them the moment he had viewed them on his camera.

The rooms, and everything in them, told stories. If he concentrated on the desk console, on its ink stand, he was sure he could read a letter scratched hundreds of years ago; if he imagined the taffeta curtains being pulled away, he could see sexual playmates chained to the supports. There was no end to the dark secrets and virile pleasures hiding in all corners of the rooms, waiting to be unwrapped like a divinely decadent chocolate box.

A third knock, the hand thuds louder.

And most fascinating of all was the plain wall mirror in the salon. There were no stories, no secrets here, yet his eyes were drawn to this wall above all else, as a dark vortex in a raging sea. He longed to be able to look at it.

He smiled, wistfully. His favourite film of all time was Blade Runner, his career in *Review* having been built on a seminal article he had submitted on the cultural impact of the film on pop culture. There was a scene in that film which was physically impossible, but that was so well-executed no one realised it to be so: a scene where the main character manipulates a photograph of a room so that he moves inside that room to find reflections in mirrors.

"Enhance fifteen to twenty three ... stop ... pan right..." Tom muttered dreamily. He wished he could do the same with the salon's photograph, so that he could step in front of that mirror and understand its secrets. Once more he cursed the photographer for the careless angle of the shot.

A fourth pounding knock brought him out of his trance. At the door he looked through the spy hole: London's agent was captured in the concave glass, as if she were twenty feet away.

"Miss Tamirov?" he asked, with a mix of excitement and concern.

Her face was impassive as she waited.

"Yes," she answered simply.

He looked excitedly at the floor. This was the break he had been hoping for: perhaps the agent could actually get him into the apartment; far better than that hair-brain scheme of Josie Hannah to get in through that new tenant, a no-hope actor called Kris Knight. He turned and breathlessly considered the wall photographs. "Can you give me a few minutes?" he called. "Just want put to put some clothes on."

"I wait. It matters not."

He went to the wall and carefully unstuck the photographs. Without folding them, carrying them as if they were ancient papyrus, he took them into the bedroom and slid them carefully under the bed. Then he composed himself, splashed on some aftershave, put a comb through his shoulder-length hair and opened the door. Renka walked straight in and sat down on the sofa in her hunched manner. She was thoughtful for a moment, then her eyes went to the bedroom with the glimmer of a smile.

He turned to look at his bedroom in spite of himself. "So you still here," she said, noticing his mis-step.

He brought his hands together. "Yeah, just thought I'd turn the interview into an excuse for a mini break. Have a chance to see the Millennium Centre…"

"So you were curious?" she said bluntly.

He smiled with confusion. "Curious?"

Her expression was like stone. "In spite of my warning." She paused. "My very clear warning."

As she considered him, he shivered with delicious embarrassment, imagining her seeing him naked. "I don't know what you're talking about," he murmured vacantly.

Shortly she tapped her cheek. "Would you like to see more?" she asked.

He smiled salaciously as he, in turn, considered the Russian, imagining her sinewed frame underneath those loose army issue fatigues. The photographs had occupied him so completely he wasn't even aware of Josie Hannah, one of the most beautiful women in the world; Renka Tamirov, while sexy in an athletic fashion, was not in the same league, but she was stretching his body like a pleasure rack. His mind was empty with nothing but the wish to please her.

"More?" he replied hopefully.

"The mirror. I have *face-on* photograph of London's mirror. That is what you want?"

His jaw dropped as she produced the photograph from

the large square pocket on her thigh. It was about six inches by four inches. He took it uncomprehendingly, then dumbly collected his hard-backed chair.

"You will need these," she added. She handed him two thin Japanese chopsticks ending in points. He took them without question, then went to his seat.

She waited patiently. Shortly he began to moan. Then he yelped and was up and running around the room, his hands over his eyes, banging into walls. Still the Russian maintained her composure, observing his progress with amused fascination as if she were watching a demented firefly. Eventually, with much of the furniture broken, he found his way back to his chair, knocking it over. His feet rolled over the chopsticks on the floor.

"There, you find them," she declared.

He moaned with relief, taking a chopstick in each hand. He pushed them quickly, neatly and simultaneously, through his eyes.

XIII

Siege

*W*HO MOVES BLACK?
 Kris was staring into the alcove, seated and alert, sharing none of the delirious fascination that had prompted Tom Singer to set up in a similar position. His vigil was more of a siege, driven by a stubborn insistence that he receive an answer to his question.

Who moves black?

The mobile was on his lap, the display showing the dark pagoda, the chess move schematic yet to arrive. The message was, simply:

Three

His chair was positioned at a sufficient distance to enable him to observe the chessboard, though his eyes only briefly settled on the game: the board carried the same aura of privacy as the wall mirror and so the pieces were largely blurs, recreated in his memory and imagination. With this method of reconstruction he was considering the black castle that had previously moved. The pagoda on his display was surely signifying a move for the same castle, the fortress of the BBC, as the other black castle was blocked. Perhaps 'Three' represented a move of three squares, which could be managed horizontally, although four spaces would be the better move, taking the white bishop.

But he wasn't going to move it, he thought grimly. "Come on, come on," he muttered to the automaton: it was in the service of Gathering and so presumably only had a licence to move white, the civilised Europeans. If so, he was determined to discover how the black pieces were moved.

He briefly considered his mobile without fully taking his eyes off the Turk. Then again, perhaps the game wasn't so much about winning or losing, about white against black; perhaps there were objectives the game wished to play out. Castling was the obvious example, although he also had the notion that capturing the BBC castle was a pre-condition for the acceptance of his screenplay.

He nodded thoughtfully, thinking that there was still a distinction to be drawn between the white and black pieces. Again, friends and enemies was too simplistic a definition, as was the divide of who was in the service of Gathering and who was not. Fabrienne and the Goof were white pieces, while Chelsea London, a clear supporter of Gathering, was a black piece. No, black and white meant something different in this context. White meant friendly or helpful to *him*, in whatever quest this game had set, while black signified enemies or obstacles he had to overcome. Buoys was an obstacle for his screenplay, while London might have the right to object to his tenancy.

With this theory taking shape he recalled that the game had begun with a white knight. He assumed this piece represented himself, not because of Fabrienne's comment that the game might have been made for him, but because of his singular experience, that surge of creativity, that sense of destiny, when it had moved. He wondered why the knight hadn't been transferred to his address book.

These reflections now had him looking at the ceiling, then with a start his eyes snapped back to the Turk. His siege had begun this morning after receiving the castle's message, prompting him to wander the salon in a despondent haze, certain that the move would happen when he was in work. He decided to call in sick, leaving a stomach bug with reception, even though Dylan had warned him yesterday that the end-of-year stats were needed today and everyone would have to work through lunch.

"I'm going to see you move it," he muttered to the automaton. The contraption remained in its lifeless crouch, its eyes somewhere on the third row out from the white ranks; the mobile display seemed frozen, a signal that the move was awaited.

Occasionally his eyes flittered to the salon door, half-expecting the black player to enter unannounced to make his move. After all, someone had been in here to plant the Moor pawn with the eyes drilled out, unless, he now realised, it had always been that way. The black pieces had their backs to him and he had merely assumed they had eyes because he was cross-referencing the pieces on the display. All the same, he had no inclination to get up and examine the board to test his theory.

An hour passed. Then another. The sun was hitting the windows as his vigil reached mid-day and it dawned on him that the Turk wasn't going to move.

"Three," he muttered, understanding forming in his expression. The message was telling *him* to move the piece: to move it three squares. With resignation he got up and approached the board. Getting this close, he allowed himself a quick glimpse of the white army, his eyes passing over the beautiful Marie Antoinette queen with her elaborate jewelled coiffure. He tentatively reached for her, wanting to touch her, but hesitated when his hand was a few inches away, imagining that he was reaching for Fabrienne, to stroke and caress her. The sense of shame at this violation was similar to when he had looked at her photographs. He pulled his hand back.

He supposed the psychological message that he shouldn't tamper with the pieces was rooted in the research he'd undertaken on Kempelen's Turk, the one that had toured Europe: that Turk would sweep the pieces off the board in fury if someone cheated. Perhaps this machine's computer program was wired in the same way.

He took the pagoda and slid it three squares across. Something jarred inside the Turk, but it wasn't the crank of the arm lever. The Turk's eyes lifted briefly to consider him, then returned to the board.

"Fucking creep show," Kris muttered, unnerved as he stepped away and closed the panel door. He slumped down on his chaise longue, wondering what it signified: the fact that *he* had moved this piece.

He closed his eyes to clear his head.

The black castle represented a place, an institution: the BBC.

And he had moved it.

He had *control* of the BBC...

He felt his mobile throb and was given the chess move schematic.

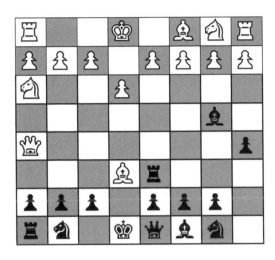

The menu appeared: a fifth icon, the writing bureau where his texts were stored, was represented by a painting of an ink pot that had downloaded in the bottom right corner. He stored this for future reference because he first wanted to access the Goof in his address book. He smiled with satisfaction to see that the Goof's chess icon, the white grenadier, was flashing. He pressed the icon, which transferred him to a call.

It was his first call on the mobile to someone in his address book and was symbolised by a picture of the battery monitor, the large, red cartoon heart beating to the pulse of the ringtone, a traditional bell and electromagnetic clapper. "Come on, come on," he muttered. Eventually the call was answered.

"Hi, Mason?"

"Kris, is that you?" Mason asked breathlessly.

"Yeah, it's me," Kris replied with a frown.

"How'd you do that?"

"Do what? What are you talking about?"

There was an uncomfortable silence.

"Mason?"

"Kris, I'm glad you called."

"No problem. Where are you?"

There was another pause. "At home, of course. You called me on my landline."

"Eh, yeah, right. Anyway, what's up?"

"That letter you gave me…" Mason began breathlessly.

"What about it?"

"It's genuine, Kris."

Kris sat back with an air of satisfaction. "Of course it's genuine. I told you: this place is like a museum."

"I'd like to see that Japanese cabinet," Mason squeaked. "To make thure…"

"Just tell me what you've got," Kris said impatiently.

"Easier if I thow you. Can I come round?"

Kris sucked his teeth. "No, I'll come to you. I've got to pick up my post anyway."

"But you haven't got any…"

Kris terminated the call with a quick shake of the mobile. It was something that seemed appropriate to his opinion of the Goof and it worked perfectly.

★

The news teams had finally dispersed from The City Plaza, the story of a macabre suicide linked with the starlet Josie Hannah finding national coverage. The crisis had allowed Erika to prove why she was worth every cent of her six-figure salary as she fielded the police and the reporters respectively with reticent frankness and solemn indignation. To the police she explained that the *Review* man had met them quite by chance in The New Theatre and they had spent a little time exploring the possibility of an article for his magazine. To the press she announced that Josie's presence in the same hotel as the deceased was purely coincidental; she was here to see family and friends, though she had also hoped to catch up with Chelsea London, an actress she had long admired.

"I wish I had my theatre," Josie whispered miserably after the last reporter had gone.

"The New Theatre, honey?" Erika asked, misunderstanding her meaning.

Josie didn't comment. She was referring to her gift from Temple 113, Precious Cargo, a 1920s puppet theatre that prefigured her future as an actress. From an early age the stick figures in the Agatha Christie-style murder mystery play had put her into character; more importantly, the theatre protected her, the play's characters telling her who to trust and who to fear.

When the temple fell her theatre became lifeless wood. The temple had also given her beauty and talent; fortunately they weren't seized as well, though she understood why when she learnt of the first death: the writer, Carl Tyrone, in London. Tyrone was the last of the children to have survived the temple's savage induction and as she became aware of the murders she realised that the youngest were falling first. She, as the oldest, the first graduate of the temple, would be the last to die.

Mikey sprang to the telephone barely as it rang. "Okay, I'll tell her," he muttered. He put his hand over the receiver. "Man downstairs to see you, Josie. He won't give his name but he says you'll know him as the Baptist."

Josie let out an audible moan.

"Tell him to beat it," Erika said, marching out of the bathroom. "Last thing our girl wants is some vulture minister trying to cash in."

Mikey nodded, taking his hand from the receiver.

"No, wait," Josie said. "Send him up."

"Josie!" Erika protested. "After all we've done to defuse…"

"Send him up," Josie repeated calmly. "I know who he is and I want to speak to him."

Erika's expression softened. "Oh, is he someone from back home, honey? Sorry, I didn't realise he was from your church."

He's not from my church, Josie thought gloomily. "Mikey, could you go down and bring him up? Don't let him see the security code in the lift."

"Sure, Josie."

Honeyman was sitting opposite her five minutes later. They considered each other awhile in silence, Josie having instructed her agent and bodyguard to leave the room. She was the first to speak. "You can't protect me, if that's what you're thinking."

He briefly closed his eyes at a painful memory. His right fist tightened. "I know," he said. "I made that mistake before, thinking in my pride and vanity that I had such power. Only those involved with the temple can alter its path. I tried to help a young man call Franklyn Tyde and … well … that turned out badly. I'll spend the rest of my life regretting that decision."

"Franklyn Tyde?" she said darkly. "He's the cause of all this, isn't he? The one who destroyed the temple?"

"*Helped* destroy it, yes. The temple had marked him for death: he refused to accept that."

"He's the one doing the murders?"

Honeyman sighed. "I believe so, yes. With an ex-Trustee turned renegade."

"Lauren Mays, you mean?"

"Yes, Dr Lauren Mays."

Josie digested this information. "Do you think they killed Tom Singer?"

"Temple Thirteen Thirteen, *Gathering*, is one of the coven's oldest temples. Franklyn has no jurisdiction here."

"So why does he have jurisdiction over *me*, and the others he killed?" Her voice was trembling. "Why does he want to kill us…?"

Honeyman grumbled with weary resignation. "Perhaps it's because he thinks you no longer exist. Temple One Thirteen conceived you. Who can you be, where can you go, if the temple no longer houses you?"

She made full eye contact. "I'm going to *find* a home, Baptist."

"But where?" he asked gently. "Do you think Renka Tamirov will stand aside and let you take a room in Gathering?"

"No of course not," she muttered.

"This isn't your temple," Honeyman reminded her. "You'd be trespassing, you see, just like poor Mr Singer."

She shook her head vehemently, fully aware of the trespassing law which allowed the Trustees to take life. "I can do it in a way that wouldn't make it a trespass: I can be invited to take the room that's become available." She shrugged. "I'm suitably qualified."

"The Trustees have already made their selection."

She looked away angrily.

"Help me find Franklyn and Mays," he suggested. "That's the key to your safety, I'm sure of it."

She shook her head again.

"If I can find…" He hesitated, then considered his right fist.

"What is it?"

"You'll excuse me but I have to leave."

She looked at his hand. "What are you holding?"

He opened his hand to reveal Gracie's figurine. As if it were a matter of courtesy, he stood it up. Josie leaned forward and her expression turned to one of disgust. "Oh, what have you got there?" she groaned.

He didn't reply, his small dark eyes on the figurine.

"Oh, oh, it's *her*, isn't it?" Josie wailed. "Franklyn's other one. The other one. Still here!"

"Yes, still here," he said sadly, wondering whether Josie's outrage was over how a teenager had become a figurine in a doll's house, or because she still retained a measure of existence. Gracie had lost her gladiatorial contest with Franklyn Tyde, as laid down by their temple. As such, she needed to be dead. Extinct.

"That's disgusting. That's disgusting!" Josie shrieked, loud enough to bring Mikey bursting out of the next room.

"Okay buddy, meeting over," he said, hauling Honeyman to his feet. The minister allowed himself to be pulled towards the front door as he carefully returned the figurine in his waistcoat pocket; then he decided to stop. Mikey shuddered as his progress faltered. "I said we're going," the bodyguard growled, his hand going roughly to Honeyman's shoulder. Honeyman caught it in a huge vice-like grip: Mikey gave a fleeting look of agony before he was released.

"I return your hand to you, young man," Honeyman said. "You'll forgive me if I am not suitably intimidated: I have after all had both my legs broken in many places while being buried alive. And worse is in store for me, no doubt."

"You're leaving, now!" Mikey growled, thinking that he might need to find a weapon.

"I was already leaving: I was about to ask you to kindly take me down in your lift. I looked away when you entered your code, you may recall."

Mikey turned suspiciously to Josie. "Why's the lady upset?"

Josie was sobbing quietly but waved him away. "It's not his fault, Mikey. It's just the stress of everything." She took a calming breath. "This is the Baptist, Mikey, and you mustn't threaten him."

"Well I've always had respect for the church…" Mikey muttered, pleased to have a reason not to have to go the extra mile with this stranger.

"That's not what I mean," Josie said irritably. She glanced up at Erika who was standing in the doorway, warning her not to interfere.

"No, that's not what she means," Honeyman agreed. A grumble sounded deep in his throat. "There are only certain people, certain powers, that are permitted to harm me. And they will finish me off, no doubt, before all this is over." His hand went to the pocket in his waistcoat. "But now, while it has been a pleasure, I really must go." As the door was opened he paused, and turned.

"One last thing," he said to Josie.

She looked up.

"Your bodyguard and your agent seem like decent people. It's time to send them home."

XIV

Snake charmer

THE GOOF'S GOT company.

"So, the Snake Charmer's found you again," Kris declared as he entered the front room of Mason's house.

Honeyman rose from his armchair, the loose spring pinging at the release of his weight. "Snake Charmer? I'm intrigued, but sadly I have no such skill."

Mason's eyes showed his distress over Kris's confrontational manner. "Why do call him a Snake Charmer?"

Kris considered Honeyman for a moment, the hoop-ringed witch doctor flashing across his vision. "That's his chess piece."

"Ah, so I'm a chess piece?" Honeyman said with a smile.

"Don't try and pretend you don't know. Tristyn Honeyman," he added.

"And you've been given my name. But it's just Honeyman."

"He's interested in my essays," Mason protested. "We were having an interesting discussion on…"

"Don't tell me: Charlemagne," Kris said sarcastically, only narrowly resisting the temptation to say 'Tharlemagne'.

"Mirabeau, actually," Honeyman said.

"Mirabeau," Mason confirmed.

"Yes, he died in his bed: a rare feat for a French politician in 1890. Too much good living and a fondness for actresses,

I believe: he, eh, preferred them two at time." Honeyman winked at Mason, who smiled back. "But our discussion more concerned the frail quirks of fate that made the French Revolution possible; whether it would have taken its violent turn if Mirabeau hadn't died, if the Cordelier Club would have found in him the orator to take on the Enragés such as Hebert and..." Honeyman turned to Kris "...Chaumette."

Mason beamed. Many middle-aged men professed an interest in history, but when tested it was confined to battles and generals. Socio-political events were the real catalysts of history.

Kris was unimpressed. "I'm just going to get myself a glass of water." He addressed Honeyman. "Any chance I can have a quick word?"

In the kitchen, Kris, after quickly failing in his attempt to find a clean glass, made an expressive gesture of stand-off. "Look, I don't want argue with you," he said. "After all, I know you're working for Gathering. Checking up on me."

"Checking up on you?"

"Yeah, play dumb if you want. That's fine. I knew my references would be pulled, I just didn't know I'd be followed. That's thorough."

"It is indeed."

"But I don't mind. I'm playing along, okay? I just wanted to say I think you're a fucking shit for involving the Goof in there."

Honeyman didn't answer; he drew the profanity through his nose, neutralising it with a brief closing of his eyes. "What did you call him?" he said at length.

Kris was already regretting swearing in front of this man; it didn't feel right. "Yeah, play dumb on that too. It's just that he probably thinks you're actually his mate; you know, that you're actually interested in what he's got to say."

"Oh I am, Mr Knight. I'm extremely interested."

Kris smiled sarcastically.

"You might find him more interesting yourself if you could just get past outward appearances," Honeyman suggested. "Although I'm pleased to see you taking an interest in his welfare," he added warmly.

Kris made a gesture of weary placation. "Whatever. I'll play your game, no problem. Let's agree that it's just a coincidence that you seem to be hanging around whenever I've got important stuff to discuss with him."

"No, that's not a coincidence," Honeyman conceded.

"Right." Kris paused. "Why do they call you the Baptist? Are you a churchman or something?"

"I was, yes."

"So is that why they make you a bishop in the chess game?"

Honeyman's eyes flickered. "Why not tell me about this chess game, Mr Knight?"

Kris waved him away, making to leave the kitchen. "Oh no, I'm not falling for that one. I know this is all a test to see whether I can keep my mouth shut."

"I know about the contraption in your new home," Honeyman said to his back. "The Kempelen machine."

"How do you…?" Kris bit his lip.

"Is a film reviewer called Tom Singer in your chess game, by any chance?" Kris turned without replying. "Check the news reports, Mr Knight."

"Why, what's happened?"

"Mr Singer was found dead this morning."

"Dead?"

"His eyes were gouged out."

Kris twitched with involuntary shock, then collected himself with an annoyed expression of disbelief. "Okay, Mr Honeyman…" he said as he returned to the front room.

"Just Honeyman."

"Yeah, whatever. Look, I've got some business I need to discuss with Mason and I'm afraid you can't stick around."

"Confidentiality agreement," Mason explained sadly.

Honeyman nodded, putting on his heavy overcoat. "This, I take it, is the letter you found in the salon?" he remarked.

Kris looked accusingly at Mason, who anxiously shook his head.

"I have my own access to information," Honeyman clarified with a reflective grumble. "I imagine you're hoping this letter will validate your Dauphin dramatisation?"

Kris's patience was running out. "Okay, I'm getting sick of this. You know about the letter because you're working for Gathering. Just like you know about the Turk. And I suppose you planted that pawn with its eyes drilled out so you could freak me out with that story about that reporter."

Honeyman considered this. "Mr Singer was a pawn? An enemy pawn?"

Kris shook his head, refusing to engage.

"Who else is in this game?" Honeyman asked. "Is Mason, here?"

"Out, please," Kris replied.

"What's this chess thing?" Mason muttered. "And did you say the *Turk*?"

"Out!" Kris repeated.

Honeyman buttoned his overcoat. "Enjoy your letter, Mr Knight." He raised heavy eyebrows. "Just remember that it's a lie."

"No it's genuine!" Mason blurted, then covered his mouth.

Honeyman's smile was signalled by a shift of his huge moustache. "I'm sure it *is* genuine, Mason. But it's a lie nonetheless."

The Snake Charmer's wrong.

The letter's as true as a virgin's heart.

Kris was sitting in his favourite Cardiff Bay wine bar with a half-empty bottle of Rioja. As he drank, he noticed a woman paying him some attention from a far table and he threw her a smile and a half-wink. She returned to her friend, prepared to let the dice roll.

He considered her without looking at her. Taking her back to Gathering was obviously ruled out, though he could always go back to hers. Maybe he felt disorientated because he was in his cups on the back of his unbelievable news about the letter, but he didn't relish the prospect. He only wanted to be in his own home, with Fabrienne, the only woman who could share that with him. Maybe that's what being a queen signified.

The emptying of his glass and a refill had him pondering on this; if he was right, then logically the black queen could also be allowed into the building, whoever she might be. The woman at the bar glanced over again but he didn't acknowledge her, now seeing that she was rather plain.

Well it certainly isn't *her*, he decided, to close down the subject of the identity of the black queen. His thoughts returned to his meeting with Mason with a triumphant mutter to his glass, "Fucking genuine."

Mason had had the letter carbon-dated, or whatever historians did to date documents. It was written in 1795 and was from the doctor who had been summoned to examine the Dauphin in the prison, then had conveniently died the following day. The doctor, Desault, had written a letter to the Committee of General Safety, the Revolutionary executive.

"13th Prairial?" he had asked Mason. "That's a date, right?"

"Correct. The Revolutionaries created their own calendar. That's the first of June." Mason paused. "The day Desault died, a week before the Dauphin died." He paused again. "The doctor was a brave man, writing to the committee in that way."

The letter confirmed that the rickety, ulcerated teenager he had been treating had been given fusions of hops and a massage of the joints with alkali. He had tuberculosis and it was feared he wouldn't survive in that damp cell. Indeed, the doctor queried why he was being held at all. The boy of course, Desault confirmed almost as an afterthought, was not Louis Capet, formally Louis-Charles, the Dauphin.

"The doctor was a brave man," Mason repeated.

"You're sure it's him?"

"We have samples of his handwriting elsewhere." Mason was animated, saliva dribbling down the side of his mouth. "Desault was a leading physician: that's why they called for him in the first place."

Kris considered the flowing, elegant hand of the physician. "This letter killed him, right?"

"That's conjecture, but it's possible," Mason conceded. "The important thing…"

"Is that we have proof of the substitution. Goof … Mason … this is huge!"

Mason was shrill with excitement. "I know, but it still doesn't explain how the Dauphin's heart came to be embalmed;

the heart the second doctor, Pelletan, said he removed from the child in the Temple prison."

"Pelletan was a revolutionary, Mason. All signed up. He would have lied. That's why the committee removed Desault and replaced him with Pelletan."

"No argument there, but the DNA testing doesn't lie. The heart that Pelletan had in his lab was the Dauphin's heart. No doubt of it."

They had sat and stared at the one page letter awhile.

"Tell me again where you found this?" Mason asked incredulously. "It's a thame we can't get more…"

"Mason, if I could get you more, I would. Look, I'm sorry the assassin didn't write a confession, and all the other players for that matter: the student who stole the heart from Pelletan's lab; the cobbler's wife who knew where the Dauphin had been held, the death confession she's said to have given to the nun, Sister Augustine. Whatever. But this is dynamite: it proves the kid was substituted. It *proves* it." He tapped the letter, to Mason's horror. "We need to get this into my documentary. It can be the main driver of the narrative: we need to write parts for the two doctors."

Mason continued to stare at the letter, but nodded slowly.

"Fucking genuine," Kris repeated to his wine glass. In his jacket he felt the mobile throb and, disabling it, he left the bar and found a quiet place in the street to read the message. The display was illuminated; taking care to avoid the thumb latch, steadying himself in his wine stupor, he pressed his address book to see if the Goof had a new message.

Lisa Man-suit
The Goof

Fabrienne
Little Tommy Snoop
Second Trustee of Temple 1313
The Baptist
The guest of The Perfumery

He hesitated, realising he was a little drunk, then pressed 'Little Tommy Snoop'. Nothing happened: Singer no longer had any details. He raised his eyebrows, also noting that Chelsea London was now 'The guest of The Perfumery'.

"We're just guests," he murmured, remembering her words, then recalled Fabrienne's remark about the hosts of literary salons entertaining their guests. Then something else caused him to almost drop the mobile, catching it just in time with his left hand.

Singer's black pawn icon was upside down.

The mobile had refused to show him anything else until he was relaxing in his copper tub. The lights were dimmed when he returned, the bath run, steaming enticingly.

The lights, the bath: the salon must have some intuitive software program that understood his mood. Either that or it was the guy watching the security camera, he thought, deciding that was the far more plausible explanation. Anyway, this bath was exactly what he needed on his return from the wilderness of the Cardiff Bay bar circuit.

He would make some inquiries on that Tom Singer tomorrow; the man had said he worked for a film magazine, *Review*, and if something had happened to him there'd be a record somewhere. In any event, Singer meant nothing to him: he'd just met him the one time, fleetingly at that. He had no idea why he was even in the chess game.

As he slipped into the bath his thoughts returned to the message 'Three', and where that might fit with the Desault letter. He groaned with pleasure; just as the onyx console had some kind of refreshing soap dispenser, there must be some special bath salts in the water: it felt as if he was having a rub-down with aromatic oils. It was so good it was almost like a massage; the water smelled divine, his nostrils flaring with pleasure.

Attached to the tub was a shell that served as a soap tray. He was using it for his mobile and in the steamy gloom he noticed the display illuminate, the invitation to access. Sinking deeper into the water, again careful to avoid the thumb latch, he surfed his address book, looking for anything new. There were no new messages but under Fabrienne and Lisa Man-suit the sealed letter icon gave him the option of sending a message.

This time he prepared himself. He accessed Lisa Buoys first, banishing the nickname Man-suit and the mobile's official description 'ugly lesbian bitch' from his mind; with his eyes on the ceiling he reordered his opinion of her. It took a while, until he had the impression of a talented, highly original woman who was loved and respected in the society in which she moved.

"Dear Lisa," he said gently, recalling she had signed herself off with her first name on her last message, "as promised I'm now in a position to show you the important historical document that gives authenticity to the theories raised in my screenplay." He was concentrating fiercely on the Buoys positive image, keeping his voice steady. "It is all very exciting and the treatment will be with you shortly."

As he heard the distant gallop of hooves he breathed a sigh of relief. It only vaguely occurred to him that he had complete faith that the mobile would somehow reorder his thoughts in accordance with his mood.

He soaked for a good ten minutes before he turned to Fabrienne, having banished all sexual thoughts of her and focussing on two key images. The first placed her in a library, reading something cerebral and French; he put some reading glasses on her for good measure. The second had her in a wedding dress; he sprinkled this image with confetti.

"Hi Fabrienne," he said, his mind's eye alternating between these two images, "just wanted to say it was nice to see you again. Hope you can show me the bedroom soon. As an estate agent, of course," he added quickly, shaking his head to lose an image of Fabrienne patting down the bed sheets. "Anyway, hope to see you soon."

He groaned at the sound of the hooves, thinking he had probably sent an even worse text message than before, that he was really cooked with her now. The display went off and he lay back in the water in reflective resignation.

He became aware that the water wasn't getting cold. Also, he was getting very, very tired. His eyes settled dreamily on the five porcelain taps, noticing for the first time that the harem women were different nationalities. Buxom in the blue silk was caucasian; elegant in the red was Indian; diminutive in the green was Japanese; athletic in the yellow was African.

"Well variety *is* the spice of life," he murmured, thinking that the fat eunuch of the fifth tap was probably the unhappiest guy in the world. As he fell gently asleep he had the vague impression that he dreamed of the four women, that they bathed and massaged him, eventually returning to the shadows as the water emptied.

When he woke it was morning, the tub was empty. The bathroom was awash with cold sunshine.

The dream prompted him to look at the taps. The harem women were steamed with condensation but the eunuch tap was loose: the figure was showing its back, having been twisted around.

Kris gave it a twist to turn the figure back around and it came away. A copper pipe with a screw rivet was revealed.

He grunted with surprise as he got out of the bath. Tucked inside the pipe was a rolled parchment, secured with a red seal.

XV

Castling

*A*ND THERE'S ANOTHER *one to follow!* was Kris's boast to
Mason. He had worked out why he had been instructed
to move the castle three spaces: the BBC would be conquered
with three documents.

Because his image of an academic was someone who
never went to work, he assumed Mason would be at home.
Fortunately it turned out to be true: while Mason spent
much of his time in his favourite corner of the university
library, this morning he was found in the front room
surrounded by copious notes and reference books. With an
appropriate sense of guilt, Mason admitted that he had put
aside all his paid research, before his expression changed to
something approaching delirium as he was handed the rolled
parchment.

Kris beamed, asking him if he was going to open it.

"Seal has to be broken under lab conditions," Mason
dribbled.

"Right," Kris agreed, only able to focus on the Goof's
saliva beard, notwithstanding that he might be standing at a
historical crossroads. As with his opinion of the homosexual
Buoys, an uncomfortable moment of introspection told him
he might be too fixated on outward appearance.

"You found this in the same place?"

"Sort of."

Mason gave a groan of ecstasy. "And you think there's a third?"

"I'm positive. Just not sure when it will turn up." He waved away the inquiry in Mason's eyes. "Don't ask. Confidentiality and all that." He tapped his forehead. "That reminds me," he said, producing another confidentiality agreement which he had dutifully collected from the Japanese cabinet.

Kris was late at his workstation, immediately accessing his e-mails: Mason had promised he would e-mail as soon he knew anything. He blinked as he saw an e-mail from Lucy, asking him why he hadn't rung her. He always rang her on a Monday; he had missed last Friday too…

He sent back a long, grovelling reply; a word search would have told him that he used 'sweetheart' fourteen times and 'promise' seventeen times. In truth, his beloved little girl had just popped out of his mind; not just two nights ago, but since his last hurried call from a payphone. He sighed, thinking that it must be stress, though one positive by-product was that all thoughts of Trish and her personal trainer boyfriend had also fallen by the way.

He returned with anticipation to his inbox. He had told Mason not to ring, saying there was an office policy about taking personal calls, but in truth he didn't care for speaking on the phone anymore, for any reason. He felt as if he was cheating on the needy, jealous network that now steered his life. Maybe that was why he was conveniently forgetting to ring his daughter.

In fact, he had to ditch this job because he needed something without phones; he thought about this for a moment then smiled, thinking that frying burgers wouldn't necessarily be his only option. With all the historical nuggets being supplied by the salon, and with Mason on hand to tart up the style, he now had every possibility of getting his screenplay on television.

For the first time he felt a rush of genuine excitement, the prospect of success no longer fanciful or remote. When he got home, and the salon was now most definitely *home*, he had the notion he would look in the mirror. That it would be time.

"You're late today, Kris, and you didn't even show yesterday." Dylan was standing at the door.

Kris acknowledged him out of the corner of his eye. He was googling Tom Singer, *Review*.

"I'm speaking to you, Kris." The young man's voice was quivering with anger, his accent pronounced. "I told you how important those stats were yesterday; your absence had me and the rest of the team working here until eight."

"I was ill," Kris murmured absently. "Didn't you get my message?" He froze: he had found an article in *The Western Mail*; it had a road view photograph of The City Plaza.

"When I got your message I decided to come and fetch you myself. But there was no one home," he added pointedly.

"If it's the Roath address, I don't live there anymore," Kris remarked. Shortly, he smiled. "You actually came to pick me up?"

"I most certainly did."

"What, you're saying I pulled a sickie?" he asked humorously.

"I most certainly am. I think you're lazy, deceitful, and you've got a kingsize chip about having a boss who's younger than you are." He paused. "I'm sorry to see you're not taking this seriously, Kris. I've already recommended that personnel send you a warning letter..." His voice tailed off. "Are you even listening to me?"

Kris was reading the article with a dark expression. He learned that Singer, a visitor to Cardiff, had died in macabre circumstances. The film star Josie Hannah had been questioned because she was the last one to see him alive. Kris nodded to himself: he was right, that *had* been Josie Hannah under the baseball cap.

"Kris! Look at me!"

The police were saying that all the evidence pointed towards it being suicide, notwithstanding the horrific and bizarre manner of his death. Kris cursed uncomfortably under his breath. A pair of chopsticks had been thrust into Singer's eyes.

He turned from the computer as Dylan pounded a small fist on his desk, then stood up menacingly. He was a good foot taller than his supervisor. "Fuck off you gimp, or I'll knock that golf ball in your neck right down your throat."

Dylan put a protective hand to his Adam's apple, almost tearful in his rage. "You're finished here. D'you understand? Finished!"

"Don't need your poxy job anymore." Kris grinned. "Besides, you'll be working for *me* in six months' time."

Dylan made a swift and determined exit as Kris felt the warning tremor of a message. With the fire of rebellion still in his blood he let the first discordant gong sound before he answered.

"Yes!" he whispered, as he saw both a white king and a white castle on the display. The king had a crown and sceptre, formally attired as if for a coronation. The castle was the typical high tower of a chess set, except that it had a number carved into its bricks: 1313.

He pressed the display and the schematic showed the king and the castle swapping over.

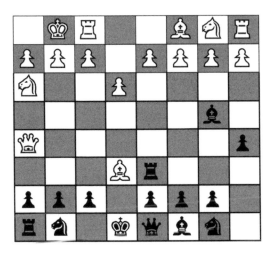

The message read:

Canteen. Now.

Notwithstanding the imperative within the message, with the display illuminated he jumped on the opportunity of accessing his address book. As he suspected, the castle wasn't recorded in the address book but the number told him what it represented: his home, Gathering. After all, Renka was a Trustee of Temple 1313, whatever 'Temple' might mean. Perhaps it was just a reference to the medieval fortress prison where they had locked up the Dauphin, which happened to be called the Temple. He still had no idea what 1313 might be: it wasn't a telephone number as he had hoped and it hadn't produced anything on Google. But he had guessed correctly over the identity of the king:

Lisa Man-suit
The Goof
Fabrienne
Little Tommy Snoop
Second Trustee of Temple 1313
The Baptist
The guest of The Perfumery
Kris Knight

Next to his name were two chess icons: the white knight and white king. He supposed that the knight was his legs, his method of getting around the board, while the king represented the things he needed to protect. That was probably why his name had only now appeared in the address book, because he was completed by the two pieces. Pressing his name and the icons revealed no information or messages; he wondered what his name would mutate into when the next entry appeared.

The display dimmed. He was thoughtful for a moment, thinking that he knew the answer to that question, then hurried to the canteen.

The breakfast shift was just shutting down and only a few tables were occupied, one of them by a tall, athletic woman with pale skin and cropped black hair. Her hands were placed on the table; she was looking straight at him.

"Renka Tamirov," she said as he approached.

"Kris Knight," he confirmed, half-offering his hand but seeing she had no intention of taking her hands from the table. "Eh, the canteen's closed now but there's a coffee machine. Can I get you something?"

With her eyes, she answered in the negative. "Nothing consumed when on temple business."

He shrugged and sat down, again assuming that she was referring to the Dauphin's Temple. "Yeah, thanks for all your help with that." He froze momentarily. "You *are* helping me, aren't you?" he muttered. "With the letters, and my housemate and Lisa Buoys and everything…?" He winced, again unsure how much he was allowed to say and whether he was breaching any rules of etiquette.

"Yes, we help. And everything you find is yours."

He breathed a huge sigh of relief, then gave her a thoughtful glance, shy at looking at her too directly. "I've seen you before, haven't I?" he said. "Yes – at Pier 64 that time?"

"At harbour restaurant," she confirmed.

"I *thought* you were looking over. Why didn't you come over and say hello?"

"I was watching over our mutual friend. Making sure no harm come to him."

Kris decided to chew on that statement later. "Yes, he's useful, isn't he?"

"You will find him increasingly so, now that Gathering is your home."

"My home?"

"Fabrienne will visit this evening to open final door."

"I really am so grateful…" He smiled amiably, though his attempt to break the ice failed, her expression remaining neutral. He looked away thoughtfully.

"You have question," she said.

"Tom Singer," he replied. "Who is he? Did you know he's dead?"

"Yes, I know he's dead. It was suicide."

He nodded. "You read the article too. Look, I just want to know in case the police find out he's on my mobile."

"They won't find out."

He shifted uncomfortably on his seat. Games and mysteries, even insults, were one thing; this was very different. "Why was he in the chess game anyway, when I don't … didn't even know him…?"

She removed her hands from the table. "Because he is pawn, and he is taken."

"I don't understand."

"His importance is that he was *taken*, Mr Knight. It is important you know *how* he was taken. What it *means* to be taken."

His body went cold, every fibre screaming at him to stop this line of inquiry. A thin smile appeared on the Russian as she noticed the conflict.

"Anyway, just want to thank you again for this opportunity," he muttered.

She tapped her cheek as she registered the satisfactory outcome of his sudden, private war. "There is one condition."

He sighed with resignation, having been in timeshare long enough to spot the set-up to a con. He knew they really wanted him as a caretaker: this was going to be a job with lots of strings attached. Maybe he would be taking shifts watching the surveillance cameras or running other residents' hot baths; after all, someone was running that place, keeping it clean and maintained…

"We expect you to do well," she said.

"What?"

"We expect you to become everything your self-image and ambition demands of you. We expect you to … complete yourself."

He frowned, perplexed.

"You read inscription on ceiling?"

"Sure…"

"When you gather at the hut, the world will gather to watch you." Her precis of the inscription was thick with her accent. "You wish to be admired above others?" she added.

He nodded in spite of himself; it would have seemed wrong to attempt to prevaricate with this woman when he knew, in his heart, she spoke the truth. "Did you offer the same opportunity to Chelsea London?"

Renka nodded briefly. "Chelsea London: another needful, mediocre talent."

"Hey, hold on…" he began, then shrugged as he acknowledged the assessment of his ability, while realising it didn't really matter. All that mattered was success: the fame.

"Yes, take pride in your mediocrity," she remarked, noting with approval the robust manner in which he had accepted her barb. "It makes your achievement all the more potent; your self-image all the more greedy."

He opened his mouth to speak, then looked away again.

"You have another question?"

"Where is this chess game going? Now that I've castled, is it over?"

"The game has several objectives. Castling only the first."

"But why a chess game at all…?"

"Because host of salon is chess master, and only *he* can invite you as guest." She paused, to look up at something behind him. Kris turned to see Dylan standing at the table, an envelope in his hand.

"You're fired," the young man declared, dropping the envelope onto the table. "There's a letter from personnel with your P45." He noticed the woman looking at him intensely and involuntarily retreated a step. "Sorry, do I know you?" he asked, the quiver in his voice returning.

She muttered something in Russian.

Whatever she said, Dylan took the time to think about it. Shortly he raised his eyebrows then crawled under one of the tables. He quietly curled up into a foetus position, his hand in his mouth.

"While you are guest of Gathering, you will always be protected," Renka explained as she got up to leave. "There may come a time when you must protect *me*," she added.

"Protect *you*?" he asked incredulously, thinking that the Russian wouldn't need help from anyone.

"I am part of chess game?"

"You're a bishop," he confirmed.

"So, I am vulnerable." She acknowledged her attire. "When in combat zone…"

He frowned. "You mean you can be taken too?"

She didn't answer, instead letting him consider this question in context of the revelations on Tom Singer.

"Why are you a bishop?" he asked.

"Because I am holy, Mr Knight."

She now indicated her farewell with a flicker of her eyes. She hissed briefly at the cringing Dylan as she left the canteen.

He also glanced at Dylan as he left, barely registering an emotion, not even one of satisfied revenge. As he left the canteen he realised that the man meant nothing to him, that he was now so meaningless to his life that he didn't even dislike him.

The thought bothered him, allied with the realisation that he was forgetting to ring his daughter.

★

"Do you want me to sign anything?" Kris asked Fabrienne as they walked through the foyer.

"They didn't say," she replied. "I think they must trust you." As they stood in the lift, the doors closing, she smiled. He smiled back.

"Can I move some stuff in now? A TV? My CD system?" He sighed, his expression wearying with the exertion of the ascent and wondering why Fabrienne didn't feel the effort too. "My sofa?"

She laughed quietly. "I don't see why not. If you really want to," she added.

The lights in the salon blazed in greeting as they entered. She unlocked the double doors, returning the key to her bag.

"Glad to see you're not angry with me anymore," he ventured.

She nodded. "That was a nice message you sent me," she said quietly. "Lovely message," she clarified.

He beamed with relief, wishing he could run out and access his writing bureau. "You haven't forgotten I promised you my Thai curry when I moved in?"

With her amiable shrug he thought that a few more presses of the button might just do it, yet something was telling him to wait.

Something has to happen with the white queen, he thought.

"Shall we?" Fabrienne asked, having opened the double doors with a vague expression of pleasant surprise: she had been expecting him to use that moment of vulnerability to make a move; she wasn't sure what her answer would have been but she was nevertheless impressed by his reticence. Perhaps he meant what he said in that text…

The bedroom was roughly the same size as the bathroom

and again one piece dominated its centre, a huge four-poster bed. Its curtains were taffeta silk, pale blue like the wallpaper. A monster of a wardrobe was at the far wall, another commode in a near corner. There were no other doors.

"Hey, wait a minute..." he said.

"I know," she muttered, taken aback. She hadn't been given a description of either the bathroom or the bedroom and had made the same incorrect assumption as Kris.

"Where's the kitchen?" they said together.

They both considered the bedroom. "Well, they obviously didn't cook for themselves back then," she suggested. "You needed floors of space to cook efficiently. They must have had food brought in."

"I'll just have to live on fast food," he remarked, refusing to entertain any negative thoughts about his new home. "Maybe I can get one of those microwave cookers in here or something."

"Looks like your Thai curry will have to wait for a while." Her eyes searched for a reaction.

He merely nodded.

"But you need to get it organised quickly. You're wasting away." She had noticed that he had lost a lot of weight since their first meeting: it had improved his appearance considerably, but weight loss at such a rate was unhealthy.

He barely heard her: he was inspecting the wardrobe and once again experiencing that cool breeze of familiarity. "Wallace collection," he murmured appreciatively. His finger traced the gilt-bronze mounts on the centre of the doors, one of the figures bearing a flailing Marseillaise. "Apollo and Daphne," he said, tapping the figure with the flag.

She looked at him questioningly, once more thrown by this unexpected display of knowledge.

He carefully opened the wardrobe to reveal an interior lined with peach blossom silk, fitted with gilt-bronze brackets and hooks. A few of these hooks were in use: he stroked a purple taffeta coat with silver embroidery; another hook held a lace ruffled shirt. He opened the second door to see that all the hooks on the right of the wardrobe were in use. The owner of these clothes would have been small, they looked as if they were sized for a young teenager. Boxes were neatly stacked on the shelf above and on the floor. Opening one of the boxes revealed a powdered wig.

"Am I all set for a fancy dress party, or is this heritage property again?" he wondered.

"I suspect the latter."

"Yeah, me too." He made to close the wardrobe; before doing so he took a sniff of the garments, expecting to be confronted by over two hundred years of fusty, moulding cloth. Such was his expectation that his face instinctively recoiled as he breathed through his nose, but the clothes were fresh.

"Whoever looks after this place does a good job," he remarked to the inside of the wardrobe. "Not even a trace of mothballs."

"What do you mean, 'whoever looks after it'?"

"Well someone's here, Fabrienne. Turning on the lights, running baths, operating the lift. Just haven't seen them yet. Maybe they're like office cleaners: they just nip in when we pop out." He peered over at the bedroom window, which was high up from the floor and permitted sunlight but not a view. There was no sign of the open window he had been expecting.

"No one's got a key apart from you and Miss London," Fabrienne replied. "Renka Tamirov was very clear on that point."

"I think she meant that we're the only two residents with keys. After all, you've got a key, haven't you?"

"Not anymore."

He detected a trace of regret in her answer as he closed the wardrobe door. He hesitated as he did so, catching sight of something inside.

"What is it?" she asked.

"Nothing at all," he confirmed. He turned and beamed. "First my microwave oven,' he declared, "then the Thai curry."

Mason's third document was on a shelf inside the wardrobe.

XVI

Home comforts

"THIS IS TOO big, too important, for just a thort play," Mason insisted.

His front room was in chaos, photocopied pages tucked under cushions, books on the floor and whiteboards with marker notes parked against the walls. When Kris had asked whether his two student tenants had complained, Mason muttered something about putting them up temporarily in a hotel while they found new digs. Kris smiled knowingly; he had never even seen the two party-loving students, just their debris, but suspected that Mason had finally cashed in his investment with his two new friends.

"It's not a play, it's a dramatised documentary," Kris corrected him. "A docudrama. I've already submitted the treatment to the BBC. We've got a meeting on Friday, okay?"

Mason looked at him with concern.

"Don't worry, it'll just be me. Just write something up for me to show the documents are genuine."

"Okay, but the BBC will do their own tests."

"Even better."

That morning Kris had delivered to the third floor a sealed envelope containing his treatment and photocopies of the three historical documents upon which it was based. Buoys' PA had dutifully returned with the signed confidentiality agreement.

He asked her if everything was in order. The mobile was yet to allow him to access his message to Buoys and she hadn't replied: perhaps his message was in French again and she was planning to give her answer in person. He didn't relish the prospect of a one-sided conversation in French.

"Ms Buoys is on the phone, but she did ask me to pass on her regards." The PA smiled in an attempt to relay her boss's goodwill and confirmed he was in the diary for 10a.m. that Friday. He had floated out of the building, barely noticing a contemptuous Dylan Hughes as he passed.

"Don't you understand how big this is?" Mason insisted. "This is history, Kris. History! It changes over two hundred years of conventional thinking." Mason paused, breathlessly. "We have to be thure everything is properly researched. Imagine how the French will react when they hear about it?"

Kris was grinning. "I know, I know…"

Mason's frustration had gone to his nose, which was running profusely. Kris looked away, considering the papers on the floor with distaste.

"Kris, I want to arrange a conference, then possibly a tour, before anything goes into the general media."

"No conference, no tour," Kris snapped. "I'm not interested in what a group of boggle-eyed academics have to say. No offence. This is television, pure and simple." He raised his arms with delight. "Television," he repeated, drawing out the word to give it all its culturally multi-functioning context.

"But…"

"And I'm grateful to you for testing the documents. Really, Mason, I am. But the academic side's only important in that it gives the docudrama authenticity and so will generate interest before it's aired: you know, mentions on Newsnight and stuff like that."

"Kris, let me thow the documents –"

"You're not showing anyone *anything*. Nor any of your university mates. If you do, I'll sue you and the university on the confidentiality agreements. I'll sue for the lost profits on the show, and just about my whole future career. Got it?"

Mason nodded in a subdued fashion. Kris considered him awhile then smiled, patting his shoulder. "Mate, you'll get all the research time you need. I'll give you full rights over the documents after we've run the programme."

"The full rights? I can lead the research?"

Mason smiled faintly, unsure whether this would satisfy him; whether the screenplay was really the thing he was searching for, that allusive vocational beacon that Kris had somehow illuminated.

"Provided you help me with the screenplay: sharpen up the dialogue, especially Chaumette's dialogue; get all that background detail in. You know, all that History Channel stuff..." He reached into his coat as he felt his mobile throb. It was only a mild tremor: not the warning of the message gong, rather the tingling scout party of a call. He was already walking to the kitchen for privacy: perhaps it was Buoys.

"Ghastly little man."

"Who's that?" Mason called from the front room.

The display showed a black pawn but the voice belonged to Chelsea London.

"Ghastly little man!"

"Miss London?" he muttered, touching the display. The schematic identified Chelsea's pawn, as before, only flashing, not moving.

He heard angry breathing.

"Miss London? Are you there?"

"There are tradesmen outside the building," she said.

Kris nodded. "Oh right, that must be my furniture."

"Your what your *what*?"

"Well, it's a sofa; the only decent thing I managed to salvage from my marriage."

"I'm not interested in your *pointless* marriage."

He chuckled at her outrageous manners. "Look, it's only a sofa. And a TV and my CD collection," he conceded.

"But they want to leave it in the foyer!"

"Have you let them in?" he asked cautiously.

"Of course of *course* I haven't let them in! Strangers can't come into the foyer! But they're knocking and knocking and knocking…"

He realised she was deadly serious. "Okay, I'll be right there. I'll get a taxi."

The two removal men standing near the front door looked bemused; his leather sofa was on a protective mat near the door, the CD tower on one of its cushions, a portable TV on the other. "Eh, I'll take it from here lads," he said.

As he unlocked the door he wondered why his instincts had made him tell those two guys to leave, but his question was answered as he imagined them pushing his sofa down the foyer, the thirteen chairs watching with disdain. London was right: just having them waiting here was vulgar and obscene.

Just like this garish sofa, he realised. It didn't matter that he and Trish had only bought it a year ago from the top range in John Lewis, at a sum which required interest-free credit that he was still paying off.

He took the sofa by one of its armrests. With the CD system clanging, he pushed it a little way down the dirt track until he managed to position it in some long grass. He stretched his shoulders, thinking he would decide what to do with it later, then reached into his pocket, feeling his mobile throbbing again.

Chelsea's *Ghastly little man!* was almost hysterical; he had waited until he was on his floor before he answered her call.

I haven't brought the stuff inside, he thought. She can go and jump.

"Yes!?" he snapped, activating the display.

There was a long pause before she answered. He waited.

"Are they gone?" she asked quietly.

"Yes. Yes, they are."

He was back in his salon, tired and irritable from his journey in the lift. He heard her breathing as he waited for her to speak.

"The answer is 'yes'," she said eventually.

"What?"

"You will become that person. The person you see in your mirror," she clarified.

He eyed the wooden frame of the mirror: he had planned to look at it the other evening, but at the last moment lost his nerve. He was now making a conscious effort to avoid its reflection.

"What is it that you want, Kris Knight?"

The glimpse of the mirror, combined with her question, was enough to energise him. He felt that rush he had experienced when his white knight had moved: exhilarating, yet full of portent, as if he had injected himself with liquid destiny.

"I want to be famous," he said, his words finding flight in a voice he hardly recognised as his own. "I know I'm not beautiful or brilliant, that there's nothing which puts me above the rest, but I want ... everything. I don't care how, but in this one chance I have at life I want to be recognised and admired; and I want to have that singular power created exclusively for this modern age, the one that comes with celebrity."

She gave an abrupt gasp, which passed for a laugh. "I think I said almost exactly that," she recalled, "those forty years back. The salon has eaten you up quickly."

He shook his head: the words, with their elegant declaration, had felt as if they belonged to someone else. "And it came true for you. Will it for me?"

"You are the guest of a salon in Gathering, Kris Knight, and Gathering was created out of the need to be celebrated. It's not possible for you to fail."

His heart was beating as he recalled the condition laid down by the Russian.

We expect you to complete yourself…

"Why are you telling me this?" he muttered.

"Let's just say it's in my tenancy agreement, so to speak. I am your only neighbour; one day you'll do the same for some eager new guest."

She hung up.

Some time passed before he felt himself again, his strange dialogue almost a dream. *Weird old coot,* he decided at length, then smiled with anticipation as he saw the chessboard menu displayed. He wanted to access the writing bureau, to see the filed message he had sent to Fabrienne, but as his thumb went to the ink pot icon the thumb latch changed colour.

"No, no!"

He was sure he hadn't touched it by mistake; the thumb latch app had activated automatically. This time the illusion was even stronger than before: bricks were noisily thrown up around him, putting him into darkness as his fingers found the rusty iron of the door latch.

It wants to show me something. Something that needs this app.

He steadied himself, determined to make the best of it. Perhaps it wasn't all bad: perhaps he could still access all the mobile's features in the same way, it would just be an immersive experience. Perhaps one day he could even access pornography. He cheered up at the prospect.

"Can I read my texts?" he asked the darkness. "My letters," he clarified, pressing down on the latch. A splinter of light took him to his writing bureau. This time he could feel the knotted lines of the wood on his fingers, the cold stone floor through his shoes.

Holding his candle steady, he pulled out a drawer to read a letter that was illuminated in its own ephemeral light. It was his latest text to Lisa Buoys and quite lengthy: an erudite analysis of the Desault letter which might have been written by the Goof if it didn't contain the occasional worldly witticism. It went on to offer a succinct appraisal of Buoys' skills and experience, sufficiently measured so as not to be sycophantic, to explain why she was exactly the right producer for this type of work. The letter ended with a salutation in French.

"Good letter," he murmured approvingly, trying unsuccessfully to remember exactly what he had said as he soaked in the bath. He returned it to its drawer and smiled with anticipation as he found his letter to Fabrienne. It merely read: 'Just wanted to say that I admire and respect you.' At length he sighed, supposing that at the moment of receipt it was precisely the right thing to get past her barriers, into her psyche.

He put the letter away and waited. Nothing happened and eventually he turned in order to distance himself from the bureau. Whether he actually turned he wasn't sure, but the shard of light had him back in the darkness of the bricked room.

"Address book?" he asked hopefully. He fumbled for the thumb latch but was unable to find it; he shivered, sure it was getting colder.

What does it want to show me?

"Chapter Emile?" he asked weakly, in the hope of escape. He found the latch and heard the door of the lift. The cage had opened to his right; this was his own floor but he was standing in front of the boarded-up door.

In Chapter Emile's address book he focussed on the first name, The host of The Magic Room. He mentally pressed the name, with no result.

No ringtone, he thought. He turned a half-circle and was in the ascending lift once more; the door he reached was polished and in use. He recognised London's plaque, La Parfumerie.

He waited, then in his mind reluctantly located and pressed The host of the Perfumery, to hear the handbell which accessed the veiled actress in eighteenth century clothes. The handbell was getting louder. She wasn't answering.

Ta-ding!

"Answer," he muttered irritably.

TA-DING TA-DING TA-DING

"Answer!" he shouted.

The ringtone ended as before with its clattered echo, but this time didn't disconnect.

"Hello?" he whispered.

The female voice had a frail breathy timbre.

"Qui sont vous?"

There was a pause.

"Who are you?" he translated fearfully.

The door opened and the eighteenth century model appeared. Behind her, he saw only darkness.

"Qui sont vous?" she hissed from behind her veil.

"I shouldn't be here," he muttered, holding up his hands in his manner of placation. He was vaguely aware of someone screaming in the distance; he imagined himself in an old asylum.

From behind her back the woman produced a glass vial filled with a colourless liquid. She carefully poured some of the liquid onto her slippers; it burned through the silk.

His eyes widened and he backed away. "Don't," he whispered, protecting his face.

And then there was nothing but the screams. He was back in his salon, listening to a ringtone.

The black queen was calling.

XVII

Black queen

THE BLACK QUEEN'S ringtone was a distant scream, but controlled and repeated at intervals. It was as if she were testing her lungs: there was no anguish in the scream, just a tormented insistence to be heard.

So far the black pieces had been ugly caricatures, perhaps the best resemblance to Moors that the untravelled and culturally prejudiced craftsman could conjure; by contrast the black queen was beautiful and sultry. The craftsman, in his attempt to portray an alien non-Christian culture was apparently content to abandon racial stereotype for age-old feminine wiles; she was suitably voluptuous in a low cut dress, the small crown seated on top of her looped curls more of a fashion accessory, an ornamental tiara. Her sultry lips were parted slightly with invitation, her large, heavy lidded eyes carrying schemes of sexual depravity.

More of a houri than a queen, he thought, comparing the chess piece with the elaborate coiffure of the white queen: the Queen of Sheba meeting Marie Antoinette. He touched the display and the scream's echo found several seconds of life in the salon.

"Hello?" he said.

There was a short pause. "Hello Mr Knight," a young woman said at length in a jauntily confident voice which seemed vaguely familiar. She had the faintest of Welsh accents. "This is Josie Hannah."

A shiver of excitement travelled down his spine. He hadn't been able to recognise the scream but with her low, husky timbre he realised it was indeed the movie star.

"*The* Josie Hannah?"

She acknowledged the compliment with a polite laugh. "The actress Josie Hannah, if that's what you mean. I'd like to speak to you, if that's possible."

"Sure…"

"I mean face to face. Can I come up?"

He hesitated.

"I *can* come up, if that's what's troubling you," she added in a tone charged with meaning. "I'm not some passing stranger, you know."

"No, you're a queen," he muttered, almost to himself. "Eh, I mean a queen of Hollywood," he added with a grimace of embarrassment.

"What a guy! You're a real charmer."

She seemed to understand his need to process as she waited patiently for him to speak. He believed her when she said that she could enter the building: Chelsea, during her rant over admitting strangers, was referring to removal men, and women picked up in bars; he suspected that the building gave at least a limited pass to anyone involved in his chess game.

"You can't come up to my rooms, but I can let you in to the foyer," he said cautiously.

"The foyer it is," she agreed, accepting the compromise.

There was no chess schematic as the call ended; instead he was taken to his address book.

Lisa Man-suit
The Goof
Fabrienne
Little Tommy Snoop
Second Trustee of Temple 1313
The Baptist
The guest of The Perfumery
The guest of The Chess Room
Josephine Hannah

He saw that Josie's real name was Josephine, recalling the queen Napoleon had cast aside. Under her details he found:

Cum-faced whore

He stretched his shoulders uncomfortably at this brazen attack, his theory that internet geeks were sending these messages losing more ground. He returned to the address book to see if Josie's chess piece icon, the black queen, contained a message.

Danger. She can go anywhere.

He mulled this over as he walked slowly down the foyer, regaining his breath from the journey down. As he had suspected on his last visit to the address book, he was now The guest of The Chess Room, and perhaps the 'danger' was warning him that Josie, as a queen, could enter The Chess Room. After all, Fabrienne had free access there. In chess, a queen was the most powerful piece because she could move in all directions: she could go anywhere.

But a king could also move in any direction: the queen was powerful because of her reach. The greater significance of being a queen, why she was a danger to *him*, was that she represented desire.

Good and bad desire, he thought. *Fabrienne and Josephine.*

Today Josie wasn't dressed for discretion; she was in tight jeans and a low clingy top, and although her skin was flawless, a hint of mascara enhanced the glitter of her blue eyes. As he opened the door his heart skipped a beat: she was the most beautiful woman he had ever seen in the flesh.

"Mr Knight," she said, offering her hand.

"Kris, please," he replied, smiling shyly as she held it a little longer than necessary. His hand was trembling. "Please, come in," he muttered, inviting her to step into the foyer. "Are your friends with you?"

"There's only little me. This is all a bit desperate, so I sent them home."

"Desperate?"

"Don't worry, I'll explain." She took a few paces and looked admiringly at the ceiling. Several concealed lights faded, then blazed with annoyance. "Extraordinary," she whispered, her hand going to her bare décolletage, attempting to cover it. She had wanted to ensure she got through the door but was wishing there was less of her cleavage showing. This was a holy place, even if it did desire her destruction.

"Would you like to sit down?" Kris asked, indicating the row of thirteen chairs.

She smiled with bemusement, as if he had just made her coffee and forgotten to boil the kettle. "We can't sit there, Kris," she explained to his look of bewilderment. She glanced at the chairs, her eyes narrowing. "I suspect you'll find you can't even *touch* those chairs."

She jumped as shadows raced across the walls and along the floor, as if people were running for cover. His eyes darted around the foyer as she tried to catch them.

"Valuable are they?" he asked, misunderstanding her.

This prompted a sigh, the comedic nature of the question diverting her from the anger of the foyer. "Perhaps we could sit on the floor?" she suggested, sitting down fluidly in a yoga position. He shrugged and complied, his legs sprawled in front of him.

"You're probably wondering why I'm here," she said. "Why I'm interesting in this building?"

He nodded mutely, still in awe. In the flesh, out of role and character, she was more desirable than he could have imagined; face to face she had a charismatic power that went beyond mere beauty and sex appeal. He was trembling, every fibre in his body wanted to please her.

Danger! he reminded himself. *This is a test…*

"This building is owned by, well, what I would call my extended family."

"I … I don't understand…"

"Yes, it is a little difficult to explain. Let's just say that I've sort of fallen out with that extended family. And they've left me homeless."

"You? Homeless? But…"

"Yes I'm rich and all that, but that's not really what I mean." Her eyes went to the ceiling as she searched for the words, wrapping her straight blonde hair around one hand. "Let's just say I have a claim on this building. A claim on the rooms. In fact, I'd like to *take* one of the rooms."

He nodded cautiously. "So this is a legal dispute?"

"No, it's a family matter."

He shrugged. "Which room are you after?"

"Yours," she answered, "if you're prepared to give it to me."

He recoiled suspiciously. "Why would I do that?"

"Because I'm trying to help you, Kris." She paused, sadly. "For better or for worse this extended family is *my* family, so I have to deal with them. But you still have the chance to run. Take my advice: run as fast as you can and don't look back."

She looked down now as she gently twisted her hair, aware that he wasn't convinced. "The Trustee, Renka Tamirov, is a murderess, you know," she continued. "Oh yes. She was a hired assassin for the Russian Mafia before she became involved with Gathering."

Kris digested this information with an air of disbelief. "Whatever her background she seems to have had a change of heart. In fact, she described herself as 'holy'. Maybe she's a born-again Christian or something?"

Josie put away her hair and offered him an ironic smile. "She certainly is *born again*, Kris, but if you think you'll see her in church on Sundays you're very much mistaken." She was thoughtful for a moment. "I knew someone, very briefly. Tom Singer, *Review* magazine. You knew him too: he talked to you the other day." She looked up, taking her hair again. "Tamirov killed him. Oh yes she did. Stuck chopsticks in his eyes."

"Paper said it was suicide," he remarked uncomfortably.

"I don't believe that. And neither do you." Her expression was reflective. "So you have a chess game?"

"How do you know about the game? And how did you get my number?"

She indicated that she found his abruptness a little hurtful; that it scared her. "I've got your number because I have the number of everyone involved with the coven," she protested gently.

"With the *what*?"

"The coven, Kris. It's a society totally devoted to the Father. It builds temples on the foundations of crimes, in a perversion of the number thirteen: the number of Christ and the Apostles. The Baptist will explain it all to you, when you're in the mood to listen."

"The Snake Charmer?" he muttered. He shook his head. "I mean that Honeyman character?"

"That's him. And to answer your other question, I know you have a chess game because I'm aware that the original occupant was a chess player … chess director … whatever they're called: a curious little man called Florian Mollien. That and the fact that you called me a queen when we spoke on the phone. Which I found very flattering by the way." She flashed her eyes enticingly as she stood up. He stood also. "I would imagine that Tamirov is a bishop in this little game?" When he nodded, she added, "Did she ask you to protect her from me?"

Kris shrugged uneasily, unhappy over revealing anything about the Russian assassin. "She might have said she might need my help at some point … maybe."

"Hmmm, that's a lot of mights and maybes. She's frightened of me, Kris; frightened of the truth, which is my gift to you. Which the Baptist, who I suspect is an *enemy* bishop, will confirm."

He made to speak but was pre-empted by her brushed cheek against his in a half-kiss of farewell, her hand briefly resting on his shoulder. "Thank you for helping poor little me. If you let me have your rooms, if you give me your key, perhaps we can spend my first evening here together. You know…"

He swallowed with anticipation.

Cum-faced whore.

He smiled but pulled himself away, his body jarring with shock as he heard the network's warning.

"Anyway, you have my number," she said, a twinge of suspicion hardening her expression. She paused at the foyer door. "You won't mention our little chat to Tamirov, will you? If you do, I won't be able to help." She waited for his acknowledgement, which he gave as a reluctant shrug. "Do you promise, Kris?"

"I promise."

Outside, she leaned against the closed door and took a deep breath, then exhaled in fear and relief. She had parked a holdall discreetly on his sofa, in between the TV and the CD system, from which she took a baseball jacket and cap, then slipped off her heels and replaced them with pumps. She pulled the holdall over her shoulder and made her way down the coastal path.

Her bodyguard met her at the footbridge to the inner harbour, taking her holdall and leading her quickly and discreetly to the chartered speedboat where her agent was waiting.

The puzzle of *who moves black?* was answered in the lift as Kris heard the creak of the Turk's arm.

So the Turk moves all the pieces, he thought, relieved at the certain knowledge that no one was sneaking into the salon after all. As the lift opened, he paused at the second creak. He qualified his assessment. The Turk wasn't in total control of the game: there were times when *he* had to move a piece, as he had done with the black castle. He wondered why that was; perhaps it was required as a proof that he had committed to the move; that it was *his* move, not the automaton's.

My action, my responsibility, he thought grimly as he stepped unsteadily into the corridor, the journey in the lift, coming so quickly after the first, having exhausted him. With the third creak, the mobile at last provided him with the chess move schematic, delayed, he suspected, because his conversation with the black queen would dictate what that move would be. He nodded, thinking that the black queen would move either one or two spaces. She moved two.

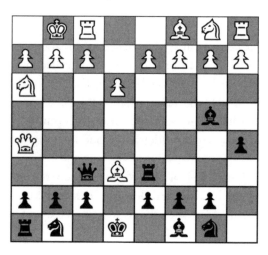

Josie had intimated that Renka was afraid of her; had attempted to turn him against her. As he predicted, Josie's black queen was threatening Renka's white bishop.

The strange dynamics of the game were making sense, he thought. In a normal chess game the black castle or pawns would have taken the bishop, but that couldn't happen here. The castle was the BBC and had no reason to threaten Renka; the pawns, meanwhile, didn't even have identities yet, were possibly not even in the game. No, the only piece that could threaten the Trustee was the woman who had just dared to expose her.

214

He opened the alcove door to see the move on the schematic had been replicated on the Turk's chessboard.

As was now his habit, he left the alcove door open and sat on his straight-backed chair some distance away, as if in contemplation of the game but with his eyes only momentarily settling on the pieces, like a bird wary of predators.

His gaze drifted upwards, feeling safer in the air of his imagination. Renka's bishop could always beat an ignominious retreat, but that was to assume she would move at all: he had no control over the bishop. Or did he? Perhaps he was expected to pass on Josie's comments to Renka: to alert Renka of the danger and *that* would make her move.

It occurred to him that he would be breaking his promise to the actress to keep their conversation secret.

"Whore," he muttered, attempting to fortify his resolve. She was lying about the Russian and the building: she simply wanted to trick her way in. He also put aside the knowledge that her ringtone, which Renka said translated emotion, was a scream, completely at odds with her confident, seductive air.

Renka's bishop must move out of harm's way.

He looked at the Turk, its glass eyes staying on the game. Kris sighed; with his move decided upon, he now had to work out how it was to be implemented.

The lights of the salon dimmed in respect for the concentration he applied to this question. The chess moves signified important events in his life, he reasoned, so he had to translate the move into something tangible.

The chess move involved protecting Renka. With this thought crystallising, the display of his mobile illuminated. He held his breath as he touched the address book icon, the horror train that was the thumb latch thankfully bypassed. He accessed Second Trustee of Temple 1313 and nodded with satisfaction to see that the network had understood his requirements, with a letter ready to be sent.

"Dear Ms Tamarov," he said, "I think you should know that Josie Hannah has been to Gathering. She wants to take rooms here and she said some unkind things about you. She says I should speak to the Baptist about you. I pretended to believe her, to throw her off her guard, but I await your instructions. Kris."

As the sound of hooves retreated he wondered how his letter would be translated by the app that appeared to understand his mood and desires, or which sometimes translated the text into French. He went to the writing bureau and accessed the file letter, but found that the text was exactly as he had read it.

He sniffed with disappointment. Maybe the bishops were immune to such passions, just as the address book declined to offer any information on them. His musings were cut short as the mobile throbbed with a message, Renka's friendly, bespectacled parson briefly revealed as the sender. The message read:

Understood. Await instructions.

As he read it he jumped, the Turk's arm shuddering into life to begin its three-stage sequence. He watched uncomfortably, with the alcove door open the noise being almost unbearable, as Renka's white bishop was moved back as far as she was able to go. His schematic simultaneously showed the move.

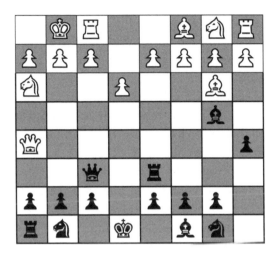

With the Turk's hand coming to rest on its cushion, he recruited the new 'strange event' rationalising muscle in his brain. Moving the bishop out of harm's way was the obvious move and one that any semi-proficient chess player could have predicted; as soon as he had sent that text message to Renka, someone in a control room somewhere had pushed a button to operate the Turk.

He smiled and sat back. All this white against black business was nonsense. Honeyman was probably an actor and Josie Hannah was doing an edgy reality drama thing to give her some art school credibility. Tom Singer meanwhile wasn't really dead – the newspaper article was a set-up. Maybe this was an elaborate psychological experiment.

He sighed, not sure if he really wanted to believe this. If this was all a hoax, then the eighteenth century documents he had found were hoaxes too and he was just an unwitting member of the public.

It was late. At the door of the bedroom he considered the huge four-poster and decided he wasn't ready to sleep in it just yet, that he needed to familiarise himself with it. With a smile he heard his bath being run instead. So there wasn't a valet: the building was definitely being operated via cameras and remote control.

That night he would again dream of the harem women, emerging from the shadows in reward for his loyalty with sponges and oils, their toned skin glistening with perfume. They would remove their silks and dance for him, their fingers and mouths occasionally finding the water; at some point his erupting orgasm would send him into the deepest, contented sleep.

He would totally forget about his furniture delivery that had brought him home so abruptly. Someone would steal the CD system and the portable the following day, while the sofa, vandalised and weatherbeaten, would remain. Kris, as he walked the track to and from his home, wouldn't notice.

XVIII

Chapter Emile

"I T BECAME CUSTOMARY to gather in front of the huts," Mason recited, to Kris's twitch of surprise and annoyance. Buoys, a woman transformed on this their second meeting, was listening attentively. "Rousseau was referring to the time when human society was created, when 'amour soi' turned into 'amour propre'..."

She tapped the three-page treatment with her finger. "That's 'self-preservation' becoming 'self-love'?"

Mason nodded, animated with excitement. "Rousseau believed that man in his natural state was effectively a bundle of appetites driven by self-preservation, moderated perhaps by a basic instinct for pity. Society created identity: people become part of a group and inevitably compared themselves with others in that group."

"And this, according to Rousseau, is the reason why we're evil," she concluded. "Man in his natural state is innocent: it's the world that corrupts him." She shrugged good-naturedly. "I'm only familiar with Rousseau's political writings, but that's very interesting. And perhaps still relevant in Warhol's world of fifteen minutes of fame, where celebrities exist purely for the purpose of being celebrities."

Kris shifted in his seat, feeling outside the discussion and resenting Mason's last-minute decision to come to the meeting, provided they went straight there and straight back.

For someone who was supposed to be shy he hadn't shut up from the moment he sat down.

He also didn't care for this new sensation: being presented with a friendly, intuitive Lisa Buoys who clearly wasn't perturbed by Mason's appearance and manner. He gave a mental grumble at having his perceptions challenged: *Gathering's* perceptions challenged; he rebelled against it as a religious convert rails against reason.

No! She's an ugly, lesbian bitch…

An enemy…

"But this philosophy," Mason continued, "was central to Revolutionary thinking. Society was evil by its very nature. What was it Saint-Just said? Whether the king has ruled badly is irrelevant: he had to die because he was the king." Mason in his excitement had forgotten to wipe his saliva from his mouth and Kris threw her an apologetic smile in Buoys' direction, which she didn't acknowledge. "Of course the whole thing was flawed. They thought with the Terror they could wipe away the old regime and create a…" and at this point he paused as he attended to his beard, Buoys pretending to concentrate on her papers while he wiped away the saliva "…a republic of virtue."

"And where does *Emile* fit into this?" she asked.

"*Emile* is Rousseau's work," Kris interrupted, calling on his own research. "Emile was a kid and Rousseau had the notion that if he could be educated in complete isolation to the world, locked up with the right tutor, then this systematic evil thing, the amour propre, would never intrude." He cleared his throat, hoping she didn't ask any questions, for his knowledge didn't go much beyond that explanation. "Anyway, it explains the name of the chapter."

"Yes indeed…" she said, taking the rolled parchment he had found in the bath tap and carefully pressing it out on the desk once more. "And you're sure this is genuine?"

"It's been radiocarbon dated," Mason confirmed, "which ties it down to a range of around thirty years. But we also recognise two of the signatures. Thaumette and Pelletan."

"So the date on the document has to be accurate," Kris clarified. "Chaumette was the jailer, Pelletan the Revolutionary doctor who replaced the Royalist doctor Desault. Pelletan did the autopsy, took the kid's heart, wrapped it in a handkerchief and pickled it as a curiosity."

The document was a charter entitled 'Chapter Emile': as with any modern company it recited its objects and listed its members, all of whom had signed their names. It was a horrific document.

"I'm still having trouble believing this," she conceded.

Mason and Kris merely nodded, having walked through the fire of disbelief themselves.

She sighed and shook her head, her red cheeks blowing with excitement. "So, let's recap. We have Desault's letter confirming, just before his untimely death, that the child he was treating in the Temple wasn't the Dauphin. Okay, that proves the Dauphin was substituted, and we have that from a source who isn't connected with … these people." She turned distastefully to the rolled parchment. "Then we have this charter. This licence for murder. And finally, we have *this*."

It was a memoir written in late 1795 by a representative of Chapter Emile, the handwriting identical to the one of the signatures on the charter lower down on the list. The narrator declared himself as a Christian Royalist who, with the help of a society of Welsh priests drawn to Paris by the political and religious upheaval, had managed to infiltrate Chaumette's private chapter in order to rescue the abducted Dauphin. Sadly Chaumette and Simon hadn't revealed his location; only when Chaumette and Simon fell had the narrator managed to persuade Simon's wife to reveal that he was hidden in an underground cell outside Lyons, but by then the Dauphin was dead, horribly mutilated. Mason's screenplay postulated that the narrator's society must have been removed the Dauphin's heart and at a future date arranged to substitute it for the pickled heart in Pelletan's lab. The Dauphin's heart must have been deliberately pickled to avoid anyone noticing the substitution.

The narrator ended his memoir by recording that the chapter had been dissolved and he had hidden its revolting charter and all other proofs of its crimes. Certain 'passionate' members had been 'removed' in the process. The screenplay had a bloody finale: Kris was delighted to see that Mason was prepared to get his hands dirty when it was necessary.

Certain parts of the story remained between Kris and Gathering. He had checked the names on the charter, the original roll call, and had been shocked to see Claudine de Tour du Pin on the list; he suspected that the other twelve members of the chapter, the 'hosts' on his mobile, were included too. He guessed that the narrator only knew part of the story; that something of Chapter Emile survived, or perhaps emerged from its destruction. The society of Welsh priests, probably the 'coven' Josie had referred to, had given them safe passage to Wales, with accommodation thrown in.

Buoys addressed Mason. "The BBC will have to carry out their own tests to establish their authenticity."

Mason nodded, having expected this.

"Subject to my confidentiality agreements," Kris added. "I'm bound by the rules of the Trust that owns the building where they were found."

"Where *did* you find them, Kris?" she asked incredulously.

"I'm sorry, I can't go into that. But I think it's the building where the survivors of Chapter Emile came to hide."

"After the chapter was destroyed?" she pressed, nodding to herself at a section of the story which would make particularly good television. Chapter Emile was a matter of public record, though it was described merely as an early Parisian club inspired by the writings of Rousseau. The club was closed during the backlash after the Terror, many of the members being murdered. What wasn't a matter of public record was Chaumette's initial involvement and the chapter's secret agenda, as now revealed in the charter.

He shrugged. "The building's derelict, there's nothing to see," he lied. Seeing she wasn't satisfied, he said, "I'm sorry, Lisa. This is non-negotiable. If the Trustees give me permission to let the cameras into the building then that's fine, but I think that's unlikely; you can use the documents, with my input, but that's all. I'm sorry."

"Your input?"

"I want to play Chaumette," he said with a measured voice.

She sat back, the frosty, dogmatic woman of the first meeting briefly returning. "Kris, I think you've got some good ideas here, but this is going to be an important drama

223

which the BBC will be trying to sell worldwide. I've no problem if you want to be an extra, even an extra with a few lines, but for such a key role I think we're going to need..."

"Little Capet will lose his idea of rank," Kris replied. "Better he be a cobbler than a poet."

The statement was uttered with cold menace, the nuances just enough to give the frisson of a French accent without turning to caricature. It nevertheless had a slightly operatic feel, as if the speaker was a demagogue.

It was good.

Buoys hesitated. "Well, I'm sure the producer will be happy to audition you," she remarked slowly. "I'll pass on a recommendation, okay?"

"Thank you, Lisa. I'd ... well I'd hate to have to take this to an independent film company. This was made for the BBC." He smiled reassuringly but shivered inwardly, seeing his reflection in the salon's mirror. That voice, the magisterial Chaumette, had come straight out of the glass.

"But we're getting ahead of ourselves," she said, processing Kris's last comment about independent film companies and resolving to give the casting director the full benefit of her views. "We'll need a script of course, but I've got enough to run the project past Finance." She again tapped the treatment with a short, unpainted fingernail.

"Mason will write the script as soon as we've been given the green light," Kris said. "Right, Mason?"

Mason nodded mutely, quiet now that the conversation had drifted away from the historical subject matter.

"You're not writing it yourself, Kris?" she asked casually.

"No, I've decided my talents don't really lie in that direction. Mason's the historian: he'll do a far better job than me."

She sighed. "I think you're making the right decision. And I have to say it's refreshing to meet someone with a clear understanding of their strengths and weaknesses."

He nodded with a degree of solemnity, as if she had offered him a holy mantra. In that moment he realised how impossibly far from success he had been in the lead-up to their first meeting: how the congested road that was his ambition had been miraculously cleared of all traffic.

"Rousseau must have overlooked me when he gave out his amour propre," he joked. "I don't do personal glory."

Kris suspected that he didn't share his professed self-effacement with the thirteen members of Chapter Emile, all of whom seemed to have considerable ambition. That evening the Chapter Emile address book released some of their details. As he discovered their names one by one, he cross-referenced his photocopy of the charter, confirming in each case his suspicion that they were on the roll call.

He had already been introduced to the novelist who once occupied Chelsea London's salon, whom Gathering for some reason had reconstructed with an actress. He was now introduced to The host of The Chess Room, but as when he first viewed the details of Mme de Tour du Pin, the details were confined to a name, a lifespan and the scantest of professional descriptions.

Florian Mollien
1750-1810
chess

Seven additional members of the chapter were accessed with a greater level of detail. There was an experimental balloonist who believed he had discovered an alternative to hydrogen; a classical actor who became so submersed in his method acting techniques that he was unable to obtain roles; a magician who refused to join any professional body for fear that his tricks would be stolen; a poet with a penchant for realistic dialogue found laughable by his peers; a sculptor with a strange inclination for abstract shapes; a theoretical mathematician with ludicrous ideas on centrifugal forces; a physicist convinced he could harness sunlight to create energy.

These seven, he discovered, had no ringtone. He wondered if they had once occupied the salons that were boarded up.

He glanced at his salon door. Yes, the magician would have been the host – to use Gathering's phrase – of The Magic Room, the boarded up apartment on this floor.

And there was something else that distinguished them from the novelist and chess player. In the comment below their names, the mobile attributed a number of obituaries and reviews, all of which ranged from the bland to the negative: a miniature treatise to their mediocrity.

"Nasty," Kris muttered, reading the epitaphs as he reclined on his chaise longue, wondering why Gathering was so keen to write these people off as mediocre failures. Reading between the criticism, some of them might not have been appreciated simply because they were ahead of their time. After all, no one could call the brilliant Florian Mollien a mediocrity: he was just someone who didn't achieve the recognition he believed he deserved. The aggressive bias of the network increased as he continued through the reviews, many of which, he noted, were from the same contributors.

The last four members of the chapter also had no ringtone, and only the basic informational layout of the novelist and the chess master: their name, lifespan and occupation. He lay back, thinking that perhaps these were the hosts of salons yet to be boarded up. There was no one at home, but equally there was no obituary.

They were for the future...

He thought about this, sure now that he and Chelsea were the only occupants of the building. In their last conversation she had mentioned something about 'handing over': maybe there was only meant to be one tenant, or 'guest', at a time.

He yawned and walked to the door of the bedroom, considered the double bed, then the wardrobe, and decided he wasn't ready. He took off his clothes and huddled up on the chaise longue.

As sleep came, he considered the curious question of why these thirteen artists and scientists were involved with Chaumette's Chapter Emile at all. On the details given, they seemed to have no political aspirations; there was certainly nothing that suggested they were evil, or criminals.

"Florian Mollien," he murmured dreamily, wondering why such a little guy had needed such a big bed.

Mason worked furiously to prepare the first draft of the screenplay, which Kris proudly presented to Buoys as if it was a newborn baby. She confirmed the documents had been established as being genuine; all that remained was to approve the script.

The next two weeks passed uneventfully. No baths were run in his honour; there was no lift blackout. His mobile didn't ring and he continued to sleep on the chaise longue.

He was unemployed now. With his meagre savings and stretching his credit card to its limit, he calculated he could last two months, maybe three if he didn't go out. He regularly checked the Turk's alcove to see if he might have missed the expected black move, but the board didn't change.

On the fourteenth night, in frustration, he set up a chair vigil. He was on his second bottle of red wine and sipping bitterly.

Am I being punished? he wondered. *No mobile: no texts, no calls. Everything's on hold.*

Shortly his eyes softened. Perhaps he wasn't being punished, but directed. If black was going to move of its own volition, it would have done so by now.

He frowned, remembering that he had been here before. He had moved the BBC castle to his own advantage on the prompting of the mobile. This time he was wasn't being helped: he was expected to work it out for himself.

"'Three' gave me control of the black castle," he reminded himself, putting down his wine glass and approaching the board. "With three historical documents delivered to the third floor with a three-page synopsis," he added thoughtfully. In his mind he carefully examined the schematic, glancing at the chessboard only to ensure he wasn't in error. He mentally moved the black castle two squares towards the white ranks, to the square where Mason's white pawn would be in a position to take it. Taking the castle was a key objective and it was okay, because the castle wasn't a person. No one would get hurt.

Against this barrage of self-interest and logic he still hesitated, seeing Singer's pawn with its eyes bored out. Eventually he took a breath, stepped into the alcove and moved the castle.

His mobile throbbed as it provided the schematic.

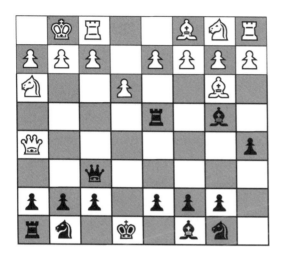

He waited for the message or the call, but nothing arrived, the display dimming. Shutting the panel door with a feeling of anti-climax, he decided it was time to have a good night's sleep.

Marching with determination into the bedroom, he found it warm and safe under the sheets.

He woke with a start, to the third bell of the discordant message gong. It was louder than he had ever heard it, the bed actually shaking, and as he reached, squinting, for his mobile to deactivate it, he estimated it was on its third, possibly fourth cycle.

It was mid-morning and the bedroom was pierced with a beam of light from the high window, but his forty-year-old eyes still took a few moments to adjust. He saw a white chess piece on his mobile display: he grinned as he saw it was the white grenadier.

He jumped out of bed to the creak of the Turk's arm.

"Yes!" he shouted jubilantly.

He checked the message. It was from Mason.

"The Goof's pawn. Yes!"

The message read:

Buoys has emailed. They loved my script. We've got it!

"Yes! Yes! Yes!" he shouted, hurrying to the alcove and making a fist of triumph as the schematic presented itself.

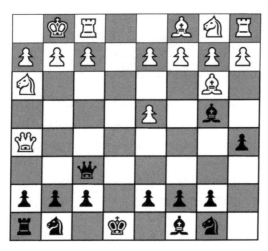

The Turk's gears were grinding. He swung open the panel door to see the Turk toppling the black castle with the white pawn. Somehow, against all odds, it rolled off the table avoiding the other pieces.

"Yes!" he muttered for the final time, reaching down to pick the castle off the floor as the Turk's hand made its way back to its cushion.

On first inspection the castle seemed unchanged, although it felt lighter than when he had moved it. Turning it upside down he saw that it was almost hollow; black scorch marks suggested its inside had been burned out.

He shrugged, thinking that it must have been like that before: it felt heavier because of some magnetism in the board. As he returned the castle to the nearest edge of the chessboard he jumped back in shock.

"Fuck me!" he shouted angrily.

The Turk was studying the third row of the chessboard in its usual, benign manner, but this morning was celebrating the christening of the bedroom by having accessed the Wallace wardrobe.

It was wearing a white powdered wig.

XIX

Faceless PAs

FABRIENNE CONSIDERED THE so-called theatrical agent in the intercom camera, then looked thoughtfully at the floor as she buzzed him in.

Chelsea's call during his last visit was stamped indelibly on her memory, while time and reflection had allowed the scene to be relit and recast. She now believed the timing of the call had been staged. Kris had mentioned a man who was stalking him; someone who had been designated as a bishop in the chess game. This, combined with a retrospective study of his manner, led her to conclude he was some kind of churchman nosing about Gathering. Instinctively, she knew that Renka would disapprove of her talking to him.

"How do you find working for Chelsea London?" he asked, deciding to get straight to it, the sales office empty apart from the two of them. His observation of her routine with The Pavilion had her working only on Mondays and always alone, though she had no hesitation in immediately locking up and leaving when she received a call on her mobile: the mobile that otherwise rang very rarely. He supposed she had a special arrangement with her employers; he was unable to discover where she worked during the rest of the week.

"I'm sorry!?"

He turned from the glass case model. "Chelsea London of The Perfumery, in Gathering." He grumbled gently. "Originally occupied by one Claudine de Tour du Pin."

"Who?!"

"Claudine de Tour du Pin," he repeated. "Known to her readers as Madame Claudine."

"I have absolutely no idea what you're talking about." As she straightened her papers she pretended to accidentally find his business card. "Mr Honeyman…"

"Just Honeyman." He glanced at the pocket of her jacket. "I heard Ms London's ringtone when I was last here. Gathering's network is unable to hide the emotions of the caller, as no doubt you're aware. Do you know why she hates you?"

Fabrienne made an attitude of surprised confusion, then at length looked down uncomfortably. Chelsea's unaccountable hostility was something that deeply troubled her. "She doesn't hate me. She just doesn't like being dependent on anyone…"

He breathed an inward sigh of relief at having straddled the first defensive barrier. "Indeed. You'll be aware that through her career she's had a marked absence of an entourage. Plenty of agents, lawyers and accountants, but none of the domestic apparatus that normally surrounds celebrities."

"She's a very private person. But she's getting older now."

"Though still fit enough to spring around on stage, take long-haul flights to the States for television serials with punishing schedules. You must have noticed that she's only lethargic when she's at home? You're a companion who's been foisted on her, by the building, by the Trustees. That's why she hates you, you see. After all, she wouldn't dare resent Gathering or its servants."

"I don't understand."

"Your presence in the building is necessary," he explained. "Especially now, when it's time to lock up."

"Why am *I* so necessary?" she asked uncomfortably.

"Because the salon needs to visualise the host in order to generate its power. In this case Madame Claudine." He paused. "To the building, you *are* Madame Claudine."

She hesitated, then laughed. "What, Pakistani was she?"

"No, but she was beautiful." He cleared his throat with embarrassment. "And she was scarred; scarred down the right side of her face."

Fabrienne's good humour vanished. Her hand went bitterly to her hairline.

"But the physical touchstones are only part of it. You also speak French and you're an aspiring novelist." Her eyes widened with surprise. "All this makes you an ideal candidate for a companion of the guest of The Perfumery. Why do you think Ms London insisted on you changing your name to Fabrienne?"

"That was my choice," she replied weakly. "What do you mean by 'time to lock up'? Chelsea isn't leaving."

He sighed. "A new guest has arrived. She has no choice."

She considered him suspiciously and said, "Why does the building ... the charity, I mean ... need to find someone who resembles the French woman ... Madame whatever?" She was in a daze, trying to work out how he knew about her novel, the most important thing in her life. "Besides, I'm Pakistani!" she repeated.

"Ah, but the main character in Madame Claudine's last novel, her most important novel, was an heiress from India," he remarked. "Would you care to venture a guess at that fictional character's name?" When she didn't reply, Honeyman returned to the glass case model. "The building finds points of recognition as a ship finds lighthouses in the fog. Mr Knight is just beginning his journey but he's already found someone with an uncanny resemblance to Florian Mollien." He placed a hand on the casing. "Renka Tamirov gave you Mason Flower's details, didn't she? Told you to give them to Mr Knight?"

She nodded mutely to his back, incredulous and frightened, but wanting to hear what the man knew.

"It's my belief that Ms London has always had a companion such as yourself. I've met with her unofficial biographer, you see, and he was of the impression that throughout her entire career she had someone in the background helping her; a sort of faceless PA."

Fabrienne had a sceptical expression. "How would the biographer know if no one ever saw her?"

Honeyman turned to acknowledge a reasonable question. "He referred me to the production notes of her first film: London mentions that she has a female companion working for her, but whom no one ever met. Mention was made that she was afraid to go out." He took out a folded page of A4 which was presumably an extract from these notes, but she didn't acknowledge it. "There are other references, years later. It's no coincidence that Gathering finds private, solitary figures for the companions. Mason Flower, painfully shy and socially awkward is such a person; you are too, I believe, though for very different reasons…"

She now considered the folded page of A4. "What happened to Chelsea's recluse friend? And all the others for that matter?"

He didn't reply.

"Seriously, I'm interested," she pressed. "If you've tracked down her production notes you must have tracked down at least some of her entourage? At least one of those women must be retired now, ready to talk about what it's like to work for a diva…?"

He shook his head meaningfully. "I couldn't find any of them, Fabrienne."

She laughed again, this time nervously. "So what are you saying? That I'm going to disappear too?" Part of her brain registered this as a joke; another part throbbed with alarm.

"Do you have dreams?"

"What?"

"Dreams of murder. Of human sacrifice."

Her hand went trembling to her chest. "Tell me what you know?" she demanded. "What happened to the PAs?"

He looked deflated, Gracie having led that last exchange through a tingle of insight; he was now back with his paper research. "I don't know," he conceded. "My research goes back a little further. The guest of the building before London – a popular radio broadcaster who occupied a salon called The Hydrogen Room, once the home of an experimental balloonist – is also credited with having companions whom no one ever saw."

"Perhaps they signed confidentiality agreements."

He hesitated. "Have *you* signed such an agreement?"

"Yes. With the Trustees. I'll never be able to talk about my work with Chelsea. Thinking about it, that explains your 'faceless PA' mystery, doesn't it?" She handed back the page of A4. "What happened to this broadcaster?" she asked casually.

"He disappeared too: his lawyers said he went abroad to preserve his anonymity in retirement. This was just after London moved in. I take it you'll agree that *that,* at least, can't be explained by confidentiality agreements?"

She regarded him for a moment, then smiled. "I'm sorry,

I really do think you've got the wrong impression about me. I'm a part-time PA to a demanding celebrity. That's it. End of story." She shrugged. "Okay, the charity who arranged the job for me is a little unusual, I'll grant you. They've got this private telephone network and seem to be fascinated with a historic building." She straightened in her seat, deciding to say no more. "Whoever they are, they pay well," she added.

"Is that how this started, Fabrienne? With money? With your need to escape your old life?"

"I'm independent, if that's what you mean." She was unnerved by his suggestion that Chelsea was planning to move out of the building, more so than his mention of the dreams. The thought of being separated from the building was a lead weight in her head. "I needed to get away from certain people. I needed money to pay for the lawyers." She paused. "And I think it's time to end this conversation." She got up and walked to the intercom.

"Chelsea London and Kris Knight both have mobile phones, don't they?" he called after her. "Given to them by the building?"

"By the charity," she clarified, buzzing the lock open.

"No, by the building," he confirmed.

"I've got an alarm which goes straight to a police station," she warned him.

"The mobile is the source of the salon's power." He hesitated as he made to leave. "You do know what the mobile is, don't you? What it *really* is…?"

The question was rhetorical as he hastily left the office, noting her hand going for the alarm.

"It's just a phone," Kris repeated, rotating the ivory mobile in his hand. "Albeit with some odd ringtones," he conceded.

They were sitting in Fabrienne's Fiesta, talking to the windscreen. Fabrienne had arranged this meeting by calling him, this time with a ringtone that was a persistent 'Answer me!' Out of amusement he allowed it to ring for a while, her voice becoming more raucous as her accent emerged and only answering when it was a shaking squeal. He grinned at his private joke as she demurely announced that it was her, suggesting they meet up for a quick chat.

They had arranged to meet at the car park behind the Norwegian Church, but he hadn't expected that the meeting would be in the car itself. He felt like a cop speaking to his informant.

"But what did he mean by 'what it really is'?" She had recounted her meeting with Honeyman in detail.

"Who knows what he meant? He's a basket case."

She squeezed the steering wheel with concern, then manipulated it in contemplation.

"Hey, you'll damage the tracking," he said. She retrieved her hand. "Are you really a novelist?" he asked slyly.

"Not published or anything," she muttered. "Just scribble a bit as a hobby." She raised her eyebrows at this gross understatement. Her novel occupied all her free time and her initial submissions had already generated excited interest from a publisher, who described the outline and initial chapters as 'remarkable'. However she was having trouble finishing it.

"You're not really worried about this Honeyman character, are you?" he asked.

She shrugged. "Just wanted to know if Chelsea had mentioned anything to you about leaving. The minister said she had to move out."

He shook his head, turning over her phrase 'locking up': he was sure he'd seen a reference to that under Madame

Claudine's entry. "And you've really been working for Chelsea?" he asked after a time. He had been considering the interior of the car with interest; for some reason it seemed vaguely familiar, as if he recognised the scuffs and stains on the upholstery. It was a similar sensation to that with the salon furniture and he wondered if this rush of recognition had something to do with his being in close proximity to Fabrienne.

She sighed. "Renka approached me in my French diction class. Said she was looking for someone fluent in French, though now I think about it I first noticed her in my creative writing class about six months before." She looked round furtively. "The money's good," she whispered guiltily, "and I owed so much money to lawyers and other professionals who helped me with ... my problems. Kris, I'm not supposed to be telling you any of this: I've signed this confidentiality agreement."

"Yeah, they're fond of those." He opened the glove box, then closed it when he noticed her look of disapproval. He frowned, sure he had seen something that he recognised in the glove box. "So why are you telling me now?"

"Because I trust you!" she blurted, horrified at the prospect that her assessment might have been wrong.

"Hey, of course you can trust me," he said with a smile. He made a conscious effort to relax, reminding himself how wonderful it was speaking to her without any undercurrent of tension: that last text message had clearly hit a sweet spot. "How long have you been working for Chelsea?"

She smiled. "What, as her faceless PA?"

He smiled too. "Right."

Her smile faded. "It feels like a lifetime."

"Really? That bad?"

She didn't answer immediately; she seemed to be in deep concentration. "If you'd asked me at the beginning I'd have said she was horrible. Really, really horrible. Not at all like she is on the telly."

"But now?"

"I've come to realise she's not really nasty or rude or anything. She's just completely self-involved."

"Well she is a diva…"

"No, it's more than that." She slowly shook her head. "It's as if she isn't even aware of other people." She shrugged helplessly. "I can't really put it into words… Don't misunderstand me, I love this job. I didn't at first, but I do now." She looked down. "In fact, I'd be devastated if I lost it." She looked out of her window and dabbed a tear from her eye.

"Why's it so important to you? It sounds like a hard gig."

She shook her head, unable to explain. Gathering, the building, had become a big part of her life, and while she had had aspirations for years, the ideas for her novel as well as her creative flow had only come to her when she started working for Chelsea. What if it was the building that was supplying the inspiration, even her talent? What would happen if the building shut its doors to her?

She groaned in the realisation that she seemed unable to finish the book, the end chapters remaining enticingly in her head, her craft insisting that she simply edit what she had written. Was Gathering playing with her?

"Fabrienne?"

"Do you think it's possible Chelsea might move out, now that you're moving in?"

Kris decided to tell her what she wanted to hear. "Not a chance. She's part of the bricks. Honeyman's just confusing things with that broadcaster you mentioned: it was just a coincidence Chelsea moved in around the time the broadcaster went abroad. There was no 'handing over' or anything. Why should there be? The building's huge."

She nodded thoughtfully. "And what's your opinion of this ex-minister?"

"Well he lives round here. He's got one of those new-build apartments opposite the Millennium Centre."

"How do you know?"

"Spotted him a few times." Kris smirked. "He always nips into a shop when I see him. But to answer your question, I think he's employed by Gathering."

"You really think he's following you?"

"Oh, I've no doubt of it, but that's okay. I know I'm being watched and tested. The chess game, the cameras in the lifts and the foyer…"

"I agree there must be secret cameras. How does that lift work otherwise?"

"Right." He considered her with a thoughtful air. "Okay, time for me to trust *you* with something."

He told her about the historical documents, then much of what had occurred with the salon and the chess game, including his meeting with Josie Hannah. Seeing that she was clearly spooked over the minister's reference to people disappearing, he left out Tom Singer, mentioning neither his pawn nor the manner of his death; he had also left out the woman with the acid slippers.

"Part of me is even wondering whether the whole thing's a set-up," he continued. "I'm not taking anything at face value. Hollywood stars turning up; a Kempelen machine; furniture which I seem to know all about… Maybe they've given me some form of subliminal hypnosis…"

"Hypnosis?"

"Yeah, I'm not kidding. Or maybe it's drugs. I tell you, every time I use the lift I feel like I'm being put through a wringer…"

"Yes, Chelsea always looks worn out in the lift."

He nodded. "Right. And … and…"

"And what?"

"Well, just lots of weird stuff." He stretched his shoulders; one of the most disconcerting things was that none of this was really bothering him. In fact he felt detached from it all, as if he was watching a movie. "Anyway, the drugs and hypnosis are just theories. Could equally be my overactive imagination, that this is just an old, mysterious building and I've taken a huge whiff of déjà vu." He simulated a long breath through his nostrils. "The way I see it, the important thing is that I've got free digs and I'm going on television."

She shrugged at this assessment and managed a smile. "Oh well. It's not as if anyone has died, is it?"

He looked out at the car park, then nodded. "What do *you* think's going on?"

She didn't answer immediately. "I've no idea what's going on now, but I think bad things happened in that building long ago. I think people were killed. Sacrificed, even."

"What?"

"Their hearts were taken."

"What?!"

She shook her head, having omitted Honeyman's references to the dreams. "Kris, is there anything on your phone about this Madame Claudine woman?"

"Yeah, but just her date of birth and stuff."

"No description?"

Kris grimaced slightly, then shook his head.

"Maybe I should mention all this to Renka," she suggested.

He turned to her. "Well you can, but Josie Hannah reckons she used to be a hired assassin."

"You believe that?"

"I don't know what to believe," he admitted, "but I saw her turn someone into a nervous wreck the other day." He immediately regretted saying this and threw her a reassuring smile. "Let's just see how the whole thing plays out. We'll keep comparing notes. Okay?"

They sat for a while in silence, considering the windscreen, until he estimated that it was time for him to leave. There was an awkward moment as he turned to say goodbye, resulting in a polite kiss on her cheek. The moment was so quick he wasn't sure whose body language had initiated it.

"By the way, you're looking good," she said with a casual air as he opened the car door.

He got out and patted his stomach. "Lost some weight. Just don't seem to find the time to eat."

"Really?"

He exhaled with a sense of exhaustion. "Think I need a faceless PA too, just to remind me to eat my three square meals every day. If Chelsea does move out, perhaps you'd fancy working for me?"

Her face was partly obscured as he shut the car door; he wasn't sure if she appreciated the comment or not.

X X

Hungry

KRIS HAD, IN fact, lost almost two stone in the weeks he had spent in The Chess Room.

"Hungry," he muttered.

He was lying on his four-poster bed, his hands on his stomach, waiting, as every evening, for the sound of his bath being run. Just as the wash basin console had a cleaning agent, there was probably some variation of a Viagra hallucinogenic in the bath water, his imagination somehow finding a fit with the houri taps. Whatever it was they had invented they could sell it for an absolute fortune.

He rubbed his stomach thoughtfully. Maybe that was why he was here, to unwittingly try out all these new inventions as the prelude to a huge marketing campaign: the magnifying windows, the furniture he seemed to recognise, the wall mirror that had a mind of its own, all patentable luxuries. But sales gimmick or not, tonight there was no sign of his bath. He clutched his ever-reducing stomach: this evening there was only hunger.

"Hungry!" he repeated, this time to the bedroom. With an effort of concentration he tried to remember when he had eaten last, the meals occupying no place in his short-term memory. He remembered drinking coffee with lots of sugar, but that was about it. A subliminal brake in his head warned him that eating outside the building was prohibited, just as using a landline phone or going online was prohibited.

These weren't things that were gifted or controlled by the building.

He wasn't even able to bring food back to the salon. The only thing tolerated was alcohol, even then only wine, the Japanese cabinet having produced two spectacular bulb-shaped glasses, though the empty bottles had to be left outside the salon the following day. Someone was picking them up.

He was sure that he was being watched through hidden cameras. That episode with Debbie and Tracy, the punishment administered by the building for breaking the house rules, might have affected his psyche. As he considered the taffeta curtain ceiling, it dawned on him that there were a lot of other pleasures he had forgone since moving in: not only music and television, but even newspapers and magazines. He frowned, realising that he didn't miss any of it; that he had absolutely no inclination to bring any form of modern media into the salon.

He briefly considered his sofa, going mouldy on the dirt track, then stretched; perhaps it was something in the air but within these walls he also felt lethargic. It was different when he was outside, where he was driven and energised: in the salon the appropriate activity was to relax in indolence, the lazy salad of his existence peppered only with alcohol and sexual fantasy. It was no wonder that Chelsea had Fabrienne as her companion, or 'faceless PA' as the Snake Charmer had described her.

With a contented smile he resolved that when he had enough money he'd get some help himself: someone who could enter the building without consequence; perhaps Fabrienne would take the job, once she was finished with Chelsea. His smile widened, liking the idea that had germinated as a joke when he left her in the car earlier; he brought his mobile to his chest as he tried to doze.

Gradually his smile faded and he opened his eyes. He was hungry. In fact, his mind was sending warning signals: he hadn't eaten a proper meal for almost a week. He did some mental calculations on how long it would be before he died, actually *died*, the urgency of his situation gradually finding its way to his face.

He slid off the bed and groaned with shock. His legs were weak, barely able to carry him.

"Hungry!" he said to his mobile, but the display looked back with a dead glare. He struggled into the salon, taking frantic breaths, the effects of his fast now dispelling whatever hypnotic trick had convinced him he didn't need food.

"Please help me! I'm so hungry!" he shouted.

The display reluctantly illuminated.

Mason dropped his notes on the marble floor as he considered the foyer. Kris bit his lip to hide his annoyance at the man's clumsiness, while breathing an inward sigh of relief that the lights were still on and the foyer wasn't showing its displeasure. He had rung Mason on the pretext of working on the script at his new home, ending the conversation with an abrupt suggestion that he should bring food.

His nose alerted him to the McDonald's bags in Mason's holdall, but it would be wrong to eat the food on the move, in the foyer, dropping crumbs on the beautiful floor. His body maintained the second wind it had discovered after his call, giving him the energy to walk.

"This is amazing," Mason gasped as he collected up his papers. His eyes went to the ceiling, where he squinted as he attempted to read the inscription.

"Yeah, I know. Come on, before the food goes cold."

Mason nodded. "Where are we going?"

They were at the lift and Kris hesitated, unsure what to do. He wasn't sure if Mason was allowed in the salon itself. Fabrienne had got that far of course, but she was a queen: Josie had hinted that she would be able to come up too, if invited. But queens could move anywhere. He breathed a mixed sigh of relief and confusion as the cage opened.

Perhaps pawns can enter too…?

Or maybe they go somewhere else…?

Mason's awe-inspired curiosity now went to the cage as he looked in vain for the controls. He touched the bars then pulled his hand back, as if it was hot. His eyes returned to the foyer; the darkness was approaching.

"Who's that?" Mason asked to the gloom.

"What do you mean?"

"That person in the chair."

Kris followed his stupefied gaze and they both stared awhile; the seventh chair – which, numbering against the ascending doors from left to right, Kris imagined to be Florian Mollien's chair – was casting long erratic shadows under the disappearing lights.

"Must have been a trick of the light," Mason said at length.

Kris nodded in agreement, his hunger creating waves of irritation. "Hungry," he murmured under his breath, but the lift didn't respond.

"It's voice controlled?"

Kris shrugged without making eye contact, wishing the little man would shut up. His irritation arose from more than just his hunger: he resented the fact that he was dependent on him, that he couldn't just go out and buy the food himself. He didn't understand why the building was doing this to him.

The darkness was almost complete. "Are you having a power cut?" Mason asked.

Kris shook his head, feeling faint as his intense hunger returned. He took hold of the cage to steady himself.

"Food?" he asked, hopefully.

The lift liked this question.

The floor they were transported to was at the very top of the building. Kris counted thirteen doors on his ascent but the deciding factor was that this was an attic room, small holes in the pitched roof letting in wafers of light. Today they dripped with rain and he had to traverse the puddles in the windowless gloom.

"What is this place?" Mason asked. "Who looks after it?"

Kris took a while to recover from his worst case of exhaustion yet. "I don't know, I haven't been here before. I thought the lift would take me to my salon."

"Your salon?"

"My rooms, my apartment," he groaned with annoyance, a cold wind finding its way through the ceiling and ruffling the damp air. A turn in the wall revealed a narrow L-shaped room and Kris guessed that there were bricked-up rooms on this top floor where no one could go, the accessible area tiny in comparison to the ranging salons below. This second half of the L had a secure roof and a long dining table scattered with candelabras.

Mason paused; Kris could almost see the question and exclamation marks in his mind. The candles in the candelabras were lit.

"People service the building," Kris explained, recruiting the new muscle in his brain. "They must have known you were coming and got the dining room ready. After all, they knew where to take us, didn't they?"

"What do you mean, knew where to take us?"

"Someone controls the lift. Come on, Mason, that's obvious."

The dining table was made of the same teak as the doors. There were no settings.

"Thirteen," Kris said, counting the chairs.

"Is that number significant?"

"There's thirteen hosts. I mean this building was once occupied by thirteen people. I think they were what remained of Chapter Emile. They escaped from Paris."

"Political refugees?"

Kris shook his head, the hunger now stabbing at him. "No, I think Chapter Emile lost its political aspirations; it turned into something quite different."

Framed oil portraits of the thirteen émigrés stared back at them out of the frail gloom, in the half-light the faces looking eerily lifelike in their oils. They were all aged, although a woman with a veil still bore a startling resemblance to the actress posing with the acid bottle: the same white, freckled skin and intense blue eyes, albeit with grey hair. Another portrait caught Kris's attention: a gormless, bald old man with buck teeth. He suppressed a smile as he glanced at Mason, recalling Fabrienne saying that Honeyman had explained the companions were chosen because they resembled the hosts.

He looked thoughtfully at Mason as he processed this.

"Do you play chess, Mason?" he asked casually.

Mason looked around with interest. "What, is there a set here? Thow me."

"No, no," Kris muttered, attempting to contain his annoyance. "I'm just asking."

"Well I can play," Mason answered with a quizzical expression.

"But you're not at tournament level of anything? You can just play in the sense that *I* can play: learnt it as a kid, know all the moves and everything, but that's about it?"

Mason shrugged. "Been years since I played," he conceded. "Prefer computer games really. I've got over a hundred online friends…"

Kris switched off, returning slyly to the portrait he was sure was Florian Mollien: the man was much older but there was a definite resemblance. The Goof didn't play chess: he had presumably been chosen primarily for his appearance. That and the fact he was a brain box, he added as a concession. After all, Florian must have been a brain box too.

"Are we eating here?" Mason asked, so overwhelmed that he couldn't think of anything else to say. Kris looked at his rucksack and nodded eagerly; having found the dining table, it at last felt right to eat. They sat down at one end and Mason brought out the plastic cartons. Kris snatched his. The food was all but cold but he didn't care as he guzzled down the burger and the fries, groaning with pleasure, no meal ever having tasted this good. He considered Mason's Big Mac meal for a while with a predatory patience, then without apology snatched that too.

"Guess I'll eat on the way home," Mason remarked to the fries he was holding. He popped them in his mouth and brought out his notes to lay them carefully on the table. Then he brought out his laptop, to find it wouldn't start up.

"The building doesn't like gadgets," Kris muttered between bites of the fries. "Put it away." He couldn't be bothered to offer an explanation: he suspected that the Goof was already developing that new muscle in his brain.

Mason put away the laptop and brought out a copy of the screenplay. "I thought we could make some notes for the redraft."

250

"Agreed," Kris confirmed, reaching in to Mason's rucksack for the two large shakes. He gulped them down greedily. "We'll work here every day, okay? And bring food."

Mason shrugged his agreement.

Kris considered the shy academic, who was too gentle to be annoyed; his look of aggrieved bewilderment at being suddenly appointed to the role of domestic servant was the closest he could achieve. "Look, Mason, it's difficult for me to explain. I can't get the food myself."

"Why not?"

"This place has done something to me. Made me really lethargic."

"What, like ME, that chronic fatigue thing?"

Kris sighed. "It's sort of like ME," he conceded. "ME in my head, maybe. Mason, look at me. Can you see how much weight I've lost?"

Mason nodded thoughtfully, in the excitement of entering the building only now registering the dramatic weight loss. "I'll bring food," he confirmed. "I've taken another week's leave and I'll bring food. Lots of food. Do you need anything else? Clothes? Laundry?"

Kris sat back with a frown. For the first time he realised he hadn't washed any of his clothes since he had moved in, but they were always clean, neatly folded in the spare compartment of his Wallace wardrobe every morning. "No, I'm okay in that department," he said slowly. "I think whoever services the building takes care of that." He shook his head decisively. "No, just food," he said.

"Just food," Mason confirmed. "But why doesn't whoever runs this place get you food too?"

Kris was asking himself the same question. Mason was

right: the building could easily have provided him with food. Was this just a trick to ensure the Goof regularly visited?

He contemplated the shadows dancing around Florian Mollien's chair, the experience reminding him of the hooks of recognition the first time he had stood in the lift. The building liked to recognise and understand the people who entered, sometimes just a surname ... 'Knight' ... or an idea ... 'the Dauphin' ... being enough. That was why his companion needed to be brilliant and buck-toothed; why London's companion had to be literary and scarred. The similarities were like ID cards, though it didn't explain why the building needed these companions here at all.

Kris frowned, thinking that this was a question he would quite like to put to the Snake Charmer, if he wasn't worried about the bad press he might receive from Gathering. Josie Hannah had urged him to speak to the minister and as far as he was concerned that was a clear signal it was something he *shouldn't* do.

His thoughts were interrupted by the sound of footsteps. They turned to see Chelsea march around the corner, then freeze when she saw them. Her face became a fury of indignation as she turned on her heels and left.

"We're not alone!" she called to her companion. "I'll take this up with Renka Tamirov! I will I most certainly *will!*"

The companion had only a moment to peek around the turn of the wall to see the cause of the commotion. It was Fabrienne, carrying a tray covered with a white cloth, which smelled of chicken.

Her eyes momentarily caught Kris's. She wasn't sure how she should react, managing only an uncertain glance at the ceiling before she ran back to the lift, the water splashing as she inadvertently found the puddles.

Mason wasn't sure what to make of the interruption and he returned, in a daze, to the screenplay. The words were merely lines of ink, Kris's question a moment ago having turned on a switch charged with fascinated curiosity.

He was thinking of chess.

X X I

Line of sight

IT WAS FRIDAY and his mobile was throbbing. It had been a blisteringly exciting week, his future having homed into view.

Monday was a strategy meeting with Buoys. The following day he had been introduced to the head of production. By the afternoon he had received the formal offer: two 90-minute slots to be shown on a consecutive Monday and Tuesday evening in the autumn, to be kept under complete secrecy until the weeks leading up to its broadcast. Advance listings would only announce a dramatised documentary concerning the French Revolution with some interesting surprises. As soon as the story broke that the revision came with authentic, irrefutable historical evidence, the US networks would be all over them for the rights.

Wednesday was spent with the lawyers, Kris engaging a £500-per-hour London QC who travelled to Cardiff on short notice, all paid for by the BBC. Along with a share of the royalties, the contract provided him with a £30,000 advance – enough to clear his credit cards and free him up for acting tuition before filming started in June. A non-negotiable condition imposed by the BBC was that the director would have full artistic control: while he was guaranteed the role of Chaumette, if it transpired he couldn't act then his role would be pared to the bone.

He decided that he'd engage Carl from the Chapter Arts Centre, this time on a one-to-one basis with no audiences putting him off his stride. It troubled him that Gathering hadn't recognised his chosen tutor, its refusal to assign him a chess piece indicating that it considered him unimportant.

Well, perhaps that would change when the classes started, he thought, after he came off the phone to a very excited Carl, having booked his first session. There were plenty of white pawns in the game waiting to be activated.

His next call was to Trish, to tell her bluntly that she could have the house and the mortgage. Her solicitor should send the papers to the BBC. She'd heard he'd resigned? That was true, but he'd just landed an acting contract that was going to set him up for life: he couldn't tell her about it, but she'd see his face on the cover of *The Sunday Times Magazine* in October.

He drank in a few moments of her silent disbelief before he put the phone down.

A final call was made to his daughter, but just to receive a dressing down from her mother for having left it so long. He shouted back that he wasn't going to take her abuse any more, that he'd just stay in touch by e-mail from now on. He was shaking with anger as he put the phone down, but shortly he decided it was all for the best. He was just too busy at the moment to give his little girl the attention she deserved; he'd make up for it once the drama had been shot.

These calls were made at the BBC, the only place he felt remotely comfortable making a landline call. Phoning people now was a complicated business: when he held the vulgar plastic handset he also clutched his mobile to ensure it approved. He couldn't be too careful: a breach of protocol could always result in a dark night in the lift.

On Thursday he had spent a full day clothes-shopping in town for a long overdue overhaul of his wardrobe, but on his return home he received another call from Fabrienne to say she was in the car park. He had his clothes bags with him when he found her car in the same parking spot behind the Norwegian Church; she remarked that it was good that he hadn't become completely indolent yet.

"Like Chelsea London, you mean?" he asked, putting the clothes bags in the back. "How long have you been bringing her food?"

"For about a year." Her tone told him she had no wish to discuss the episode in the dining room. "She doesn't eat every day. Sometimes she goes a long while. When she remembers, she calls me. I just started out with the food, but in the past few months I've been doing everything for her." She glanced pointedly at the clothes bag.

He got in and closed the door. "Sounds like a full-time job. Do you have one of their mobiles?"

She shook her head. "Only the guests have those."

"Is hers different to mine?"

She seemed uncomfortable with this line of conversation. The last time they had spoken she had been open and frank, in shock from her meeting with the minister, but he was getting the distinct impression she had called this meeting to reset their relationship. He cursed, thinking that with every two steps forward he was going one step back. "Chelsea's mobile looks like it's made of brass," she said, "and there's an almond perfume smell when it rings. But the network's the same, I think."

"So no chess game?"

"No chess game." She threw him a glance. "It's good to see that you've put some weight back on. I was getting worried about you." She glanced once more. "You're finding trouble taking food back?"

He grimaced. "I told the Goof that I've got some sort of mental ME when it comes to eating."

"The Goof?"

"Mason, my ex-landlord."

She nodded. "You're using him for your food? What's he like?"

Kris grinned. "Okay, let's cut straight to the chase. He's a lot like Florian Mollien, the original occupant of The Chess Room. The *host*, as Gathering puts it. Okay? The guy squeezed inside the cabinet while Kempelen was being hailed as a genius."

"Like him how?"

"Just looks like him. The Goof doesn't play chess."

She put her hand on the steering wheel to manipulate it, then remembering his previous rebuke about the tracking, retrieved it. "Why do you think Gathering finds them … finds *us*?" she corrected herself. "What do you think they're trying to achieve?"

He stretched his shoulders. "When I was lying in bed the other night I had this brilliant notion that it was all some sort of marketing ploy, to test and film all these new inventions. You know, the lights and lift which work by themselves and … and everything…"

"That sounds plausible."

"Yeah, but then I remembered how long the building had been here. How many people have come through it: we know that Chelsea has at least forty years under her belt. That would be a marketing strategy with a very long budget." He sighed. "I think there's some kind of cult surrounding the building and its history; they find people who resemble the people who once lived there…"

They sat in contemplation for a time until he broke the news of his BBC contract. She wasn't as excited as he hoped, though she promised to watch out for it in October. As she checked her watch, the signal that it was time for him to leave, she inquired where *he* would watch it, given that he didn't have a television.

He answered only with a bemused grin. He was sure that Gathering had made provision for the lack of a television; he was taking bets with himself as what part of the salon would miraculously turn into a plasma screen in October.

He hesitated as he made to leave. "Any particular reason for you wanting to see me?" he asked, reminding himself that she had called this meeting.

She nodded. "Just wanted to tell you that I'm not working at The Pavilion anymore."

"Oh right. Why's that?"

She merely shrugged in response. The Trustees had organised that job for her and had now informed her that the sales team wanted to open properly on Monday. She suspected that she had been planted there solely for the purpose of meeting Kris.

She smiled as he opened the door, but there was no kiss.

Friday was the first read-through session.

There were three professional actors, none of whom he recognised but who were highly experienced, Buoys assured him. A woman in her late twenties, who fancied herself as being far more seductive than she actually was, took the part of the Dauphin's sister, Marie Therese. A man of the same age, a stick-thin thespian with hollow cheeks and fedora took the doctor, Pelletan. An older man, overweight and sporting a paisley scarf, was to play the cobbler, Simon. This man spent considerable time clearing his throat and massaging his vocal cords.

Bastards, Kris thought. When he had attempted to inject some characterisation in the opening scenes the two young actors had exchanged glances. The older actor paused a little too long, as if he had found something distasteful in his mouth, before delivering his line.

Kris was sipping his third glass of complimentary squash, now saying his lines in a neutral voice: the actors – who he had secretly named Missy, Stick-Insect and Big Fat Luvvie – would assume he was going to be replaced but he'd surprise them all when he came armed with his acting lessons. He knew his inflection was almost there and he could see Chaumette in his head: it just needed that final winkling to get it out.

The actors did compliment him on the script. He had a joint writing credit with Mason, though Mason had written everything apart from the directions to camera, which Buoys had said the director would ignore anyway.

His mobile was throbbing in his jacket on his chair, though not to the extent that it was alerting him to a call. Perhaps it was just trying to decide which of the actors needed to be allocated a black chess piece.

They shook his hand as the session ended, the insincere sweat of their palms not assisting him on the question of who he disliked the most. When he complimented them on their reading they acknowledged the compliment gracefully but without returning it. They were all going for a drink somewhere; they hadn't decided where yet and had to make some calls first.

He didn't care that he wasn't invited. On his downtime, the only person he wanted to be with was his queen, Fabrienne.

Walking home along the coastal path he was again turning

over his two meetings in her car. Since he had sent her that second message he was sure he was making inroads, though even during the first car meeting he got the feeling that a request for a date would have resulted in disappointment. Maybe it was the problems with her ex-husband, the stuff that made her move around the city clandestinely. Or perhaps it was that she didn't want to mix business with pleasure; that she was under strict orders not to. He grunted, thinking that was probably it. Well, she wouldn't be working for Chelsea forever; besides, in October he'd have enough money to offer her a job to…

"Hello Kris."

It was a low, husky voice he recognised immediately: Josie Hannah was waiting for him in her baseball cap.

My *other* queen, he thought, feeling his heart go off like a pneumatic drill. The image of the dark temptress that was her chess piece flashed in his subconscious, his flesh quivering with desire.

She was sitting on the arm of his abandoned sofa, her raincoat sparing her designer jeans the pale fungus the brushed leather had contracted. "Hope you don't mind me using your furniture," she said, a shard of double meaning in her tone.

"I don't want it," he muttered. "The council just haven't picked it up yet."

"I suspect they haven't even seen it, Kris." She glanced back at the door. "No one sees this place too well. You must have noticed it was difficult to get your head round it when they first brought you here?"

He frowned, struggling to remember. It seemed a long time ago, when he was a different person.

"So have you made up your mind?" She crossed her legs with a shy smile.

"Made up my mind on what?"

"If I can have your rooms. I'll be grateful, you know." She briefly pinned him with her eyes. "I'll be *very* grateful."

He made to speak, but no words came.

"You know how important it is to me, don't you?" she pressed, examining her hands. "I'm not safe anywhere else. I'm too deeply involved with those people. But you can run, Kris. You've still got time." She gathered some of her hair. "Did you speak to the minister?"

"No."

"Why not?"

"Because he's an enemy."

And so are you.

There was a flicker of irritation in her tone as she released her hair. "You need to speak to him, Kris. He'll tell you about this place and these people. Things that I can't tell you."

"Why can't you tell me?"

"Because I can't, Kris. I'm part of the coven and there are rules which gag me. Even telling you about the Russian's history, even before she became involved with the coven, was difficult for me." A cold rustle of wind had her considering the sea and she shivered a little theatrically. "Can I come in, at least? I don't mind sitting on the floor again."

He closed his eyes. "No, I'm sorry." He nodded to himself to confirm his decision, his eyes remaining closed. "And I'm not prepared to give up my rooms." He opened his eyes and made for the door. "And I don't care how grateful you can be…"

"Hey buddy!" a man shouted. As Kris unlocked the door he turned to see Mikey emerging from the side of the building. "You should give the little lady what she wants," Mikey suggested.

"There's money in it, sweetie," Erika confirmed, stepping out from behind the bodyguard. "Plenty of dreamy real estate you can find with the sort of cheque Josie's prepared to write."

He shrugged, a dull knock of surprise telling him that the offer of cash carried no temptation value whatsoever.

"I'm sorry," he repeated. He dared a long look at Josie, who was considering him with a mournful expression.

"I *will* live here, Kris," she said. "One way or another."

He stepped quickly inside and shut the door: he was expecting the darkness but the foyer lights were already approaching him energetically. The lift door was open at the far end of the foyer, enthusiastically awaiting his approach.

And inside his salon, as he heard his bath being run to ease the aches of his ascent, the mirror allowed him a viewing.

It would be the best Friday night he had ever had. And it started with a glimpse of himself, as he would be when famous red and white blood cells coursed through his veins. When his ego gorged and soared; when he was a modern pharaoh, worshipped by the world.

The weekend passed. He was sure he was drunk for most of the time; he might have gone for a stroll along the harbour, to sit under the anchor and watch the sea. He might even have eaten without the assistance of Mason, such was the delight of the salon, its total joy in his success with the black queen. The weekend was a dream montage of warm comfort and delicious sex.

He woke too early on Monday, to the sound of the message gong.

With a hand on an ear he saw Josie's salacious queen. He touched the display to produce a message:

I want your home

"Fuck," he muttered. He accessed his address book, to find without surprise that she was now called, simply, Josephine. He clicked her name to find her details had been slightly amended.

The cum-faced whore wants your home

He clicked her chess icon.

Move!

He rose from his bed with a puzzled expression and took his neatly-folded clothes from the wardrobe, dressing with an air of contemplation. Was the mobile telling him to move out? Is that what the network wanted?

The thought appalled him.

His expression steadied as he entered the salon. If Gathering wanted him to move out, it wouldn't have rewarded him over his rejection of Josie's advances. The chess game wouldn't have classified her as an enemy.

His eyes went to the black wallpaper panel. No, the mobile wanted him to *move*.

He opened the panel door, and jumped. The bewigged Turk was staring right at him, his hand hovering expectantly above its cushion.

Kris looked briefly at the chessboard, blinking to avoid the pain of too long a study. It hadn't changed. With a deep breath he took stock, then checked his watch. He didn't have long: another script read-through was scheduled for 10a.m.

"Your move," the Turk said.

Kris jumped again. The Turk's voice was deadpan with the electronic buzz of a voice synthesiser, though it had a high inflection and a French accent.

"So you can speak, you son of a bitch."

With another glance at the board he found his straight-back chair then considered the game dynamic in his head. He had been willing to move the black BBC castle because he knew that it was in his interest to do so, that he had been empowered to control, to manipulate the castle. But this was different. Josie's queen had only one logical move on the message he had been given: to move her the five squares across the board to threaten the King's white castle, which must represent the building. After all, the king had castled with that piece, which had allowed him to move in.

He shook his head. Not only was he concerned at the prospect of Josie threatening his home, but it would be a stupid move on her account. If she took the castle, the white king would simply take *her*.

No, he wanted Josie to go home. He wanted to move her back to her starting place.

"Your move!" the Turk repeated in an even higher voice.

The lights in the salon were dimming with warning as he approached the board. He took the black queen and slid her carefully back towards her own ranks.

The lights went out for a full second. Even the glass in the arch windows went black. When the light returned he felt the salon's chill.

He had kept his hand on the piece, aware that the rules of chess didn't confirm a move until the hand had left the piece. He now moved it carefully back and waited, feeling the Turk's glass eyes boring into him.

"Okay, I get it," he muttered eventually, and moved Josie's queen the five squares so that it threatened his castle. He was sure that he momentarily felt the impression of her breasts, pert and flesh, as he moved the piece. He felt the mobile throb with the chess schematic as he did so.

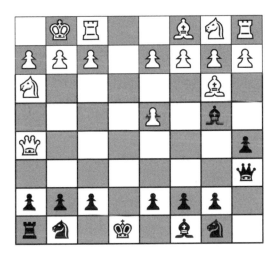

With a slight creak in the neck, the Turk returned to its pose of thoughtful contemplation of the white ranks. Kris cautiously closed the panel door, prepared to play along to this extent: the move had perhaps been triggered by his rejection of Josie on Friday, the exercise of his will over hers, but he had no intention of allowing the queen to actually take the castle.

All the same, as he left the building he was wondering what it meant that the castle was now in the queen's line of sight.

That she was threatening his home…

The question was answered when he joined the actors in BBC Llandaff. Big Fat Luvvie and Stick-Insect were elated, Missy morose. Buoys' red cheeks were puffing with excitement.

"There's been a most exciting development!" she declared.

"Really?" Kris muttered, with a suspicious glance at Big Fat Luvvie eagerly rubbing his hands.

"Exciting for you, maybe," Missy muttered. "She's taking my role."

"Who's taking your role?" Kris asked.

"There'll be other roles, Christina," Buoys said impatiently. "I've told you we'll prioritise you."

"What's going on?" Kris asked.

Buoys took a self-satisfied breath. "I don't know how she found out about our little project…"

"*Who* found out?" Kris pressed.

"Josie Hannah, Kris," Buoys said. "*The* Josie Hannah wants to play the part of Marie Therese."

"Josie Hannah…" Kris murmured to himself.

"Hello America!" Stick-Insect declared.

Buoys acknowledged the statement enthusiastically. "Her agent contacted me on the weekend. The confidentiality agreement's already signed."

Kris sat back, shell-shocked. "Well, I suppose it will make the US distribution a doddle," he said at length, warming to the idea.

Buoys' eyes widened. "Absolutely. Her agent will take care of that." She made to speak, but hesitated.

"What?" Kris said.

"But she has laid down a few conditions," Buoys said.

"What conditions?"

"Artistic conditions," Big Fat Luvvie clarified.

"*What* conditions?" Kris pressed.

As if in answer, Stick-Insect picked up the script.

"Shall we start?" he asked the table.

XXII

Check

"MY ROLE'S BEEN reduced to a walk-on part!" Kris protested in the angriest voice he dared. "My lawyer says they can do it. The contract I signed says they can do it. I've been sitting like a lemon in rehearsals all week, with nothing to say. I'm going to sue the BBC and that muppet of a barrister."

"Ah, you are fuelled indeed, Capet," said the old man Renka had introduced as Mr Ovenstone. "But you're here to see my winged Valkyrie, are you not? Are you contemplating litigation with her as well?"

Kris warily considered the old man with the bad wig. Valkyrie was his name for Josie Hannah, while he insisted on calling him Capet; he had decided it was better not to protest. "I'm not sure if she's still here, but yeah, I was hoping to see her." He shrugged uncomfortably at the prospect of suing a Hollywood star; he'd need very deep pockets indeed.

Mr Ovenstone returned to look into the hearth fire. They were in the lounge of The City Plaza on a busy Saturday afternoon but Kris had noticed the Russian when he came storming in; she didn't beckon him over, barely acknowledged him, but he shrank from the idea of just walking past.

"Litigation is out of the question, of course," Mr Ovenstone said to the fire.

"Well then I'll pull out of the contract and go to another production company. The BBC hasn't got a monopoly on…"

"Then dear old Auntie Beeb will sue *you*, Capet."

"So? I haven't got any money."

Mr Ovenstone warmed his long, liver-spotted hands. Kris glanced uncomfortably at Renka, who had been looking at the old man throughout the entire exchange with an air of obedient fascination. "Any legal dispute inevitably leads to the documents; the documents your salon has so considerately provided for you," Mr Ovenstone said. "Temple Thirteen Thirteen has no intention of explaining where it obtained such treasures. No, we would have no hesitation in withdrawing our licence."

"You evicted," Renka clarified.

Mr Ovenstone considered the coal flames with a philosophical air. "Yes, I'm afraid so. I fear your acting career might stall in the process, unless you have forged other contacts, of course…"

Kris looked at the ceiling, picturing the room where Josie Hannah was holed up with her entourage, enjoying her little victory. "But I don't understand why you're protecting her," he muttered. "I thought you wanted me to succeed. Sure, I'll make a packet with the writing credit, but I want to be an actor. I want to be on television."

"I can assure you, Capet, that we want you to succeed too. *Gathering* wants you to succeed."

"So why…?"

"The Valkyrie is part of the game. It has to play out."

"You *take* her," Renka said.

As Kris considered her thin smile, he was prepared to believe she had once been an assassin: behind her eyes he saw only an animal's instinct, with no concept of right and wrong. "Well it's the Turk that moves white," he remarked. "It's out of my hands…"

Renka tapped her cheek. "No, you move white. You move everything now."

"What do you mean? The Turk…"

Mr Ovenstone turned away from the hearth. "It's not a question of sides, but one of control."

"Control?"

Mr Ovenstone had an amiable smile. "I know you understand, Capet. You moved the black castle because you conquered the BBC. You moved the black queen because you resisted her advances."

"Yes I understand that, but…"

"You have no control over the bishops on either side. You will never have control over them because they serve only one master, although of course they may move in accordance with events you direct. But the white pawn, for example, is yours. You can physically move that piece."

"Mason?"

"Mason become companion," Renka confirmed.

Kris nodded slowly. "What, like Fabrienne is to Chelsea?"

Mr Ovenstone pulled and clicked on a long forefinger with amusement.

Kris digested this information. "And what about Fabrienne? Do I control … can I move her piece too?"

"Not yet," Mr Ovenstone replied, "although I'm sure she's in your sights, so to speak." He smiled salaciously and Kris contained a nauseous shiver. "The Turk may well decide to move her in front of your castle, to protect you."

"But he won't," Kris muttered dismissively, picturing the chess game. "There's two possible moves that puts the white queen between the black queen and the white castle, and with both moves black queen takes white queen without putting herself in danger."

Mr Ovenstone nodded with cheery encouragement.

"The best move is the white queen's pawn moving forward one space to protect the castle." Kris paused. "Who is that white pawn?"

"No one," Renka said abruptly. "The only white pieces that are people, are the pieces that have already moved."

Kris looked to Mr Ovenstone for confirmation; he had hoped that the queen's pawn might have been his acting coach, Carl, stepping forward to restore his part in the drama by turning him into a brilliant actor. That would have made sense...

"Yes I'm afraid that's correct," Mr Ovenstone said. When Kris's face dropped he added, "Ah, were you hoping it was that little thespian you have acquired?"

When Kris shrugged, Mr Ovenstone briefly flashed a look of pure hatred; with the flames behind him the effect was demonic.

"Do you think you have a shopping basket, Capet? That you can choose who you want to play with? There will be many games during your tenure of The Chess Room, all with different objectives, but the pieces will always be chosen for you. Now do you understand?"

"I understand," Kris replied nervously, avoiding Renka's contemptuous glare.

"Good," Mr Ovenstone said. "On that happy note of

accord, I will tell you something that you need to know, given this is your debut game. Everything you need for victory is already in play."

"All white pieces, you mean?"

"Of course. Black is the enemy, though there will be more black pieces put into play, as I believe you suspect." he paused. "You have questions, Capet."

Kris nodded slowly. "Why have you manufactured this chess game...?"

Mr Ovenstone laughed with a chesty cough into his fist. "We haven't manufactured anything. The host, Florian Mollien, was a chess master. His vanity, his self-image, is stored in that contraption in the alcove."

Kris signed with resignation. "Why you're playing out this charade is a mystery to me. That and all the stuff you've rigged in the apartment." He paused for a response but was met with silence, Mr Ovenstone contemplating him with a delighted squeeze of the eyes. "I mean I'm not complaining or anything," he added, "but is this a test? If so, just tell me what I've got to do."

It was Renka who answered, her eyes pinning him.

"Take black queen."

Kris hesitated. "No," he said. The Trustees exchanged glances. "But I won't let her take my rooms, either," he said warily.

"So what will you do?" Mr Ovenstone asked.

"I have to move the white castle." Kris's eyes narrowed. "Move the *room*..."

"Move the room," Mr Ovenstone agreed.

"How do I do that?"

Mr Ovenstone looked up. "You may wish to tell her there is another room she can take. That will allow you to…" and he coughed another laugh "…move the room."

"Another room. Whose?"

"Just say that, Capet. The Valkyrie is upstairs, waiting for you. She'll understand."

"Bodyguard, guarding lift," Renka remarked, looking down the lobby. "Perhaps you give message to him?" She raised her eyebrows. "We know you don't trust yourself with pretty film star."

Kris stretched his shoulders, eyeing Mikey sitting in a chair by the lift door, reading a newspaper. The large American was facing in their general direction but the newspaper made it difficult to tell whether he was watching them.

Kris had a cold sense of foreboding. "Why don't *you* tell him?" he suggested, but already knowing the answer to that question.

This is my game, he thought, as he travelled up in the lift. He was considering the white castle that bore the number 1313 on his mobile display, the marking which indicated it represented the building. The message read:

Josephine looks forward to inspecting the room

The schematic had showed the movement of the white castle two spaces to its left, out of the line of sight of the queen, though the better move would have been to move it one square, so that it put the black king into check and gained the initiative.

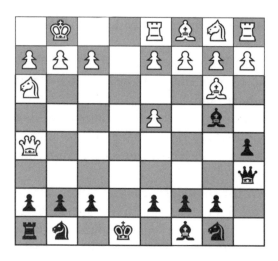

But if it's my game I can move where I like, he thought, thinking that all he wanted to do was to make his home safe. He stopped outside the door of the salon. He could hear a voice from inside, so faint it was just a bell tingle in the distance. He put his ear to the door and screwed up his face in concentration.

Check…

"Oh no," he muttered, opening the door.

"CHECK!" came the French electronic squeak.

The Turk was looking down, contemplating the white ranks. Kris studied the board breathlessly.

"No," he groaned.

The black queen had travelled to the white back row, parking herself between the king and the castle. If the queen wasn't taken, it would be checkmate. He turned back into the room, feeling the throb of his mobile.

It was a call, the black queen showing on his display. The ringtone was Josie's scream but so quiet it was a distant lament.

"Hello?" he said, pressing the display.

"Hi, it's me," Josie said.

"I know."

He watched the schematic moving the queen. The white king, in check, was blinking on and off.

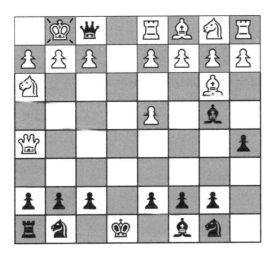

"Check?" she inquired playfully.

He closed his eyes. "How did you know?"

"Oh, call it intuition. Mikey noticed the Trustees in the lobby. It takes something rather important to get dear old Mr Ovenstone out of mothballs."

He shook his head wearily.

"Anyway, I'm just ringing to make arrangements to come and see the room," she said jovially.

"Josie, go home. You're in danger."

"I can't go home, Kris." She paused. "I really didn't want to pressure you the way I did: I'll get my agent to ring the BBC to pull me out of that silly old history thing you've got going. No hard feelings, okay? Especially as it looks as if we're going to be neighbours." She paused once more. "Look, I'll give you a little time to get yourself organised. I'd rather move in at night, stop prying eyes, so I'll be outside Gathering at ten o'clock, say, the day after tomorrow? Will you let me in?"

He didn't comment.

"Kris?"

"Please Josie, go home. I'm worried about you."

Her tone hardened. "You're the one in check, Kris. I suspect you need to be worried about *yourself*."

He frowned with confusion. "You've seen the layout of the chess game?" he asked cautiously.

There was a moment's hesitation. "I don't need to," she replied, but with a tremor of uncertainty.

He pictured the chess game.

She doesn't know, he thought.

She's walked into a trap and she doesn't know.

"The day after next, at ten," she said, and hung up.

He considered the Turk that evening from his straight-back chair, the hours passing quickly.

It dawned on him that the Turk wasn't going to help him. There were only two moves to avoid a checkmate: the king had to take the queen, or the castle had to take her. There was no block or escape. He had to take the queen.

He was the white king: the thought of him 'taking' the queen, with all the connotations Renka had offered in the canteen, made him shudder. No, it had to be the castle.

The castle is just the building, he thought, but still uncomfortable about the prospect. *Are they trying to frame me or something? Perhaps Gathering is some Russian Mafia murder syndicate.*

His eyes settled briefly on the black bishop, closing his eyes to prevent the pain of a lengthy observation. For the first time it occurred to him that he should take the Snake Charmer seriously.

That time, at the Goof's place, he was trying to warn me...

He got up and grimly approached the board. In his fear he had forgotten about being famous and, with a sneer of bravery, he snatched up the black queen. The Turk shuddered at this gross faux pas; a lever in its neck cranked as it looked up.

The chess piece was heavy between his fingers.

"Fuck "

The black queen was still provocatively buxom, but her face was hideous: not the steaming beauty on his mobile display, but a boil-ridden hag with screaming eyes.

The piece might have always been like that, he reasoned, recalling Singer's mutilated pawn, though he hadn't noticed it when he had moved her before. More likely, this piece had been substituted in the last 24 hours. It was some kind of obscene hit contract message; a sort of black spot.

"She's going to be killed," he whispered, thinking that Singer's pawn had probably been substituted too, just in time for his murder.

He was aware that his fingers were aching. The chess piece was very heavy and it seemed to be getting heavier by the second, unless he was more tired than he realised.

"Well, fuck you," he said to the bewigged Turk and placed the black queen next to her own king on her home square. He stepped away and waited.

A full minute passed before the Turk's eyes returned to the board. The automaton stayed in position for a few moments, then with a long, efficient sweep of its arm knocked all the pieces off the board.

Kris was awoken by the cold.

His first instinct had been to pull the heavy woollen blanket up to his neck, then to tighten it around his shoulders, but it wasn't enough. The cold was unbearable.

It was the middle of the night, the windows capturing just enough light from the dull March morning to allow him to navigate his way by the shadows. In the salon, the blanket around him, he shivered deliriously. It was getting colder still: the bastards must be operating the air conditioning and turning it to freeze mode.

"Put the heating on!" he moaned to the corners of the ceiling, the places where he imagined the secret cameras were positioned. "Put the lights and the fucking heating on!"

The room went colder still, now so cold he detected a glimmer of heat coming from the bathroom, as a starving man smells a crust of bread. He shambled into the bathroom and saw that the bath was run. The water was steaming.

He considered the bath suspiciously. This was the place where the salon rewarded him with comfort and sex, but it was angry with him. It wasn't just the cold and the darkness that told him this: for the first time in weeks he realised he was thinking normally, the muscle that rationalised the odd workings of the salon refusing to work. He didn't want to step in.

He groaned, the air now so cold that his chest was aching. With a moan of agony he let the blanket slip from his shoulder and stepped into the water.

XXIII

Morning frost

"Look, I know that things aren't right, that there's some weird cult, maybe even a criminal conspiracy, surrounding the building…" Kris began.

"Indeed," Honeyman remarked.

"…but I've got it under control."

Kris had been sitting under the anchor, braving the cold, waiting for the Snake Charmer to emerge from his apartment complex, aware from previous observation that he rose early for brisk constitutional walks. Kris hadn't needed to say anything as he quickly approached him, the large bearded man merely grunting and returning inside, holding the door open. The complex was asleep and their footsteps tapped like hammers on the stone steps.

"And what is the character of this conspiracy?" Honeyman asked softly, his Welsh lilt accentuating the word 'character'.

Kris lowered his voice as he climbed the steps, the hard echo telling him that he was speaking too loudly. "Oh I don't know. It's something to do with showbiz, and with history. They make people famous but keep a hold over them."

"Indeed?" Honeyman repeated, climbing quickly but with a slight drag in his right leg.

"Yeah. I get the feeling they set Chelsea London up, all those years ago. She seems pretty scared of them."

"And who are *they*?"

"Well there's two of them. This Russian bird, who I'm told used to be an assassin. And this creepy old geezer. Ovenstone. They've got this chess game which they say needs to be played out. They've told me that if I don't play ball, I'll lose my rooms."

"Lose them? Who to?"

"Josie Hannah. The film star."

"Ah yes. And that worries you?"

"Well, yeah. It's free."

And I love it. And I love what it gives me…

They came to a stop on the landing of the top floor. Honeyman searched for his door key in his ranging overcoat pocket and in doing so brought out his bible.

"Oh, sorry," Kris muttered. "Were you going to church? It's Sunday, I should have realised…"

"No apology needed: I wasn't going to church." He offered Kris a slow squeeze of his eye. "No church will have me."

"No church…?"

"The coven has cursed me, you see. Cursed me with profanity when I'm in God's house." He grunted a qualification to that statement. "Only when I'm on its scent, as I am now. I receive a temporary reprieve in between our trials."

"You've completely lost me."

"I know." Honeyman found his keys and replaced his bible. As he opened the door he offered Kris another encouraging squeeze of his eye. "It's good that you're fighting it, Mr Knight. You may still find the strength to break free."

Kris shrugged uncomfortably. "Look, it's Kris."

"Ah, does that mean I'm no longer the Snake Charmer?"

Kris nodded with a shrug of apology. "But I'm not fighting anything," he clarified. His mind was operating on two levels for this meeting with the minister. Logic told him that all information on Gathering was important, so if the black bishop was prepared to talk to him then it was his duty to listen, while his subconscious presented Singer's eyeless chess piece, with Renka's imperative that he 'take' the black queen.

Honeyman went to the smallest of kitchens to boil a kettle. Kris looked around and rested against a wall: the studio apartment wasn't furnished; the room was bare except for a camp bed installed in the corner and several packed suitcases and files stacked neatly against the skirting, under a large handwritten wall chart. This chart had thirteen names written in thick pencil, some of which had arrows underneath with further names scribbled. There was a photograph of The Pavilion sales office, and of a busy university campus, students pouring out of the Humanities building.

"I see you know my friends," he remarked to Honeyman, returning with two large mugs of tea, "but you don't seem that good at photographing them." He smiled. "Was Fabrienne moving too fast for you when you tried to snap her coming out of the sales office?"

"They are elusive," Honeyman admitted, sitting carefully on his camp bed so that it accepted his weight without buckling.

"No photo of me?"

Honeyman considered the chart. "No. Nor Chelsea London. I know who you are and you'll find your photograph in my files." He indicated the ring binders. "No, I'm interested in the companions. They're up there because I don't quite understand their purpose yet: I want Gracie to see them."

"Gracie?"

"She's a friend. It doesn't matter."

Kris put his mug on the floor, then decided it would be easier if he sat on the floor. "Fabrienne told me the companions bear a resemblance to the person who originally occupied the room. Fabrienne speaks French and has some facial scarring, just like the novelist who lived in Chelsea's room."

"And of course Fabrienne isn't her real name."

"I think she might have changed it because of a bad marriage. She's very cagey about being outside. About being seen."

"It doesn't concern you that only the Trustees and Ms London know about her employment with Gathering? That she has no family to protect her? That if she disappeared the police would assume that her family had caught up with her? No one would think that Gathering..."

"Fabrienne's fine. She's not going anywhere. I'll see to that."

Honeyman sounded a melancholic growl deep in his throat. "Tell me about your new drama," he suggested. "It might help me piece things together."

"Sorry. Confidential." Kris smiled. He wasn't quite sure what had possessed him to come here but that last comment was an alarm bell: the Snake Charmer was working for a rival network, or perhaps some library or university or something, trying to steal Gathering's secrets. All this stuff about companions disappearing was designed to scare him, knowing that he'd want to protect Fabrienne. He touched his mug, deciding he should leave; he would do it in a casual manner that wouldn't result in confrontation.

"Well, when you're ready to tell me, then perhaps we can work it out together."

Kris nodded and finished his tea.

"You have a Kempelen machine, I believe?"

"The Turk," Kris confirmed. He bit his lip. "Eh, that's confidential too…"

"But it isn't the Turk, is it? It's a prototype."

"Whatever."

"It was the machine that housed a small genius called Florian Mollien."

"Right, the chess guy."

"The nature of the invention sadly prevented his ever being recognised as a genius."

"Well, yeah. It would have rather defeated the purpose if little Florian had jumped out at the end, wouldn't it?"

Honeyman nodded, his moustache twitching with a smile. "Florian didn't quite see it that way. He wanted to finish the European tour and then have Kempelen reveal the illusion. Florian wanted to be recognised, you see. He wanted to be celebrated…"

Kris found his name on the wall chart, the inscription on the foyer ceiling flashing in his mind's eye with that last remark. "And Kempelen said no. So Florian stole the machine?"

"Correct."

They waited for a while, considering the chart.

"Your tea is finished," Honeyman remarked. "Do you want to leave?"

Kris cleared his throat uncomfortably. "Well if there's nothing more that you can tell me…"

"You're worried about the movie star, aren't you?"

Kris hesitated.

"Do you believe that the film journalist was murdered?" Honeyman pressed.

Kris checked his watch. "Look, I don't know, and I don't really *want* to know…"

"Because you want to be celebrated too." Honeyman stood

up. "Believe me when I say that your hunger for celebrity is merely a pang of the appetite you will acquire. I've studied Chelsea London's life, you see, and the broadcaster who preceded her: like them, your obsession with fame will turn to insanity."

Kris hovered suspiciously at the door. "Actors, broadcasters. Are we all media people? Gathering's guests, I mean?"

Honeyman nodded in appreciation of the question. "Yes, you're thinking that the hosts were scientists and artists, pursuing more worthy vocations..."

"Well I wouldn't go that far..."

"...but the twentieth century has polarised the meaning of celebrity, has it not? And Gathering isn't interested in talent..."

"Yeah, thanks a bunch."

"...in fact they actually resent artistic talent, one of God's gifts to the world. I'm guessing that your mobile indicates they have nothing but scorn for the thirteen's achievements?"

Kris's eyes darkened as he recalled the obituaries. He didn't answer.

"No, Gathering is only interested in fame. Their ideal guest is perhaps a talk show host made famous through one of those reality programmes. Something that reduces celebrity to its lowest common denominator. You've always understood that, haven't you? That when it comes to fame, there *is* only television."

"I think you're being a little unfair," Kris remarked, but remembering that he had arrived at exactly this conclusion the first time his mobile had rung. He looked for somewhere to put his mug and Honeyman took it from him. "And anyway, that isn't true for Chelsea London, is it? She's got an impressive back catalogue."

"True," Honeyman confirmed, returning to his small kitchen and swilling the mugs. "Ms London has worked very hard for her credibility: to prove Gathering wrong. As will you. Gathering would derive little amusement from making you famous without an extreme effort on your part."

"Amusement?"

"Oh yes, Mr Knight," Honeyman said, deciding he wasn't ready to use the man's first name, notwithstanding the earlier invitation. "This and all their other temples are just sources of amusement for the coven. They worship by way of the ironic joke."

"Worship? Worship who?"

Kris heard a moment's hesitation in the washing-up process.

"But in respect of Ms London," Honeyman continued, "none of her achievements will have satisfied her. She will always doubt her talent, will always suspect she was simply lucky, chosen just because of her name." He returned to the room, wiping his hands with a tea towel.

Kris glanced at the front door. "Look, I'm just going to use these people for the help they can give me, and once I'm on the box, with a few quid in my pocket, I'll move out." He stretched his shoulders to indicate his determination. "I'll give them back the mobile and just move out."

Honeyman sighed. "Do you really believe they'll allow you to leave?"

"Well they won't have any choice. How will they stop me?"

"I suspect you already know the answer to that question. I imagine they've already given you a warning fright."

Kris swallowed. He had been terrified getting into that hot bath last night but to his relief he had simply fallen asleep.

When he woke, the salon was warm again. They wouldn't spook him a second time with that trick.

"But before long, they won't need to scare you. Before long you'll be so addicted to the salon and its gifts that you'll be prepared to do anything, without question."

"Well, we'll see." Kris now turned pointedly to the door.

"Yes, just one last thing before you go." Honeyman opened the door to reassure him. "Your chess game has left me intrigued. Perhaps you could tell me its present set-up and what the moves have signified?"

"The game's over. The Turk had a tiff last night and knocked all the pieces off the board."

"Ah, so you made an illegal move?"

"Yeah, I suppose so."

"Something to do with protecting Ms Hannah?"

"Look it doesn't matter. I'm just saying the game's over."

Honeyman affected a serious expression. "I'd be very interested to learn the set-up before it concluded, nonetheless." He reached under his camp bed and produced a whiteboard with a chessboard and pieces marked in a black felt pen, the black pieces carefully shaded.

Kris considered the board, suspecting that the game would also find its way onto Honeyman's wall. "Okay. So why do you want to know about the game?"

"Well, let's just say for the sake of argument that when you return home you find the board has righted itself and the game is still proceeding." He waved away the protest. "Let's further assume, purely theoretically, that you decide you want my help; that you're prepared to take at face value everything I tell you."

"Okay, so?"

"At that point I will tell you that your deliverance lies in the chess game itself. You might be glad that I've taken a little time to study it."

Kris thought about this, deciding it couldn't do any harm. "The chess game's on my mobile; I can't access that unless it wants me to."

"Would you let me try?"

Kris's hand went protectively to his jacket pocket. He was sure the minister had known it was there all along, his small dark eyes occasionally veering to the inside pocket.

"I can see you're reluctant to produce it," Honeyman said hastily, anxious not to unsettle his visitor. "No matter. Can you remember the moves?"

Kris touched the edge of the door, then nodded.

"So who moved first?"

Kris hesitated, his face a mask of indecision. "I did," he said eventually.

"You did?"

Kris shrugged, deciding there was no harm in telling him this: the game was over, after all. He closed the door.

"White knight moved. I'm white knight…"

"Check."

As Kris's eyelids flickered, his sleeping memory told him this was the latest of many electronic instructions from the Turk. He lay awake in the darkness. Once again, it dawned on him that he was freezing.

"Check."

He crawled out of bed and groaned, sure that he was on the verge of a heart attack, such was the vice that had snapped around his chest. With his heavy blanket over his shoulders he staggered to the door, hearing his bath running.

"This is … getting boring … now…" he muttered with chattering teeth.

He stopped in the salon. Someone had come in while he was sleeping: the panel door was open as he had left it, but the chess pieces were back in place. He shuffled towards the board, his breath coming in white clouds. Josie's queen was once again pinned between his king and his castle.

"Check," the Turk squeaked as it studied the board.

Kris shook his head, too cold to think about this now, and followed the heat into the bathroom. He groaned with relief as he saw the steam rising from the tub.

Slipping into the water, he felt himself starting to relax, feeling his muscles loosening, a film of sweat beading his forehead. He sighed, supposing Gathering was angry with him for talking with the Snake Charmer, but he'd hardly jumped ship. Besides, if this was the worst their caretaker could dish out, a little fiddling with the air conditioning, then he'd dare them to do their worst.

"Check."

"Look, I'm not taking that queen," he called defiantly to the ceiling. "If you're planning to do something to the actress I'm not going to be a part of it. Do what you've got to do," he added with a tremor of guilt, "just leave me out of it."

The lights dimmed further. There was no light whatsoever coming through the windows, the glass panes appearing as if they had been painted black.

"Check," the Turk repeated from the salon.

His heartbeat stumbled and he gripped the sides of the tub. Something was wrong; last night he had immediately felt drowsy when he stepped into the bath, but tonight he was wide awake. The cold was intensifying. He had the vague impression that his nose had gone numb, that he was in a freezer.

"Check!"

The automaton's voice was a squeal. It almost sounded frightened.

"Look, this isn't funny anymore!" Kris called. "Turn the fucking heating on. Let me get out."

He noticed that the four houri taps were missing. He blinked with confusion, then splashed in surprise as his four concubines emerged from the shadow, visible in the darkness only by the wax candles they each held in cupped hands. At first their naked bodies seemed to be swaying gently, then he saw they were covered with worms, wriggling in the candlelight.

They opened their mouths seductively to produce their tongues. More worms were revealed, these thin and hairy.

"Christ," he whispered. He tried to shout for help but his chest was too tight.

The petite Japanese concubine raised her free hand to her throat.

"Asphyxiation," she said.

The athletic black concubine covered one eye.

"And mutilation," she added.

Kris groaned, his throat contracting with the cold. One of his eyes was closing. He tried to concentrate. This was just the hallucinogenic in the water and he was having a bad trip: if he concentrated, it would end.

The buxom white concubine touched her crotch.

"Then castration," she declared.

He shook his head violently.

The elegant Indian concubine pointed to her heart. She smiled widely before she spoke, the worms climbing up her long perfect teeth.

"And, finally … your very painful death," she explained. "CHECK!"

They retreated into the darkness.

His face, one eye screwed shut, was numb, the constriction in his throat making it impossible to speak. In desperation he pulled his head under the water and kept it there for as long he dared, until he felt his blood pumping again. Through the shimmer of the water he saw the four women looking down at him.

With a watery gasp he pulled his head up. Two of them had their hands on his shoulders and pushed him back down. Through the choking water he saw the blurred grey lines of a serrated knife.

He was bursting out of the water again. The knife was in the water, moving up his leg.

"CHECK!"

His throat now released him, letting him scream for it to stop, that he would do anything they ask.

He went under again.

XXIV

The Perfumery

THE UNDERSTUDY WONDERED if tonight would be different.

Once again the audience was on its feet. Even the critics were being generous over Chelsea London's stage performance in *Mousetrap*, confounding the predictions that the actress, stripped of her skilled US directors and those moody, esoteric scripts which so suited her enigmatic character, couldn't act.

The old girl has proved them all wrong, the understudy thought on the third curtain call, the theatre refusing to be silenced. Chelsea, ecstatic, was hugging and kissing her fellow actors and throwing flowers of her bouquet to the audience. This sixth and final night had been the same as before, with her lighting up the stage with a charming, amusing persona that went far beyond the parameters of the play.

The understudy beamed as the curtains finally closed; she made ready to take the flowers that Chelsea would hand to her as she left the stage.

Surely tonight would be different... It *was* her final night...

"Oh you were wonderful Miss London!" she said, hurrying to keep pace as the actress made for her dressing room. "Your best performance, I'm sure!" They would be inside the dressing room, the door closed, the sound of the audience barely audible, when Chelsea's warm, generous smile would drop like dead flies from her face.

In her head, the understudy sighed with disappointment, seeing that tonight was no different. She pretended not to notice the transformation as she put the flowers in the watered vase already in place; she knew that the actress had already forgotten she was there, would ignore both her presence and her praise. Once more she wondered at the stark contrast between her stage and off-stage personality; perhaps the American celebrity machine did that to you, after a time...

"Thank you," Chelsea murmured.

The understudy, so startled that she dropped one of the flowers, turned and beamed.

"Thank you," Chelsea repeated to the dressing mirror, looking not at her reflection but at the two photographs she had now fixed under the wire of the mirror lights. "Thank you for letting me finish it this way; not with tricks or disguises, but with the talent I always knew was mine."

"You're not retiring, are you?" the understudy asked, tentatively approaching and attempting a peek at the photographs. Perhaps she had family no one knew about. Chelsea stiffened and turned, her eyes taking a moment to focus on her understudy, to remember who the woman was.

"Leave," Chelsea said abruptly, returning to her reflection, not caring if the understudy left quickly or slowly, in confusion or in anger. With a smile she recalled countless audiences in front of her salon's mirror as her career had been plotted. She always knew this time would come: the Trustees had told her that when the new guest arrived, it would be time to lock up.

Her reflection smiled in a resigned state of grace. The fear had left her now for she understood what *Locking Up* meant; Claudine would be trapped forever in the salon, while she would escape. It didn't matter whether she spent the rest of her life in anonymity, not even if she died: just so long as the building released her.

She heard her dressing table rattle and she rapidly unlocked the drawer with the key secreted in her costume. In her travelling life she had found many safe places where she kept her mobile, this drawer in The New Theatre dressing room having been specially adapted by Renka to incorporate a steel lock.

She glanced at the dressing room door in a moment of irritation. Where *was* Renka? The Trustee hadn't come to any of the performances.

As she opened the drawer she winced at the trapped cloud of almonds created by her throbbing brass mobile. The call was a message of congratulations, though with a breath of dismay she saw that the heart monitor was transparent, the blood having all but drained away. The mobile needed charging. It had taken over forty years for the battery to fail, but it had happened at last.

As if to emphasise the point, the mobile was slightly sluggish as she went to her address book. That aside, it still worked normally, with a different perfume scent for every name her thumb ran over: every person in her life had a different aroma.

Her address book was huge, almost a lifetime's work, for she had possessed this line to the Gathering network when the rest of the world was stuck with wires and dials. The broadcaster she ousted had mentioned that he had started out with a gramophone, then a radio, before his mobile telephony arrived.

She regarded the names, all given aliases through the fictional characters in Claudine de Tour du Pin's romantic novels.

The handsome cad, LeClerk…

The trustworthy farmer, Pierre…

The virtuous heroine, Mimi…

Only one of Madame Claudine's novels had survived in print, a novella preserved in a curiosity compilation, but the network was able to access them all in an elegant computer font, together with pencil sketches of the characters as they had appeared in the novelist's imagination. A few were in colour and highly realistic. These colour images postdated Madame Claudine's disfigurement with concentrated sodium cyanide, an acid that smelt of bitter almonds: they were from her final novel, *The London Address*.

Chelsea's expression turned to alarm. The aliases were reverting to their real names, their character pictures fading. Instinctively she knew that this regression was part of Locking Up; she also knew what she had to do.

Her thumb found Vaishali Iqbal, previously Mlle Fabrienne, the star-crossed heroine of *The London Address*. The character was loved by Madame Claudine, though she was one of the principal causes of the manuscript's rejection, the publisher's letter a prominent feature on the display.

This work is too dark, Claudine… You can't have a story set in both Paris and London, not with war with England on the horizon. But these are trivial concerns compared to your choice of heroine. The illegitimate union of an Indian servant and a duke, a girl who becomes heiress to his fortune and position. How will your readers react to such an abomination?

She considered the colour picture of a proud, striking Indian woman. She pressed the name to a squeak of arid cologne.

Fabrienne answered almost immediately.

"Miss London?"

Chelsea considered her companion's voice, rolling it over on her tongue.

"Miss London, are you hungry? Shall I bring food?"

Chelsea regarded the picture of the Indian heiress, as imagined by Madame Claudine as she wrote her final novel in a state of psychotic depression. A story of a woman entering society in the face of extraordinary prejudice and surviving with the help of a London correspondent, a man she had modelled on the enlightened English satirist Henry Fielding. It was a visionary work. "I'm not hungry, but bring food if you wish."

There was a pause of uncertainty. "Of course…"

"I just want to see you. This time you'll come to my salon. To The Perfumery."

Again, Fabrienne hesitated: she hadn't been inside Chelsea's rooms before. "Of course. Shall I come now?"

Chelsea rose from the dressing table and carefully took her photographs. Her eyes were dead. "One hour."

The dawdling tone, morose even by Chelsea's standards, gave Fabrienne a twinge of foreboding. "At ten thirty then," she confirmed.

★

Kris opened the foyer door at two minutes before ten. He stepped aside with an air of defeated exhaustion to let Josie enter, Mikey and Erika behind.

No one spoke. As he accompanied them to the lift he regarded the entourage: both had looks of intense concentration and were holding a colour print of a photograph in front of them as they walked, as if they were studying a map. His glimpse of these pictures reminded him of his salon.

"What are they?" he asked Josie when they were in the lift, the doors waiting to close.

"They're photographs of the rooms we're taking," she said distractedly.

"I don't understand."

She considered him for a moment, deciding that perhaps an explanation would be necessary before the lift decided to move. "I suspected the Trustees wouldn't give me your rooms, Kris. After all, you're the next big thing, aren't you? No, I guessed it would be Chelsea's rooms I was offered, especially as they're becoming available. Renka left Tom Singer's photographs in his hotel room for me to find."

The memory of last night was thankfully dulled by his extreme fatigue, his mind soggy with lack of sleep. "So why did you ask for my rooms?" he slurred.

"I needed your help. I had to get you to offer me Chelsea's room in your place, just as the Trustees planned."

Kris glanced at her agent and bodyguard. Notwithstanding the intensity of their glares, their eyes didn't blink; they seemed heavily sedated.

"Why didn't *Chelsea* offer you her rooms?"

Josie's eyes flickered. "She has, hasn't she? You've got her permission, haven't you?"

The cage closed and the lift travelled up. It opened on Kris's floor.

"Well, this is me," he murmured, his exhaustion complete.

Josie was looking at him suspiciously as he stepped out. "Wait…" she began, but the cage snapped quickly shut and ascended quickly.

He considered the bare wall of the lift shaft, the black cable tightening as the cage found its floor, then shuffled back to his salon. The lights in the entire building were failing and he took one last glimpse of the chessboard before he closed the alcove panel.

The white castle had taken the black queen.

"Take care, Josephine," he said mournfully. He considered his mobile, the display frozen on the schematic.

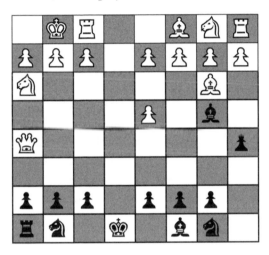

The black queen was prone on the edge of the chessboard. Perhaps it was a trick of the alcove lights, which were flashing on and off under the disruption to the building's lighting system, but her face seemed to alternate between temptress and witch.

★

"There's nothing to be afraid of," Josie assured them as she jovially stepped backwards out of the lift, concealing her unexpected sense of weariness at her ascent. Mikey and Erika were reluctant to leave. "This is our new home," she explained. "Don't you want to see our beautiful new home?"

She smiled encouragingly as their eyes returned to their pictures, their stares intense with wonder. "This is where we'll live. Where we'll be safe," she added.

This was only partially true. Gathering's salon was her refuge from the renegade assassin Franklyn Tyde, a sanctuary where she could hide until the Trustees tracked him down, but she had no idea what would become of her entourage. Perhaps they would find a place here, become servants, just as she had spied an Indian woman visiting Chelsea London with food. Then again, perhaps the room would have no use for them and spit them out.

Josie didn't regard this as an immoral gamble. She had been conceived in violence and had grown up with death, within the rules of combat laid down by her temple Precious Cargo. It was a calculated risk made necessary by events: Erika and Mikey had started talking in secret and she knew they were planning to leave. To bring them here she had shown them Singer's photographs.

The lift door closed. Mikey and Erika looked up from the photographs but didn't move.

"Well stay in there, then," Josie said. "I'll find a way of getting you out."

"Sure thing Josie," Mikey droned.

"Okay honey," Erika agreed, also in a dazed monotone.

Perhaps they're not meant to be here after all, Josie thought. She briefly considered the contradiction of their casual turns of phrase within their trance-like condition, then put them out of her mind. She approached the door.

La Parfumerie

"The Perfumery," she said approvingly, liking the name.

She put a finger tentatively on the thumb latch and felt the strength in the mechanism. It was strong but it could be pushed. As she tested it she heard the lift rattle forcefully. "Won't be long," she said, assuming that Mikey was waking up and shaking the cage. She took a breath, then pushed heavily down on the latch.

It didn't go down all the way, finding a knot of resistance. She jumped away from the door as the lift whined into life: it was not so much the noise that had startled her, which was soft and efficient, but rather the splashes of blood which shot down the corridor.

The left and right sides of the cage had come together with a snap, razoring effortlessly through Mikey and Erica. Bodyguard and agent tottered momentarily in long slices, before the side bars snapped back and the front and rear walls met with a clang, then again and again, quicker each time, turning them into red mist.

The thumb latch sprung up and the lift plummeted.

★

"What's going on?" Fabrienne asked as Kris admitted her into the foyer. She struggled to keep her balance: the floor was whirring with water.

"It's either a plumbing leak, or some maintenance cleaning," he replied. "You here to see Chelsea?"

Fabrienne nodded as she followed him to the lift, the water charging across the marble with such speed it was creating vortexes. She noticed the water escaping through drain holes under the lift.

"Chelsea's got company," he replied.

"Really? That's okay, I'll wait."

"They looked like they're going to make a night of it."

She shook her head. "I don't understand. She told me to come." He considered the satchel she was carrying; her arm tightened around it protectively.

"Well, she probably forgot," he sighed, gesturing to the cage suspended a few feet above the floor. "Anyway, you're not going anywhere in that. It must be on a maintenance program or something; don't know how long it will take."

She considered the cage suspiciously. "I suppose…"

He yawned. "I'm stuck here too. The lift brought me down when I heard all the commotion, dropping like a stone and stopping in that position. I had to lower myself out." He shook a leg, which was soaking. "Look, why don't we walk down to the Bay and find somewhere warm while the building does its business?"

"Kris, I can't…"

"Chelsea's got your number. She'll ring you if she wants to know where you are."

Fabrienne looked up at the ceiling, cursing her bad luck at not having arrived sooner, before the lift went out of action: she was desperate to see Chelsea's salon. The decision made, she considered Kris properly for the first time. He looked drawn and pale. "Are you okay?"

"I had a bad night."

"Really? What happened?"

He shook his head slowly. His recollection was continuing to fade, his vague sense of apathy a sort of homespun aesthetic: oil of cloves for the memory toothache. If he dipped into his memories he would find pain. Extreme pain. All that was clear was something bad had happened last night, that it had lasted a very long time, that he had passed out on occasion, to be revived; that he had been almost ecstatic with relief when he eventually managed to crawl to the chessboard, to pick up the white castle and knock the black queen off her square.

"Forget about that," he said. "Let's get a drink." To her look of inquiry he added, "Yeah I can get a drink, so long as it's coffee or red wine."

"No bars," she said cautiously. "We can sit in my car, if you like. I've got a flask of coffee." She motioned to her satchel. "And Chelsea's sandwiches," she added mischievously.

He suppressed the urge to ask her if she wanted to stay the night with him, though he glowed as he imagined her naked body wrapped around him. He even gave himself a mental warning not to try and kiss her in the car, even if she was expecting it. He wasn't going to risk moving her chess piece.

"Flask coffee and stolen sandwiches sound great," he said.

★

Josie decided she had waited long enough. Reluctant to touch the thumb latch again, she had stood here waiting for Chelsea to come out and investigate the noise of the water jets.

A tremor of anticipation made her realise there was no turning back. If this was trespass, as the Baptist had warned, then it had occurred in the lift: that sense of weariness after Knight got out, as she travelled to this floor, made it seem as if she was pushing through some invisible barrier. Anyway, she had been in the foyer without consequence: the fate of her people demonstrated that the lift was the threshold.

She whispered a farewell to Mikey and Erika and steeled herself. Their death merely proved that *they* were trespassing, but then they hadn't been invited. Her pulse quickened. Knight was wrong: Chelsea *must* know she was coming. She had Knight's king in check, after all: whatever that might mean within the dynamics of the game, she had obviously manoeuvred herself so that the advantage was hers.

She checked her watch: it was gone 10.30. She knocked.

"Come in my dear," came Chelsea's voice from within.

Josie exhaled with relief and pressed down the latch. This time it released easily as she opened the door.

Chelsea was standing in front of her wall mirror, carefully considering her reflection as if she were checking an expensive gown for its fit. She was naked, her skin leathery and wrinkled.

And dirty.

There was dirt, possibly excrement, on her skin, in her hair, in her long fingernails.

"Oh no," Josie whispered.

The salon was barely recognisable from its photographs. Brown filth was smeared on the walls and walked into the floor, the air heavy with damp. Fungus and heavy dust covered the furniture. Only the full-length mirror seemed untouched by the decay, its plain wooden frame polished.

Chelsea turned with welcoming eyes, which quickly became hostile. "Who are you?" she snarled.

"I'm here for the room," Josie sputtered, her hand going to her nose. The stench was unbearable.

Chelsea's expression gradually softened. "For the room?" She returned to her reflection. "For *this* room?" she asked at length.

Josie nodded with a grimace. "Just for a short while," she clarified. She now reminded herself that she was a survivor, that she had committed the most terrible acts against her own heart to survive Precious Cargo. She only needed the room long enough for the heretic, Franklyn Tyde, to be caught.

Chelsea stepped away from the mirror, while Josie looked

fearfully at its frame. "Then come in and look," Chelsea suggested. Her expression hardened. "Leave, or look."

"I can't leave," Josie said. She stepped in.

Chelsea beckoned her to the mirror, showing no embarrassment over her nudity. She was always naked in this room, had been so for years. "You're exceptionally beautiful," Chelsea remarked. "I'm sure the mirror will eat you up."

The smell receded as Josie looked into the glass. Though her attention was wholly on her reflection, she knew that the room had taken on a different aspect, was immaculate and fresh as it gloried in the power of the mirror.

"I *am* beautiful," Josie muttered to her reflection. "It would be a crime to kill me."

It was difficult to imagine Josie Hannah as more ravishing than she actually was, but the mirror succeeded, casting light and shadow on her bones for dramatic emphasis. Josie moaned with pleasure; without taking her eyes from the reflection she adeptly slipped out of her clothes.

"Yes, it's better naked," Chelsea agreed from the other end of the room. She was holding her mobile to her chest like a crucifix. "You learn fast: you would fit in here quite easily."

Josie nodded slowly in agreement to all these observations. "Oh, Father Below, it's so wonderful," she groaned, seeing herself amplified beyond the scope of all human possibility. She was both myth and history, all that could be imagined: a goddess worshipped by ancient tribes who had once looked at the stars and tried to rationalise life and beauty.

"Yes you would fit in well," Chelsea clarified, "if this mirror was for *you*..."

Josie's eyebrows creased, her concentration broken as she

briefly looked at Chelsea. When she returned to her reflection she screamed. Something hideous screamed back.

"That's not me!" she shouted, but she knew she was lying. The reflection held her every sinful thought and deed; from her first memory of plotting her mother's death, to her ambivalence a moment ago when her friends were killed; the seed of evil in her character that in different times would have made her a monster; the face she imagined at the seat of judgment.

"That's not me," she moaned, yet with resignation. The reflection was getting uglier. So ugly it went beyond understanding. And she knew it wouldn't stop. She knew it couldn't stop…

"Help me…"

Chelsea was at her side, a hand on her shoulder. The shoulder she touched with delectation had delicate bones and soft skin, but the reflection was a mass of sores with the crouch of a beggar thief.

She placed two hatpins in Josie's hand.

XXV

Voices from abroad

"I WANT TO move forward," Buoys declared. "How long do we have to wait?" The BBC's solicitor grimaced uncomfortably as the table, which included the executive producers, turned to him with impatient expectation.

It had been two weeks since Josie's visit to Gathering. On the first Monday, Kris was jubilant to hear that Josie had e-mailed from America to say she couldn't make the play after all. So, not only was she alive, but the production was back on track.

Another week passed and he received a text message from Buoys' leering Moor. Whatever she had meant to text had obviously been garbled by the network's software, for it read simply:

Or the Snake Charmer?

It hadn't been until today, with this meeting organised at short notice, that he had understood why the network had sent him a message that involved Buoys and the minister. The actors had been informed last week that the production was stalled due to legal difficulties, but a thump of understanding now arrived with Buoys' imperative: 'I want to move forward!'

He had given the minister the set-up of the chess game. He

had done it casually, even scornfully, as if his attitude made what he knew to be a gross act of indiscretion excusable. The minister had ignored his manner, happily marking the schematic on his chart, scribbling hurried notes as he was provided with the context. He had pondered the diagram for only a few moments before he said, "You have a possible checkmate in three moves."

"Checkmate?"

"I'm assuming that's the end of the game," Honeyman said. "Putting the black king in checkmate." A concerned raise of his eyebrows offered a postscript: *That it's the end for you...*

Kris had paused by the door. "Three moves...?"

"Provided black makes certain safe moves," Honeyman clarified. He flattened the chart out on the bed. "Let's see. Now, white can only move the pieces already in play. Yes?"

"That's what they said. They said there might be new black pieces."

"Very well. Now for black, we know for certain that we have black bishop, that's me, and black pawn, your TV executive."

"Okay..."

"I can go several ways, but preferably I'd just move forward one space, away from the defence of the king. So..."

He rearranged the black bishop on the chart.

"While black pawn..." he continued.

"Just moves forward," Kris confirmed.

Just moves forward...

Kris glanced at Buoys, who was listening with restrained anger as the solicitor nervously read out the letter from Josie Hannah's Los Angeles attorney. The film star had pulled out of the production because there were doubts over the authenticity of the material: the lawyer was insisting on bringing historical experts over from the States. The solicitor's eyebrows rose fretfully as he came to the paragraph that intimated there would be a breach of contract if it was found that Ms Hannah's schedule had been compromised through misrepresentation over the source material. Damages for disrupting the artist's schedule would be colossal.

Gathering's waiting for me to move black, he realised. *It wants a safe move: Honeyman's bishop or Buoys' pawn.*

Honeyman had demonstrated the double-prong checkmate. White castle would put the black king in check; if the black king moved right, the white queen could put the king in checkmate without taking any further pieces. He marked it out on his diagram.

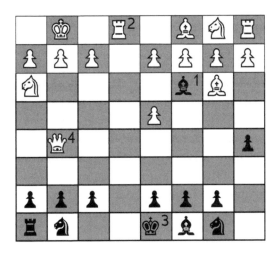

"That's not the end," Kris had remarked. "There's a black pawn that could block the queen."

"I agree, but that pawn's not in play."

"Okay, then the black knight could block the queen." He marked the move on the diagram.

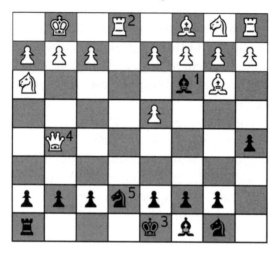

"Why do you think the black knight is in play?"

"I just know."

Honeyman looked at him thoughtfully. "Again, I agree. White queen takes black knight," he said. "Checkmate."

Kris considered the chart. "The white queen is Fabrienne," he murmured, thinking she wouldn't harm a fly. He had glanced at Honeyman, wanting to ask him more questions, but deciding instead to leave. He would remain neutral: he wouldn't fight the Trustees, but he wouldn't co-operate either. Things would just have to play out.

His attention briefly returned to the meeting, then wandered again.

"Can you give me an indication of the nature of these historical documents?" the solicitor asked.

Kris's hand touched the soft utility case where his mobile was hidden. The network was giving him a clear message: it

308

was his move, with Buoys and Honeyman being offered as possible pieces. But while the network might be hoping for Honeyman's quick checkmate, it didn't really matter: white had complete mastery of the game. The important thing was that he allow the game to progress.

He frowned uncomfortably, wondering how they had discovered his nickname for Honeyman. He shrugged, thinking he must have let 'the Snake Charmer' slip somewhere.

I said the name when I was with the Goof that time...

"Kris?" Buoys repeated.

"Yes," he said, rising from his thoughts.

"Are you prepared to say what the documents reveal?"

Her eyes darted to the lawyer.

"Oh right," Kris said. "Eh, has he signed a confidentiality agreement?"

"The meeting is minuted and confidential," a producer confirmed.

Kris nodded. "Okay. We've got three documents. The first is a letter from the Dauphin's original doctor to the Commune. It proves that the kid he examined in the prison wasn't the prince."

The solicitor was scribbling furiously.

"That proves all the conspiracy theories were correct," Kris added, following the solicitor's pen. "That the Revolutionaries had no option but to substitute him, to scotch rumours he'd escaped."

The solicitor paused. "But didn't they do a DNA test on the heart...?"

Kris nodded, impatient now that he had explained this so many times. "That's where the other two documents come in. We've got a charter for a Revolutionary club called

Chapter Emile that Chaumette belonged to. Its origins were Rousseaun and atheistic: they wanted to prove kings weren't chosen by God; that the Dauphin's 'royalty' was just a product of the systemic evil in society. Chaumette had already been tinkering round the edges with this, giving him over to the cobbler Simon to try and bring him down to his level or whatever, you know the bawdy songs and everything, but Emile was designed to go a lot further."

"How much further?"

"It wasn't just imprisonment, solitude and deprivation; they could have done that in the Temple prison. They wanted to *change* him. They were basically trying to remove the influence of society, just as Rousseau had done with his student Emile, but of course that was impossible with someone who had already lived in the world. So, they decided to remove his memories."

"How?"

"Torture, basically. Mental and physical. Through brainwashing and some primitive brain surgery they were going to extract the royalty from the royal." He paused. "The drama's going out after the watershed," he added meaningfully.

The lawyer waited for him to continue, then looked up. "Really? That bad?"

"That bad," Buoys and her producer said together.

"Anyway," Kris continued, "they didn't succeed. Chaumette got the chop and a small Royalist section of the chapter took it over."

"Royalist? I thought you said…?"

"Yeah, these guys were working pretty much undercover, pretending to go along so they could get the Dauphin to safety. But Chaumette and Simon hid the kid, then they went to the guillotine. Anyway, Madame Simon later told the Royalists where he was, which is why she went to her grave believing the Dauphin had been rescued, but the kid was dead by the time they got to him. They removed his heart, then later arranged for a student to replace it with the heart of the substituted kid in the Temple."

"Why didn't they reveal that the Dauphin had been murdered?" the solicitor asked.

"To keep Royalist sentiment alive. Better to have rumours of his escape."

The lawyer considered this. "Why not do so at the time of the restoration of the monarchy?"

"Too late then. They might have been tried themselves for conspiracy: Louis XVIII was very twitchy about pretenders. But the diary gives a different reason: it records that the Dauphin was so heavily mutilated that they didn't want to distress his family. That might be true. The narrator didn't seem to care too much about his own skin."

"And that was the end of this Chapter Emile?" the solicitor mused.

Kris cleared his throat. "I suppose," he replied.

The solicitor mulled this over. "The French will be very unhappy about this."

"Let them be. It's their history."

"But I can see why Ms Hannah is so keen to establish its accuracy."

"Look," Buoys said, bringing the flat of her hand firmly down on the desk. "Make this go away, Robert. We're already behind schedule."

The solicitor nervously scratched his neck. "But we have to be careful…"

"Make this go away," she repeated. "I want to move

forward." She looked at Kris, with a secret wink of encouragement. "Right, Kris?"

Kris returned an uncertain smile.

The Turk hadn't pulled its eyes away from the chessboard since the night he had taken Josie's queen. The black queen piece had been missing in the morning, frustrating Kris's inspection to see whether she really did have two faces.

He studied the board, thinking that perhaps he should just give in to the inevitable and move one of the black pieces. He didn't have control over the Honeyman bishop – Ovenstone had explained that no one controlled the bishops – but he supposed if he made it clear to Honeyman that he wasn't interested in his help that might result in the Turk moving the bishop itself.

But Buoys was the better option. She wanted to be moved and he had control over her. Perhaps he could just move the piece now…

He made a fist of his outstretched hand as he changed his mind. No, he'd made a plan and he'd stick to it. And he wasn't going to be coerced anymore: he'd vowed to the salon that if it frightened him again, like that night in the bath, he'd just leave and check in to a hospital to get force-fed.

He nodded grimly to acknowledge his temporary victory. In the final analysis the building was just a nasty box of tricks, but he was also aware that he had stepped back from something and was thinking differently as a result. In the last few months he had started to see people in different ways: people didn't anger or excite him anymore, they were either relevant or irrelevant, that was all. He recalled his last conversations with both Trish and his first wife and, with perplexed dismay, thought how easy it had been to take a timeout from his daughter. He was like a drug fiend steadily descending into a hell where no one could follow.

The mobile throbbed in his hand. The display showed a black pawn and he assumed it was Buoys. The ringtone told him he was wrong.

"Ghastly little man."

"Hello Chelsea," he said wearily, taking the call. He watched the chess schematic flash with Chelsea's pawn, which guarded the king's castle, but it didn't move.

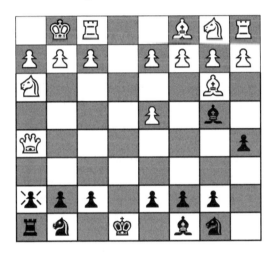

Chelsea *never* moves, he realised, thinking that Chelsea's pawn could now have been one of Honeyman's safe moves to progress to the checkmate.

He wondered if that signified anything. Perhaps it meant that she was trapped: trapped in The Perfumery.

"I've been instructed to tell you that the Trustees are waiting," Chelsea said in a stressed voice. "I don't know what that means," she added. "Are they waiting for you to move *in*?"

"No, I know what they mean."

There was a pause. "I'm supposed to be handing over. Why the delay?"

"Handing over?" he muttered, walking around the salon, his shyness with the international star having completely vanished. "To Josie Hannah you mean? When she comes back from the States?"

Chelsea gave a short gasp, which was her laugh. "Why would I hand over to Josie Hannah?"

A cold tremor took him to the windows where he thoughtfully observed the view, the people dots growing in size until he could see their faces. He blinked and pulled back, yet to come to terms with the magnification feature of the windows. He was gaining the feeling that he would spend a lifetime discovering this place: the prospect both frightened and excited him, as a drug is sampled, its addictive power understood.

"I thought she was taking *your* rooms?" he said.

"Taking my rooms!" she snapped back. It took a moment for her to retrieve her calm and her disinterested drone. "I'm handing the building over to *you*, Kris Knight."

"To me?"

"There can only be one guest at Gathering. The building is private and house-proud."

Kris frowned. "Well I've already moved in. I've got a key."

"If you had moved in, as you call it … *really* moved in … then I would know."

"Look, I've got a few issues I need to clear up before I … eh, commit."

"Oh. At the precipice, are we?"

"What?"

The short gasp of laughter again. "I was there once. Take my advice: save yourself the time and trouble. Commit."

He didn't answer. He was waiting for her to hang up, but clearly she had more she needed to say.

"Have you spoken to Bonaparte yet? To Saint-Just?"

"Yeah, good one."

"The network allows you to access such people."

"Really."

"Just as you accessed the real Madame Claudine with the thumb latch. The building finds and preserves them. Anyone in the circle of the chapter, who had a strong self-image... The building finds them all..."

His eyes narrowed, wondering how she knew about the French actress with the acid slippers. "What *is* the thumb latch?" he asked warily.

"The latch," she said dreamily. "Do you care for the latch, Kris Knight?"

"No."

"One day you will, I promise you. The latch is the key to the building. It takes you in, or it takes you out."

"So is it some kind of special software? A hypnotic program or something?"

"Are these modern terms? They sound meaningless."

The seconds passed uncomfortably as each waited for the other to speak.

"Is Josie Hannah dead?" he asked at last, his buried fears rising like bile. In his mind he saw the chess schematic: the white castle taking black queen. "Did they kill her?"

She didn't answer.

"Then tell me what you mean about the latch: that it can take you *out* of the building."

"I think you misunderstand my meaning of 'out', Kris Knight. Do not confuse it with 'escape'."

"Then what do you mean?"

"The latch opens two doors. Either way, you see the building differently."

"Two doors? I don't under-"

She hung up.

Josie Hannah is definitely back in the States, he decided, playing prima donna with her agent and lawyers. He wasn't going to let his demented neighbour unnerve him.

After the call, the mobile had stayed bright, allowing him access.

"Bonaparte, Bonaparte..." he muttered, scrolling the address book. He came upon his name, to be told, "The colonel is busy".

"It figures," he said. He found Saint-Just, the second name Chelsea had mentioned: the fiercely idealist young Jacobin executed with Robespierre at the end of the Terror.

When he tried to call he was again told, "The esteemed Saint-Just is busy". This time however he was given the option of sending a message.

"So how do you feel about being guillotined?" he asked with a smirk. "Who do you blame?"

The message went off with a clatter of hooves.

Shortly the mobile throbbed, angrily.

Kris waited for a while, eventually deciding he wouldn't receive a reply. Any software Gathering had built in clearly wasn't clever enough to answer random questions. He felt rather disappointed at their lacklustre performance.

He sat back on the chaise longue and considered the black flower wallpaper. Beyond the panel, in its alcove, the Turk awaited his move. He had the sensation that the automaton was looking directly at him, through the wood.

"No way," he said to the ceiling. "You know my terms."

He nodded to himself, the courage of his convictions empowering him. Perhaps some things were more important to him than success, and all that success entailed.

First I see Josie Hannah alive.

Only then do I commit.

XXVI

Eighteenth-century reflections

A s KRIS STEPPED into character, with Chaumette's mirror reflection silhouetted in his imagination, his concerns over the network fell away. As he recovered from his creative high, now becoming an addict's fix, he wondered if he could ever bring himself to leave the salon.

"Yes that's good, that's very, very good," Carl enthused quietly.

"You don't think I went over the top?" Kris asked, leaning against the one prop on the Chapter stage, Chaumette's writing desk. He took a needful swig from his large water bottle, as if he had just been laying paving slabs.

"No, not at all," Carl replied. "It had the necessary venom, but the menace was understated." He returned to the selected sections of the script Kris had brought to the rehearsal, the Japanese cabinet having failed to provide a confidentiality agreement suitably tailored to the tutor. "I'm not quite sure of the context, but shall we move on to the next scene?"

Kris's attention went to the back of the small auditorium. "Any chance of a coffee break? I think I've got company."

Fabrienne was standing at the door at the far end of the auditorium. She shyly raised her hand and left as soon as Kris acknowledged her.

"Eh, sure, ten minutes," Carl agreed, following his eyes.

Kris quickly trotted up the aisle after her, his slimmer physique having made him agile. In the lobby he looked round, then groaned, realising she was outside. He found her in her Fiesta, parked on the street.

Perhaps he was still in character, the Commune leader darkening his mind, but he didn't smile as he half got in to the passenger seat, leaving the door open. There was a moment of uncertainty while neither spoke.

"What am I thinking?" he said. "Great to see you. Faaaaantastic," he added, realising he hadn't used that expression in a while. It reminded him of his old self, before he wore the grim, professional cloak of the salon, and somehow it no longer felt right. He leaned forward to peck her on the cheek. She put her hand on the right side of her hair and leaned forward too, but got the angle wrong. Their lips met briefly.

"Sorry,' they said simultaneously. She shook her head, embarrassed and confused.

He pulled himself fully into the car and shut the door. "You okay?" he asked.

She shrugged.

"What's wrong?"

She sighed. "Chelsea hasn't been in touch."

"So?"

"It's been too long. Something's wrong. Something's happened, I just know it."

"Maybe she's giving you a holiday."

She shook her head despondently. "No, the money's stopped."

"Oh, well no need to worry about that. I've got plenty right now. Seriously, Fabrienne: anything you need."

She smiled in gratitude, then shook her head once more. "It's not that. I think Chelsea's found a new PA."

"In that case I think you're well out of it." He hesitated. "I saw you with her, in this car, last time I was here. She was in the back, wasn't she? And she hit you, didn't she?"

Fabrienne looked at the windscreen. "She gets angry with me sometimes. It's probably my fault…"

"It's not your fault! Fabrienne, get out of there. The last thing you need is more grief, what with this trouble you've got with your family. *That's* the problem we need to sort out."

They sat in silence for a time. "I don't know how to explain this," she said at length, "but I miss the building. I hated the place when I first saw it, it gave me nightmares and everything, but I've got used to it. And it gives me something … something I need." She took a deep breath. "Kris, I've stopped writing."

He grinned. "What, bit of writer's block?" She banged the steering wheel in frustration and he raised his hands. "Whoa! Sorry, didn't know it was so important!"

She put a hand over her eyes to regain her composure. "So you know now," she said at length.

He threw an embarrassed glance down the road. "What's your book called?"

"*The London Address*," she said.

Kris considered this with a pragmatic stretch of his shoulders. "You'll get the muse back, don't worry. You certainly don't need to continue to be Chelsea's PA to write a bestseller: you must have more than enough dirt on her by now." He was assuming from the novel's title that Fabrienne's novel was loosely based on the actress, hence the need to stay close to her. Perhaps it was an unofficial biography. "Anyway, does this mean I can call you *Vaishali* now?"

"No!" she snapped.

This time he merely groaned, not even making an attempt at placation. She put her hand to her mouth. "Kris, I'm so, *so* sorry, I don't know where this is coming from, but please, keep calling me Fabrienne. It's, like, *her* name for me."

He nodded, his question having been a probe: he was wondering whether the minister was right, that the name had an association with Madame Claudine, or if she had changed it to disassociate herself from her family and her background. "You'll get over this, Fabrienne. And when I've got this TV thing under my belt, I'm out of there too. Believe me."

She looked at the Chapter Arts Centre. "How's it going?"

"Good." He rolled his eyes. "Better than I could possibly have dreamed. And I'm not just talking about the lucky find with the historical stuff. The Goof's turned out to be a brilliant screenwriter, and even my acting has improved."

"The Goof's your ex-landlord, isn't he? I remember you saying he's in your chess game...?"

Kris tapped the glove box, resisting the urge to open it and get a better look at that thing he had recognised. "Renka gave you his details, didn't she? Told you to give them to me?"

She nodded darkly. "I don't know why, but yes."

"What did Renka tell you about the chess game?"

She sighed. "Not much; just that you'd be set a task of completing a chess game, that I shouldn't be surprised if you made references to it. When I asked, she said she had no conception of what the game would involve."

"Well that's bullshit. The whole thing's been rigged from day one."

She considered him with an uneasy expression. "Kris, can I ask you something?"

"Sure."

"When we first met, and for a time after, I had the impression that you ... well ... liked me."

"I do," he said to the glove box.

"No, I mean really *liked* me..."

He looked at her. "I do," he repeated emphatically.

She took the steering wheel but resisted the urge to manipulate. "That's nice. Thank you. And you know my opinion of you has, well, improved..."

He chuckled. "I hope so, yeah. Couldn't get much worse."

She made to speak, then shook her head.

"You're wondering why I haven't done anything about it?" he said. She made eye contact again. "Now you're going to think that *I've* lost my marbles..." he began.

"No, tell me."

He pulled his right knee close to his chest; it had been a long time since he had a flat stomach and he was enjoying this new flexibility with his body. "You know that you're one of the pieces in the chess game, Fabrienne. One of the most important pieces, in fact."

"So?"

"So I don't want you to move. I don't want anything to happen to you."

"I don't understand."

"Look, I'm worried that if we get together that something will happen with the game. Don't you see? Gathering wants us to get together; they're expecting it. Why else would they make you my queen?" He turned to her. "No, I just want you to stay put until the game's over; not to be threatened, or to be put in a position where you're threatening anyone else." He groaned. "I was worried enough about Josie Hannah, and I don't even like her..."

322

Fabrienne nodded with a mix of concern and relief. "What, you think Gathering has done something to her?"

"No, she's gone back to the States."

"How do you know?"

"Because her lawyer's crawling all over us. Wants to close us down."

"But you suspected Gathering? Before, I mean?"

He shifted in his seat, releasing his knee, not wanting to tell her about Tom Singer. She might have heard of his suicide on the news but Singer had only briefly muttered his name outside the building that time and she had darted off anyway. He glanced at his watch. "Looks like my ten minutes is up. And it's my dime. Or the BBC's, I should say."

He made to kiss her goodbye but she recoiled. "Wait, I've got something for you. It's why I came." She presented him with what looked like an envelope. Closer inspection revealed that it was a page of handwritten parchment, folded and sealed. The seal was made of black wax with an imprint '1313'.

"What this?" he asked, taken aback.

"I don't know. Renka told me to look in your pigeonhole."

"I have a pigeonhole?"

"In the foyer. There's an ingress in the wall behind every chair. Yours is behind Florian Mollien's chair."

"Really?" he asked suspiciously. He recalled Josie saying that he couldn't touch the chairs but he was yet to test her theory: that part of the foyer with the chairs had the same unwelcome chill he experienced with his alcove. "How did you find the recess? Did you pull the chair out?"

She had a puzzled expression. "I'm not sure really." She

frowned as she gave the question some thought. "No, I just knelt down and reached for the letter. The ingress is virtually at the floor: the chair puts it into shadow, which is probably why you haven't seen it." It had been a pleasure to run Renka's errand this morning; anything to get her back inside that wonderfully elegant building, her literary inspiration fleetingly returning. Her eyes creased; perhaps she *had* tried to pull away the chair. Something was telling her that it was the obvious thing to do…

Kris broke the seal and unfolded the paper.

"Who's it from?" she asked.

He sighed with exasperation as he read the signature. "Saint-Just," he replied.

She didn't answer immediately. Shortly she smiled. "What … *the* Saint-Just?"

"The very same. It's dated ten Thermidor, the day he died: 28 July, 1794."

"I'm impressed."

He shifted again, not knowing where that information had come from but supposing he must have read it somewhere. Either that or he was spending too much time in the company of Mason Flower. He handed her the letter, which was in French. "Can you translate that for me?"

She took the letter. "To answer your question," she read, "I go bravely." She looked up. "I don't understand…"

He froze momentarily. "I asked him how he met his death," he muttered.

"Asked who? Saint-Just?"

"It doesn't matter. What else does it say?"

She returned to the letter. "And to answer your second question: it was both the people and the church who moved against me, shrouded black with lies and fear."

He regarded her with an ironic grin, then took back the letter. "That was clever of them," he muttered.

"Clever of who?"

"The people and the church: the pawn and the bishop. Shrouded black. The network want me to move either the black pawn or the black bishop."

"People and church…?"

"This is the real Saint-Just," he said.

"What?"

"I'm telling you, the Goof will check this against his handwriting and confirm it. I *know* it."

"Oh … rubbish!"

"They wouldn't send me a fake, Fabrienne. They're serious people. They know I'll check it out."

"But how…?"

"They've probably got loads of stuff like this. Whatever Gathering is, it was around in Revolutionary France and knew a lot of people. You wouldn't believe the number of contacts in my address book." He paused. "This only means something to me because I've just texted Saint-Just and I'm thinking about enemy bishops and pawns: Saint-Just was obviously referring literally to the people and the church when he wrote this, but it just so happens that with a contextual leap the letter fits." He looked down the road, momentarily sharing Fabrienne's paranoia. "They must have boxes of letters if they can afford to give them away like this."

She looked at him aghast, then took the letter again, this time with reverence. She noticed the discolourations on the parchment, perhaps caused by sweat, or tears.

"I'll get the Goof to check it out, of course," he said, "but I'd bet my life it's genuine."

"I revel … in my flesh…"

They both looked around to find the source of the voice, one that belonged to a frail old man.

"I *revel* in my flesh."

The voice was more assertive. Kris's eyes widened in recognition as he reached for his mobile. "It's a call," he said. "It looks like Renka Tamirov," he added, the display throbbing with the friendly country parson, "but that's not her ringtone."

"No, she just laughs," Fabrienne agreed, with a tremor of fear.

"Does she?" he muttered, recalling that her ringtone had something to do with 'eyes'. "The voice sounds like her boss, Ovenstone. But it can't be a move: the other bishop *can't* move, it's got pawns in front..."

"I REVEL in my FLESH!"

Kris touched the display, but there was no move: the white bishop on the far rank flashed without moving.

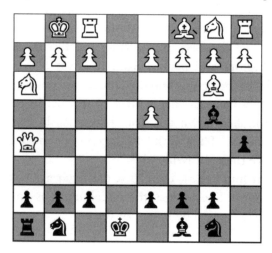

"Mr Ovenstone?" he asked.

"Capet," the old man whispered in response.

There was a pause.

"Can I help you?" Kris asked.

"It seems you are more intent on obstructing us."

"I don't understand."

"My chess piece is blocked. Is it your wish that I put down roots, Capet?"

"You can do pretty much whatever you want, I'm guessing."

"But this is *your* future, not ours."

Kris didn't reply.

"You prefer the counsel of Saint-Just, perhaps?"

"Yeah, nice trick. You must have gone through quite a few boxes to come up with that one."

Kris now heard the man's breath.

"Oh, I see. You believe that letter was written two hundred years ago, and stored away just for today?"

Kris nodded, but something bad and undigested was floating around in his stomach; Chelsea had insisted that he had accessed the *real* Bonaparte.

"I have another letter you might be interested in."

"Another?"

"It is in front of me, in fact: I wonder what your BBC dignitaries would make of it?"

"Go on…" he said cautiously.

"This is very high up: from the Committee of Public Safety and signed by Robespierre himself. Your Goof friend will confirm its authenticity."

Kris swallowed with premonition. "What does it say?"

"It discusses the Desault letter you acquired, deliberating on why the doctor needed to be murdered…"

"Well that's great! I need to tell…"

"While resolving that the committee, after due deliberation, prefers the Beatles to the Rolling Stones."

Kris looked as if he had been slapped. "You're telling me all these documents are fakes?"

"I'm telling you to banish any thoughts of leaving us, Capet. If you wish to leave, do so now as the failure you came in. Leave the stage and your ludicrous tutor, who I don't even honour with a name, and tell Man-suit that you're taking an early retirement." He gave a tedious sigh above the rustle of papers being pushed aside. "In the meantime, while you're pondering on your future, my colleague is expecting you this afternoon at the BBC offices. As your agent she will help you through this difficult time."

"Help me with what?"

"The police wish to question you over the disappearance of Josie Hannah."

"Josie Hannah…?" Kris returned, but the call was terminated.

"What's the matter?" Fabrienne asked.

Kris didn't reply. The display was still lit and for the first time since he had last seen Josie, he accessed the address book. He moaned mentally as it appeared.

Lisa Man-suit
The Goof
Fabrienne
Little Tommy Snoop
Second Trustee of Temple 1313
The Baptist
The guest of The Perfumery

The guest of The Chess Room
Josephine
Rufus Ovenstone

Kris considered the list for a while. In order to delay the inevitable he accessed the new name first, Rufus Ovenstone, to find nothing in the name or the parson icon. He returned to the address book with a crestfallen expression.

"Kris?"

"I think she's dead," he said. The black queen icon was upside down.

"Dead? What do you mean?"

"I *knew* she was dead. Deep down, for all that American lawyer bullshit, I knew it. They've killed her." He accessed Josephine, then frowned. The epitaph read:

But behold! Her heart still beats.

XXVII

An intervention

R ENKA'S MANNER DURING the interview at the BBC made him feel as if it was taking place under caution in the cells.

She's even making me believe that I'm guilty, Kris thought, as the plain-clothed CID detective looked with surprise at his notes as another question was closed down by the Russian.

This is another message, just like old Ovenstone's fake letter this morning. That they can destroy me.

But these were secondary observations. His primary concern, trumping even the police investigation, was the realisation that Josie Hannah was, most certainly, dead.

The detective had explained he was working with the Los Angeles police in attempting to ascertain the whereabouts of the movie star, who had disappeared along with her bodyguard and agent during a short holiday in Cardiff. When Kris corrected him, saying that the BBC was in contact with her US lawyers, the detective shook his head. It appeared that whoever was responsible for the actress's disappearance had put up a cover story through a fictional firm of LA attorneys.

Fictional?

The law firm didn't exist: the construct had been rattling off numerous complaints and inquiries on behalf of its client Ms Hannah. Why? Because it delayed her being registered as missing.

Kris accepted this information with a blank expression.

Renka, sitting next to him, was eyeing the detective with bored disdain.

So was Josie Hannah dead?

All they knew was that she had disappeared, but she had recently been questioned in connection with a death: a film journalist in The City Plaza. When Kris mentioned he had read about that, the detective confirmed it was initially believed to be some sort of macabre suicide, though Hannah's disappearance had prompted them to reopen the case.

"On insistence of American police," Renka remarked.

The detective paused, in confused bewilderment at yet another jab, then returned to his notes. "Yes that's correct," he muttered.

"They call you incompetent. They say no one kill themself with spike in eyes."

The detective smiled, pretending to take this in good part. "As I said, Miss Tamirov, it's the disappearance of Josie Hannah that makes Singer's death suspicious."

"Why are you questioning *me*?" Kris asked, again making an apologetic face for his agent.

"We're questioning everyone she was in contact with during her time in Cardiff." The detective shook his head as Kris made to speak. "I appreciate you wouldn't have met her, Mr Knight, but as I understand it you're involved in a play, a television drama, in which she expressed an interest. Ms Buoys talked to her agent."

"Yes … yes, that's right."

"Is there anything you can tell me about that?"

"What do you want to know exactly?" Kris asked guardedly.

The detective gave him a quizzical look. "Well you tell me. What was the play about, for example?"

"Confidential," Renka broke in.

Kris sighed with exasperation. "I'm sorry, officer, but my agent is right. It *is* confidential, though if it helps I can tell you that it's a historical dramatised documentary."

The detective's expression inquired as to what all the fuss was about. "Can you tell me the part Josie Hannah was going to play?"

Kris turned to Renka again, who shrugged with boredom. "The Dauphin's sister." Kris said, turning back to the officer.

"Dauphin?"

"Yeah, son of Louis the Sixteenth. Look, I really don't think this is relevant. It's just a play with an interesting historical twist based on some new research."

This didn't satisfy the detective. "It's relevant in that it seems odd that an A-rated actress out of Hollywood would involve herself in a small local production."

"It's the BBC," Kris replied, smarting at the inference. "And she was also Welsh."

"Was?"

"I mean ... *is.*"

The detective carefully wrote something on his pad, paused, then underlined something he had written.

"Did you meet her, Mr Knight?" he asked casually.

"Don't answer that," Renka said.

The detective put his pen down. "I think you *will* answer it," he said.

Several wheels turned frantically in Kris's head. In the moments allowed to him he tried to remember who had seen him speaking to Josie: where he had been, who had been watching; all the threads of his existence that led him to the movie star; that led her to Gathering.

"Mr Knight?"

"No," he replied.

Almost immediately after the meeting concluded, Kris became desperately hungry. He raced home, the mobile inviting a call to Mason.

They ate pizza in silence in Gathering's L-shaped dining room. Eventually Mason asked him what his crazy app was.

Kris didn't answer, instead considering his crusts. He had asked Mason to bring three large pizzas, encouraged by Fabrienne's remark that Chelsea's eating habits were erratic: perhaps he now had a camel's digestive system which would allow him to stock up for days. He was disappointed, barely managing a few slices before he became unpleasantly full; he would need Mason again very soon.

"Who's Goof?" Mason asked, when his question about the app was ignored.

"Hmmm?"

"That app you use, when you ring me," Mason clarified.

"What do you mean?"

"I mean it's the first app I've seen which affects someone *else's* mobile. How does it do that?"

"Mason, what are you talking about?"

"The ringtone."

"What about it?"

Mason chuckled. "It sounds like your voice and it says, 'Hey Goof!' It gets louder and angrier. How did you do that?"

Kris cleared his throat uncomfortably: he had assumed the voices only worked on Gathering's mobiles. "Believe me, Mason, it's not mine. It's this crazy network that I'm connected up to."

His hunger satisfied, the melancholy returned. Josie and her entourage had been killed on the night he had taken them up in the lift and a sickening deduction told him that the water in the foyer that night might not have been maintenance at all, rather a means of the building losing the evidence: of washing out the blood.

My poor Josephine. My beautiful black queen…

"Kris? You okay?"

Kris nodded. He considered his mobile, on his lap in case Mason should try to reach for it; it was still lit. "There's someone I've got to see, but I want Fabrienne to be there too." He paused, thoughtfully. "Actually, it's *your* mate, that Honeyman guy. Maybe you'd like to come as well? More heads the better."

Mason nodded but wasn't really listening. He was considering the thirteen framed wall portraits, having noticed they were all painted by the same artist.

"Mason?"

Mason started. "Thure, whatever you say."

Kris called Fabrienne. When she answered, a thought occurred.

"Fabrienne, do I have a strange ringtone?"

She laughed quietly. "Don't you know?"

"No, Mason just told me. So what is it?"

"I won't embarrass you if your friend is there."

Kris groaned. "God, don't know what you must have thought of me," he said, imagining the possibilities.

"Don't worry, all Gathering ringtones work that way."

"All of them?" he asked at length.

"I'm guessing the software records your speaking voice, then synthesises it somehow."

He accepted this theory with a tick of dissatisfaction, the

call from the French actress having been a handbell, not a voice, but he felt too exhausted to raise the inconsistency. He mentally prepared himself for his journey back to the foyer, the prospect making his bones ache. "Anyway," he said wearily, "I'm going to see the minister again. Will you come?"

Honeyman was found in one of the tourist restaurants, struggling with a rather sloppy bolognese. When he noticed the three people standing outside he immediately got up and went to the door, leaving a safe amount of cash to the surprise of the waiter. Without speaking, attending only to his beard with a serviette, he beckoned them to follow. He didn't speak until they were in his studio.

"He only has milky tea, I think," Kris whispered to Fabrienne.

"Indeed," Honeyman called from the kitchen, returning shortly with four mugs and a sugar bowl on a tray. The three visitors took the mugs, the minister's brusque sense of purpose making it inappropriate to raise any objection to his choice of beverage. He beckoned for the three of them to sit on his camp bed, but only Mason accepted the invitation, the bed easily managing his small frame. Kris and Fabrienne chose the floor.

Kris was admiring the new large poster that occupied another wall of the studio. It was a schematic of the chess game prepared with great care, the pieces hand-drawn with meticulous detail, the squares neat and measured. Each of the pieces he had described had a face. It must have taken the minister hours, perhaps the attention to such detail helping him to concentrate.

"Your game, as it presently stands?" Honeyman asked the room.

Kris nodded, sipping his tea in appreciation of the effort. He leaned closer as he noticed Honeyman had anticipated the taking of black queen by white castle.

"Black to move?" Honeyman pressed.

"Yeah, but how did you know the black queen would be taken?"

Honeyman turned to the diagram, though he had studied it long enough that it was branded on his memory. As if in answer to the question, he said, "So are you ready to accept you need help? An intervention, to use the addict's phrase?"

There was a long silence. Fabrienne looked at Kris with concern, Mason with confusion.

"Yeah," Kris said eventually. He played with his shoes, shaking his head with bewilderment at his admission. He was giving up so much...

"The beautiful actress is dead, I take it," Honeyman said quietly. He took something out of the pocket of his overcoat, then folded the overcoat and laid it on the floor. "Yes," he sighed, returning to the diagram.

Fabrienne considered the photograph of the open door of The Pavilion with suspicion. "Honeyman, who *are* you?" she asked. "Who are you *really*?"

Mason looked from the woman to the minister with an increasing sense of mystification, then returned to the schematic.

"That doesn't matter," Honeyman answered. "All you need to know is that the coven has selected me as their nemesis; that I've been tasked to hunt them, which they consider to be a test of their faith. For that reason they can't kill me, though they take great delight in wounding me whenever I trespass."

"Trespass?" Fabrienne asked.

Honeyman hesitated, thoughtfully. "Is it still Fabrienne, or Vaishali?" he inquired.

"Fabrienne," she snapped.

Honeyman nodded once more. "The Trustees believe themselves holy, Fabrienne. They have no worldly ambition: they are far more complicated that. They have rules. One rule is that their places of worship, their temples, cannot be desecrated: the intrusion of someone who is uninvited *is* such a desecration." He paused. "Tom Singer, Josie Hannah, both died for that reason."

Fabrienne glanced coolly at Kris. He had reluctantly brought her up to speed with Singer's involvement when they had a debriefing earlier in the Fiesta in its usual parking place, the space he had started to think she had rented. He had shrugged off her frosty "Anything else I should know?"

"But Singer didn't enter the building," Kris said. "Not even the foyer. He tried to, but I didn't let him in." Fabrienne nodded, recalling the meeting she had overheard as she hugged the wall.

"But he trespassed nevertheless," Honeyman replied simply. "Like a spy, he secretly photographed Ms London's *own* photographs of her salon." His fist flexed once more. "I tried to warn him. Perhaps I should have been more forceful, though that would only have strengthened the temple's hold over him, I think." He seemed to be speaking to himself. "I need to be careful; my interference, no matter how well-intentioned, has cost people dearly in the past." He nodded slowly to himself.

"There was nothing clandestine about Josie," Kris remarked. "The Trustees knew she was coming. They even seemed to encourage it."

"Yet she wasn't invited," Honeyman remarked. "She used

wiles and pressure to get inside the building. As I've said, the Trustees are bound by rules, but they take great pleasure in interpreting them in their favour."

"What do you mean?" Kris asked.

The minister shook his head, his expression becoming grave. "Do you really believe the building will let you leave? You have enjoyed its gifts, witnessed its abominations. It has a claim over you now."

"A claim?" Fabrienne muttered.

"Mr Knight wouldn't be able to just walk out of the door. That's impossible now."

"Why not?" Mason asked.

"No, he's right," Kris murmured. He tried to imagine himself living without the building, without the mobile, and couldn't visualise it. Like a drunk at his first meeting at Alcoholic Anonymous mourning a frosty beer, he thought of that recent moment of exhilaration on the Chapter stage. He should just get up and leave; this was all a waste of time...

"It's not too late, Mr Knight," Honeyman said in a loud voice. "You need all your strength now."

Kris gasped and closed his eyes. When he opened them, he looked up sheepishly. "It's Kris," he said.

"Kris," Honeyman repeated, with a smile.

"Honeyman, I've seen thirteen portraits in the dining room," Mason said. "Are these the same people Kris and I have been writing about? Chapter Emile?"

"What remained of the chapter, yes." Honeyman glanced at the window. "Chapter Emile was conceived in misguided principles of equality, but its midwife was violence. There, in that place entrusted to the émigrés by the Welsh priests, the violence, the madness, continued."

"What happened?" Mason asked, his knees shaking.

Honeyman hesitated to answer. "Torture and murder, Mason. The horrific crimes that give the building its power, that created the chains for you and Fabrienne."

"I just take Kris pizza!" Mason protested.

"That will change, Mason. Your fascination with the building will grow, as will your fascination with the salon's host, Florian Mollien. You will begin to want what he wanted."

Fabrienne's eyes widened as she looked at the floor.

Kris shook his head. "Look, I just want to know how I can get out of the place." He considered the chess diagram with a frown. "Get out, without going to prison, starving to death, or being bumped off by that crazy Russian," he clarified.

Honeyman regrouped, feeling Gracie's figurine throb, warning that he had said too much. He stepped back to observe the diagram from a distance. "The answer is in the chess game, I'm sure of it." His head tilted slightly as he considered his handiwork. "The game brought you in; it will bring you out."

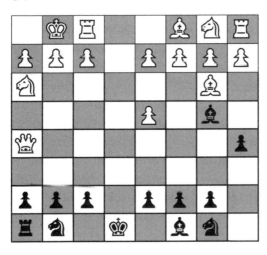

"Who's black and who's white?" Mason asked. Kris had brought him quickly up to speed with the mechanics of the chess game.

"Black is most definitely the enemy," Honeyman said to Mason, "but you must remember it is Gathering's game, so the terms 'friends' and 'enemies' are misleading. I'm an enemy, for example. And from Kris's description, the game isn't as straightforward as winning or losing. Kris moves pieces on both sides, while there are pieces he can never move: the test is whether he has control over them. Also, there are events in this game that appear to have their own relevance." On the chart he indicated Mason's pawn. "You took the BBC, Mason, which coincided with the BBC confirming the contract for the dramatisation. The dramatisation that will make Kris famous very quickly," he added.

"*Took* the BBC?" Mason asked.

"With your authentication of the documents and your screenplay. The chess game recognised your importance from the outset: your importance to Kris's career. Perhaps that's why your pawn is the *king's* pawn."

Mason nodded slowly with a mix of wonder and exhilaration, while Kris eyed the diagram with grim resentment; Fabrienne still had her eyes on the floor. "So how do I get out?" Kris asked.

With a grumble of reflection Honeyman brought out his notebook. "I mentioned the game has specific events. Every move has been significant..." and he presented his notebook to give a physical illustration of his thought processes "...but without doubt the most significant to date has been *castling*."

"Right," Kris agreed. "That's when I moved in."

"Exactly. The white king swapped places with the white castle..."

"Which represents The Chess Room?" Kris asked.

Honeyman paused and tapped the white castle. "No," he decided. "You said it had the number thirteen thirteen, so I think it represents the entire building. The temple. Remember that Josie's black queen threatened that piece when she was trying to take Chelsea's room. And..." he tapped the castle again "...I suspect it is the building itself that has *taken* Josie and her friends, just as Renka's bishop has *taken* the journalist."

There was another silence as they considered the chart and absorbed this information, the word 'taken' dissolving maliciously in their imagination.

"Okay...?" Kris said eventually.

Honeyman turned to him and winked. "So, I have an idea," he said. He tapped the black king and the black king's castle. "What if *black* castles?"

Honeyman didn't need to explain the rules of castling: an excited Mason did that for him. A king could swap with the castle provided the king hadn't already moved or been placed into check, or if castling wouldn't put the king into check.

"So, we move the black knight to set up the castling," Honeyman declared. "If we move the knight here..." and he scribbled its new location "...then it prevents white stopping the castling by putting the king immediately into check, whether it be with its castle or queen." From under the camp bed he produced a smaller photocopied chart which showed the potential moves. He wasn't sure what white's move would be, but outlined the option with the white castle.

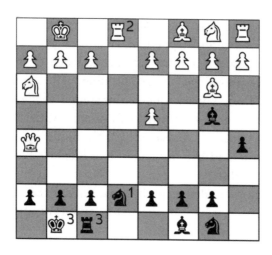

Mason studied the new diagram. "That's good, Honeyman: black bishop also protects the knight if they decide to take it. But they can still put the king in check before he castles. The queen or bishop takes bishop's pawn." He sprung up from the bed and put a finger on the black pawn three squares from the left.

"Right," Kris agreed, shaking his head despondently.

"I think not." Honeyman's eyes darkened. "Taking a pawn would be murder and no one else has trespassed. Remember the rules." He nodded, but to himself, to satisfy himself that his logic was watertight. He had made such deductions before with the coven, to find nothing but pain.

Kris briefly considered Fabrienne, wondering why she was so quiet. She didn't acknowledge him as she looked suspiciously at the wall diagram.

"Okay, I get it," Kris said, breaking himself away from Fabrienne and returning to Honeyman. "But what does it mean? So *what* if black castles?"

Mason answered for him. "It's a reverse castle," he said, his eyes widening. He blushed as he noticed the room looking at him. "I mean … I mean…"

"Our history professor is absolutely correct," Honeyman confirmed. "Remember that the temple works on ironic logic. If white castling is moving *in*, then black castling is…"

"Moving *out*."

It was Fabrienne who spoke. She continued to look sullenly at the wall, oblivious to the others.

Honeyman tapped the black king. "That's my theory, yes."

The room was silent for a time.

"But who's black knight?" Mason asked at length. "And how do we move it?"

With Mason still hovering by the chart, Honeyman took this opportunity of sitting down on the camp bed. He was tired now and it creaked under his weight. "Your mobile phone. Will you show it to me?"

Without hesitation, Kris shook his head. Out of the corner of his eye he noticed Fabrienne briefly shake her head too.

Honeyman seemed unsurprised by this response. "Is there anything in the building that makes you feel … how can I put it? … as if you are travelling?"

Kris shrugged. "The journey in the lift always exhausts me. I feel like I'm breaking through some kind of barrier."

Honeyman nodded thoughtfully. "And what about software, in your mobile? The mobile is the method by which the building travels with you outside."

"The latch," Kris confirmed. "Anyway, that's what Chelsea calls it. It's a sort of door key: it makes the mobile an interactive experience. That's how I met Madame Claudine: the novelist who used to occupy Chelsea's room. Or rather some actress playing her, pretending to burn herself with acid."

Fabrienne twitched at hearing this further piece of information he had concealed from her.

"Why do you call it a door key?"

"The app only appeared when I used the thumb latch to open the door to the salon. The first time I went there, Fabrienne opened the door." He flashed a smile at Fabrienne, which she didn't acknowledge.

Honeyman's eyes went to the ceiling. "That's it," he said eventually. "That's the pulse."

"Pulse?" Mason asked with a bemused smile, breaking away with difficulty from the chart. The dynamics of the chess game were fascinating him. "Seems like an odd description."

Honeyman's eyes landed on Fabrienne. He spoke directly to her, though the question was for Kris.

"Who do you think black knight and black king represent?"

"It's me," Kris answered immediately, having given this a lot of thought. "Black is the old me, white the new."

"But why a knight and a king? Why not just one piece?"

"The knight is like my legs; the king is what I have to protect. Sort of attack and defence."

Honeyman nodded with raised eyebrows. "Do you think that's correct?" he asked Fabrienne.

The woman slowly shook her head. At length she looked at the diagram.

"The knight is your life on earth," she murmured. "The king your immortal soul."

XXVIII

Locking up

T O THOSE IMPERVIOUS to the illusion generated by the memories of the thirteen émigrés, the hosts to the salon, the building was a cold ruin. The bronze foyer was now a grimy brown, the chairs torn and mouldy, their cushions homes for bugs, the hidden candles in the ceiling recesses stubs of wax.

There was no other light source in the foyer – except for the peek of the sun from the upper windowed floors, the illusion of light within the building's imagination. Renka, as a dispassionate caretaker, led Mr Ovenstone carefully through the semi-darkness with a gentle hand on his shoulder.

At the far wall she found the severed body parts of Mikey and Erika, which she bundled into black bags and placed in the cage lift. These were the bodies the building imagined it had rinsed out, which in fact had been severed in two with the razor-sharp scythe fitted to the bars of the cage lift like some Aztec temple trap.

The cage lift was an iron platform with a wheel mechanism, operated manually to pull it vertically on coil ropes. The mechanism was well-made but time and rust had made it stiff, requiring vigorous winding. Renka, unlike most who twisted and strained as they imagined the lift miraculously rising, turned it effortlessly with one hand.

The black bags were destined for the top floor, to the bricked-up rooms reserved for trespassers. Every coven temple had such a place, be it a room or a pit, and here the building was unable to maintain the illusion of graceful opulence, the decay being apparent to all. For that reason Mr Ovenstone particularly enjoyed this section of the building, studying the portraits while Renka opened a section of the wall, brick by careful brick, until she was able to step through.

This was in fact the only place where Mr Ovenstone was able to picture the building as the wondrous, tranquil affair it once had been, when the émigrés were attended to on their every whim. As they sat in the foyer, drugged to delirium, actors would come and play out their works, or debate their theories; thirteen disillusioned artists and scientists, their egos now fattened like foie gras with the amour propre created through the adoration of others. So they were each given their own Emile: a baby brought to the building and raised to know nothing of the world but the host and his or her craft.

Renka would leave the wall undone because her next trip was to The Perfumery, a dark, rotting shell of a room bearing the evidence of a longstanding resident blissfully unaware there was no plumbing. Chelsea, believing it to be a playfully opulent salon, wouldn't see the eyeless body of Josie Hannah, certain she had been sucked into the wall mirror. The mirror was unaffected by time and decay: it was a window into Hell, which even the Trustees dared not look upon.

Though she was dead, Josie's heart still beat inside her corpse, her neck, temple and wrists occasionally pulsing with the cold blood being pumped through her cadaver. It was a feature of this particular temple, where the original crime's signature was the ritual removal of a heart, that no human heart could perish inside these walls.

Renka effortlessly pulled Josie over the shoulder, great strength a gift given to all junior Trustees, and stepped around the elegant bookcase that contained the original manuscripts of Claudine de Tour du Pin's novels. Claudine was here herself, her bones and still-beating heart stored in jars of varying sizes that served as bookends; every host's earthly remains remained with the object of their creative desire.

This was the reason nothing could leave this room, except for The Perfumery's preserved heart. This heart was pickled in vinegar in remembrance of the Dauphin, the inspiration for Chapter Emile, now the source of the building's power; that allowed the building to remember.

"You're coming back?" Chelsea asked.

"Of course. Time to lock up," Renka replied.

Chelsea nodded cautiously, her belongings, such as they were, in a suitcase near the door. In her hands was the heart of Madame Claudine's devotee, which pulsed as if it was alive. To Chelsea it appeared as a portable object of communication, for being pickled it could endure for a time outside the building, though it always yearned to return.

Josie found her resting place with her entourage on the top floor, Renka wading through the skeletons as she progressed through the walled-up rooms, ribcages bottling hearts so numerous that their collective thumps were a faint murmur. Before the bricks were replaced, she collected her tools: half-a-dozen wooden boards, around two dozen long iron nails, and the square stone which had been adopted by the Trustees over the centuries as a crude hammer.

"Have patience, we'll lock you all up in time," Mr Ovenstone said to the portraits as he heard her emerge, the likenesses having been taken on their deathbeds when they were told what awaited them. The bricks would go back in place once the holy ritual of locking up was completed, the hammer stone thrown back into the room to be found in later years by their successors.

Ovenstone turned from the portraits to smile approvingly at the observance of the ritual. This was of one of the coven's earliest temples, numbered 1313 because of its thirteen émigrés, and it had begun in France. Welsh priests had infiltrated a chapter seeking to decant the Dauphin's personality, pure and marinated with royal essence, through torture and experimental surgery, to establish the existence of the Rousseau core of being. The *soul*, that would reverse the tide of atheism in French society and, as a by-product, bring some long overdue divine fortune to its members.

Renka waited patiently for Mr Ovenstone to acknowledge her, then they both turned in the direction of the lift. Mr Ovenstone didn't look back at the portraits, though he basked in the intensity of their eyes as they followed him with futile longing. Safely removed to this building while the French chapter was being hunted down, the priests had declared that the experiments would continue, but there was no more talk of God. It was the Father, the only deity to be trusted, who would help them, in return for a small token of their commitment.

"Are we leaving now?" Chelsea asked as the Trustees returned, getting up from her grey chaise longue to the vapour of dust and the irritation of fleas. Renka didn't answer, carefully laying the boards and the nails on the floor outside the room as if she were studying a complex instruction sheet. Chelsea went to the suitcase which contained only the possessions she had brought with her when she moved in forty years ago; clothes that no longer fitted and toiletries and cosmetics long gone bad. She had never been sure why she had kept them, though in recent weeks she had come to treasure them, the few mementos of her life before Gathering. "I can leave? And Madame Claudine will stay?"

"You want to leave, Feather Lady?" Mr Ovenstone inquired, using the name he had given her forty years ago when he had spotted her potential in a London burlesque bar. Even then, as she flirted with the punters for tips, she had the embittered weight of circumstance in her eyes.

Chelsea nodded, summoning her courage. Her relationship with this building had been a lifelong addiction to a drug a hundred times stronger than heroin; something that had cost her family, her friends, and eventually her sanity. "I just want to be free of her now. To retire and live somewhere alone, to enjoy my success," she added, though not really caring about success at all. She had changed in the last few days; she felt as if she was coming out of a mental coma.

"Ungrateful," Renka remarked. "Claudine reason you success. You failure, you *nothing* without her."

Mr Ovenstone coughed a laugh into his bony, liver-spotted hand as he stood at the windows, attempting unsuccessfully to look through the grime-smeared glass. "Do you really think you could bring yourself to leave, Feather Lady?"

Chelsea turned to him with a face of concern. "No, I *can* leave. Not before, perhaps, but, but now." She took a breath of horrified realisation. "I don't even want my career anymore. Not really. No, no, I don't, I really don't. Just want to rest. I'm so tired, Mr Ovenstone. Tired, tired, tired…" She put her mobile carefully on the floor, where it pulsed for a while with energy. Eventually she shook her head and picked it up.

"It ending soon," Renka confirmed, noting with approval the fact that Chelsea was unable to be separated from the preserved heart. "New tenant moving in. Locking up now."

Chelsea suspiciously eyed the Russian, then the boards in the corridor. "When?"

Renka paused, thoughtfully. "You have been hearing handbell recently?" she asked. "The ta-ding ta-ding."

"Yes," Chelsea whispered. "That's her ring. I heard it first during that interview, in The New Theatre."

Renka nodded. "That ringing means Claudine waking up." She looked at the floor, to the rooms below. "She waking up *now*."

★

"Can't you just move the piece?" Fabrienne asked. She was standing a little distance behind Kris, both looking into the alcove.

"I honestly don't know," he admitted, all too aware of the power the physical representation of the game exercised over his subconscious.

"I don't understand."

Moving the black knight would set up the reverse castle. Furthermore, the knight would protect the king, preventing a check which would stop the castling. It was not a move Gathering would wish him to make.

"Kris?"

A deep breath took him a long step into the alcove, his eyes blurring around the image of the black knight, a turbaned cavalryman snarling his charge. He took another breath, his vision deliberately keeping the piece out of focus as he reached for it.

He snatched his hand back as Fabrienne let out a yelp. The Turk's head had snapped up to look at them; its eyes were rolling in consternation and warning.

"Oh God what made it do that?" Fabrienne whimpered, her hand at her mouth. She yelped again as the lights in the room quickly dimmed.

Kris stepped out of the alcove. "Sorry, not going to do it."

"What?"

"I mean I'm not going to do it this way." He took out his mobile. "I can't do it this way," he clarified. He sighed with relief, finding the display lit. "Honeyman said I've got to use the latch to get in."

"Get in? Get in to what?"

His thumb hovered over the icon of the thumb latch. "The knight's an important piece in this game. It represents a part of me. How did you describe it? The knight is my life, the king my soul?" He hesitated. "What made you say that?"

She considered this awhile. "I just knew the answer to the question," she said at length.

"You were quiet the whole time. What was wrong?" He was contemplating the display as a reluctant swimmer stands at the edge of a high diving board.

She sighed. "I just had this huge sense of foreboding. As

if I was about to be given a big gift of knowledge that was going to change my life. I was excited and frightened at the same time." She shook her head with confusion. "It was as if everything he was saying was dragging me somewhere; somewhere I wanted to go, but I didn't."

"You understand I have to get out?" he asked again. "That we both have to get out? Before it's too late…"

"We've got no choice, have we?"

He nodded, noting that the icon of the app had gone a deathly grey. "If white knight is my life, is black knight my death?"

"I don't think so, Kris."

"How can you be sure?"

Her voice was vaguely trance-like, her words collected from a store of lethargy. In fact she hadn't been herself, had been quiet and distant, since they had left the minister. "The white knight represents more than just earthly life. It represents a life where you're successful; famous, where you've … completed yourself."

He returned to the display, thinking that Renka had used the same word: *completed*… "So black knight is just…" he smirked ironically, "…well, it's just me, isn't it? The real me, I mean. The jerk. The loser. The nobody."

"Don't say that, Kris. It's not true."

"Isn't it?"

"No, it's just what Gathering wants you to believe."

In the mounted Moor he glimpsed his future life outside Gathering: moving on to a menial job; all sense of creative ambition slowly fading; getting older, the aspirations eventually no more than the folly of youth.

With a startled blink, he also heard the laughter of the Trustees at his tiny human dilemma. Then he felt the malice of the temple walls closing in, in its obscene power the building not even wishing to pretend anymore that it was anything other than a prison.

With an air of annoyed courage he pressed the latch.

This time there was no scramble of bricks that walled him up in a dark room; no writing bureaus or other physical representations of the mobile's software. In fact, he was still in his salon and at first thought nothing had changed. But he was aware that he had the power to move the black knight.

He touched the chess piece and his disappointment and failure rushed through the skin, into his veins. It filled up his arm, making it numb and heavy with regret.

"Mon amour…"

He turned. Fabrienne was dressed in the white finery of Claudine de Tour du Pin, one of her white slippers bearing an acid burn. A veil covered the right side of her face, red lava veins under the lace. She smelled of almonds.

"Déplacez la pièce, mon amour," she whispered.

Move the piece, my love…

"Fabrienne?" he said. "Is that you?"

In answer, she slowly raised her arm and pointed at the Turk. The automaton was studying the board in its normal poise, its glass eyes somewhere on the third rank, but the board was shaking. Kris touched its edge, then realised that it wasn't the board that was moving, but the Turk, or something inside the Turk. The tremor was working through its hand, into the cushion.

"Florian!" Fabrienne declared ecstatically. "Florian est venu!"

Florian has come…

The ebony porcelain skin began to crack. The head split in two, the wig sliding off, then the arms and torso cracked. The skull and skeleton of someone small, though with a beating heart, was revealed inside the automaton: for a moment it stood preserved in shock, as if it still had its sinews, then dropped to the floor.

Kris closed his eyes to remove the scene, then opened them.

A whimper came from inside the Turk's cabinet. It was followed by muttering. It was the voice of a young French boy.

The boy now hammered at the cabinet, before a shrill adult voice silenced him.

The scene changed, the door of the cabinet swinging open merely to show the artificial gears. The little boy reciting Florian Mollien's algebraic mantras, the theories that made the chess master unbeatable, was gone. He was down in the foyer, on the floor before the thirteen, drugged and masked. The boy was grown now, a young man aged before his time.

Kris felt his stomach turn as he saw the young man's heart being removed, to be handed still beating to one of the masks with grey, wrinkled hands. He recognised the small purple taffeta coat with silver embroidery from his wardrobe.

"With this token of devotion from the world," the priest had said, "you will return to fulfil your destiny, Florian Mollien."

Kris closed his eyes again. When he opened them, the child was locked in the cabinet, barely a toddler now.

"Aidez-moi, Papa Florian. Aidez-moi!"

With a shiver of disgust, Kris moved the black knight.

The display was illuminated when he opened his eyes. The Turk and the room were back to normal, but the black knight had moved. The mobile's schematic mirrored the configuration of the board.

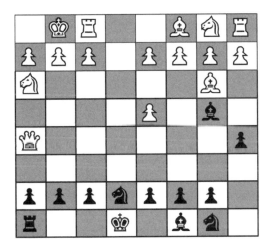

He wasn't sure whether he had been sleeping, but he was on the floor. Fabrienne was prone too, her hands in her hair. She was looking at him.

"Did you pass out too?" he muttered.

"I don't know," she moaned.

"I've done it. I've moved the knight. They can't stop the reverse castle now." His eyes widened as he realised that both of them were naked. She gave a shy smile as she saw his look of recognition.

"How did we...?"

"It doesn't matter," she whispered. She inched closer. "Now move *me*..."

He groaned with pleasure, swallowing her with his eyes.

"Let's finish this, Kris." She kissed her finger and planted it on one of his eyelids. "I'm tired of waiting. Tired of their games. We've done it. We can leave. So move me."

He touched the right side of her face. She flinched but resisted her natural impulse to pull away. "Don't, Kris," she implored.

"It's okay. Trust me, it's okay."

He could feel her shaking as he gently pulled back her hair. He kissed his finger, and with it he touched her blistered scars.

It took several finger kisses before her body eventually relaxed. He felt the resigned surrender in her muscles.

"It's been ... years," she admitted.

"Forget the past, Fabrienne."

"D'you think that's possible? I mean, really?"

His fingertip now dabbed the little wells of tears in her eyes.

"Move me," she repeated, as they reached for each other.

XXIX

Waking up

MASON HAD STAYED in Honeyman's studio after Kris and Fabrienne had left, shyly accepting the offer of another mug of tea. He was now on his fourth mug, the minister's trip to the kitchenette, the sound of the steam kettle, the mug returned to his waiting hands, prompting a twinge of déjà vu.

"Do you do that a lot?" Honeyman remarked as he sat on the camp bed, referring to the confused blink of Mason's eyes as he wandered to and from the chess wall chart, unsure where to plant himself. Once again, with the mug warming his hands, he sat cross-legged on the floor. "That double-take, if I can describe it as such," Honeyman clarified. "You've performed the same set of movements every time I've made your tea."

Mason was wondering whether he was drunk. His thinking was fuzzy.

Concentrate, Mason. Remember why you're here…

"Just worried about Kris, that's all."

"Of course."

"Are you thure it was safe to send them back?"

"Kris has no choice, Mason. The thing he carries will always take him back."

"You mean his mobile?"

Honeyman grunted as he contemplated Kris's mobile

phone. His careful questioning of the young salesman in the Apple store had confirmed Gracie's suspicions.

"Don't you see it as a mobile?" Mason asked dreamily, interpreting Honeyman's response.

"I'm in the chess game, so I see everything projected by the temple. But I'm also a bishop," he added thoughtfully, recalling that Kris had explained there were no nicknames, no details, on the bishops in the address book, just formal titles. "I think the bishops have no fantasies: they see only the reality. If I enter that building, I will see it as it really is, just as I would see a preserved heart if Kris were to produce his mobile phone."

Mason sipped his tea, attempting to concentrate. He didn't quite understand why everything Honeyman was telling him, all this nonsense, was making complete sense.

"You'll become more disorientated, I suspect, with time," Honeyman reflected.

"I have been working too hard," Mason conceded.

"Ah yes, with your research. Is this Kris's screenplay, or your series of acclaimed academic papers?"

Mason wiped tea from his beard. "Eh, both, really."

Honeyman put a hand lovingly on his overcoat, folded carefully next to him on the camp bed. "Do you really remember writing the screenplay, Mason? Are you sure it wasn't provided to you?"

Mason looked at his tea. An alarm was ringing inside his head.

"You know that you're *not* published, don't you? After our meeting in the restaurant I tried to look you up, but I couldn't."

Mason struggled to find his words.

"Don't try to speak," Honeyman said gently. "I'm being

unkind and you don't deserve it. It's just that I know who you are, you see." He sighed and took Gracie's figurine from his overcoat pocket, placing her carefully on the floor. "At least, *she* knows."

"Knows what?" Mason asked, moving closer to consider the figurine, though instinctively understanding he shouldn't touch her. The girl with the tightly-pinned red hair stood with aloof reserve, her hands behind her back, one finger in the other hand.

"You were never destined to be a historian, published or otherwise." Honeyman shrugged pragmatically. "It's simply convenient at the moment to have an intellectual occupation that is relevant to the new tenant, which also minimises contact with the outside world, to suit your rather convenient agoraphobic shyness."

"Convenient?"

"You strike me as something of a social animal, Mason. But you would shortly have found your true vocation and put your history books aside."

It was some time before Mason spoke. "What vocation?"

"Chess," Honeyman confirmed. "That's why you've been disorientated since you've been here: the wall chart has accelerated the process. At the moment I imagine you're studying the game on my chart, calculating the value of each piece, classifying it by its position on the board and sifting through thousands of move permutations. You're started to realise that if you played you'd be unbeatable."

Mason shook his head. "No, I just played a little in school."

"You never went to school, Mason. Your father made you work with your hands until you ran away."

"Who's she?" Mason asked, referring to Gracie with a forced change of subject.

Honeyman settled back with a resigned smile. "Someone else who is unable to leave, just yet. Her memories keep her here too."

"Memories?"

"Memories of her love for a certain young man: she's searching for him in the coven's temples, the only place where she can pick up his trail." Honeyman adjusted Gracie's figurine slightly, as if this action made her more comfortable, having rested too long on one foot. "We are but the sum of our memories, Mason. One life is meant to be no more than a touchstone, just a pausing breath of revelation in that long journey through eternity. A fixation on one life puts a pot-hole in that journey: that's what keeps ghosts haunting the objects of their love, and their anger." Honeyman paused. "It's what allowed the coven to find thirteen brilliant artists, ill-used by fate and society, and bound them in servitude to that building on the coastal path. The building is just a raised fist, railing against the divine purpose."

Mason's eyes were scanning the chess configurations on the wall chart. He realised his brain was working like a computer, shooting out permutations to every move that were scored with mathematical efficiency against the strength of each piece. He held out his mug. "Can I have a cup of tea please?"

"No. Enough tea."

Mason staggered slightly, the answer upsetting his equilibrium.

"Did you know what Florian's Mollien's occupation was before he ran away to Paris?" Honeyman asked.

Mason didn't answer, his eyes remaining on the wall chart.

"Like his father, and his father before him, he was an artisan. Manual work that he despised. He was a stonemason."

Mason looked down.

"I was trying to work out why you chose your first name, you see," Honeyman clarified. "*Flower* of course was more obvious: Florian is derived from the Latin for flower."

A few minutes of silence drifted by.

"Mason … Flower…" Mason murmured eventually. His hand went to his face, where he felt his features with bemused wonder.

Honeyman collected both Gracie and his overcoat. "Will you come with me to Gathering, Mason? Come and try to remember?"

"Won't you be trespassing? You haven't been invited."

"I'm in the chess game. That means I'm allowed to enter the foyer at least." Honeyman put on his overcoat, his expression dark with uncertainty. "We need to go: I was watching Fabrienne carefully during our meeting and I believe Claudine de Tour du Pin is finally waking up."

Kris wasn't sure if it was the creak of the Turk's arm or the freezing cold that woke him. He pulled the blanket up to his neck with a muttered curse.

"Mon cher…"

The Turk was moving, he realised. This would be a white move – inevitably a redundant move now that he was protecting the king – which would then leave the black king free to castle. That meant he would be walking out of this place without looking back. He shivered; perhaps the salon was bitter about letting him go.

"Mon cher."

Fabrienne was lying next to him. His logic told him they

361

had made love, but he couldn't remember them coming to bed, or anything else, though the fact that he had slept in the middle of the day suggested the right kind of exertion. He exhaled, pulling the blanket tighter, his breath white with frost; perhaps the memory removal of a wonderful experience was another product of the salon's resentment.

Fabrienne, at his side, whispered:

"Tu m'avez réveillée, mon amour."

Florian Mollien's salon understood French. The translation drifted easily across Kris's imagination.

You've woken me, my love.

Another creak of the Turk's arm brought him fully awake. He turned, to see Fabrienne looking directly at him, the right side of her hair swept completely off her face. She was wearing thick white face powder, an ornamental heart pencilled just above her mouth. Against her brown neck, shoulders and ears, the exquisitely applied white face made her look like a marionette, though her scarring, greatly accentuated, was rippling the skin.

Her glorious perfume filled his nostrils as she leaned forward to kiss him, but he jumped out of bed, pulling the blanket with him. He gasped as he wrapped it around him: Fabrienne, though naked, was gently stretching herself awake, impervious to the cold.

"What's wrong with you?" he whispered.

She smiled dreamily as she rolled, the white mask elastic around her mouth. "Pourquoi parles-tu l'anglais, André?"

Why are you speaking English, André...?

"I'm not André," he said, his teeth chattering,

The third creak echoed through the salon. She didn't seem to hear it, settling on her front and considering him with an expression of bemused, childlike curiosity.

"We have to leave," he said. "I don't know what this place has done to you, hypnotised you maybe, but we have to black castle and leave." He glanced at the door. "Did you hear the Turk? The chess board's been made ready for us. White has moved."

She gave him a quizzical look, then considered the bedroom. "Ce n'est pas ma chambre," she muttered.

This isn't my room…

"No, it's the bedroom of Florian Mollien, a chess master."

She nodded thoughtfully. "Florian," she said, the name slotting in to her memory.

"His bones are through there, hidden in an automaton. He had this little kid, which he sacrificed. This place is evil, Fabrienne. We've got to leave *now*."

"Fabrienne," she mused. A finger went to her mouth and she sucked the end. "Oui, j'aime ce nom."

Yes, I like that name…

He sidestepped towards the door. "Aren't you cold?" he groaned. "Get dressed, we've got to go."

"André, où vas-tu?"

André, where are you going…?

"I am not André!" he shouted. "Fabrienne, snap out of it!"

Her quizzical eyes followed him as he staggered into the salon, towards the Turk. He frowned: a black pawn was face down on the floor. Picking it up, he saw it had no face, rather the back of the Moor head. It was a piece with two backs.

Someone who's locked up…

He looked up to see Fabrienne walk past the window in a lace nightshift, into the bathroom. Hopefully she was coming to her senses, the salon having somehow convinced her she was Madame Claudine; presumably André was the lover who had disfigured her. With concern he placed the fallen black pawn on the side of the table, wondering if it had always been two heads stuck together. The piece gave him a panicked twinge of claustrophobia.

He shuddered, the salon's cold stabbing him as he realised why the pawn was on the floor. The mobile was alerting him to the move he now saw represented on the Turk's board.

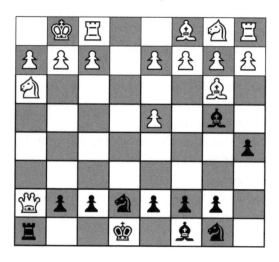

Fabrienne's queen had taken Chelsea's pawn.

I moved you, he realised from inside his blanket. *Last night when we kissed, I moved you…*

A shriek came from the bathroom.

His eyes darted to the bathroom door, then back to the chessboard. His jaw dropped as he realised that black could no longer castle: the black king would move in to check with the white queen. Honeyman had been both right and wrong: the white pieces couldn't take a black piece that wasn't allocated to something or someone, but Chelsea's pawn had revealed itself early on as being part of the game, just as Mr Ovenstone had revealed himself as the second white bishop. These were chess pieces that were perhaps never meant to move, but were in play nonetheless.

He looked up at the ceiling, imagining Chelsea's room and wondering what it meant for Fabrienne to have *taken* the old diva. The room went colder still, his hands going numb, before he was thrown to the floor, Fabrienne on top of him, her face paint smeared.

Above them, if they had been inclined to listen, they would have vaguely heard the sound of Chelsea's struggle.

The Trustees were outside The Perfumery, Renka nailing the boards into its closed door. Chelsea was alternately pounding on it with the flat of her hand and pulling at its latch.

"Door won't open," Renka barked with irritation. "Claudine awake. It sealed now."

The latch suffered one last futile rattle before it went quiet. Renka put the last board in place, Mr Ovenstone obligingly holding it as she hammered in the long rusted nails with the flat stone. She didn't care too much about the fit: the process of 'locking up' was purely symbolic, for no power on earth could now open this door, sealed as it was with the temple's ironic malice.

"How long will I take to die?" Chelsea whimpered through her exhaustion. "How long did the *others* take?" She was now sitting on the floor staring into her mirror, her horror turning to serene resignation as she regarded her reflection, her only one true friend these last forty years. It had been explained to her that *she* wasn't being locked up, just the preserved heart of the devotee, for it belonged to Madame Claudine. Indeed, she had been given the option of leaving without it; it was her choice entirely, the Trustees had explained, as they waited patiently for her to make her decision. Eventually she had nodded mutely and stepped back into the salon.

"You won't die until you're ready to do so, Feather Lady," Mr Ovenstone answered. "The salon will care for you: you are its guest, after all." He leaned away as Renka hammered in the final nail, then stepped back to admire his assistant's handiwork. He tested the firmness of one of the nails, then noticing a cut, offered his finger to Renka to kiss and soothe it. "Your earthly body will perish in this room, as Claudine de Tour du Pin perished, but the memories will sustain you both for as long as the building stands."

"And its foundations are as iron," Renka remarked, banging a board with the flat of her hand in farewell. Faint screams from the depths of the building, from its many floors and rooms, reverberated from the wood.

"I am not Andre!" Kris insisted. His arms were pinned to the floor, unsure whether it was the cold that had completely sapped his energy or whether Fabrienne had acquired superhuman strength.

She shivered, perceiving the cold for the first time. She looked at the Turk, then at Kris, her expression softening with recognition. Her eyes went to the ceiling and she released his wrists. "Je dois revenir à La Parfumerie. Pour finir l'oeuvre de ma vie."

I must return to The Perfumery…

To finish my life's work…

She stood up and cast a thoughtful glance at the door. "Comment est-ce que je pourrais oublier qui j'suis? Et permettre à quelqu'un d'autre de prendre ma chambre aussi?"

How could I have forgotten who I was? To allow someone else to occupy my room…?

Kris retreated to a chaise longue, taking some cushions for warmth. "Do you want to leave? Shall I open the door for you?"

"Je ne peux pas partir par là."

I can't leave that way…

She wrapped her arms around her shoulders and approached the chessboard. The Turk lifted its head, Kris imagining the click of Florian's vertebrae inside its neck.

She thoughtfully touched the white queen, her finger briefly caressing the elaborate hair creation, then collected the black pawn with two backs. "C'est de nouveau ma propre chambre maintenant."

The room is mine again now…

Clutching Chelsea's pawn to her breast, she walked out of the salon. He waited for the sound of the lift, but it didn't arrive. Eventually he got up and peered into the corridor, but she was gone.

X X X

The players revealed

CHELSEA HAD SAID that the latch opened two doors. Perhaps this second door didn't lead to another imagined place of immersive experience, but to the very opposite.

Perhaps it led to reality.

This was Kris's assessment based on a mounting suspicion that his senses were deceiving him.

He squinted as he considered the hidden lights in the foyer, the lift that operated without controls, the attentions of the harem women as he relaxed in the copper tub. The memory of it all jarred in his vision like a television set being banged. It had all seemed so logical at the time.

Now Fabrienne was possessed by an eighteenth-century novelist, vanishing in corridors.

"Take me out," he murmured.

His mobile display was lit, the thumb latch icon a resentful grey. He pressed it, repeating, "Take me out," and closed his eyes.

He waited. The intense cold, the salon's primary weapon, retreated, to be replaced by something far more familiar: a moderately uncomfortable tingle created by March winds and damp walls.

He opened his eyes to see his home.

★

The foyer door was unlocked. As the door closed behind them Honeyman took Mason's elbow, explaining that he couldn't see, shaking his head when Mason mentioned the approaching ceiling lights.

Mason stopped at the beginning of the Rousseau inscription, turning towards a bright light at one of the chairs. Fabrienne was seated on Madame Claudine's chair, dressed in her jeans and sweater, her mobile a beacon of light.

"Don't know what's wrong with it," she muttered, referring to her Blackberry. "It's going crazy. I'm seeing Chelsea's call sign, the perfume burner, but she's not getting through."

"That's because she's locked up, my dear," Honeyman said.

Fabrienne shook her head as she punched the buttons, choosing not to hear him.

"Are you okay?" Mason called, too shy to look at the beautiful woman directly. "We were all worried about you."

She put her Blackberry away with a sigh of exasperation. "I think I've been sleeping. I can't remember anything." A few moments of reflection had her eyes widening with concern. "No, I mean I can't remember *anything*!"

"Oh but you will find that you can remember *everything*."

The voice belonged to Mr Ovenstone, who was being helped out of the lift. Renka pulled a lever in the wall and its mechanism took it up, screeching and shaking on the release spring that allowed it to travel when not weighed down with people.

The Trustees approached, Mr Ovenstone smiling as he

noticed Honeyman through the gloom. His eyes invited an observation of the floor in front of the chairs; here the marble was stained with blood.

"Your time is very short," Mr Ovenstone said to Fabrienne. "Madame Claudine is looking for you."

★

This was reality.

Kris was sure of it. It was too depressingly miserable to be anything else.

The first thing that had struck him was the lack of light. The glass in the windows was caked with dirt, obscuring the view and putting the salon into a grey pall.

The second thing was the smell, which he discovered originated in the commodes in the bathroom and bedroom. Both were full. He was unable to recall using them.

He was in a derelict building. The copper bathtub was black with rust, as was the onyx washbasin, though a large bar of soap and pitcher of water, neither of which he remembered seeing before, were obligingly on the console.

He paused as a flash of recognition had him scrubbing feverishly at the basin as he imagined a miraculous water source making him clean. He had a similar experience in the bedroom a moment ago, when he had come across the old, fusty clothes in the wardrobe, which he once imagined to be fresh.

He was in the salon. The etched marble floor, the only durable feature of the room, attested to the fact that it had been beautiful in its day, but the walls were damp, the furniture rotting. He went to the alcove, to find the Turk and the chessboard.

His fear issued from the fact that there was *nothing* to fear:

he found himself able to look easily upon the game, without consequence. With raised eyebrows he carelessly knocked over a chess piece, which rolled obligingly and knocked into another. He regarded the Turk and touched its hand, then pulled it, jumping back with alarm as the hand came away to reveal a wrist bone sticking out of the sleeve.

After taking a few moments to regain his breath, he gingerly put his hand to the automaton's chest. Against his palm, faint but unmistakeable, he felt a heartbeat.

With a shake of his head, he decided it was a trick: a science student's skeleton and a pneumatic pump.

He considered the chess game, configured exactly as he had last seen it, Fabrienne's queen having taken Chelsea's pawn. There was one piece in the game he was yet to see.

He picked up the black king.

★

"I don't remember anything," Fabrienne answered weakly, to Renka's ironic smirk.

"Take a little time," Mr Ovenstone suggested, "because soon you'll be bones in The Perfumery. You bargained for a life, so at least try to remember it. Perhaps you should start with your precious little novel."

"My novel...?"

"The one which only survives in your memory." The Trustee paused. "How long have you been writing it?"

Fabrienne made an expression of discomfort. "A year..."

"I think you should try again."

Mason looked inquiringly at Honeyman, who responded with a resigned expression.

"A year, it's almost finished..."

"Try again. When did you start working for my Feather Lady?"

"She arrive in building forty years ago," Renka added. She took Mr Ovenstone's elbow as he wobbled slightly with suppressed mirth.

Honeyman's eyes narrowed. "Don't listen to them Fabrienne."

She turned to him in a daze. "Are they lying?" she asked.

"We have to get back into the chess game," Honeyman clarified. "Only *then* must you remember." He paused. "Mason too."

Renka made to approach Honeyman, hatred in her eyes. Mr Ovenstone stopped her with a hand on her shoulder. "You're meddling again, Baptist," he remarked laconically, translating the Russian's anger.

Honeyman grumbled and nodded, his eyes going to the lift shaft.

Kris paused at the lift, the black king in the palm of his left hand.

It was an ordinary chess piece. There was no unexpected weight, no scorch marks or mutilations, no sensations of flesh. But the piece was him, Kris Knight, wearing a laurel crown, seated on a throne with a mix of concern and bemusement.

"A throne of vanities," he muttered, but unsure where that description had come from. There were markings on the chair but too small to make out.

In his right hand was his mobile, now a shrivelled, preserved heart, which nevertheless carried a faint pulse. In the corridor he had stopped, realising he couldn't leave without it; returning to the salon he found in its place this dry piece of meat.

The lift was also perplexing him as he manually pulled

open the cage and stepped onto the platform. He heard voices from the foyer and he waited impatiently for it to move. Shortly his attention veered to the wheel in one of the corners and he followed the coil rope, wrapped around the base of the wheel, through the platform and into the shaft.

He closed his eyes and recalled his journeys in this cage. With a groan of weary understanding, he pulled down the cage, went to the wheel and turned it.

The lift moved slowly at first and he turned the wheel with greater force, sweat dampening his hair. His exertion was partially inspired by excitement: no matter how miserable, this at least was reality and neither he nor Fabrienne were prisoners anymore. When he found her, Honeyman would help him snap her out of her hypnosis.

He was on the floor below, presented with boarded-up doors. Momentarily he paused, unable to remember Fabrienne's face. All he could remember was her words.

He twisted the wheel again. This was a trick of the temple, who wanted to steal Fabrienne away. He growled, every muscle in his shoulder aching.

Finally, in the foyer, he pulled the cage up.

"Fabrienne, are you here?" Kris called.

As his eyes adjusted to the gloom, he saw the Trustees approaching. Honeyman and Mason were standing further down the foyer.

"Fabrienne not for you," Renka declared, stepping in front of Mr Ovenstone. "She belong to The Perfumery."

He blanched and looked at the floor. His surprise at seeing so many cracks in the marble was only fleeting, as he found the loose, broken edge of a tile. "Enough of this bullshit," he said, picking up the marble shard and wielding it like a stone. "No more games. I'm serious, and don't think I won't hurt you. Tell me what you've done with Fabrienne."

Renka seemed to find this development interesting. She stepped forward and raised her arms in invitation.

"Don't Kris!" Honeyman shouted in warning.

Kris shook his head, attempting to maintain his composure. "Shut up, we're doing this my way now. I'm sick of being pushed around." He advanced on Renka, who with effortless speed took the wrist of his hand carrying the tile. He froze momentarily in agony, before she snapped his wrist and sent him hurtling down the foyer floor, yelping as his body snagged on the sharp edges of the tiles.

Honeyman held Mason back, then hurried to Kris and laid a gentle hand on his wrist. "I have to get into the chess game," he whispered. Through his pain, Kris looked at him in confusion. "Give me your chess piece, and your heart," Honeyman explained.

The foyer was bright once more, the hidden candles in the ceiling lit. The marble was also sheen and unbroken, Kris realised, as he pulled himself up from the floor and slumped, holding his wrist, into his large chair.

He frowned, seeing this chair for the first time. It was the throne of his chess piece, his aspirations and ambitions recorded in the wood with symbols like a Sioux totem. His ambition to be famous was recorded with a rudimentary television box with his face inside; his wish to be admired, a handclap; on the arms, his sexual ambition, phallic figures chasing each other energetically. This was his throne and he understood them all.

But the biggest symbol, the large carving which he

could feel with his back, was the desire for contentment; to understand himself. This symbol was a circle, simple and complete; it dwarfed, made somewhat ludicrous, the other busy activities driven frantic and giddy by media distortion.

He looked up, thinking at first that he was in a hall of mirrors, because he saw himself, again seated on a throne, looking back at him down the foyer. But the reflection had an elaborate crown and the throne was of solid, unmarked gold.

"The throne of blind ego," he murmured, the words coming from the same place as the 'throne of vanities'.

Emerging from his disorientation he realised the foyer had become his chess game. He saw himself as black and white knight in a waiting crouch. With a sigh of relief, he saw Fabrienne on his left. She shook her head to say he shouldn't approach her, her eyes directing him to the rest of the game.

He located Honeyman, who was holding his mobile. He instinctively knew he was studying the chess schematic, which now flashed in his mind.

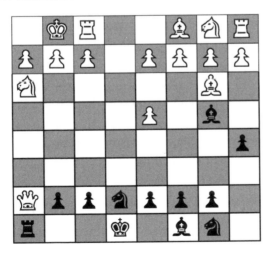

Mason was in the centre of the floor, looking at the ceiling in dazed amusement. The minister, to his left, was standing in front of an imperious Renka. With a stretch, Kris saw Mr Ovenstone's head further down the foyer. The stretch, the need to look over an obstacle, made him realise that there were life-size casts of the remaining chess pieces in the foyer, perhaps the pieces that would never be in play, or at least not in play here. He noted there was no sign of Buoys, her place occupied by an ivory black Moor.

"It's the six of us," Honeyman called in confirmation. "We're going to have to play this out, Kris."

"How have you managed this?" Kris called back. "The chess game's for me..."

"But you've given me your mobile, the king being your password. And I have Gracie to help me activate the latch."

"It's not as simple as that, Baptist," Mr Ovenstone said from behind a white grenadier pawn. His hand gripped the soldier's bayonet. "You have called this game, so you have to start it. You start it at your peril, Baptist," he added.

"You trespass," Renka said. "We *take* you."

Honeyman nodded. "Then perhaps it's time for it to end," he conceded. "God knows you've wanted it enough." His fist tightened, where he held both Gracie and Kris's king, and took a few steps sideways towards Kris, ending in front of Mason. Mason now noticed him, no longer interested in the ceiling. The mobile schematic flashed.

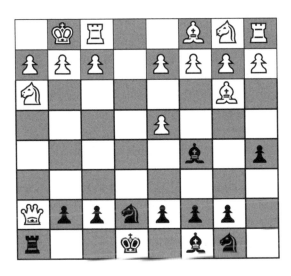

"*Take* him," Mr Ovenstone called.

From a large trouser pocket Renka produced a Uzi machine-gun, which she slid across the floor to Mason. He picked it up immediately and aimed it at Honeyman.

"I'm meant to kill you, Honeyman," Mason said with a face of apology. "Why did you have to move there? You *know* a pawn takes sideways."

"Don't Mason!" Kris and Fabrienne called as one.

Honeyman opened his overcoat to reveal his waistcoat. "I'm an easy target, Mason. You'll either remember who you are, or you'll kill me."

Mason hesitated, his finger pressing on the trigger.

Honeyman's eyes darkened. "You've seen people killed in this room before, haven't you, Florian Mollien?"

"Florian…?" Mason hesitated, his thoughts returning to his strange discussion with Honeyman in his studio. He lowered his weapon.

"Don't listen to Baptist," Renka snarled. "You have life

here. You are entitled to a life – you have *bought* it. You want to give it back?"

"I did buy a life," Mason muttered. He turned to Florian Mollien's chair with a look of horror.

"You were promised another life where you would fulfil all your aspirations," Honeyman said. "But the priests deceived you, Florian. The coven lies, without lying."

"We never lie, Baptist," Mr Ovenstone clarified. "We are holy."

"Mason, you're a construct of Florian Mollien's memories," Honeyman continued. "You will have that life they promised you, but it will be unfulfilled. Now listen to me. From what I have learned from Fabrienne's experience, I believe you'll move in short, one-year cycles: you'll discover your love of chess, discover your extraordinary talent, be poised to exploit it, just to be returned to the beginning, your memories erased. In the meantime, you'll be the willing slave of the guest of the room you once hosted, who will be totally dependent on you." He paused and cast a glance at Fabrienne. "Why do you think Chelsea hates Fabrienne? Fabrienne was foisted on her through the building's weapon of starvation and she's had to endure forty repetitious cycles of Fabrienne and her novel…"

Fabrienne frowned and turned to Kris in confusion, who frowned back.

Honeyman spoke to Mason's back. "Florian had his chance at fame and fortune, Mason, and fate decided it wasn't to be." He paused. "But Florian was brilliant, nonetheless, and no one can take that away from him. Even if he was hidden in a box, he was the one responsible for the magic."

Mason's machine gun clattered to the floor as he looked on Florian's chair. "I'm thure I must have been quite mad," he conceded.

"This is a temple of power. And the priests were persuasive, no doubt."

Mason nodded slowly. "But I'm sorry for it all, and for the poor boy who died." He turned to the Trustees, briefly considered them, then slowly shook his head. He became a life-size white grenadier.

There was silence as everyone processed this development.

"No! Mason's real!" Kris called eventually.

"Real to you, certainly," Honeyman agreed. "Real to anyone connected to the temple's memories. But Mason was merely a modern equivalent of Florian. Mason mentioned the portraits: I suspect Florian made Mason an exact physical replica of himself."

"No. Lisa Buoys saw him."

"And she was a chess piece, connected to the demonic broadband of the temple. Believe me, when the next game started, with Buoys abandoned as an irrelevancy, Mason would have been invisible to her." Honeyman sighed. "Why do you think Mason developed this fantasy that he was agoraphobic? It was to create a defence mechanism that allowed him not to be seen: a mechanism he would need once he became your faceless PA."

"No, you're wrong," Kris muttered. "He had tenants and everything…" He took his wrist uncomfortably, realising he had never seen the students. His old boss Dylan had gone to his house when he had pulled a sickie, to find no one lived there. "We went to a restaurant…" he added weakly, then rubbed his wrist as he remembered the strange looks directed at his table, which he thought were prompted by Mason's lack of social skills. He cast a suspicious glance at Renka, who smiled back as she read his thoughts; the Russian had been there on the deck terrace to ensure nothing interfered that might break the illusion.

"You're close," Honeyman said with an air of encouragement. "Concentrate now, Kris."

A gasp jarred Kris to the lungs as his memories returned. Mason hadn't got him Big Macs and pizzas at all: he had collected those himself, in his dream-state buying food which he dutifully took to the top floor.

"Yes, you know what's next, don't you?" Honeyman said sadly. He looked at Fabrienne. Kris looked too, his face downcast.

"Fabrienne," Honeyman said, "we need you to move. Move so Kris can castle."

Fabrienne had been processing furiously during Honeyman's exchange with Mason. Certain unwelcome memories had brought tears.

She had been working for Chelsea London from the day she had moved into Gathering, forty years ago. Even then, she had been on the run from her family, the reason why she rarely went out in public. Even then, she had been working on a manuscript entitled *The London Address*, the story of an Indian heiress thrown into French eighteenth-century society.

An heiress called Fabrienne Lafayette … the name her French father had given her in his will with her inheritance. The character's real name, the name her unmarried servant mother had given her, was Vaishali Iqbal.

Her tears were of frustration and anger. She had never been allowed to finish the book. Just as she was close, about to write her final chapter, she would be returned to where the novel was just a seed of an idea, something that would grow in importance as she worked as a PA to a needy celebrity in order to raise sufficient funds to leave the country, to escape her violent ex-husband and his family.

A family that didn't exist.

"There's more, Fabrienne," Honeyman said sadly. "If you're to be free of this place, you have to remember it all."

Her eyes widened, then she gasped with despair as she pictured the child brought to her more than two hundred years ago by the priests. Her own little Emile, raised in her salon and taught merely to read and admire her novels, treats and torture being administered according to the standard of her critique. The child became a woman, an ashen-faced zombie who could recite *The London Address* almost word-perfect.

"Oh God, what did I do?" Fabrienne wailed.

"You bought a life," Mr Ovenstone returned.

With a wince of pain Fabrienne's hand went to her chest. Her recurring nightmare was not of her own sacrifice, but that of her Emile, as her heart was taken.

"And you've had that life in full," Ovenstone said. "In return for the life you took."

The heart was still beating: the heart that would power The Perfumery and her own existence when it was found by Chelsea London.

Ovenstone nodded with grim satisfaction as he savoured the final drip of realisation. "And now it's time to pay for that life: to return to your salon and be boarded up with your guest, my Feather Lady."

Fabrienne turned tearfully to Kris.

"Don't say it!" Kris shouted, rising from his chair. "You're not like Mason. You exist!"

Fabrienne shook her head with regret, then smiled as she mouthed the word 'Goodbye'.

"No!"

Fabrienne transformed into the woman with white freckled skin and auburn hair Kris recognised from the latch. Veiled, she turned to face the Trustees and from her lace shroud produced a small handbell, which she rang.

Ta-ding.

"Et maintenant je me suis réveillée," she said, making to step forward.

And now I've woken up…

"Fabrienne, come back!" Kris implored.

She stopped, bringing her slipper back from her step. She turned to look inquisitively at Kris.

"Kris, you have to let Fabrienne go!" Honeyman called. "You have to remember too!"

Kris grasped his wrist in agony when in his confusion he tried to move it. "She drove me here that first time in her car. How can a ghost drive a car?"

"It's *your* car, Kris," Honeyman said. "You must try and remember. We haven't got much time." His face revealed his burden as he put the mobile on the floor, now too heavy to hold. "Gracie can't maintain this image much longer. This is your only chance for escape."

The word 'escape' lit a beacon in Kris's mind.

"But there is no escape for *you*, Baptist," Mr Ovenstone rasped. "Not this time."

"Remember the photographs on my wall?" Honeyman pressed, ignoring him. "The one of the empty office, and of the university students? Fabrienne and Mason were in those photographs, in my lens, when I took them. They were missing, when I developed them."

Kris closed his eyes and opened them. He repeated the motion, repeatedly testing the new muscle in his brain that allowed him to fantasise.

It began in The Pavilion. He hadn't wandered there out of chance at all, but had been given the address by his agent, telling him they'd been approached by a Russian theatrical agent who might be interested in giving him 'small part'. He had been given the code to open the door.

The Pavilion was in fact a sales office, closed on Mondays, but he had found a preserved human heart on the glass case surrounding the model of the development.

When he picked it up, Fabrienne had come from behind the counter. He had immediately forgotten about the audition, believing he had wandered in out of boredom.

He blinked.

Later in the salon he had taken the heart out of his puffer jacket and placed it on the chessboard. It had become a mobile phone.

He had driven himself to this building, the red Fiesta salvaged from his marriage, just as Trish had maintained outside Chapter. He blinked, and he saw himself driving to Chapter on that day, returning on the bus when he imagined Fabrienne arriving. He came back for it later in his dream-state, to park it behind the Norwegian church, where it would remain until his next journey to Chapter.

He blinked once more, processing every meeting with Fabrienne in The Pavilion, in his car, and in this building. Eventually he turned to Madame Claudine and simply nodded. She produced her handbell.

Ta-ding.

"In case you wonder," Renka said, "the bell is ours, not Claudine's. It tolls her damnation march. All hosts have bell, at end."

Claudine nodded solemnly in acceptance of this fact.

Ta-*ding*.

"I think not, young lady," Honeyman said.

"Silence, Baptist," she returned scornfully.

"Ah, but you cannot silence me: you have made me part of your society; the test of your faith." He grumbled both his satisfaction and his discomfort at this notion. "This game has released Florian Mollien. He has confessed his crime and sought forgiveness. God has heard him. He has forfeited the second life he bought." He glanced at Florian's chair. "And if Florian is free, then this temple is finished. You cannot have only twelve hosts."

Renka turned furiously to Mr Ovenstone for his confirmation. The old man glowered back.

Honeyman beckoned Madame Claudine forward. "Vous pouvez partir maintenant," he said.

You can leave now...

She stepped forward. The display of the mobile at Honeyman's feet blazed with anger.

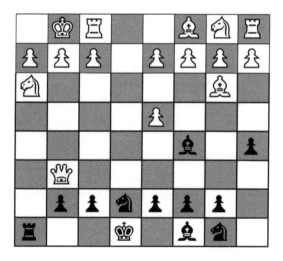

"Castle!" Honeyman called to Kris. "Quickly, while you have time!"

"There is no escape for *you*, Baptist!" Mr Ovenstone repeated. Renka spat in his direction.

Kris looked left at the black castle, now a projection of the foyer door, open wide. Then he noticed the white castle next to his image on the gold throne. The chess piece had gone and was now represented by the Turk, pounding incessantly on the chessboard.

An icy hand went to his shoulder, urging caution.

It was wholly appropriate that the game should be finished in his salon. This would ensure all the mysteries of his life would be revealed, eventually allowing him one day to sit, victorious, and consider his extraordinary life.

His huddled form in front of him, which was his black knight, was standing up. If he moved himself out of the way, the next move could be the Turk, to put him in check.

Yes, he wanted to be put in check.

That was the object of the game. When he was put in check, the temple would have its claim over him. The psychological hooks in his skin would be buried too deep to remove.

There would be no more talk of escape: no more confusion, no more regrets…

"Kris! Focus!" Honeyman shouted.

Kris turned to the projection of the foyer door, which was closing. A squeeze of his wrist returned him painfully to his senses.

He ran through it.

★

The black castle seemed to swell with outraged surprise as it accepted Kris's leaping form. The illusion of the chess game found a few seconds of existence in its powered malice before all the pieces blinked out with a dead pop.

The foyer was empty. The Trustees turned to Honeyman with hatred.

"That was not an escape, Baptist," Ovenstone snarled. "Merely an exchange."

Honeyman nodded slowly, but was observing Kris, who had picked himself up from his leap to find himself in a state of complete amnesia. He was stumbling towards the foyer door, his stomach instinctively taking him in that direction, as a baby turtle emerges from the sand.

The foyer door opened easily and he was outside, gazing without comprehension at the sea. Shortly, a sigh of relief announced the return of his memories, his disorientation passing.

Yes, he was parked behind the Norwegian Church and had an appointment with his agent High Hopes. He was late.

He briefly considered the building he had just left, then shook his head.

The building was simply walls in his mind.

EPILOGUE

THE DAUPHIN'S MURDER never saw a television screen. Production of the docudrama ended abruptly when glaring anomalies were discovered in the historical documents. The historians abandoned their dramatic revision in dismay, wondering how these forgeries could have fooled the radiocarbon dating. The consensus opinion was for a synthetic ageing formula.

Lisa Buoys was the first BBC executive to condemn the project, warning all concerned about the confidentiality agreements they had signed, now designed to protect the corporation from embarrassment. She attempted to contact Kris, but he had disappeared; he had a researcher friend, she seemed to recall, who was credited on the screenplay, though she hadn't met him. Perhaps this Mason Flower was also a figment of Knight's imagination, as fanciful as the Dauphin's abduction.

Kris was living very much under the radar with Trish, who had come to realise their separation had been a mistake. She would have told him as much during their last phone conversation if he hadn't been so abrupt: her persistent wish to stay and watch him in Chapter that time was, in hindsight, a wish to be with him. The relationship healed quickly, working easily now that Kris had unaccountably overcome his need to be feted, content with just an understanding of who he was, of his qualities and limitations.

He certainly had no further interest in achieving celebrity, though a different passion would soon invade his life. He had no memory whatsoever of Temple 1313, his brief stay in Florian Mollien's salon a hole in his life that would never be filled, but a year on he discovered in a Cardiff junk shop the original manuscript of Madame Claudine's last novel *The London Address*. After researching her extensively, both here and in Paris, he found a connection with twelve other talented émigrés originating from an odd Jacobin chapter. He arranged for the novel's publication; it met with critical acclaim and its adapted screenplay made him sufficiently wealthy to enable the creation of a foundation uncovering, explaining and promoting the works of the thirteen émigrés.

He would explain his strange path to Trish, and to himself, as the need to 'give something back', referring to their windfall with Madame Claudine's lost manuscript. In truth it was an obsession he couldn't even begin to explain, though when the last émigré was produced to the world, a lonely magician's extraordinary tricks and illusions fully catalogued and researched, his fascination with Chapter Emile would fall from his mind like a stone.

But even during his obsessive years, he never returned to the building. Gathering was emptied now of its hosts and guests, yet it retained the bitter memories that shielded its existence and gave power to its Trustees.

"I bring you food," Renka muttered to Honeyman, on his third day in the dining room on the top floor. He was ravenous as he sat at the head of the table, the only place he could sit when he was not sleeping on the floor, but he took the stale bread crusts reluctantly. "I will wait until you starving next time, if you don't eat," Renka warned him.

"Perhaps I won't eat even then," he muttered, though unable to resist gnawing at the bread.

"Then you die," she said, producing a flask of rainwater collected from the ceiling. "You die and we take your little companion and throw her in room with bones." She turned briefly to the bricked-up rooms, where the hearts were rotting. "And don't think of escape. You chose to make exchange, to offer yourself to Temple in place of Capet. This is holy bargain, Baptist; the building will keep you to it."

He sullenly looked away. The thirteen portraits of the émigrés were gone, replaced with alternating photographs of himself and Gracie as she was in life, the thirteenth portrait showing them together. All the likenesses were unflattering, the eyes too close together or off-angle; the last painting was from a distance and depicted them sneaking through a door like thieves.

"I am still Trustee," Renka confirmed, "so I will visit you regularly. You're building's pet now; perhaps Mr Ovenstone come too."

"Aren't you concerned that Franklyn Tyde will find us?" Honeyman asked, his hand going protectively to Gracie's figurine by his side on the table. He felt the glow of anticipation at the question.

Renka didn't answer.

"Don't underestimate the bond Franklyn has with Gracie," Honeyman remarked sadly. "You created it, after all."

She considered him awhile, unwilling to look beyond Mr Ovenstone's assurance that Temple 1313 had now changed in its object, was now the living prison for the Baptist. She was still smarting from having to remove the boards of

The Perfumery, to release a dazed Chelsea London with amnesia, but transformation was not the same as defeat. With a parting spit to the floor, carefully aimed – given that it was a protocol of the imprisonment that no part of her, not even her saliva, should make contact with him – she returned to the lift. Wheeling herself down to the foyer, she pondered on the little tortures the Proctors' protocols would allow her to perform.

Honeyman finished his bread and turned Gracie slightly to face him, offering a look of apology as he brushed away the crumbs.

Perhaps it was a shiver of the candelabra flame, but a light passing fleetingly across her face gave her the appearance of a smile. He was unsure whether it was a smile of encouragement or resignation and once again he lamented the loss of Gracie's book, confiscated by the Trustees.

Without that dialogue to sustain him, he felt adrift. He wondered if anyone from the three temples he had opposed would remember him, would hold him in their memory for the services he had performed. The notion of unacknowledged achievement provoked a moment of empathy with the émigrés, powered by a trace of resentful ambition that always glittered in the air of this building.

With a grunt of wistful acceptance he sat back, deciding it was enough to have given some service to people when they had needed him, conducting himself with as much courage and fortitude as he could muster.

Armed with that truth, and in the sure knowledge that Gracie would have chastised him for this indulgent self-analysis, he prepared to meet his captivity. He closed his eyes to pray silently, swearing as he did so, the curse of profanity when talking to God an added manacle to his prison.

Gracie's figurine observed the candelabra with a series of thoughtful reassessments on their predicament, until the candles eventually burned out. The darkness closed like a tomb.

THE HONEYMAN SAGA

The Vanity Rooms is the third encounter between Tristyn Honeyman, a de-frocked Baptist minister, and an old, demonic Welsh priesthood.

In the first instalment, *The Mourning Vessels*, the priests are the Trustees of a charity visiting the recently bereaved and offering to *solve* their grief... Honeyman must rescue the deceased from the objects they coveted in life: in dolls, clocks, even a bespoke Cluedo board

In *Precious Cargo*, events have taken another sinister turn. Now the Trustees have set up a charity offering children to couples desperate to become parents, but these gifts from Heaven come at a terrible price. When the children reach sixteen they are forced to fight for their survival, with the assistance of the malevolent hand-crafted toys given to them at birth.

With the Honeyman saga, nothing is as it seems for this secret society is playing its own game, twisted with an evil logic and ironic humour:

"The Trustees believe themselves holy. They have no worldly ambition: they are far more complicated that. They have rules..."

Visit the author Peter Luther at
www.peterluther.co.uk
or join him on Facebook.

Also by Peter Luther:

PETER LUTHER

PRECIOUS
CARGO

Most childhoods end too soon.
Some never begin.

y Lolfa

£8.95

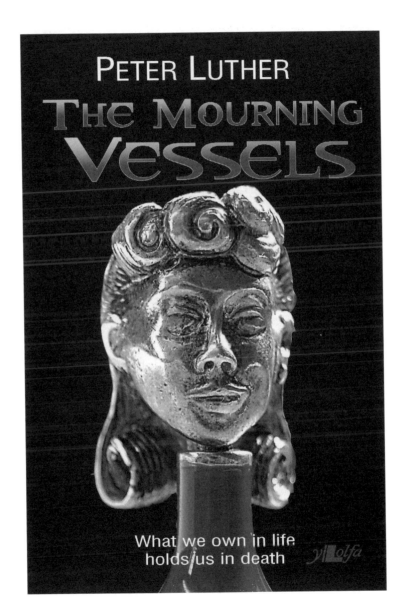

PETER LUTHER

THE MOURNING
VESSELS

What we own in life
holds us in death

£7.95

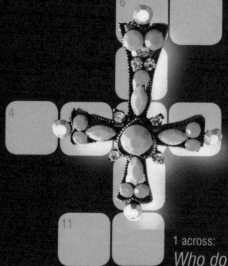

PETER LUTHER

DARK COVENANT

1 across:
Who do you bring?

"Powerful, mind-blowing stuff... a book that once opened,
does not want to leave you" – GWALES

y Lolfa

£7.95
Also available as an ebook £1.99